THE
TIMEPIECE
PROTOCOLS

J. Mark Hart

Jack of Hearts Publishing

.

A government should not infringe the liberties of its citizens under the guise of keeping them safe

THE
TIMEPIECE
PROTOCOLS

PROLOGUE

In the gray mists of the early 20th century, as governments struggled to rebuild civilization from the barrenness and devastation of the Great War, those governments also sought to control radical political theories and activists rising in the vacuum left from toppled monarchies. Red and White Bolsheviks battled in Russia. Fascist philosophy spread through beer halls in Bavaria. Even the democracies of England and France saw the rise of domestic communist parties with signs and picketing as their memberships swelled. Public rallies and protests could be controlled well enough. It was the secret meetings that kept Ministers awake at night. So it was decided.

The secret meetings must be infiltrated. Careful watch of the leaders must be instigated.

So it began.

Though primitive by modern standards, governments developed means of spying upon disfavored groups. Some departments simply kept dossiers and careful watch over those with unsavory opinions. Others were not so benevolent. Overtime, these efforts spread beyond disfavored groups to those who were simply odd, different, off-beat, or did not toe the party line.

Gradually, the hard-liners, preaching fear and doom, acquired pockets of power. They were not shy about overstepping bounds and trouncing the privacy of the innocent.

Protest began appearing in the papers and occasional speeches, but no strong group arose to call for investigations and the return to sensibility. But in that environment, two physicists at Cambridge with prescience of how a threatened democracy could over-react, took action.

They formed an organization—the League of Privacy Sentinels—to work for protection of personal privacy and the right to individual thought. But the organization arose not from their political observations, but from an incredible discovery that they harnessed into a practical device. The device would enable them to extend their work into succeeding generations past their own mortality. It was a watch, a special

Watch, that could travel across time. And those holding the Watch could travel with it.

At first they almost destroyed the invention. The ability to travel in time and disrupt the natural course of events was too frightening to consider. They finally, however, compromised on strict protocols for use of the Watch.

The First Protocol was that the Watch must always stay securely locked in a hidden location known only to the physicists.

The Second Protocol was that they would always work in secret never calling attention to the League. That would insure their effectiveness over time and protect discovery of the Watch by curious outsiders.

The Third Protocol was that the affairs of the League would be run by a board of the two physicists and senior agents they recruited and trained. The board would direct the actions of the League's agents and operatives. It soon became apparent, however, that new personnel must be recruited over time as agents and operatives aged or retired.

The Fourth Protocol, then, was that Nigel and Cuthbert would use the Watch to travel ten years forward at the end of each decade to select and recruit new agents and operatives into the ongoing activities of the League. These recruits would pledge an eternal oath of secrecy and loyalty to the League.

The Fifth Protocol limited the Watch's use to protect its secrecy. The Watch could be used to time travel only to select the new "decennial" personnel, and then, only five times in that "decennial year."

The Protocols were rigorously observed. It was imperative the Watch not be discovered—or stolen. An unscrupulous person could wreck humanity with the ability to time travel and interfere in events. Even a well-meaning person could unknowingly set off catastrophic consequences. A government certainly could hardly refrain from using the Watch for its nationalistic purposes.

The Protocols worked proficiently and effectively producing outstanding results.

Until 1969.

One of the candidates selected for induction into the League that year was questionable. The board as a whole thought that Manfred Redford would develop into a fine agent in time, but some members strongly dissented. They thought Manfred too rebellious and invested in the American counterculture to be a solid agent they could trust. However, the majority view won out as it usually does.

But all were stunned when a team went to induct Manfred in December 1969. They arrived at Oberlin College where Manfred was a student. They timed their arrival for the day fall final exams ended. But Manfred was not there. The college administration had no idea where he was. It seemed he had simply disappeared without a trace. Gone—poof!– into thin air. That had never happened before!

His disappearance threw the League into frantic disarray. Had some dark mischief befallen him? Had an enemy penetrated the secrecy of the League? Had there been a criminal agency? It was imperative for the safety of the League and its operations to find out.

The League was able to trace Manfred to the Woodstock Music Festival in August 1969, but there he simply vanished. The League suspended the Fifth Protocol limiting the number of times the Watch could be used that decennial year. With the Watch, the Agents crisscrossed time searching for Manfred in frantic trips forward and backward in time. Then a breakthrough, and finally, finally, they found him.

But when they found him, it was fifty years into the future at the worst possible time and the worst possible place.

I.

THE GEORGE DOUGLASES

CHAPTER 1

THE DOUGLASES HAVE A FAMILY DINNER
April 9, 2019
The George Douglas Home
4729 Fairhope Drive
Birmingham, Alabama

6:00 p.m. CDT

George Douglas, Jr., or simply "Junior," as his family called him, raced into the family's keeping room off the kitchen, slung his school backpack across the floor, and demanded, "What's for supper, Mom?"

Virginia Douglas, his mother, turned from the kitchen island with a stern look. "Junior, put your backpack in the cubby in the hallway. How many times do I have to tell you to put it in the cubby? That's why I paid a fortune to the carpenter to custom build it for you and your sister. I don't want ya'll cluttering up our family room with your school junk."

Junior's older sister Carmen smirked at him from the kitchen table. He hated that smirk. It was one of his earliest memories, and he was powerless to do anything about it. Worse, she knew it tortured him.

"I'll end the suspense, Sherlock," she teased through her smirk. He also hated when she called him "Sherlock." She'd started that when he spent one summer reading the complete stories of Sherlock Holmes. He had annoyed the rest of the family all summer vacation by constantly making deductions about anything and everything and repeating *ad nauseam* his favorite Holmes saying, "Watson, when you eliminate the impossible, whatever remains no matter how improbable, must be the truth."

George, Jr. ground his teeth.

He knew there was no aid from his father. George Douglas, Sr. ignored Carmen's mistreatment of her brother, attributing it to sibling squabbles. His mother would side *with* Carmen, her "pet" for whom she had great ambitions.

"So what's for dinner *Miss Know-it-All?*"

"Junior, don't be smart to your sister."

"Urban Cookhouse—something yummy with all those different type greens you just love," Carmen informed him.

"You mean that looks like the green yucky stuff that gets stuck underneath the lawnmower."

"Junior, those are *healthy* meals," Virginia corrected him. "They buy from local markets and farmers, and it supports the 'go local' movement. They're really nice restaurants and the people running them are very friendly."

George, Jr. rolled his eyes. "I get that, but can't we just once in a while get Milo's burgers or a chicken basket with French fries and a gallon of the sweet tea?"

Virginia glared at him over the top of her reading glasses. He knew his mother's I-will-brook-no-argument look. Bending for his backpack, he turned, and with slumped shoulders, walked away.

Virginia watched her son. She felt a wave of guilt. She shouldn't criticize him, she knew. But her worry for him seemed to morph into a constant nagging beyond her control.

Virginia was in her early forties, slim, with the beginning of that tanned and dried look women with money get in their middle age. She still carried it all well. She had been very pretty in her youth, and now her cheerleader prettiness had evolved into a mature attractiveness. She could turn a head or two striding into a posh bar to meet her husband for cocktails after work or to celebrate a lucrative house sale from her real estate job.

Her hair was short, about at the jaw line, with medium brown highlights, giving her an air of vitality as well as hiding any pesky gray. Her face narrowed at the chin, and her lips were still full and inviting. Her blue eyes were striking, some thought her best feature, until she stared at you long enough. Underneath the prettiness was a hard determination with a hint of haughtiness. She was lithe with an athletic figure attired at the moment in mid-calf black Lycra pants, aqua T-shirt underneath a white tank top, and rainbow-colored workout shoes all the young women wore. The color of her nails matched the aqua T. Her skin had a healthy glow from her Pilates session forty-five minutes earlier.

As she watched her son walk away, she couldn't help judging the boy. She was oblivious that she did. She was simply confident that her viewpoint always was the correct one.

2

She wished Junior had more of her athleticism. But he had too much of his dad's golf-only-on-the-weekends-at-the club genes. Her husband's body, either in a suit or khakis and golf shirt, looked soft, along with soft hands and pale skin from office work as an accountant. Maybe George, Sr. could begin going to Pilates with her.

She sighed, trying to make peace with the death of her athletic hopes for her son. They had tried rec league baseball. After watching a few games, clearly the boy needed extra work. His dad bought him a tee to practice hitting in the backyard. But they might as well have saved the money. The boy could barely dribble a grounder. The boy's only successful athletic feat—if it can be called a success—was once hitting the ball solidly, powerfully over his backyard fence straight into Ms. McGillicuddy's picture window, which turned into a really neat spider web decal before all the pieces broke free at once and fell into her azaleas. That evening the boy and his dad deposited the bat and tee in the trash can without a trace of regret.

Now he was in eighth grade, turning fourteen this summer and played no sports. At least the boy was bright, very bright. But, Virginia chewed her lip, too much brightness caused its own problems. It seemed that being too bright, in his case at least, also brought a social awkwardness.

It was not that she did not love her son, for she did, dearly. But her love was bounded by expectations and anxiety. What would the boy do with his life, would he have friends, would he fit in an organization like his father's, would he find a sweet girl that loved him? Or would others take advantage of him or manipulate him? My god, did he have Asperger's, she fretted. She had nightmares of him with some low-paying job, living alone in a dank apartment eating TV dinners. So her love and fear became braided into a habit of nagging to try to protect him.

Virginia turned to Carmen and smiled. The girl had her genes. Carmen was beautiful with shoulder-length blonde hair streaked just right with natural platinum highlights. Her hair, along with gem-quality emerald eyes, caused people passing to turn for a longer look. But if Carmen caught them—and was uninterested—the beautiful face could transform into a pouty snarl that caused the former admirers to quickly stride away.

Carmen also had Virginia's athletic body. She was a high school junior and hoped to make head cheerleader that spring. Virginia was highly invested in that achievement, for Virginia, too, had been a high school cheerleader, but had lost out on head cheerleader. She had never gotten over it.

The delivery boy arrived. Virginia sent Carmen to the front door for the bags. Carmen gave the poor guy an eat-your-heart-out look, and then shut the door in his face. She pocketed the cash Virginia had given her for the tip.

"Okay, everyone," Junior heard his mom call them to dinner.

The boy slipped into his chair, eyeing bags on the table. "What poison is it tonight?" It was fifty-fifty at best for something decent, he thought.

"Well," Virginia passed out the styrofoam containers, "I ordered the chicken salad and fruit plate for Carmen and me, the lime-marinated steak and rice with a warm orange roll for your dad, and an Urban Cowboy sandwich plate for you."

Junior nodded, appeased with the "Urban Cowboy."

The clinking of forks and knives on the everyday china filled the kitchen. Junior scarfed down his sandwich. "Junior, please don't eat like a wolf," Virginia corrected.

"Yes, ma'am."

Virginia put down her fork and looked around the table. She's going to say we should have a family dinner conversation, Junior thought. If the children complained, Virginia would answer that with all their schedules and activities, not to mention her real estate appointments, it was hard to have dinner together, so when together, they should put the smartphones away and talk, like the *Real Simple* magazine articles said they should.

Junior watched Virginia straighten up taller, asking brightly, "Well, children, how were your days?" She tried to smile invitingly. Neither answered. She looked at her husband for assistance but he was distracted with a sheet of numbers sitting to the right of his plate. "George?" she stared at him, raising her eyebrows.

"Oh, yes, sorry. A developer client has to make a decision tomorrow whether to sign onto a large open shopping mall complex up I-65 north of Gardendale and wants the figures."

"Well, can you do that after the family dinner when the children are doing homework." Virginia said, not asking, through pursed lips.

"Sure, sure," he managed, pushing the page away from his plate.

4

George, Jr. wiggled as Virginia turned toward him. "Okay, then, Junior, how was your day?"

"Okay."

He saw her can-you-elaborate look. There was no escape.

"Ah, math was okay. We're doing quadratic equations. I don't know what they're for in the real world, but it's kind of fun to work through them."

"Get used to it," Carmen said, frowning. "You'll never use half the stuff they make you learn in high school math." With that astute pronouncement she stuffed a large bite of chicken salad in her mouth, chewing nonchalantly.

"Carmen, education is important," Virginia lectured. "Math develops critical thinking skills, whether you become a mathematician or not."

"Mom, you've been reading too many parenting articles."

"Carmen, please don't talk with your mouth full. Okay, then, how was your day?"

"The usual. Cheerleading practice was pretty tough, but we're coming together. We're working on a pyramid cheer for this fall. Oh, yeah, AP American History was actually pretty interesting."

"Yes?"

"Yeah. We're on McCarthyism. Like, that was really cra, I can't believe the whole country got so paranoid, everybody saw communists everywhere they looked, and if anything went wrong it was 'the communists.' The government was spying and taking pictures with telephoto lenses, some people ratted out their neighbors, the FBI was wiretapping everybody and that kept going even into the sixties. Senator McCarthy had all these hearings, he made all these people appear, asking them if they were ever members of the Communist Party, and if they said yes or raised the Fifth Amendment, they got fired and lost their jobs, especially a lot of movie producers in Hollywood. They called it 'blacklisted.' Then they found out McCarthy was a drunk and a fraud and the government made people suffer for nothing. I just don't get it. We had oceans on both sides of us."

"It was a different time," George replied absently, concentrating on cutting his meat into little strips. He looked up. "When Russia got the bomb from American traitors, we didn't feel safe anywhere."

5

"But McCarthy was disgraced."

"Pretty much."

"Why did it take so long for people to see that? My teacher, Mr. Ramal, said lives and careers were ruined, but the government never made up for it. But it was the government, the McCarthy committee that ruined their lives!"

"Sometimes these things happen. Mistakes are made, Carmen," George answered.

"But that's not right, is it? Shouldn't the government fix its mistakes?"

"Carmen, I don't think the government likes to admit it makes mistakes."

But he couldn't put her off. George Jr. watched his mother. He thought Virginia enjoyed watching her bright daughter test her father. Since Hillary got screwed in the election, Virginia was real big on women being assertive.

Carmen continued. "Why didn't McCarthy ask about Russia? Why did he say communists instead of Russia? Was there only one communism or several types? We fought communism in Vietnam. Was communism Russia or was it Vietnam?"

"Well, Carmen, it was one communism—well maybe two once China became Red—but America was concerned it would spread over the world like a shadow snuffing out freedom. If all these other countries fell, then free countries would fall like dominoes and communism would spread over a large part of the world, and it could also hurt us, if countries became communist and wouldn't trade with us for raw materials and things we needed."

"But what communism," Carmen insisted. "China or Russia—"

"That domino thinking was wrong," George Jr. couldn't contain himself. "WWII created two superpowers—American and Russia—but left a vacuum in other places. What the American government didn't understand was that World War II destroyed the European colonial system and the former colonies, like Korea and Vietnam, weren't really fighting for communism over democracy, but for their own freedom and unified countries. It was all a big mistake, and McCarthyism fed into that mistake and made it worse for a long time."

"How do you know?" Carmen frowned at him. "You're only in eighth grade."

"I read a lot. I—"

"Well, you both had quite a busy day," Virginia intervened to prevent an argument. "This has really been an enjoyable dinner. George, you just have to start coming home by six each night, and I'll schedule my appointments around dinner. We really have to make dinnertime a family priority."

George pulled the sheet of numbers over and began reading them again.

Junior's mouth fell open. He didn't get to finish. They just shut him down like always.

Virginia said, "I am really pleased you both are getting so much out of your classes. You are getting a top-notch education at that school. Don't you think so, George?"

He looked up quickly, "Ah, yes, yes, sure."

"Well—what's that noise?" she frowned. "Is a neighbor mowing their lawn?"

"No, Mom," Junior answered. "Lawnmowers have gas engines and sound different. It's an electric motor sound. It's a drone."

"A drone?"

"Yeah, a drone."

"It's loud enough to be a giant bumblebee with a thirty-foot wingspan."

"Common now," George interjected. "My developer client uses them to scout undeveloped property. More efficient and cost-effective than walking acres and acres."

"It sounds like it's right over our house," Virginia complained.

"It is," Junior replied.

"But I don't like that," Virginia answered, looking up as if she could see the drone through the ceiling and roof. Looking back down, "What about our privacy? What if it's some predator looking for young girls coming outside that they can snatch? What if he's trying to scope out Carmen?"

"Don't worry. Dr. Reed can get her back."

"Dr. Reed? Junior, our pediatrician is Dr. Beck."

"Mom, it's a joke. Dr. Reed is on *Criminal Minds*. He's my favorite character on the show."

"Junior, I've told you not to watch that show. It's too disturbing for a boy your age." Turning to her husband, "What do we do about drones snooping over our houses and children, George?"

George looked up from the paper as if he'd missed the question.

"I could shoot it down," Junior piped up. "They make drone guns to shoot them down. I could order one from the internet."

Virginia stared at him blankly. "How do you know there is such a thing as 'drone guns?'"

"Mom, everybody knows that. But they got to be within 90 vertical feet of your property. You can pop 'em down all you want there. But over ninety feet they're like in federal airspace and you can't do it. I think I could get away with it. I could say I misjudged the distance, it's hard to judge distance looking straight up. Plus, I'm a kid. They wouldn't do anything. If they did, it'd probably be just Youthful Offender and wouldn't go on my record or anything."

"George Douglas, Jr., banish that thought from your head this instant. You are *not* buying a drone gun." Her eyes bore into him.

"Geez, it was just an idea, Mom. Okay."

Virginia shook her head as if clearing it. "Well, okay, then." She clasped her hands. "Everybody clean up the kitchen and then kids do your homework. We have a busy day tomorrow."

Turning to her daughter. "Carmen you have cheerleading practice and then your calculus tutor at five."

Carmen groaned.

"Carmen, you're looking at Sewanee, W & L, or Virginia for college— you need top scores and AP classes. If you decide on Alabama, you could get in the Honors College with a full ride. Mary Grace Kullen did that two years ago with a 35 on the ACT and a 4.25 GPA. She's getting a free education. AP Calculus separates the winners from the losers to the colleges."

"K," Carmen said, bowing her head.

"Junior, you have Scout meeting tomorrow night, so you need to get your homework done in the afternoon."

"Yes, ma'am."

"And your father and I have big days. He has the big meeting with the developer client, and I—" she beamed proudly "—have a meeting to sign the listing contract on the Featherstone house. I've worked and sweated three years to bag that listing, and tomorrow it's mine." She smiled, tilting her head, most pleased with herself.

"Congrats, Mom!" Junior beamed. "That's really sick."

"Yeah, Mom," Carmen added a half-beat later. "That's extra."

George smiled at his family around the table.

Virginia smiled back.

The Douglas family retired pleasantly that night with their plans carefully set for the coming day.

By dawn, those plans would be in tatters.

CHAPTER 2

THE DOUGLASES RECEIVE A VISITOR
April 10, 2019
The George Douglas Home
4729 Fairhope Drive
Birmingham, Alabama

1:30 a.m. CDT

It was a totally mind-blowing ride, like sitting on the front edge of a light beam rocketing through space.

The beam was a rainbow of colors, rich perfect colors, beautiful hues, glowing, humming, a living beam birthed in the crystal prism of the universe, chased by dainty, crystal notes arranging into sonorous harmonies.

Riding the beam, he felt an unimaginable freedom, the melting of all boundaries, with the pigeonholes of the mind disappearing as the self fell out of time, dissolving into the universe, until all awareness was of a vast, sweet, even oneness, a sublime, contented oneness, as if his soul had returned swaddled to the tender loving arms of the Cosmic Mother.

Of course, he would remember none of this later.

Then there was a noise, a little louder than a bubble gum pop, and Manfred Redford popped out of space-time, landing hard on his bottom in the foyer of the George Douglas home.

A short while later, Manfred would become violently disoriented and anxious, but for now he uttered merely two words: *"Far out!"*

Upstairs, Junior lay sleeping in a bed with royal blue sheets. His pillow was halfway off the bed and his body twisted as he lay diagonally across the mattress. Virginia nagged that he would get a crick in his neck sleeping like that.

A Galaxy S15 smartphone had fallen next to him, the ear buds splayed along the mattress. She also nagged him about falling asleep with his earbuds in. "You'll lose your hearing, do you know that Junior?" she had said a million times.

But he didn't care. He could hear fine.

The boy roused at the popping sound that heralded Manfred's arrival.

He raised his head a millimeter and looked at his robot digital clock, which he got as a present back in the days of robots and Bionicles. Virginia asked if he wanted a nice combination alarm clock and weather radio, but he was attached to his old robot clock. She told him he could not take it to college with him, it wouldn't do. He wasn't so sure about that.

The clock read 1:30 a.m. Good, five more hours, he told himself and was instantly asleep.

George heard the pop. But he did not go back to sleep. Although it was not terribly loud, it was terribly unusual, and so it became terribly important to investigate. And he had *it* that gave him confidence that he could keep his family safe.

George rose, slid his feet in his bedroom slippers, grabbed *it* out of the bedroom closet, and quietly padded down the carpeted hall toward the foyer.

In the meantime, a little puzzled, Manfred looked around the foyer. What was he doing in a house? Before he had time to compile possible answers, he was confronted by a man in a red-checked bathrobe with disheveled hair and glasses askew. Manfred peered at the man who had straw-colored hair thinning on top, and a little ruddiness to his complexion as if he were of some Scottish descent. The man's face was plain and square, and Manfred thought he looked trustworthy. That is, until he saw the man pointed an assault rifle at him—George's *it*.

Upon seeing Manfred, George stopped short as if yanked by strings. His eyes widened, and his face flushed.

Manfred said, "Hey, man, like, just stay cool."

George frowned, then he blurted, "I'm a member of the NRA, and I know how to use this." He waved the automatic rifle at Manfred.

Though Manfred did not find George particularly threatening, the rifle was another story.

12

"Who . . . who are you?" George tried to command with authority.

"Ah, like, dude, can you lower the rifle, man, like I don't want it to accidentally go off—at least not while it's pointed at me."

George paused, lowering his rifle. He said, "What do you expect when someone breaks into your house at one-thirty in the morning?"

"Man, I didn't break into—*what!* One-thirty in the morning! Oh, man, I didn't miss Hendrix's set, did I? He was supposed to play at midnight. Tell me I didn't miss Hendrix—please tell me."

"I don't know about, ah, Hendrix, but you have broken into a private residence in Birmingham, Alabama."

George stared perplexed at Manfred's shoulder-length hair. He said, "I demand to see some identification. Come on, out with your identification."

Manfred fished in the pockets of his faded bell-bottom jeans. He wore a work shirt with an old sixties peace sign embroidered on the pocket.

"C'mon. Hand it over," George snapped.

Manfred passed his license to George who peered at it, blinked and looked again, holding it closer as if to check what he'd seen. He looked over the edge of the card at Manfred. His face bore a pinched look.

Manfred added, "Hey, man, I got something else. It's my draft card, man, see?"

Draft card?

George closely examined the second card. Indeed, it was a draft card issued in 1966 to one Manfred G. Redford, age 18, classification 1-A. "This is impossible—these cards look new. Your . . . your name is Manfred Redford?"

"Yeah. My friends call me Greenjeans." Manfred shrugged. "But my really tight friends call me Space Cadet."

George stared at Manfred.

"This driver's license was renewed in 1969. It says you were born in 1948, you were twenty-one years old when you renewed it."

"Yeah, Einstein," Manfred said, getting tired of the whole scene, "that would be right. I turned twenty-one this year. I can vote and get an actual legal drink before they draft me to Vietnam."

The dude looked unsteady. Manfred wondered what's up.

"Ahem." George cleared his throat, rifle dropping to his side. "Well, I have some rather disturbing news for you. . . ."

"Huh?" Manfred turned solemn.

George braced himself. "It's the year 2019. You are seventy-one."

"No way, man, its 1969—*August 1969!* You're putting me on."

"Sorry." George shook his head, tiredly.

The man seemed sincere.

"Oh," Manfred nodded.

But then the realization that maybe, just maybe, he'd time-traveled fifty years into the future hit him like a Mac truck with faulty brakes. Manfred levitated off the floor just an instant, bellowed an ear-splitting scream, and fell over completely unconscious.

With frayed nerves, the scream startled George, causing him to clench his trigger finger, squeezing off a burst of three rounds. The bullets shattered his wife's étagère in the foyer.

The étagère could be replaced.

The pieces of collectible Wedgwood crystal reduced to shards, however, could not. Staring at the jutting, shattered remnants of his wife's nicer pieces, George moaned, "She's going to kill me this time. She's going to kill me."

Or at least, he would wish she had.

CHAPTER 3

DOES ANYONE REALLY KNOW WHAT TIME IT IS?
April 10, 2019
The foyer and the living room
of the George Douglas Home

1:34 CDT

This time Junior did awake. Wide-eyed. Somebody downstairs had screamed like a caveman seeing an eclipse of the sun. The boy rushed toward his bedroom door, almost tripping on a basket of clean clothes his mother had told him to put up a week ago.

He fleetingly wondered if he ought to get his Boy Scout knife. But there wasn't time to find it. Then he heard gunshots, causing him to race down the stairs, jumping the last three steps. Junior had on a pair of middle school gym pants and a Nirvana T-shirt.

Seeing his father holding the rifle and Manfred unconscious on the floor, his mouth flew open. "Did you kill him, Dad? Huh? Where's the blood?"

His father sadly shook his head. He pointed the rifle to the étagère and shattered crystal. "I killed them instead."

The boy turned to look. He slumped.

"Oh, this is bad, Dad, really bad. You should've shot the guy instead. It'd be easier to face the cops than Mom."

"I know," his father answered miserably.

Junior ran to Manfred's body, dropping to his knees on the parquet floor.

"Son, stop. What are you doing? We don't know him, he could be dangerous."

Manfred stirred, blinked, and looked up at Junior leaning over him.

"Whoa, that hair," Junior exclaimed. "Are you in a band? How long did it take to grow it?"

Manfred stared puzzled at the owner of this voice that had not yet completely hit puberty.

Junior studied him. The hair, the shirt, the bell-bottoms.

"Are you a hippie? A *real* hippie?" the boy blurted.

"What other kind would there be?" Manfred said groggily, trying to lean up on his elbows.

Manfred squinted at the boy's face. "Your eyes are different."

"Yeah, I was born this way," Junior answered.

"You got one brown one and one blue one." A memory blinked, "I was with a girl with eyes like that one time."

Junior, embarrassed about his eyes, leaned back and looked toward his dad.

George was staring down at the rifle in his hands.

"Will she make you get rid of it?" Junior asked.

George turned to his son with a sad expression. "Probably. And I only fired it this one time. Except for the time I bought it." George was not really a member of the NRA.

George bought the rifle from a man whose name he did not know and who would take cash only. George stumbled onto the gun show by accident while driving to a business appointment in a rural county and bought it on the spur of the moment. When he fired the weapon that first time, the recoil almost wrenched it from his hands, causing the seller to frantically dive away with a terse but helpful suggestion: "Shit, man, you got to hold on to it!" George got a good deal because the serial number had been etched off.

Junior's head jerked toward the hallway, then back to his father who looked stricken.

"*Oh, my God . . . George you didn't . . . Surely you didn't . . . What in Heaven have you done . . . ? George put that rifle away now. I knew you'd eventually do something stupid—*"

"*George Junior!*" Virginia Douglas shrieked. "Get away from that man." When the boy paused, she shrieked again. "*This instant. He might be dangerous—or have a disease.*"

Eyes blazing, she surveyed the foyer. "*I want that thing out of my house by daylight, George Douglas!*"

Junior watched his dad lean the gun in a corner in the foyer. He then turned to his mother who was standing over the shards of crystal, hands clasped to her mouth, devastation twisting her face. On a positive note, the boy thought, maybe they could use money from sale of the gun for a down payment on a car for him when he got his learner's permit.

16

There was a musical chime, causing Manfred to sit up looking alert. George pulled a small thin black box from his robe pocket and the chime stopped. George began talking into it.

"No, Herb, there's nothing wrong." There was a slight pause while George appeared to be listening to the device. "No." George tried to laugh. "There were no real gun shots. . . . George Jr. was playing a his new game, you know, the *Deadly Combat XXXIII* Mature-Mature-Adult version with the special surround sound internet link . . . yes, it's one that advertises the effects are so real you look for bullet holes on your playroom walls and blood really squirting from the screen . . . oh, yes, we've told him a hundred times only on Friday nights and weekends . . . yes, I think he slipped down tonight for a little extra action and misjudged the volume control . . . yes, appreciate your understanding . . . sure, we'll get the families together soon and grill out. Goodnight."

Junior was fascinated by Manfred's reaction.

"Wow, man, you got a Captain Kirk communication thing. That's something out of the fut—"

Manfred froze, eyes wide open. He looked woozy.

"Please don't scream again," George pleaded.

"It's a smartphone, dude, come on. Everyone's got one," Junior said, scooting close to Manfred, the intrigue of an apparent hippie overcoming his parents' admonitions.

"George *Junior*, stay away from that man, do not say anything to him," Virginia commanded, with her arms crossed over a lavender silk robe cinched tight at her slim waist. Her voice was a mixture of fear and protectiveness. "We don't know anything about him or his people— George, is he a burglar, should we call the police, how did he break in!"

"No, no, no police," George blurted, thinking of the etched-out serial number on the gun. "We don't know anything about him, although, well, er . . . ah, it's a bit strange, but he thinks he was at Woodstock and the next instant he was in our living room."

"Woodstock?"

"Yes. Woodstock"

"You mean the music festival?"

"Ah, yes."

"That was in 1969."

"Yes."

Virginia stared at her husband mouth open, stupefied. "George that is preposterous. He has to be on drugs."

George nodded. "That's the best explanation."

"We'll put some food in him and see if that sobers him up, and we can get some truth out of him. Then we'll either call the police or the University Hospital psych ward. George, keep that rifle near. You may have to protect us until the authorities arrive. But don't point it toward Junior."

Before George could answer, Virginia froze as she realized the implications: Flashing emergency lights outside of house in the middle of the night. Neighbors coming out in their robes, peering toward them. It would be all over Facebook before she even knew what was happening in her own home. If it leaked out the stranger said he was a time traveler, they would look like a freak-show.

Virginia, frowning, shook her head. She pointed toward the keeping room. "Everybody in there now!"

CHAPTER 4

JUNIOR AND MANFRED VISIT
April 10, 2019
The George Douglas Home
Birmingham, Alabama

2:00 a.m. CDT

"Let me get going on the cooking," Virginia muttered once they were in the kitchen area. "If I don't call the police before then, I'm calling our family lawyer at 8:00 a.m. sharp for his instructions on what to do with you—what's your name?"

"Manfred."

"Seriously?"

"Serious as a heart attack."

"You two sit at the table. And you"—she pointed at Manfred— "I want you planted at this table. If you as much as twitch I'll call the police, and I am personally acquainted with the Chief who will bury you. Time traveling, my foot. I can have you locked in a cell or maybe you need a psychiatric commitment. So, if you want to see daylight a free man, you'd better toe the line, mister. Clear?"

"Ah, clear."

George, Jr. turned to Manfred. Manfred looked scared—and pissed off.

"Better do what she says," the boy whispered.

Manfred did not respond.

Virginia stared at Manfred a few moments more, then disappeared into the walk-in pantry, calling out to George, "George, honey, can you help me find the tea?"

Joining her in the pantry, George said, "I don't remember any Earl Grey in here."

"Shhh," Virginia whispered, "that's not why I called you." Virginia looked out the pantry door to make sure they weren't overheard.

Though his parents thought they were being discrete, George, Jr. and Manfred every word.

19

"George, if anything happens, hit the panic button on the alarm system. If closer, I will—"

"Certainly, but—Virginia, the alarm—"

"What of it?"

"It was on. How did he get in our house without tripping the alarm?"

"Are you sure it was on?"

"Yes, I checked the display panel by the back door in the kitchen before coming to bed. The light was green—and it still is. It's been armed all night. I'm positive."

"How . . . how could he get in the house and not set off the alarm?" Virginia's voice rose with her anxiety. "The kids set if off every other week."

"I—I don't know?" George frowned. "This is impossible. Do you think he knew how to bypass it?"

"*Him?*" Virginia, said sneering. "He looks like he couldn't start a car with the key."

George shrugged. They stared at each other.

"George, I detest the thing, but if you need to, you get that rifle ..."

George, Jr. frowned. There went the down payment for a car.

Manfred stared forward, as if his face was cut from stone.

They had an awkward meal at an awkward hour.

Virginia had whipped up a breakfast of scrambled free-range chicken eggs, gluten free toast of ancient grains, organic cantaloupe and blueberries, and dark ground coffee from a new fashionable shop.

Eating had distracted the group from dealing with each other, but now the tension had them all shifting and fiddling.

"Can we go to my room?" Junior asked.

"No," Virginia and George spoke in unison.

"How 'bout the living room?"

Virginia passed a look with George who shrugged, welcoming a respite. She seemed to make a decision.

"Okay, for a minute. Mr. Redford, remember my husband has a rifle."

"Ma'am, that would be hard to forget." He nodded his head toward the foyer.

"I don't need a sharp remark, Mr. Redford. You just take care you mind yourself."

20

Manfred nodded. The pair rose for the living room. Manfred turned back, Thank you, ma'am, for the breakfast. It was delicious."

"Don't thank me," Virginia shot at him. "Just watch yourself. Junior, call out if he gets out of line."

As they headed through the archway, Junior whispered, "That was a good move, thanking Mom. Manners get you a long way with her. Wait here, I'm going up to my room to change."

Junior was smallish for his age with straight, straw-colored hair like his dad and brown plastic glasses. He had bright, precocious eyes that didn't miss a trick, even if they were different colors. His face was friendly, yet with a hint of reserve.

The boy turned, moving about the room toward the closet.

There was a *Rise Against* poster on one wall, and across the way, *The Offspring*. The rest of the walls were covered with pictures, drawings, pages torn from magazines, another poster, one of the robot from *The Day the Earth Stood Still*, the old one with Michael Rennie, and next to it, a poster of the Monolith from *2001: A Space Odyssey*. There were other prints and photos, including Junior's favorite, Gil Grissom from *CSI* with the caption, "Follow the evidence."

He put on blue jeans, a pullover shirt, and running shoes. He boogied back down the stairs.

Sitting on the sofa with Manfred, the pair was silent a moment. Junior looked at Manfred. "You really time-traveled?".

"Apparently, straight from 1969."

"How? I mean, how could you do that?"

"Don't know. It's like a bad trip."

"I can't get over your turning up at our house tonight? And that you don't know how you got here?"

"Dude, it's mind-blowing, that's all I can say."

"But how did you get in?" the boy pondered. "The alarm system was on. I saw the green light."

"What alarm system?"

"Home alarm."

"A home alarm? You mean you have a burglar alarm on your house? Why would you do that?"

The boy could only stare at him blankly.

"Oh, it's one of those future things I don't know about?"

The boy nodded.

"So you're saying if somebody jimmied a door or window to get in— like does the alarm go off—"

"Or breaks glass, the window."

"Wow. It can tell that?"

The boy nodded.

"So like if somebody breaks in the house, what, an alarm goes off, like a ringing bell or something?"

"Actually, a siren."

"A siren?"

"Yes."

"Like a police car siren?"

"More like a car alarm but close enough."

"You have alarms on your *cars*?"

The boy nodded again.

"Man, you guys are paranoid here in the future. You don't have alarms on the toilet seats do you, cause, like, I really got to take a leak. I was scared to ask your mom to go pee. Bathroom down the hall?"

Junior pointed his head toward the powder room door. "In there."

"Are ya'll okay in here?" Virginia, hand on hip, stood in the in the living archway.

"Yes, ma'am."

"Where is Redford?"

"Behind you, I had to use the restroom."

"Oh," Virginia said, moving to allow him by. She turned back toward the kitchen, but first stopped in the powder roof, sniffing the air for drugs and looking in the trash can for paraphernalia. Finding none, she returned to the kitchen.

Back with the boy, keeping his voice low, Manfred said, "You know I was thinking in there, like, you're saying there's an alarm on the house and if I opened a door or raised a window a siren would go off—"

22

"And it would automatically call the police."

"Police. Geez, this is like *1984*. There's not a 'Big Brother' around is there?"

"No. That was a book."

"Okay, just checking, this is all a real trip."

Junior stared hard at Manfred, judging his face.

Manfred slumped. "All I want to do is get back. You know, to Woodstock, dude, and hear Hendrix . . . and there was this chick. Man, I rode all the way from Ohio to hear Hendrix and sat through all that rain and shit, and now I'm in some tripped-out futuristic Big Brother place that's a real paranoid drag when none of this is my fault."

"Wow, this is fantastic," the boy said, excitement rising in his voice. "You may be the first time traveler. You know how cool that is? You can be famous, rich." But he frowned. "The government will want you." He shook his head. "They'll want to find out all about you and how you got here and everything and then declare it top secret classified. Plus, the tabloids and paparazzi will drive you crazy."

"I'm not dealing with the government. You can't trust the establishment, man. And who are the pepperoni?"

"You don't know how you to get back. No idea?"

Manfred shook his head.

Junior chewed his lip, deep in thought. He looked up. "I wonder if maybe someone could help you?"

"No, shit."

"Yes, it'd be really cool. I know this guy who might could help."

"What guy?"

"This guy that runs the computer and electronics store. He knows everything about electronics, computers, and physics—his knowledge is freaky, almost like he came from the future. He's way more fun than my science teacher. He helped with me with my science project, and I placed third in the southeastern regional science fair. Mom almost went to the moon she was so happy, but I never told her about that guy. I didn't feel like being cross-examined. She'd probably check the predator data base, certain that something was wrong with him for being that interested in some kid. Plus, I'd probably lose my award for collaborating with an adult."

23

They both became quiet. Junior cut a glance at Manfred. Was this guy taking him in? Maybe. But everything seemed real about him, and Manfred didn't seem to fake being shocked at the house alarms and stuff that really seemed new to him. Junior trusted his gut, like Gibbs on NCIS. He decided to go with it.

Junior thought hard. The problem was in order for Manfred to go back, wouldn't they have to figure out how he got here in the first place?

And about that, they had no idea.

The same year that physicist Richard Feynman won his Nobel Prize, a not-so-famous Manheim Schnictmann worked out a series of formulas that predicted what he came to call a "disaccordian resonance bubble." The formulas predicted that, at the subatomic level, a quantum bubble could form and in a few nanoseconds rapidly expand into our macro world. Schnictmann named this process "disaccordian inflation." He had no clue why this occurred, but he theorized that discordant vibrations in the subatomic realm produced a set of conditions that randomly produced a macro-bubble. The formulas also predicted that the disaccordian resonance bubble would be totally undetectable, except upon its demise when it popped, releasing triverticular particle perturbations over extreme distances.

The real kicker in the theory was that Schnictmann extrapolated from the equations that the inflating bubble would trap everything within its circumference. Everything inside would be subject to quantum mechanics, and due to Heisenberg's Uncertainty Principle, matter would be in a state of quantum flux, which for living things would be like a state of suspended animation. When the bubble popped, any living things would pop right out into the stream of life no older, but with an odd experience of having ridden on a rainbow light beam surrounded by beautiful melodies.

Schnictmann's theory had been impossible to test, because in the mid-twentieth century, it was impossible to build a triverticular particle perturbation detector. So, his theory became relegated to an obscure text sitting on an obscure shelf of an obscure section in the physics section of an obscure small library on the Princeton campus.

Schnictmann would have been delighted to find that, indeed, disaccordian resonance bubbles were real, and a human being, one Manfred Redford, had actually become trapped in one the last night at Woodstock in 1969. However, fifty years is a long time to wait on a disaccordian resonance bubble to pop, and Schnictmann did not make it, having died of natural causes in 1994.

Of course, Manfred and Junior knew none of this. It would have made no difference if they had, for Schnictmann's theories predicted that disaccordian resonance bubbles could not go backward. When they popped, a traveler was stuck on the flypaper of time.

CHAPTER 5

A TIME TO RUN
April 10, 2019
George Jr.'s bedroom
Birmingham, Alabama

4:00 a.m. CDT

"Think you can call the guy?" Manfred asked in a voice between hopeful and hopeless.

Junior stared at Manfred.

Manfred had chestnut hair, shoulder length and parted down the middle. His eyes were blue, but slightly unfocused, a little spacey. The boy guessed that was from drugs. Manfred wore black, low-cut Converse tennis shoes. The boy thought he was thin, could use five or ten pounds. Although spacey, Manfred also had a subtle kinetic energy. Despite Manfred's weirdness, the boy liked him.

"Are you okay in there, Junior?" Virginia called from the kitchen.

"Sure, mom, everything's okay."

"I'm fixing a plate for Carmen, do you need anything else?"

"No, ma'am."

"Who's Carmen?" Manfred asked.

"My sister."

"I didn't know you had a sister."

"I try not to mention it."

Manfred shrugged. He was becoming more anxious. "Think you can call this guy? Your mom's going to have me in jail by sunrise if you don't?"

"I'm thinking?"

"Well, call him man. Like, I don't want the fuzz sniffing me over."

"The fuzz?"

"The police, man. Don't be a square."

Junior frowned. From school, he was self-conscious about not being cool. But he had decided to call the man anyway. Things were too strange.

"Well, call man, you got a Captain Kirk thing?"

"You mean a smart phone? Of course, everybody has them. Even the kindergarteners."

Manfred gestured, like do it, then.

Junior was debating when to call. He wanted to wait to a decent time, closer to daylight. He wasn't used to calling adults. But the man had told him to call if anything really weird happened, *anytime—day or night*. The guy was really serious about that and made Junior promise, which was a little scary. But if tonight wasn't weird enough to call, it never would be.

"Okay." Junior checked his phone for the time.

"What are you doing?" Manfred questioned.

"Checking the time before I call."

"On your phone? Don't you wear a watch?"

"No. Why would I? I always have my phone."

"Oh, brother." Manfred hung his head.

Junior, more than a little nervous, pulled up the man in contacts, and tapped the number. He held the phone so Manfred could here. It rang twice, and then, "Hello, Junior."

"Mr. Bossilini, sir, sorry to call you so . . . early. You know how you told me to call you if something weird ever happened . . . well, something really weird happened at our house tonight. You're not going to believe this, but a guy just popped into our living room, saying he's from another time . . . yes, I mean the past . . . oh? He seems to be a hippie, like a real one from the sixties. You know, Mr. Bossilini, it's really probably nothing . . . oh . . . you think it really is . . . look outside, okay, hold on." The boy walked to the living room window and pulled open enough of the side of the curtain to peer out.

The boy did not know Mr. Bossilini was an Agent of the League of Privacy Sentinels.

Junior breathlessly shouted into his phone, "Mr. Bossilini—someone's on our street. There's a black SUV—and a big black van with its lights off heading toward our house."

Manfred ran to the window and peered out over the boy's head. "This is not good. I don't know what it is, but it's not good."

"What's happening, Mr. Bossilini?" the boy whispered urgently into the phone, but no so loud as to attract his parents.

Bossilini's voice immediately assumed an urgency. "Run to the alley this minute. Tell your family the weather emergency alert radio just went off and there is a gas leak on your street that could blow up the block any

28

second. The authorities are on the street working on detecting the leak but they may be too late. An evacuation team is parked in the alley to ferry people out of danger. Tell them to run, run, leave everything behind. It is urgent. You must be convincing. Your lives are at stake. Do you understand that?"

"Where will you be?"

"In the alley, of course."

"Is this for real?" Manfred asked Junior.

They boy nodded, his eyes wide.

"Let's, like, split then," Manfred said.

Junior led the way, running to the keeping room, "Mom, dad. The weather radio emergency alert went off. There's a gas leak on the block and everything could blow up. We have to get out NOW. The men are on the street looking for the leak, but it said to leave through the back of your houses now." Junior, with his eyes wide and extremely agitated, executed a most convincing performance. It didn't hurt that Manfred had corroborated the weather radio warning, too. Whatever a weather radio was, he wondered.

George and Virginia had until that moment begun to relax.

The urgency in her son's voice put them instantly on high alert.

"Out, out, out now. Leave everything," Virginia shouted. "We have replacement cost coverage on our insurance. Carmen and Junior come to me this instant."

Manfred noticed there was a girl rising from the table. The thought occurred maybe the future could be interesting after all. She was very, very pretty, about sixteen, though her face was still puffy from sleep. She had shoulder-length blonde hair pulled up, a dust of just the right shade of mascara to accent her beautiful green eyes, with a lovely sculptured neck. He quickly veered to leave with her.

He had taken two steps when Virginia sliced in a voice so sharp he thought he'd been cut, *"Don't you even think about it."* Manfred stopped short. The girl glanced back at him with a snotty look.

Manfred asked Junior in a whisper, "So that's your sister."

"Welcome to the family," Junior quipped as he moved toward the door.

"You both quit talking and *move*. We *have* to get out the house before it blows up. Hurry. *Hurry!*" Virginia shrieked.

George bellowed in support, "Come on kids, you heard your mother, get out now. This is the real thing. It's *dangerous!*"

With Virginia leading the pack, the Douglas family and guest fled through the back door, almost wrenching it from the hinges as it banged open. Junior reached down and snagged his backpack where he'd left it after his homework.

They heard a boom and splintering sound from the front of their house.

"Was that an explosion?" Virginia shouted.

George looked back, peering intently at the house. "I don't know." Then the house alarm went off with an ear-splitting shriek.

"Oh, the alarm," Virginia said.

"Don't worry about it, just *RUN*," George yelled.

"*Faster, faster, everybody*," Junior cried, taking the lead. The group bumped and lumbered, following the boy through the backyard, past the weathering wooden swing set toward the alley twenty-five yards away. They could hardly see in the dark.

George looked back. "Virginia, there seem to be people in our kitchen. It looks like they are running around." Arcs from flashlight beams crisscrossed out of the kitchen windows and open doorway.

"Dad, we really have to hurry," Junior said, fear making his voice high-pitched. "Oh, this is close, it's really going to be close," he squeaked.

Finally, the group huffed and stumbled to the edge of the grass before a black strip of asphalt, which was the alley. They looked frantically back toward the house at the people swarming the kitchen.

"Maybe those are gas company people in our house," Virginia said, her head turned back toward the house. "Do we need to go back and show them where the shut-off valve is?"

"No way, Mom," Junior shouted at her.

Suddenly, Virginia jumped from a fast whooshing sound right in front of them. Junior had the sensation of something coming to a quick stop a foot or two away. He peered hard into the dark and could barely make out a black rectangle shape before him.

"Is this the shuttle?" George asked. But he jumped back, startled, when the front passenger door swung open without warning. A head appeared from the driver's seat, and a voice as resonate as a cello, but with a trace of Hungarian accent, greeted them.

"Nitko Bossilini at your service. Please hurry inside. I am to extract you from the danger."

II.

PARTICLES

CHAPTER 6

TRIVERTICULAR PARTICLES
April 10, 2019
Cape Canaveral, Florida

2:30 a.m. EDT

Charles Carmody rubbed his face, scratching a two-day stubble of beard, and wearily glanced at the clock, though he needn't have looked. He knew that two-thirty-in-the-morning-on-night-shift feeling. Four hours to day shift, four months till retirement. He noticed the symmetry in the numbers, but felt no thrill. Unlike detectives in crime shows, he believed in coincidences.

Carmody was shift supervisor for the South Florida Detector Facility, a super-secret operation of the Department of Homeland Security. The equipment in the Facility detected unusual phenomena related to subatomic particle bursts, waves and emissions.

The Department, along with its cousin the NSA, was dedicated to detecting *every* human communication that it could, collecting those communications and preserving the data in perpetuity in mammoth storage facilities. Carmody's section was tasked with eliminating signal interference so the conversations stored in perpetuity were crystal clear, clear enough to hear a pin drop, like in the old Sprint ads.

But Carmody at the moment didn't give a whit about any of that. He was trying to decide whether if he had a cup of coffee it would keep him from sleeping when home. Though he had been on night shift for six months, he'd not adjusted to the topsy-turvy sleep schedule.

Carmody hadn't made a decision about the coffee when through the thin glass walls of his supervisor office he saw a technician hurrying toward his office door, headphones still on his head, unplugged cord trailing behind. He's going to trip on that cord if he's not careful, Carmody thought with a shake of his head.

Then Carmody thought brightly, *maybe he will*. But he knew he had no such luck.

What the hell does Jeffers want this time? Carmody inwardly groaned. He'll bug me the rest of the shift, whatever it is. It *had* been a pleasant evening thus far.

The door flew open. "C.C—" Jeffers burst in.

"Goddamn it Jeffers, I've told you I don't like C.C. Call me Carmody or Charles, but not C.C. Got it?"

"Okay, C.C."

Carmody shook his head and regretted he had no office bottle of whiskey to pour in that cup of coffee he just decided to have.

"Spit it out, Jeffers."

"You won't believe it. You won't freaking believe it. It's incredible."

"Why don't you just slow down and tell me what it is, and I can help you assess if it really is incredible." Carmody found Jeffers scattered like so many of his generation. Carmody sighed. What do you expect from a three-second attention span?

"Okay, okay." Jeffers took a deep breath, looking at Carmody. "Detectors—the detectors went off ten minutes ago, crazy like."

"What, long wave, broadband, gamma burst?"

"No, no, none of that. You know it was dark till now. Sitting in that corner collecting dust. Floris keeps her Begonias on it."

Carmody sat up. Surely Jeffers did not mean *that* detector.

In the glare of Carmody's stare, Jeffers sputtered, "Tri-tri-the triverticular particle perturbation detector. It went off. *It went off.* Flashing lights. We have readings—"

"Where, what—"

Jeffers rattled a sheaf of print-out pages.

"Oh, hell," Carmody uttered, turning for the procedure manual listing the steps in responding to a positive triverticular particle perturbation recording. It had been nine months since the last training refresher. He tried to run the steps through his mind, but he'd never paid that much attention. To him, this was all theoretical, no one really expected to find the particles. He and other old-timers thought it was all some wild stuff from kids who had played too many video games. He fumbled with the titanium key to the titanium lock on his bottom right desk drawer.

"C.C., you need me to help you?"

"I can open my own goddamn desk drawer, thank you."

Carmody slammed the manual on his desk and ran his finger down the protocol. "This goes straight to Washington," he uttered.

"Not Atlanta?"

"Not Atlanta. Straight to D.C. Straight to the Secretary."

"Holy crap."

Carmody punched a button to activate a special line on his desk phone—the old kind with real wires connected to a real, though highly secure, telephone line. Carmody was glad it was connected to real wires and not the damn ether cloud of electron waves.

A fuzzy signal beeped three times, then a clear line opened.

Carmody spoke one word: "Wildroot." He hung up the phone.

Three minutes later his phone rang. Carmody answered. Jeffers watched Carmody as he listened intently, sweat beads forming on his forehead. Carmody relayed to whoever was on the other end the data from the detection reports.

"Yes, sir," Carmody replied, staring at the report in his hand.

"Who is it," Jeffers mouthed. "Who is it, C.C.?"

Carmody said, "Yes, sir. I understand. Yes, sir, it was good work. Thank you, sir."

Carmody hung up with a dazed look.

"Come on, C.C.—I mean—Charles, who was it?"

Carmody looked up with trepidation. "The Assistant Secretary of Homeland Security."

"Holy crap. We didn't screw up anything, did we?"

"No, Jeffers, not us. But I think the guys at the top may have a shot at it."

And the guys at the top had never read Manheim Schnictmann.

CHAPTER 7

IN THE DENS OF POWER
April 10, 2019
Washington, DC

2:50 a.m. EDT

Preston A. Ogilvie, Secretary of Homeland Security, sat in his home study in Georgetown watching by secure video conference the report from select Undersecretaries and department heads. In his moments of pique, the more immature of his staffers often whispered, "P.O. is PO'd."

"So let me understand this. This—device—"

"It's not a device, it's a triverticular particle perturbation detector. The guys call it a TPPD," Lathers, the Undersecretary of Science and Technology, corrected him.

Ogilvie stared sternly through the screen at the man. He did not like being corrected in front of his department heads, or really anyone. After a sufficient glare, Ogilvie continued. "But it's theoretical, right? Didn't the Government Accounting Office criticize us for the cost of the mainframe detector and the portable units? They were barely civil, lecturing us that the technology to even remotely approach that threat was centuries away, if not impossible altogether. I caught hell in the Congressional oversight hearing for the expense on that one." He steepled his fingers in front of his chest.

"But our guys were all worked up over the boys at Princeton who postulated these theoretical particles. Nobody even knew if they existed, and the next thing you know the Department of Defense is doing this cloak-and-dagger deal to build portable detector devices, they say are essential to homeland security. And they stuck that it in *our* budget! We took the heat for their toys."

"That's a correct rendition, sir," Lathers nodded.

"But now you are saying these particles are *real*. Our systems actually found real particles—here in America. And that's supposed to mean somebody or somebodies are opening a transport tunnel to invade here on American soil? That the tunnel when it opens throws off these, ah, particles, whatever you call them?"

"That's exactly right," Dick Chambers chimed in. He was the Assistant Secretary at Homeland under Ogilvie though the latter's senior by fifteen years. Chambers had seen a lot in Washington and had the scars to prove it. He was a hard-liner, and Ogilvie relied on him, especially when things got tough.

"Secretary Ogilvie," Lathers continued, on the edge of his chair. "The best thinking is indeed these particles signal—I know it sounds crazy—the opening of a space tunnel, a transport tunnel—"

"A tunnel opening here in America but initiated in a foreign country?"

"Yes, that's it," Lathers said. "It's a radical new weapon, sir. But the whiz kids at Princeton predicted it, and our own whiz kids confirmed the math. It should be possible."

"And what it makes possible is for the initiating country—"

"Or terrorists."

"—or terrorists—to travel instantly with troops and equipment from their country to our country?"

"That's it. Like a wormhole. No need for traditional logistics, transport delays. Boom, they're here."

"Yeah, but some of our guys are not so sure," Bob Harley interjected. "Don't they joke, calling it the BRT—the 'Buck Roger's Tunnel'?"

Lathers frowned. He had heard the reference and didn't like it.

Assistant Secretary Chambers felt the momentum in the room slipping. He did not want to lose this opportunity, for indeed there was opportunity. An opportunity for more appropriations, more information gathering, more power.

"Preston," Chambers said firmly, "we can't be caught with our pants down on this one. Chambers was the only member allowed to call Secretary Ogilvie by his first name. If it turns out to be a false alarm, we can shut it down, keep it quiet, call it a training exercise if anybody gets wind of it. But if it's real and we didn't respond, well, the spaghetti would hit the fan—and let's just say, you don't want that."

"But Birmingham, Alabama. Why would they target there? I mean, don't they grow cotton and peanuts—and play football?"

"Big thing used to be steel, Mr. Secretary, but the Germans and Japanese cut them out of the market," Bob Harley said. He then offered, "If Reagan had gotten in sooner perhaps he could've busted the Steel

40

Workers union down there and things might've gone a different way, but it is what it is."

"You're good with this, Dick? A Wildroot Alert—the emergency team deployed to Alabama?"

Ogilvie turned to Chambers, who nodded to signal that he was. "Preston, you can't take chances with this—an invasion on American soil through a revolutionary new weapon whose full capabilities we don't know. We have to act." Chambers knew if he was firm, Ogilvie would go along.

"Agreed. Wildroot it is. I'm good to go," Ogilvie decided, quickly. "Get it done."

"Ah, Mr. Secretary," the Department General Counsel interrupted. "The White House?"

Ogilvie looked at Chambers, then shook his head vigorously. "No."

"But sir—"

"That will take too much time. The President will want to vet this with the full Cabinet and then run it through the spin control cycle for the media. You're talking days. If this is real, and you're telling me it looks like it is, then an Iranian regiment at any moment could pop out of a space tunnel in Times Square and start shooting."

"Well, I *guess* you could say that," Dave Whitmire, the Department Press Secretary said, not trying to hide his skepticism. He'd have to clean up the mess if this blew up in Secretary Ogilvie's face.

"Or, Dave, maybe you'd like better a terrorist popping out in San Francisco, say on the Golden Gate Bridge, and blowing himself up with a suicide vest? Or maybe one pops out in Anytown, USA, rents a car filled with fertilizer crap like McVeigh, and drives it into a middle school? How would you like to field questions at *that* press conference when we knew *ahead* of time but didn't do anything?"

"Okay, okay, Mr. Secretary, we get it," Whitmire said, throwing in the towel. It was useless to argue with Ogilvie when he got like this.

"Or maybe the Chinese have the technology and will send two divisions of combat troops to help Mexico reclaim the southwestern United States?"

"Preston," Chambers said calmly. "I think we understand the point."

But Ogilvie was worked up.

41

"The point is they can make mincemeat out of our Department, they can make us look like clowns." He stared steadily at each in turn. "Not on my watch."

"Urgency is required," he declared. "Urgency is demanded. Better to seek forgiveness than permission." He had always liked that phrase and used it whenever he could. "We don't have a second to spare. Gentlemen, the survival of our country, our democracy, and our way of life are at stake. That is why we are here."

He was pleased with his statement. "Urgency is demanded" would be a great sound bite. He wished this moment had been recorded to capture his profile—square, strong, resolute. The kind of clip that could galvanize a campaign and win a nomination.

But he saw their reluctance. They worried, it was risky going it alone, without consultation with other agencies. Space tunnels, after all? Terrestrial wormholes? Blame was better when shared.

Ogilvie considered their nervous expressions as they pondered the loss of carefully constructed careers. If they charged into Alabama and this turned out to be nothing more than a meteorological phenomenon, then the President would leave them twisting in the wind, the press flailing them unmercifully. No campaign literature then, no great, patriotic pictures. Only talk show interviews to avoid. Maybe he should take their counsel, but with modifications.

"Okay. Here's how we will work it—we're only talking a couple of hours anyway." He noticed they sat up straighter, as if a reprieve were offered.

"We'll release a Wildroot team, our technicians will deploy. We'll turn the field work over to the FBI—I can work with its Director. He knows the score. That will drag in another agency to share the blame if needed. When it's too late to recall the deployment, we'll brief the Homeland Security Council, tell them that it an immediate response was essential for the defense of the country. They wouldn't want a delay in responding hung on *them* if a kindergarten goes up in smoke. And they will involve the President before you can say Jiminy Cricket."

Jiminy Cricket? Chambers frowned.

He shook his head.

How could a man that corny rise this far?

CHAPTER 8

"WILDROOT"
April 10, 2019
Department of Homeland Security
Washington, D.C.

3:30 a.m. EDT

Secretary Preston A. Ogilvie sat back in his leather office chair, reflecting with satisfaction upon his conversation with the Director of the FBI. He knew he could count on Bart. They had been classmates at Yale, though nowadays when speaking they kept to business and no longer reminisced about their college days.

Ogilvie glanced down at the crease in his suit pant leg. The suit was navy blue, which Ogilvie liked because he looked good in blue, but also because a blue suit was a power suit—he'd studied Reagan enough to learn that, though his tie was not red, but light emerald green with blue squares. He was more debonair than Reagan, after all.

Ogilvie liked the crisp crease in the pant legs, for it showed that quality and expensive tailoring counted. He was six feet three and looked like a middleweight in his fine suit. His jaw was square and firm, and his hazel eyes possessed a politician's range. He moved easily among people, appearing confident and in command.

Now that the night sky was fading from black to gray flannel, Ogilvie sat smugly at his desk, pleased that he was the highest ranking official in government who knew of the threat to the United States of America, and he—Preston A. Ogilvie—was taking decisive action to protect and secure this precious land. If he handled the matter correctly, which he had every confidence he would, he was very likely to gain even more power.

Ogilvie had begun his public career with a sincere desire to serve. The arc of his career began with a lowly position on the White House staff, followed by a steady rise through agencies, commissions, junior staff, senior staff, and now—head of Homeland Security—one of the most, if not the most, powerful departments in the United States government, and hence, the world.

Ogilvie was connected—courtesy of his wife's wealth—and had learned to navigate Washington. Ogilvie was pleased that he had managed all aspects of his life to advantage. Though he was idealistic when entering public service upon law school graduation, he quickly became enamored by power, its exercise and its fruits. Thus, what began as a career about public service evolved into a career about Preston Ogilvie.

And the last two hours had presented an unimagined opportunity to boost Preston Ogilvie's persona and career. As Secretary, he intended to rise on Homeland's record of keeping America safe.

Now, if there were an attack with a new and fearsome technology—an attack that Ogilvie and Homeland thwarted—then Congress and the people would give Homeland and NSA a blank check to collect whatever data they wanted. Ogilvie would have access to that data, and the power it bestowed. As a bonus, Ogilvie's face would be the symbol of victory. And with the victory he provided, Americans would feel safe to return to their travel-team baseball, reality TV, and all those singing competition shows. Ogilvie had realized some time ago people just wanted to feel safe, and if they felt safe, then they really didn't want to be bothered.

He smiled in anticipation. Perhaps he could snatch the nomination from the President at the convention the next summer, or at least, garner the Vice President spot on the ticket.

He caught a glance of his appearance in a silver water pitcher on his desk. He admired the square cut of his face and black hair with silver steaks representing maturity and confidence. He could not fail, he smiled. With those distinguished looks, he was destined for success.

CHAPTER 9

THE FBI
April 10, 2019
Washington, D.C.
Limousine of Director of the FBI
"Operation Gettysburg"

3:30 a.m. EDT

FBI Director Bart Cummings reflected on his conversation with Secretary Ogilvie as his driver whisked him through the early morning, empty D.C. streets toward the FBI building.

He thought Ogilvie's narcissism was getting worse.

Cummings was unsettled, and he did not like to make decisions when unsettled. Cummings was not flamboyant and had never liked that part of Ogilvie when they had run in the same circle at Yale. Ogilvie frequently chided Cummings with the platitude, "Nothing ventured, nothing gained." Cummings would simply reply, "Remember Icarus."

Now, an attack on United States soil with a new weapon—in Alabama? Those guys down there would love a fight, they hadn't gotten over losing the Civil War.

"But Bart, we have the data," Ogilvie pressed. He could be most convincing when he really wanted something. "This is solid science. We've been watching for something like this. Didn't expect it this quickly, really, but our guys were on top of things and had the detectors in place. Good thing, too."

"But why weren't we briefed, Preston? There's been not a whisper about this technology or threat. Not even a whisper stays quiet in this town. Now, out of the blue, the United States is being attacked through a space tunnel? It doesn't jive with our current intelligence. That would mean our whole intelligence community committed the biggest screw-up in history. Can you imagine what the 24/7 talk shows would do with that?"

Ogilvie frowned. He did not like the assertion about the whole "intelligence community," as his DHS could be construed part of that community. But he thought of a deft response, one that could play.

45

"Bart, you and I are both domestic. The Department of *Homeland* Security. The FBI by law is limited to *domestic* operations." Ogilvie could tell from Cummings' silence that the point was registering. He knew Cummings too well. "Seems to leave our friends at the CIA rather asleep on the watch, wouldn't you say, our friends who are charged with *foreign* operations. I expect *you* would never lose sleep if the CIA had a *faux pas* on its watch?"

That was true, Cummings admitted to himself, but not aloud. But he did say, "Preston, you're asking me to assemble a team immediately and fly it to Birmingham to . . . what . . . work with your technicians and locate and, I guess, apprehend Americans who are aiding and abetting the enemy, treason, really. I mean, we don't have any warrants, not even a FISA warrant for surveillance."

"Bart, Bart, this is not a violation of the federal criminal code. This isn't kidnapping or bank robbery. It's high treason and invasion of our soil by an enemy. The Patriot Act. We have plenty of legal authority under the law and Executive Orders, even the secret ones, to conduct this operation. Our guys are making a cover story if we're wrong. A training exercise on infiltration by a homegrown terrorist cell. We're making documents, creating email traffic, fictitious identities, the whole nine yards for running a training exercise, backdated and ready for upload if necessary, if this turns to be only a cosmic particle barrage or something benign. If we play the training exercise card, it will be too boring even to make *The Situation Room*."

Cummings mused that over.

He thought it through aloud. "So we're covered either way. If it's real we do our job and take these guys down. If it's not, we're covered by training and being prepared. The citizens like us being prepared."

"Yes, they do, Bart. So what do you think? You know, the Bureau can always use good press, like that was quite fine work in Boston a few years back, nabbing the bombers within a week, and busting the neo-Nazi group in Little Rock with all the weapons and bombs—that could've been a bad one. It's always nice to stay ahead of the curve. Be involved in this one, don't you think?"

Cummings was quiet. Then he answered.

"I think it can play. A lot still bothers me. But if it's real, we can't delay a minute. If not, it's training, and everybody's in favor of training. The downside is hedged."

Ogilvie smiled on his end of the call. He knew he had his old friend Bart.

"I don't have to tell you, Bart, it's important to pick the right man to lead this. Very important. Keep me posted." Ogilvie ended the call. Sitting back in his chair, he pressed the fingertips of his hands together. The next three hours were critical.

Cummings fretted over the choice of who to lead the team to Alabama. The agent would have to be loyal to the Bureau—unquestionably loyal. And he—or she, he guessed—would have to be experienced in leading a team in a rapid-fire deployment and keeping that team in line with an iron fist. There was no room for error in this operation. Cummings could feel his GERDs kicking up acid in his stomach. He'd forgotten his Nexium in the morning's excitement.

Cummings turned over several promising candidates in his mind. But as he visualized them one by one in the operation, he was uneasy. While each had capabilities, and had proven themselves many times, none seemed right for *this* operation. He was becoming annoyed that he had let Ogilvie talk him into such a preposterous undertaking. *Project Gettysburg*, Ogilvie called it. Cummings disliked that name: it was another example of Ogilvie's flair for the dramatic.

He thought about reaching Ogilvie and calling it off, but he knew, Ogilvie would erupt, and he was erratic when he erupted. Also, again, what if it was real? They hadn't seen the planes on 9/11 coming, after all. If the Bureau had a chance to protect America and abdicated its responsibility, well, Hoover would turn over in his grave. Not to mention Cummings digging his own.

He relented and returned to the task of mentally running through a stream of FBI agents and managers. The moniker *Project Gettysburg* ran through his mind again, and he said to himself, "Maybe, just maybe." Cummings thought he may have just the right Special Agent for this project.

The guy was a Marine from Pennsylvania. And had seen combat. That counted for a lot. But more important, with his straight-laced intensity, he could easily pass for the reincarnation of Jack Webb as Joe Friday. He would not question orders and would stick doggedly to the facts. Most importantly, he loved the Bureau and would protect it at all costs.

Cummings broke off his musings. He reached for the heavy, corded phone that broadcast through a V-shaped antenna off the rear top of the limousine. He asked his chief of staff to pull the file on a special agent, as luck would have it, who was presently stationed in the Baltimore field office. He told the chief to summon the agent immediately to his office for an assignment.

"Yes, I've got it. Special Agent Frank P. Imhoff. His file with be on your desk upon your arrival. See you in a few." Cummings replaced the phone in its cradle and sighed.

CHAPTER 10

THE MISSION
April 10, 2019
American Airspace
Southeastern United States

3:55 a.m. CDT

Special Agent Frank P. Imhoff finished reading the e-version action report on a secure tablet as he flew 35,000 feet in the sky toward Birmingham, Alabama with his team. Triverticular particle perturbations—space tunnels?

During the briefing before he left, Imhoff asked one of the science techs how he was supposed to find the triverticular particles, what did they look like? The tech, Smothers was his name, looked at Imhoff like, dude, how could you ask such a question, the world's no longer flat.

Smothers explained the TPP acted more like waves, but they could be detected more easily like particles on a device. When Imhoff, looking rather blank, asked are they waves or are they particles, Smother arched his eyebrows. "Think of it like light. You know, like light behaves, sometimes it acts like a wave, sometimes like a particle with a photon cell." Imhoff thought that all he knew was when he flicked the switch, the light came on.

"Don't worry about it," Smothers added. "The techs will have the detector units. You just get the bad guys."

Bad guys? Imhoff shook his head. He thought about asking Smothers whether bad guys acted like waves or particles, but he refrained. Smothers didn't have to worry about *him* getting the bad guys. He'd gotten plenty in his career. And before that, he'd gotten plenty as a Marine, though it a little different way.

"Yeah, those triverticular particles. . . ." Smothers just couldn't shut up. "You know, there's another explanation for them. There was this real obscure physicist, Manheim Schnictmann, who had some way-out theory they were produced by these weird things called disaccordian resonance bubbles like a big quantum mechanics bubble that grew in our macro world that swallowed up things, and when it popped, it gave off triverticular particles. Nobody took him seriously." He shrugged.

Imhoff scoffed. "So, if we're not fighting terrorists from a tunnel, we're fighting the Blob?"

Smothers just stared blankly at Imhoff, wondering what is the Blob?

As he flew across the Mason-Dixon line in a Bureau plane, Imhoff thought that this all way out there. He thought it sounded pretty fantastical to Director Cummings, too. An hour or more ago, Imhoff had sat across the desk from Cummings. Cummings was plain-spoken and balding with a square face. Imhoff thought he looked like Chuck Yeager in the old ACDelco TV ads.

"Frank, I know, I know. This all sounds bat-shit crazy. Maybe it is. But I've known Secretary Ogilvie a lot of years, and he is right most of the time. He's got some pretty smart techs in Homeland."

"But, sir, a space tunnel or transport tunnel or whatever it is? Transporting troops instantaneously from one place to another?"

"Well, by god, that's what we intend to find out—if it exists, and if it does, whether any Americans are behind it. If they are, you apprehend them. All of them. No one gets away. Alive . . . or dead."

Imhoff opened his mouth.

"That's an order Special Agent. It came down from Homeland."

Barely a pause. "Yes, sir."

"You will get a full briefing and strategy on the plane. Now get going. Frank, don't let me down."

Imhoff closed the tablet, and soon touched down in Birmingham and hopped into a fast Bureau car to speed to the neighborhood where DHS had triangulated the triverticular particle perturbation emissions.

The George Douglas home sat smack in the middle of that triangulation.

Out on the street, a technician turned to Special Agent Imhoff. "Sir, the strongest reading is in the middle of the street on the right coming from that house." He pointed directly toward the Douglas house.

"The particle things, you mean you actually detected them?" Imhoff asked.

"Yes, sir. Triverticular particles have a short half-life, but we definitely confirmed their presence."

"You mean with those vacuum cleaner things strapped on your backs?"

"Yes, those are portable triverticular particle perturbation detectors," the tech answered, with a sneer. "Cost a cool million each. So, I wouldn't put them in the class with vacuum cleaners, sir."

Special agent Imhoff noted the sarcasm. "Where did you find them?"

"Again, sir, that house right there," the tech tiredly pointed to the Douglas house.

"Okay, then." Imhoff rubbed his hands together. "You lead the way, son."

"Ah, what do you mean?"

Imhoff laughed. "Son, I can work a vacuum cleaner but not a machine that cost a cool million. You lead the way into *that* house."

The tech blanched. "Has it been cleared?"

Imhoff laughed. "Of course not, you're first in."

"But sir, I'm not certified for field work."

"Are you certified to run the vacuum cleaner detectors?"

"Yes, sir."

"Well I'm not, so you're first in. Don't worry. SWAT and I will be right behind you. And we shoot real good." Imhoff grinned.

At that moment, the tech and Imhoff saw a rectangle of light from a front window as George Jr. pulled back the curtain to look out.

"No more chit-chatting, get going," Imhoff barked, and after a nervous swallow, the tech took off.

Moments later, before the Douglases front door was splintered, Imhoff stood with the tech and SWAT team. The door was locked. "Sir," one of the techs asked Imhoff, "do we announce FBI before going in."

"No need, son, I said 'FBI' walking across the front lawn. We're free now to reduce that door to toothpicks."

Imhoff stood in the foyer in a charcoal gray suit directing the rapid search and occupation of the Douglas house. He sent SWAT through the house, hearing their shouts of "Moving! Clear! Moving! Clear! Clear!" He then sent the techs around the house to take samples. "Go, go, go!" He shoved the techs forward. "The house is secure," SWAT shouted.

But Imhoff was puzzled. He had not heard that SWAT had apprehended the occupants. The house appeared strangely empty, silent.

The SWAT squad leader confirmed this walking down the stairs with his weapon lowered. "It's empty. Nobody here."

"How can it be empty?"

The leader shrugged.

"Sure there's no false wall, secret hiding place?"

"Sure."

Imhoff happened to glance to his left toward the shattered étagère. "How do you explain that?"

The squad leader shrugged again.

"Are those bullet holes in the wall?"

The squad leader did not shrug this time. He said, "Looks like it to me, sir." He dug a slug from the sheetrock. "Looks like a round from a Kalashnikov." He then searched around. A few minutes later he came back. "Yep. Found it in the bedroom closet. Rounds are from it." He carried the weapon back to Imhoff.

"*AK-47?* This has to be the place. Serial number?"

"No, etched out. Lab guys can probably raise it."

"Sir, sir," a tech shouted bustling into the living room. "Positive readings, sir. Very faint, deteriorating, but definitely positive for triverticular particle perturbations."

"Search outside, secure the neighborhood. Get these people," Imhoff shouted.

"Frank," an agent called from the keeping room. "You may want to take a look at this." Imhoff hurried into the room. The agent pointed at the table with four plates and one on the counter.

"So they ran out in a rush, before they could load the dishes? They knew we were coming."

"That's not all, Frank. Count the number of plates."

"Five, so what."

"Frank, this is a family of four. What gives with the extra plate?"

"*A visitor.*"

The agent nodded.

"In the middle of the night?"

"Exactly."

Imhoff stared at the agent. *My god, was it real after all? Had they stumbled onto real traitors, missing them by minutes.* "I can't believe this is real—a tunnel—?"

"A tunnel, Frank?"

Imhoff snapped, "It's classified."

"But you said—"

"Classified. Got it." Imhoff seethed at his own breach of protocol.

"Nothing outside, front or back, sir." Another agent burst in.

"Bring in the dogs, get them going."

"Yes, sir."

Imhoff stared at the keeping room table. Five plates . . . family of four . . . before dawn . . . bullet holes in the living room . . . it didn't add up. It just didn't. But he would make it add up before he was finished with the Douglas family.

Must've been a really deep cover, he reasoned, set up over years. They were so ordinary—that was the genius of it—they were so ordinary they blended into the wallpaper, nobody paid them any attention. That has to be it, he thought.

Imhoff walked into the foyer, puzzled over the gunshots and shattered crystal. That didn't fit. Why would a deep undercover family risk shooting a gun in the living room in the middle of the night? Or shoot only crystal? That was weird, really weird. It didn't walk.

Unless? Unless the tunnel was real and somebody came out perceiving a threat . . . or on an adrenaline rush . . . and squeezed off a few rounds. He'd seen green Marines in combat do that. That walks. The extra table place could be their handler . . . or whoever came out the tunnel. But why leave the weapon in a closet? It didn't walk again.

Imhoff chewed his lip, lost in thought.

Imhoff stood about five-feet-eight inches and had a wiry build that helped in the Corps. His hair was Marine short with gray creeping in like weeds in a tailored lawn. He was tan. His eyes were gray steel with the beginning of crow's feet. He exuded potential energy, like a big cat, a panther, poised to spring.

"Sir, sir. The dogs got a scent but it stopped at the alley."

"The alley?"

"Yes, sir."

"What does that mean?"

"I don't know, sir."

Imhoff thought a moment, looking around the living room, then into the keeping room. "I'll tell you what it means. They had help. Someone picked them up. They got word we were coming. And someone picked them up. This is a conspiracy—that's the only way it all adds up. Homeland was right. It's a conspiracy against the United States."

But Imhoff was worried. How did they know we were coming? They barely got out in time; plates on the table. They had sat down to eat not that long ago. They weren't alarmed. They fixed a nice breakfast. But then they became alarmed. And they ran. But who alerted them?

Imhoff reviewed his team's actions. *We were on the street,* he thought, *but not for long, and we were quiet. We used stealth tactics so we wouldn't alert anyone.* He reviewed their approach again, his face taut. No, more likely someone warned them. But the only one who knew we were coming was the FBI—

And Homeland.

He wasn't worried about the FBI. But did Homeland have a leak, a mole? Still too early to tell. But this family got word to scram. That would walk. But he didn't want it to.

Special Agent Frank P. Imhoff was concerned. This could be bigger than they thought. With a traitor or traitors in the FBI or Homeland or someone else with knowledge of their ops. Hackers? Russians?

He stood frowning and thinking in the living room of the Douglas house.

Five minutes later Imhoff was on a secure link with Director Cummings. Even though it was a secure link, he wanted to be careful. "I didn't believe it either, Director. Yes, I know . . . I thought Homeland was mistaking seagulls for bogies on the radar. But the evidence . . . gunshots . . . compatriots . . . the quick getaway. Yes, this is now an FBI matter . . . catching the fugitives. . . joint with Homeland on lead for the technological parts. Got it. First . . .? Throw a steel curtain around the area, not even a gnat gets out . . . then transport direct to Washington for joint Homeland-FBI interrogation, yes sir. We will get the job done."

Imhoff thought carefully how to approach the next subject. "Director?"

"Yes."

54

"We need to talk."

"What is it, Frank?"

"I don't mean here."

"Well, Frank, you are there, and I am here, and time is running. What do you have to say?"

"Leaky faucet."

"Oh," the Director, paused, obviously taken aback. "Are you sure, Frank."

"No, not sure. But it walks."

"Who? Certainly not us."

"Not likely, but you never know. More likely others."

"Do I need to be careful with Ogilvie?"

"Probably not that high. But like water, information seeks its level."

"We need to think very carefully about this, Frank."

"Yes."

"May be worth engaging a systems check."

"Maybe, sir."

"We don't need this on top of everything else, Frank. This was an—unusual mission—from the outset. Surely, Preston has not allowed a leaky faucet."

Imhoff did not answer.

"Russians, Frank? Worth looking that way."

"Yes, sir, it is."

"Well, Frank, proceed apace, proceed carefully."

"Yes, sir."

Imhoff punched the off button. He stepped out into the Douglas front yard to a rising pink sky. The FBI crime scene technicians slipped quietly into the house with their gear cases.

Special Agent Frank P. Imhoff turned his face up, greeting the warmth of light from the coming day. This needed to end and end quick. He wasn't convinced there had been a leak—or a hack—but if there had been, all the better to apprehend the Douglas family and their companion, agent, collaborator, or whatever and whoever he—or she—was. By the end of that very day he planned to have them all in custody. There was no chance of escape. He was too close on their heels from the start for them to escape. And under Homeland's legal authority, as interpreted by its own officials, the traitors would be held without anyone knowing of their captivity. No ACLU or activist lawyers. They would simply disappear.

They deserved worse.

Having betrayed their country, they would get worse.

Imhoff had heard there was a place deep under a nondescript building that Homeland owned in a blighted Washington area neighborhood that you didn't want to know about.

It was affectionately called by Homeland officers, Gitmo North.

CHAPTER 11

INTO THIN AIR
April 10, 2019
Office, Secretary of the Department of Homeland Security
Washington, D.C.

10:00 a.m. EDT

Secretary Ogilvie looked up from his desk when Chambers walked in.

"Dick," he said irritably, "what is going on? This mission should have been over before sunrise. Cummings told me he was sending a crack team. We had our own people there—some of your agents from I-Division. The traitors should be in custody with every limb in cuffs and hoods over their heads on their way up here so we can deal with them. Hell, I expected we'd have a press conference at noon. McCluskey's already finished a statement. But nothing. We got nothing. Thin air, Dick. That's what we got. Thin air."

Chambers looked noncommittal.

"But thin air . . . maybe. . . ." Ogilvie chewed his lip, then brightened. "Maybe that proves we're right."

"Right?" Chambers cocked his head.

"Proof the Douglases are terrorists, combatants, traitors. Dick, it's obvious somebody tipped them. How else could they have avoided the Wildroot team with FBI support—and a couple of your people in the wings?"

"Do we have any evidence, Preston?"

"We don't need evidence." His face was enthusiastic. "That's the only explanation, and you know it."

"Preston, I don't disagree. But it would help if we had evidence. It would support our accusations and bolster the soundness of our decisions."

"I see. I see," Ogilvie, nodded as Chambers' point registered. "Yes, Dick, indeed. Can you point someone in that direction? Someone, ah, creative?" He gave Chambers a knowing look.

"You bet," Chambers smiled.

But Ogilvie fretted, and Chambers thought he looked remarkably uncomfortable. Ogilvie was hanging out there without a net.

Ogilvie, with Chambers in the background, had briefed the National Security Council at six a.m. sharp and the President at a less sharp seven-thirtyish. The briefings were back in the early hours of the mission when capture was imminent. In the briefings, Ogilvie possessed control and command, confidently waving aside any skepticism.

"My god, Dick, it's now pushing *ten o' clock*." He compulsively pressed the creases on his pants.

Chambers' phone beeped.

"Any news?" Ogilvie jumped, but quickly tried to act nonchalant.

Chambers checked his phone.

He shook his head, "No. Something else."

Ogilvie flipped a letter opener in his fingers.

"Dick, make a note, we need to go to Congress for appropriations next time for even more cameras. We need to blanket the country from shore to shore. We can work in tandem with NSA—you know they want more." Then, his mind jumping, "This Imhoff—what do we know about him—is he the right man?"

"Seems so. He checks out. Cummings wouldn't take a chance with a second-stringer on this one." Chambers noticed something in Ogilvie's face. "You talked with Cummings?"

Ogilvie nodded.

"How was he?"

Ogilvie pondered the question. He answered slowly. "I'm not sure."

Chambers raised his eyebrows.

"Right at the end of our call . . . he was casual . . . but he asked questions."

Ogilvie frowned as Chambers leaned forward.

"He asked who we had involved, saying he may have worked with some of them. He wanted to know how big an operation it was, what levels had been read in. He didn't ask much more than that. He didn't push. . . ." His voice trailed off.

The men sat silently a few moments.

"So that's it," Ogilvie said, sitting up. "He thinks we have a leak here at Homeland. He thinks someone tipped off the Douglases. He thinks that's the only way they could have escaped."

"Hmmm."

Ogilvie shook his head. "Cummings is old school. That's old cold war mentality. We have good people here."

Looking at Chambers, he said, proudly, "We take only the best. And, we check them when we hire them, and we check up on them regularly—even if they don't know it."

He looked out the window at the surrounding government buildings. "No. If there was somebody rotten here we'd know it. If there's a leak, and I still don't think there is, it's not here." He gave Chambers a knowing look. "But the Bureau's been around a long time. There could be people with a past that could be leveraged. Maybe even a mole burrowed in deep, before the Wall came down, now cashing in, looking for a big score."

Chambers watched Ogilvie's mental machinations. He, Chambers, would take this in stride however it played out. Ogilvie accused him of wearing asbestos suits. No matter how hot the heat Chambers always worked the plan, knowing there was always the next plan, the next opportunity, the next press cycle—and the public's memory was short.

If Chambers wasn't sweating this one, Ogilvie was. The ambitious ones always did, he thought. Ogilvie clearly had plans after DHS. At the right time he would suggest that Ogilvie relax. This would work out, the public would understand, they wanted simply to lead their lives, while the government kept them safe in this dangerous, very dangerous, world.

He could turn any tough questions back on the talking heads, making them seem callous and picky: "So what you're saying is you're more concerned with the cost of fuel in jetting a team to a suspected hot spot, than saving American lives. You would save gasoline over American families?"

A piece of cake.

Ogilvie interrupted Chambers' thoughts. "Let's do some checking over at the Bureau. Discretely, of course."

"Of course."

"And Dick, let's have NSA listen in on Cummings and Imhoff."

"Sounds good, Preston. Prudent. I'll get someone on it."

"Someone good, Dick."

"Sure."

"And one more thing. Just for the fun of it, let's update the cyber-checks on our people, all their computers, laptops, phones and devices—work and personal—everything. Just to make sure. Want to be ahead of the curve on this one. No surprises." He added, "And Dick, let's do this inside. I don't want NSA to be looking at us."

"Sure."

Chambers took Ogilvie's measure. "Preston, there's another possibility."

"Huh?"

"Putin."

"Putin?" Ogilvie paused. But after a moment's thought, shook his head. "Not like him. Too messy, agents who could be caught or compromised—or turned. He may be KGB, but he likes the cyber route. You can't arrest bits or bytes. They can do it all from Mother Russia."

"Still, I'll start a check of the systems for any penetration."

Ogilvie nodded. He buzzed his secretary for coffee for them both.

On the second sip he asked Chambers, "Still no evidence the media is sniffing around?"

"No."

Chambers sat impassively in his charcoal suit with crisp white shirt and nondescript tie. His white hair was receding. He wore old-fashioned gold frame glasses. He gave Ogilvie his confident look, the look he had perfected in Washington—and during his sabbatical in the executive suites of Wall Street, when he had amassed a significant fortune, before returning to the public sector where, coincidentally, he could protect the industries and companies in his portfolio.

"Preston, we need to cover the Douglases' disappearance. Why don't we send in a team disguised as pest control workers with a cover story of pest contamination, one that requires fumigation of the house. That would explain why the Douglases are gone."

Ogilvie nodded.

"If neighbors ask, the 'techs' can say that Mrs. Douglas mentioned something about a quick trip while they were out of the house. That ought to play in this community, it's posh. I bet they're always pulling the children out of school for fancy trips."

Chambers watched Ogilvie think through the plan and smile. "Perfect. Get it done." Ogilvie thought a few moments more. "I'll brief Bart when we talk next. Has NSA sent over the Douglas family's e-footprints?"

"Our boys have had them for a while," Chambers replied.

"Let's go." Ogilvie rose smoothly, and Chambers followed him out of the room.

CHAPTER 12

THE PROBLEM WITH MILLENNIALS
April 10, 2019
IT Floor
Department of Homeland Security

10:15 a.m. EDT

On another floor, a highly secure floor, Ogilvie and Chambers walked into a facility with more electronic hardware and screens than they could count. Through glass double doors, Ogilvie stared into a room, dark, cool, electric, populated by Millennials and a few of the alphabet generations—the Intelligence and Analysis branch of Homeland.

Ogilvie did not like coming to this floor. The techs seemed glued to their devices. He couldn't understand what any of them said. Apparently, they were incapable of translating a concept into plain English.

A supervisor with the name tag Marcie Beethoven quickly approached. "Mr. Secretary, may we assist you?" She wore a white coat over a purple Oxford clothe shirt with a black necktie, loosened at the collar, and thin-legged blue jeans. She had black hair, pretty eyes, and a nice smile. More encouraging to Ogilvie, she made good eye contact. Maybe there's a personality in there, he thought.

"You got all the Douglas stuff?" Ogilvie asked.

"Yes," She said crisply, nodding her head back toward an array of equipment that was blinking, whirring, and running madly across screens of all sizes and shapes. But then she then she checked a notification on her smartphone and typed a quick burst of a response.

"If it's not too much trouble for a briefing. . . ."

"Oh, yes, sorry, certainly." She looked up, her face casual. "Okay, like this is the most boring family in America. The mother's truly OCD, like she super-schedules and controls everything, she wants her kids to get every first-place award in the world, though that causes some pretty nasty cat fights with the daughter. The son just tunes her out, which drives her crazy. The husband is a partner in a profitable accounting firm, raking in the cash, otherwise standard stuff, mainstream clients, Rotary Club, kid activities, all that biz. Really b-o-r-i-n-g. Their politics are what you'd expect in Alabama. The daughter's really a piece of work."

"What do you mean?"

"Like, you'd just have to read her stuff, I mean, she's into everybody's business and everybody's into her business, like there are no boundaries—plus she's a pretty deadly cyber bully."

"What about the son?"

"Oh, he's really cool." Marcie smiled. Ogilvie thought her eyes brightened about the boy. He rubbed his chin as Marcie continued. "He's really smart. Plus, he's funny and he wrote this most incredible essay for English class . . . he's excels in math and science . . . but I didn't see anything about sports. I'm guessing he probably couldn't catch a ball if you handed it to him, and oh yeah, he's going for his Eagle Scout badge this year."

She hesitated before the next part. "And he's solid, and I think he cares, like things really bother him, things that are not true or are unfair or phony. I think he'd really stand up to what he thinks is wrong. You know he's a guy so he doesn't just come out and say his feelings, but when you read the stuff he sends, it's there."

"That's it?"

"Pretty much."

"That can't be it. They're foreign agents. They're a cell. They're traitors. Maybe they encrypted or inserted secret messages or back doors or honeypots and all that crap you guys obsess about all the time? Have you looked?"

"Scrubbed everything clean. No dirt."

Ogilvie looked incredulous.

She seemed not to notice. She paused. There was something else she wanted to say—why not? They were on the same team looking for the truth. "Sir, well, have you considered it's all a mistake?"

Chambers almost smiled.

"Do you like your job," Ogilvie asked solicitously, looking at her name tag, "Marcie?"

"Why, yes sir. It's challenging, and I feel like I'm doing good for my country, and hopefully, the world. Plus, there's good health insurance." She smiled.

"Do you like your pay grade?"

"Again, yes sir. I'm single—and I have student loans."

"Very good." Ogilvie smiled like an appreciative employer.

But then he turned sour, staring harshly at her for several seconds until she shrank back. "If you want to keep your job and benefits you will never utter that sentiment again. Now get back to work and find the Douglases' secrets. Got it?"

"Got it." She turned, blushing, head down and shoulders hunched. She scurried back through the double glass doors.

Back in his office, Ogilvie glared at the department head for IA—Intelligence and Analysis. Ogilvie had vented his displeasure over supervisor Marcie's assertion and her flippant demeanor toward him.

"Preston, she's young. The good ones down there are a different breed. And she's a good one. Besides, maybe she's got something."

"She's not old enough to have something."

"Preston, nothing's happened. It's been hours and nothing's happened."

"So what?"

"If the particles really were from a space tunnel, well, wouldn't we be attacked by now? Wouldn't something have happened or blown up?"

"We don't know. The Douglases could be assembling their team. We threw a pretty good monkey wrench in their plans this morning—"

"Assembling where? The house is clean. The particles are gone. There's no trapdoor. Maybe it's just an empty house of a normal American family."

"That would be great. Just great. We issued this big alert, blew by the National Security Council, interrupted the President, occupied a house in goddamn Alabama—now the family is missing and the media would love a sob story about the poor family hounded by the government. It's not like that movie with Tommie Lee Jones where he holds up a pen and zaps everyone's memories. You don't think this could leak out one day to haunt us? Our political geese would be cooked."

The IA director shrugged.

"Keep me posted," Ogilvie said gruffly, turning to papers on his desk.

"Will do," the IT Director said as he left.

Alone, Ogilvie felt Chambers' assurances had suddenly become pale.

Ogilvie thought of the future, his future, a path to the vice presidential nomination he had mapped out this morning. But if the training cover didn't work and the truth leaked out that he had deployed a whole rapid response task force on a Rotary Club member and his family who now were MIA, well, the repercussions were simply too awful to dwell upon.

Later, recounting the conversation with the IA head to Chambers who had come to his office, Ogilvie said, "Dick, if we don't find something soon . . . well, maybe we just have to make up something for the team to 'find.'"

Chambers nodded. He took his leave.

Walking down the hall, Chambers had no problem whatsoever with "finding" evidence." He'd studied Richard Nixon—the only thing wrong he'd done was getting caught. Also, while he did not have a campaign to plan, he did have some expiring stock options to sell while the market was at record highs. He didn't need a flap over loss of confidence in the government to suppress stock prices. He made a mental note to call his broker that afternoon.

Besides, if they played this right, they could get Congressional authority for even more surveillance, more spying, more information.

And information was power.

CHAPTER 13

YOU CAN'T GO HOME AGAIN
April 10, 2019
Dark alleys and roads
Birmingham, Alabama

5:01 a.m. CDT

Bossilini punched the gas, and the black rectangle that really was a Hummer snaked and slid along the dark alley away from the Douglases home as the SWAT team ran out of the house into the backyard.

A few blocks later Carmen whined, "Mom, change places with me, please." She was wedged in the middle seat between Virginia and George and caught shoulders and body blows from both sides as the Hummer's acceleration and turns slung the passengers like loose luggage.

A few miles later, Virginia called forward, "Mr. Bostaloni, oh Mr. Bosaloni."

"*Bossilini*." It was just one word, but it was said in a voice that carried power and was not to be disobeyed.

"Oh, yes, sorry. Are—are we safe? Has our house blown up? Can we slow down now?"

George chimed in. "Are we going to a shelter? There's one over on Greenbriar Street run by the YWCA. When can we go back home? Do we need to go to Target and get things for today and tonight?"

Bossilini cut a look at them in the mirror. Though sitting, he stood five-feet-nine and weighed 220 pounds, all muscle. His hair was thick and black with some curl, though not long. His face was square with a strong chin and dark with features reflecting his Hungarian and Italian heritage. He seemed to wear a perpetual matter-of-fact expression and was dressed in black jeans and a black turtleneck.

He knew he must handle the next few minutes carefully if he was to save all of the Douglases. If not, he would flee with Manfred and the boy. The others were inconsequential except as to how the boy would react if separated from his family. Bossilini's eyes rested on the girl squeezed between her parents. He thought nothing of her.

Bossilini focused back ahead, steeliness in his grey eyes. He shook his head irritably. Of all the places in the universe Manfred could have popped out of a disaccordian resonance bubble it had to be at the Douglas house.

"No, your house has not blown up," he answered without looking at them. "You are safe for the moment. We are not going to a shelter."

With a questioning expression, George glanced at Virginia.

"Are you a firefighter, a first responder?" Virginia asked, judging Bossilini's reflection in the rear-view mirror.

Bossilini did not return her gaze but looked ahead, expertly guiding the black rectangle away quickly from the Douglas neighborhood.

"Yes, I am a first-responder of sorts." Bossilini was not yet ready to inform them of his true employment.

"What is the protocol?" George asked. "Should I call my insurance agent?"

"No. You should not call anyone. You should pass up your phones, everyone, now, quick, quick."

Carmen gave a pissy snort, then looked alarmed. There were some texts and pictures she *really* should delete before her mom got her hands on her phone.

Virginia shifted uneasily in her seat. "Why do you want our phones?" she demanded, her face hard. "How are we to be in touch, I mean, with the authorities, neighbors? When will we know it's safe to go home?"

Bossilini didn't answer.

"I have my schedule, everything is on my phone, business, family, my *whole* life. This doesn't really seem necessary." Virginia frowned at George. She mouthed, "Kidnap?" He gave her a worried look. Then she remembered and her voice became frantic! *"I have the Featherstone house today—I can't be out of touch! And, besides, we don't really know you. You can understand that, I'm sure."*

George joined in: "My phone belongs to my accounting firm. It has confidential client information, access to emails, my firm's server. Professional ethics prevent me from turning it over."

Bossilini bit his lip. He never liked the idea of extracting the whole family. But they ordered it for the boy's sake. Bossilini turned to the side, looking out the window, angry. They had one precious chance to escape.

He knew they would not understand his commands. But the knowledge didn't help his impatience. He tried to stay calm. "Please pass your phones up."

Glancing behind, with tension in his eyes and breathing to try to calm himself, Bossilini still gripped the wheel harder, palms clammy. The government by now surely had broadcast every conceivable alarm, roadblocks rising as he drove, all-point bulletins, BOLOs blasting to precincts, station houses, and even to the lowly dogcatcher. If caught, they would never see the light of day.

The government would shut *everything* down, cordoning off every highway, street, road, alley, and sidewalk so tightly that even a mouse could not squeak through. The Feds would throw a broadband dragnet over the city with electronic watchdogs chasing every bit, byte and watt of e-communications. It would be easy to trace them with their phones.

"They can track you with your phones," he tried to say evenly, swallowing the irritation.

"Well, that is a good thing," George said. "They can text us when it's safe to go home."

Bossilini slammed his hand into the steering wheel, but before he could speak Virginia interrupted.

"We need to get back home as soon as possible—as soon as it's safe—Carmen has a math tutor this afternoon and a workout with her cheer trainer, you know, tryouts are coming up soon. I am a real estate agent with Brownell Realty and—like I said—have the Featherstone contract at three." Her voice rose a pitch. She, too, tried to speak in a calm voice, but could not hide her hysteria rising at this stranger. "I've fought for three years for his listing and I *have* to be available. So I will keep my phone, thank you." Her eyes fluttered from nerves as she finished. Bossilini could not see that she tried to surreptitiously dial 911 on a touch screen without looking down.

George backed his wife, "Yes, I have an important client meeting at eleven. He needs our figures—he's got to decide 'go or no go' on a shopping center project."

"If you do not hand me the phones now, I will rip them from your persons."

Virginia flinched. Junior and Manfred watched from the third seat, fascinated.

"Mr. Bossilini—we're approaching the *city limits*," George cut him off. "This seems rather unusual."

Junior noticed the sharpness in his father's voice. Virginia looked at her husband, her face angry. "Mister—"

"SHUT UP!" Bossilini shouted with all the volume he could muster, banging his fist violently on the dashboard. "SIMPLY SHUT UP!"

George and Virginia flinched from the force of his outburst. With a heaving chest and a wild look in his eyes, Bossilini turned toward them, daring them to talk. They cowered back, eyes wide, rigid, bodies erect.

"I am trying to *save* you—and your children. You . . . are . . . in . . . DANGER," he thundered.

Now that he had order, he shifted, trying to explain so they would comply—but not panic.

"You are in a very serious situation," he began. "One beyond your comprehension. It is important you fully understand this. Your government thinks you are traitors, that you are deep undercover agents for a foreign power or domestic terrorists. Those were government agents who broke into your home."

"That's preposterous," George countered. "Why, I pay my taxes . . . I'm a member of the Rotary Club."

"What—what do they think?" Virginia asked, alarm on her face, glancing at her children.

"They think you are assisting a foreign power with a new weapon, a weapon that can create a tunnel, through space, and transport enemies instantly through it."

"How—how is that even possible? I mean, that is ridiculous," Virginia stormed. "Why, that's completely silly. Who would even believe such a thing?" A look crossed her face, but she paused, turning back to Manfred, "Is that how Manfred got here, through the tunnel?"

"There is no tunnel. Of course it's silly. They have mistaken a natural phenomenon for a space tunnel opening in your living room. Quite preposterous, even funny if you think about it."

"I don't find it *funny* at all, Mr. Bossilini," Virginia snapped, crossing her arms. "We only need to get our lawyer Drew on the phone. He'll end this in a New York minute."

"First things first. How do you know this?" George interrupted.

"There is not time for this. But if it helps you, let me simply say it is good to spy on the government spying on you. Now, hand me your phones."

"Spy?" George looked puzzled. Trying to work it out, he asked, "The government is spying on who?" It hit him. "Oh, you mean the government is spying on people, domestic Americans?"

Bossilini nodded.

"Well, who are they spying on?"

"Everybody."

"Us?"

"Everybody."

"Everybody?"

"Yes."

"When?"

"All the time, 24/7 as you say."

"All the time?"

"All the time."

"Everybody?"

"Everybody all the time."

The passengers sat silent, stunned that their government—run by the majority party for whom they had voted, aided and abetted by big corporations—systematically, relentlessly, and methodically, spied on them and their neighbors, shredding any remnant of their privacy. And was it now accusing *them* of treason? The silence was soon broken.

Bossilini turned to Virginia. "Are you going to save your family? You have about three seconds."

Virginia blinked, sitting perfectly still. A determined look crossed her face.

"Pass me up your phones—all your devices," she demanded. "Now. Carmen, too." She handed them up to Bossilini. He threw them out the window.

"*What*—" Virginia shrieked. "Couldn't you just have taken out the batteries. We're not eligible for upgrades for another fourteen months."

They rode for miles as fast as Bossilini could take them. When colored lights and sirens did not pursue them, when the Hummer was not run down by sliding roadblocks, Bossilini began to breathe again. Miraculously, they had made it. He almost didn't believe it. He rolled his shoulders, trying to relax the knotted muscles.

Subdued from the shock and hectic escape—and still wary of Bossilini—Virginia asked in a small voice, "When—when will all this be over—when do you think we can go back home?"

George nodded with her.

"Mr. and Mrs. Douglas," Bossilini said without taking his eyes off the road, his voice soft. "Have you ever read Thomas Wolfe?"

"Well," George piped, "I read *The Right Stuff*—saw the movie, too."

"Wrong Wolfe. I was referring to the book *You Can't Go Home Again.*"

"Huh?"

"It is like that for you."

"What!?" George and Virginia uttered in unison.

"You're not really with the gas company or civil defense are you?" George said, with resignation.

Bossilini turned. "No, I am not."

CHAPTER 14

ON THE ROAD
April 10, 2019
The Hummer
Alabama back highways

7:00 a.m. CDT

"Are they going to kill us if they catch us?" Junior whispered to Manfred.

Manfred was surprised by his directness. His first thought was to protect the boy, answering in a soothing voice, "No, they're not going to hurt us. This is the United States of American. Not Russia."

But Manfred couldn't give the boy some malarkey.

"Like, I don't know what's going to happen," he counseled softly in the boy's ear. "I mean, you'd think your parents could straighten all this out. They got to know lawyers and people. But this cat's racing us out of Dodge like the James Gang is coming. Your parents are freaked out—"

The boy nodded in agreement.

"—and, like, that's not good—"

"Do you think I made a mistake calling Mr. Bossilini?" the boy whispered. "He seemed like a really cool guy. And he was really serious about me calling him."

"Little dude, did you see those cats in the kitchen with the lights and everything," Manfred said out of the side of his mouth. "They were swarming like trail hands through the Long Branch Saloon after a cattle drive. Yeah, I'd say it was the right thing to call him, and you know, I have a feeling about him, I think he will keep us safe—if he can."

"Really?" the boy looked up at Manfred for hope.

"Really."

"What are you two whispering about back there," Virginia called.

"Nothing," Junior answered for them.

"It wasn't nothing. I distinctly heard you two whispering to each other. Now out with it. I don't know Mr. Manfred—"

"That would be Mr. Redford, actually."

"It's a Southern form of address—never mind—Mister Manfred Redford, then. Now, what were you saying to my son?"

Her condescension flamed him. He decided to mess with her. "Well, I was saying to Sherman—"

"Who's Sherman?"

"Your son. It's the new nickname I gave him. With those glasses, he kind of looks like Sherman on the Mr. Peabody cartoons, remember the Wayback Machine? Wish I had one. That was a cool show. Junior sounds corny, like something out of *Leave it to Beaver*."

"My son does not look like a cartoon character," Virginia sniffed.

"He really does," Carmen giggled.

Junior did not particularly relish her attention, though he was pleased to finally have a nickname, like a regular guy.

Carmen beamed. "I can't wait to text everybody at school about your new cartoon nickname. It'll go viral."

The boy shuddered. "No, you won't. *Mom!*"

"Of course, she won't." Virginia glowered at Carmen.

Then Sherman smiled. "No you won't. *You* don't have a phone anymore."

"Good one, dude," Manfred smiled.

"Oooooh. Mom, why did you let him throw our phones out?"

"I like it, the name," Bossilini interrupted. "The name Junior can too easily be connected with him, with the name *Junior* Douglas. Sherman it is."

Virginia opened her mouth to resume the protest, but upon seeing Bossilini's hard eyes as he turned to stare at her, she crossed her arms, stared out the window and sniffed. "Well, maybe for a day or two . . . until this is cleared up."

"Watch," Sherman whispered to Manfred. "She's now going to give it to Dad."

Three seconds later.

"George, can't we go back and straighten this all out," she said irritably. "You work with lawyers all the time, and one of our Senators attends our church . . . when he's in town. Surely he has some pull to convince whoever invaded our house that it is the wrong one?"

"That's right, Bossilini," George said, firmness in his voice, glancing furtively at his wife. "The worst thing is to keep, er, running. That makes us look guilty."

"Have you not listened to a word I said?" George flinched from the contempt in Bossilini's voice. "There is no *working it out* with these people. They are not interested in *working it out* with you. You are pawns in their quest for power. You do not count."

He turned to George with a look that said, *Listen to me, you stupid fool.*

"You are liabilities. Soon they will realize that when no great invasion occurs, when no terrorist attack occurs, when nothing is blown up, that they have made a very foolish mistake."

George and Virginia eyed each other nervously.

"Think about it. The truth is they have marshaled a rapid deployment secret strike force to protect the United States against eminent attack on its soil, yet instead, there was nothing, they ransacked an ordinary household, chased a loyal American family out of their home, and then, pursued them like ICE after illegals."

Bossilini gritted his teeth before continuing. "Tell me, George and Virginia, how do you think that would look in the media? What do you think the opposing political party would do with such a blunder—all the talk shows, all the talking heads? Gail King would interview you on the CBS morning show. Trevor Noah would want you on *The Daily Show*. Seth Myers would grab you. Do you think that could undermine the public's sense of security in the judgment of those tasked with keeping them safe? The judgment of those in power—for now?"

When they didn't respond, he said, "Sure, the calmer heads will try to work the spin, use their PR resources, keep their cool. But they aren't like the darks ones. The dark ones will act outside official channels, they are subterranean. They will never permit those interviews. They will never take that risk of the story surfacing."

Manfred leaned forward to catch every word.

"So . . . so what will they do. . . .?" Virginia couldn't finish her question. Her face was pale, stricken, the lines deepening around her eyes and lips.

"To you?"

She could only nod.

He shook his head gravely.

Virginia slumped. George looked shaken. Carmen's lips quivered.

Sherman whispered to Manfred so his mother would not hear him. "I guess it was a good thing I called Mr. Bossilini."

Manfred only nodded.

Sherman's lip quivered in resonance with his sister's and he began to weep. Manfred put his arm around the boy and held him tight.

As the Hummer drove, Manfred looked down the road, wondering what the future held for them. But all he could see were the white stripes disappearing into the horizon.

CHAPTER 15

BY A PICNIC TABLE
April 10, 2019
Highway rest stop
Southwest Tennessee

Late morning

The motley pack of fugitives huddled around a weathered picnic table under a shade tree at a highway scenic overview in northeast Tennessee above Knoxville. They were haggard and exhausted from shock, frenzied driving, and hunger.

Earlier, without explanation, Bossilini pulled into a rest stop outside of Chattanooga. He had left the Hummer and walked over to a man sitting on a bench. They shook hands heartily, as if they were acquainted but had not seen each other for a long time.

Back in the Hummer with the man in the front passenger seat, Bossilini turned. "Everyone, this is Bodhi Jha."

The man nodded, smiling. "Hello everyone." He spoke in a melodic Indian accent. He was about five-six, medium build, black hair, dark complexion, even features—but his brown almost black eyes seemed to sparkle with merriment. He wore a white dress shirt with a mechanical pencil in the pocket and black pants and shoes.

Virginia stared suspiciously at the new passenger. If they were in such urgent danger, why pick up a stranger? Virginia gave George a questioning look, and he frowned in response.

Noticing, Bossilini said, "He is here to help."

Bossilini turned to Bodhi Jha and gestured that he should speak to the family. Bodhi said, "My name is Bodhi Jha."

But with his accent the syllables slurred together, prompting George to ask, "Did you say your name is Buddy?"

Bodhi Jha laughed, his face warm and open. "No, Bodhi. But Buddy is good enough if that is easier."

Now, George, Virginia and Carmen sat wearily around the picnic table. They sat with shoulders hunched and heads hung, purple circles forming under their eyes and their bodies feeling heavy and lethargic.

Sherman, propped against a tree trunk, was asleep. But a tickling sensation in his pants leg startled him awake. He realized it was a bug. He smashed his fist against his leg and smashed it again. He shoved up the pants and flicked away something black and crumpled.

Sherman watched Bossilini wave Manfred over to where Buddy and he stood by the Hummer, which Manfred called simply the "Rectangle." The boy wished he could hear their conversation, but they were too far away. Sherman worried. Manfred seemed freaked out. He was arguing with the men.

"How are you holding up?" Bossilini asked.

Manfred looked at the men with tired, harried eyes. "Why couldn't I have landed somewhere good? Like with Bridget Bardot on the French Riviera? Do you know how to get me back? If you don't, I'm thinking of just splitting. This scene with them," he nodded toward the picnic table, "is too weird. I'm not interested in going to jail for them. I haven't done anything."

"Neither have they," Bossilini quickly replied, his eyes sharpening. "But it's understandable."

Buddy stared at Manfred pleasantly with his full attention, as if Manfred were the most interesting person in the world.

"Why are you risking it?" Manfred challenged Bossilini. "You're not related to them."

"The boy."

"The boy? That's it?"

"He is important."

"How? He's a kid."

Bossilini peered at Manfred's face. "Now is not the time to explain."

"Who's the Indian cat?" Manfred said irritably, nodding toward Buddy. "Why's he here?" Manfred looked over at Sherman under the tree. "He's here to help with the boy, too?" The boy was the only one Manfred cared about. He would leave the others in a New York minute.

Bossilini nodded evenly. He did not say that Buddy was a Master Agent of the League of Privacy Sentinels sent to help.

"And you, too, Manfred, if you choose to remain with us, you must look after the boy. This family is overwhelmed. If anything happens, I need you to keep the boy safe. If necessary, whisk him away. Bodhi—Buddy—can help you. But if I—or he—cannot, then you must do so alone until other help comes. Will you do this for me? Will you do it for Sherman?"

"Man, this is getting heavy—"

"Will you do it?" Bossilini pressed.

Manfred stood perfectly still while Bossilini's stared deeply into his eyes.

"I know more about you than you can realize, Manfred. You are more capable than you realize. You are more important than you realize. This all started with you, Manfred; you must see it through.

"What started—" he tried to protest.

"Not now. *Later.*" Bossilini's forcefulness startled Manfred. Bossilini knew something about him. But he would not tell Manfred now. Maybe Bossilini knew how he could get back?

Manfred swallowed. He looked over at the boy, gazing at him a few moments with a wash of emotions he could not explain. Then he looked up, staring at shy for several long moments.

He turned back to Bossilini. "Yeah, yeah, I'll do it." Manfred looked steadily into both their faces. He swallowed again. "Yeah, I'll do it."

Bossilini clasped him on the shoulder. "Good, good." Buddy beamed.

"One more thing," Bossilini said.

Bossilini reached into the console of the Hummer and passed Manfred a large manila envelope. Inside was a wallet with a driver's license and $1,000 cash. The license was issued to Manfred G. Redford from Omaha, Nebraska.

Manfred looked at the ID incredulous. "How—there was no time—I came in the middle of the night—you didn't stop anywhere?" Then the stunned realization, his body jerking. "You knew I was coming? How—"

"Yes, we knew you were coming but not exactly when. The rest will have to wait. Buddy and I need to talk. Please join the others. We will be leaving soon. Oh, and hand me your real license and draft card." Manfred stared at him, then passed them over. "Manfred, why don't you join Sherman now."

Manfred stared at him, stunned. Recovering, he walked away to the boy. When Manfred was gone, Bossilini turned to Buddy, "Any word?"

Buddy shook his head. "There is activity at the house, of course, but nothing to suggest that they have identified you or the escape vehicle."

Bossilini nodded, thinking. "Are there new instructions?"

"No. Proceed as planned. The League can send up to two more Agents—"

"I—"

"I know. You like to work alone. But it is ordered. And Nitko—we may need all the help we can get. The critical thing for now is to keep you and your charges undetected."

"That will be become harder and harder as the government brings to bear its full surveillance powers."

"We did not plan these events. It is only fortunate we discovered them in time."

"Yes, of course." Bossilini's shoulders slumped.

"Have they discussed where to go?"

"No. But it has been planned." Bossilini sighed. "We need their buy-in. It is better if they think it is their own idea. This family is wildly unpredictable. Have the Officers and you factored in their unpredictability?"

"There is only so much we can factor in. Unpredictability is inherent in our world."

"Let us see what they have to say," Bossilini said.

Huddled again in the Rectangle, Bossilini and Buddy turned toward them. "Where do you think we should go from here, George, Virginia? Where is a safe place they will not predict you will go?" George and Virginia were quiet. They looked at each other, suddenly feeling the desperate weight of a life-or-death choice.

Silence.

Bossilini thought, *They are not yet ready to put it together.* But he had planted a seed. Finally, he said, "Okay, okay. Let's head to the mountains for now. We should be able to keep out of sight."

Bossilini reasoned they were safe for the rest of the day, based on Buddy's report. Also, the Rectangle had sophisticated and highly secure satellite radio, internet, and TV. Bossilini had checked the feeds periodically, the last time fifteen minutes ago. Nothing on them. Using the device posed no risk. Special, seemingly futuristic, apparatus randomly switched satellite feeds every two minutes and routed internet connections through a Byzantine maze both in and out of the country, all while showing a false signal of the Hummer's location. At that moment, their satellite link showed they were in Eugene, Oregon, even though they were actually approaching the East Coast.

Ten miles later, Bossilini went into a fast food joint for food. Buddy took the time to talk gently, distracting them with his soothing voice, his brown, smooth face pleasant with no sign of distress. He told them he was a mathematician and studied Zen. He was here to help them, along with Bossilini, and they must do as instructed. That was important. But, they should trust that any instruction was for their best interest and well-being. They began to relax with the melodic rise and fall of his voice.

Bossilini popped the mood upon his return with his usual brusqueness in passing out the food and drinks. Buddy gave him a stern look, but Bossilini plowed forward.

"Here, each of you take $1,000." Bossilini passed back a handful of cash.

"Thank you," George said. "I'll pay you back when we get all this straightened out."

Sherman eagerly reached for his stash.

Bossilini turned to face them. Buddy lightly touched his forearm to signal reserve. But Bossilini bulled on, "Keep half in your wallets or purses—and hide half on your persons. It will be important for you to have money if we get separated—"

"*Separated?!*" Virginia almost screamed.

Buddy shook his head slightly, looking down. He did not agree with Bossilini's approach.

"I hope not," Bossilini answered, "but we may have to take extreme steps to protect your freedom."

"I'm not letting my babies out my sight," Virginia said fiercely, reaching her arm around Carmen, pulling the girl gently to her. But Carmen quickly shoved her away.

"Mom, I'm not a baby," Sherman complained from the back. "I'm starting high school next year."

The boy has no perception of their predicament, Buddy thought. That is probably better.

"I'm still not letting them separate my family," Virginia said, her tone defiant. "They have run us out of our home, out of our city, out of our lives, but I am not letting them tear our family apart."

"Mom, we don't have a lot of clout right now, if you haven't noticed," Carmen pouted.

Buddy turned back toward the girl, sensing the turmoil in her mind. She could benefit from meditation, he thought. Maybe there will be time.

Buddy sighed as Bossilini pressed on.

"Silence. We must plan for contingencies," Bossilini insisted. "It is plausible we could become separated by events unforeseen at present. We need to plan where to rendezvous if that happens. Ideas?"

The Rectangle was silent.

"Okay, then, I will choose the rendezvous point. I have given this contingency some thought. If we become separated, everyone go to New York and meet at 3:00 p.m. at the Unisphere—where the World's Fair was—it's in Queens. I am sure you have seen pictures. If no one shows, keep coming back every day at 3:00 until we meet again."

"We will not be separated, Mr. Bossilini. I will not leave my children," Virginia snarled at him, defiant.

No one spoke after that.

Bossilini did not need to further upset, Buddy thought, for upset flames unpredictability. He shook his head. They simply could not allow chance to cast their fates. He would not permit it.

Late that night the poor fugitives poured into beds with their miserable thoughts, hope as thin as the ratty motel blankets they clutched tightly to their chest. Bossilini had checked them into to a national economy chain motel in Hagerstown, West Virginia.

Virginia and Carmen huddled in one bed, shocked and terrified. "Mom, when do you think we can go home?" Carmen whimpered.

"Soon, honey. I hope real soon. Before too long I hope we all will be back together in the keeping room with something good cooking . . . home together where we belong."

"Mom, you promise?"

"Promise."

Carmen scooted close to her. Tears ran down Virginia's cheeks as she held her daughter.

On the other bed, George was in bad shape, his mind relentlessly whirling trying to find a solution, his mind racing and racing in perverse contrast to the time barely ticking off the bedside clock. Finally, George fell into a black, haggard sleep.

Sherman, crowded into the same bed, could feel his father's restlessness, which kept him awake for some time. Sherman was as frantic as the others and just as baffled. But he had a sliver of hope, a sliver of confidence that Bossilini and Manfred, and maybe this man Buddy, would save them. Finally, after several hours, he fell asleep, his breath slow and regular.

At 2:00 a.m., when Manfred could not sleep, he stood outside on the second-floor walkway. Staring up at the stars, at the universe itself, Manfred saw a shooting star. He had only seen a shooting star one other time in his life—one night with his grandfather, long dead. And now even longer, he realized.

Manfred felt like a game piece moved fifty years forward on the board of time. Staring into the quiet sky, Manfred yearned to catch that star and ride it back, ride it back to 1969, ride it back to where he belonged, ride it back home.

But how to catch a shooting star? The song said to tuck it in your pocket and never let it go. But how did you do that?

Before reaching the motel, Sherman had fallen asleep in the Hummer, dreaming vividly.

Sherman was much younger in the dream, maybe three or four. He was outside on a pleasant day. As he looked up he saw big green stalks reaching above him toward the blue sky. At their tops he saw giant flower faces, almost as big as his head, their black faces ringed with yellow petals.

Sherman sensed that the flowers were friendly, and he liked them.

When he awoke as they pulled up to the motel, the image of the flowers lingered. He could still feel their colors, their friendliness.

Bossilini had made a final check of the Douglases' room before retiring. He again asked George and Virginia where they should go tomorrow. They shook their heads. No ideas. Sherman suddenly felt the dream flow through him. He felt the sunlight, the happiness, the marvel of the strange giant flowers. He blurted out: "We need to go to the sunflowers."

"Where is that, son?" George asked, his thoughts sluggish.

"I don't know. We need to go to the sunflowers. We must go to the sunflowers."

Bossilini shot a questioning glance at the boy's parents, who both shrugged.

"Do you know what he means by sunflowers?" Bossilini asked carefully.

"No."

"Has he ever he mentioned sunflowers before?" Bossilini eyed George for his reaction.

George looked at Virginia, who shook her head. "No, not that we know of," he said.

Bossilini sat watching them.

Suddenly, a look of recognition flashed on George's face. As the memory became stronger, he became certain.

"We need to go to Vermont," he told Bossilini.

"Vermont? Where?"

"Middlebury."

George thought Bossilini did not look surprised.

But in his fatigue, George paid it no further thought.

84

And George did not know that, while Manfred had arrived by a disaccordian resonance bubble, Buddy had traveled by other means.

III.

CAMBRIDGE AND PHYSICS

THE BIRTH OF THE LEAGUE

CHAPTER 16

WELL DONE, EINSTEIN
November 7, 1919
Buck's Club
London, England

9:00 p.m. GMT

"He was right, by Jove," Sir Nigel Clements said. "General relativity." He shook his head. "You knew he was right all along," replied his friend and scientific colleague, Cuthbert Wagnon.

"Yes, but the proof's in the pudding, and the pudding was Eddington and Principe Island."

"Well, now the proof's in the *Times*," Cuthbert said cavalierly, pointing at the newspaper opened before Sir Nigel.

Sir Nigel nodded over his gin and tonic. He still wore a severe Victorian collar framing the knot of his black and gray necktie; his graying hair was combed tightly to his head. Cuthbert wore a cravat with a gay pin, his face framed with blond curly hair and accented by two sparkling blue eyes above his moustache and perpetual grin.

"Another gin and tonic, sirs?" asked Alves, the waiter.

Nigel looked at Cuthbert, then, "Sure, another round. Alves, thank you. We've something to celebrate."

"What may it be, sir?"

"Our view of the universe will never be the same, thanks to our Swiss-German colleague, Albert Einstein."

"Oh, dear," answered Alves, "it's not looking bad for the Empire is it, sir? You know, with the Germans and all last time. . . ."

"Tut, tut, Alves, not at all, our own countryman, Arthur Eddington, did the experiment. Couldn't look better," Sir Nigel assured him.

"Mighty glad to hear it, sir." Alves turned and headed toward the bar with two empty glasses on his small cocktail tray.

"Decided not to explain the great experiment to the common man, Nigel?"

"Alves is a good man, but I didn't think he would quite follow."

"What—not follow the experiment that proved that the light rays of a star are bent by the gravity of a massive celestial body nearby; that cousin Albert was right space is curved—and it's not empty space anymore, but space-time? That the shortest distance between two points is no longer necessarily a straight line, and that common sense has flown out the window?"

"Something like that," Nigel smiled. "It's a pity that experiment was delayed during the War." He paused thoughtfully. "It's for the good that our work will never appear in the *Times*." He looked sternly at his more jovial colleague. "Cuthbert, we've agreed no one can ever know of our findings."

"Of course."

"You still abide by that agreement."

"Of course," Cuthbert answered smiling.

"No, I mean seriously, it has to live in our memories only. It's too dangerous even to write down the formulas."

"Our memories it is." Cuthbert tapped his temple. Becoming uncharacteristically serious, he said, "Nigel, you know I am the more lighthearted of the two of us, but on this you have no fear. I am linked with you arm-in-arm on my sacred honor." Seeing Nigel relax, he added with a sly smile, "But what happens, ol' man, when we get a bit daft—and don't remember the numbers so well?"

"There will be others from each generation."

"Who will they be?"

Nigel pondered his collaborator's question for a full two minutes, sitting perfectly still. Then he announced, "I don't know. We'll just have to go check one day. If we can."

"Proof's in the pudding, eh?"

The men were silent for a few moments.

"Time has nothing to do with clocks, but everything to do with light," Nigel announced.

"But not in the way Einstein thinks."

Alves arrived with their drinks, and they toasted each other and their secret pact.

CHAPTER 17

THE PRETTY BUBBLE
January 1, 1921
Cambridge Physics Lab
Cambridge, England

5:00 p.m. GMT

The lab was empty. Only dust motes dancing in the pale sunlight slanting through large vertical windows interrupted the stillness. A dusty chalk board bore equations written carefully in Sir Nigel's hand. A few feet away sat two blacktop lab tables. The surfaces were littered with Cuthbert's experimental tools: lenses of various shapes and thicknesses; copper wires; dry cell batteries; a disassembled box camera; a hardware store of screwdrivers, needle-nose pliers, and tiny screws; a soldering iron; electrician's tape; paint bottles full of metallic colored solutions; and small lead boxes with lids protecting chunks of radioactive elements inside.

The silence in the lab was heavy. A wall clock lethargically tick-tocked, time flowing thickly like syrup through the lab. Outside, the chimes sounded, calling to dinner the few students who had not left for the holidays. But college life seemed far away. If someone entered the lab, his footsteps would only echo lonely against the walls. The room seemed not just empty, but abandoned, its scientists gone away, their ideas padlocked in a trunk.

Without warning or cause, a little flicker of light arose, as if from a freshly struck match, a tiny bluish-green light that quickly snuffed out. But moments later it suddenly flickered again, this time quickly expanding, not like a flame, but like a big, translucent bubble, inflating rapidly not unlike a hot air balloon filling from a burst of the gas jets. As the bubble expanded, rainbow-like colors flashed across its surface, partially obscuring movement inside. Suddenly, the surface popped like a soap bubble, and there stood Nigel and Cuthbert. Cuthbert held a large bellows camera and laughed. "We're back, we're back." Nigel ran for a calendar. Cuthbert called after him, "Did we really do it, did we really?"

Nigel hurriedly examined the calendar on his desk. "Yes, by Jove, January 1, 1921. The new decade. Indeed, we did it!" Cuthbert beamed.

"My god, Cuthbert, we traveled years into the future and traveled back to the very same date! I mean—this is right out of Wells!"

"Yes," Cuthbert smiled, "but Wells only wrote it. We did it. Nigel, are you okay? Nigel?"

Nigel had grown pale and unsteady. He sat down. "Yes, Cuthbert I am fine. It's just—I think the enormity of what we've done has hit me."

Cuthbert smiled. "You mean the enormity of irradiating a series of metallic coated lenses with radium emissions, producing a concentrated photon perturbation into a different spectrum than white light—a perturbation that quite unexpectedly revealed a type of wall, for lack of a better term, a wall composed of honeycombed, lighted cells with grainy 1's and 0's appearing in discrete quanta, that when radiated produced bubbles that allow one to go forward or backward in time...." Out of breath, he had to pause.

Nigel couldn't answer at first. Finally, he collected his thoughts. "Ye gods, Einstein thinks light governs time as a constant speed throughout the universe, but in truth, time is governed by these super-photon perturbations of non-white light."

"I wonder if it is something more than those photons?" Cuthbert said.

Nigel shrugged. "At least we can make it work now. The full explanation may have to wait until we understand better. But, Cuthbert, this is serious, very serious business."

Cuthbert nodded. His face was solemn. He stared at the camera he had built, which was no longer a camera, but rather contained a series of metallic coated lenses inside. When the shutter was pressed, the top of a lead box within the camera opened, emitting a radium burst through the series of lenses. Incredibly, the burst made visible the "wall."

Studying their invention, Nigel pointed at the camera. "This camera device is too bulky. It's too easy to break or lose . . . or to be confiscated." Nigel pondered, "We need something smaller, more private, a device that can be concealed about the person if we are to travel with it."

Cuthbert smiled. He had an idea. Pulling an object from his vest pocket and holding it up, he said with a grin, "Say, a pocket watch, for instance?"

CHAPTER 18

NIGEL'S MALAISE
October 1925
The Marlborough Cafe
London, England

10:00 p.m. GMT

The mathematician Zen master known as Bodhi Jha was positioned at the University of Oxford in 1929. In addition to his duties in the mathematical department of the University, he gave lectures on Zen. While attending a reception hosted by Madame Channing Wadsworth following one of his Zen talks that nobody really understood, he suddenly disappeared from the room.

He had been told to expect a sensation of a bubble encapsulating him followed by a brief, unusual ride to his destination in time.

Madame Channing Wadsworth had turned, reaching for a guest to introduce to Bodhi. But when she turned around, saying, "Mr. Jha, I'd like you to meet—" Mr. Jha was gone. Perplexed, Madame Wadsworth anxiously scanned the room for the Zen master, her head swiveling jerkily in all directions. She could not fathom where he had gotten off to—and just as she was about to enjoy the satisfaction of presenting him to her snobbiest friends.

A short distance away at the bar, two professors from Cambridge could have explained the sudden disappearance of the mathematician master. But they had no intention of enlightening Madame Wadsworth. They nodded to each other and left the room. Cuthbert patted his vest pocket safely holding the large, gold pocket watch resting securely inside. By 1925, Sir Nigel and Cuthbert had successfully minimized the device from the bellows camera to a personal, ubiquitous pocket watch. But it had not been easy.

During their work, they began pondering what to do with "the Watch," or whether to do anything with it, for its existence posed the gravest danger in wrong hands.

For a difficult spell in their collaboration, Nigel thought that they should destroy it. Cuthbert, who enthusiastically supported the device, quarreled with him and became quite cross. For several months, they barely spoke and did no effective work.

One afternoon after tea, Cuthbert had had enough. He said, "Nigel, you can't destroy it. You simply can't. It's one of the most remarkable devices created by mankind ever, as consequential as the sextant, microscope, and Roentgen machine for X-rays. Mankind's destiny is forward, toward knowledge, toward understanding the universe— suppressing the device is suppressing our *raison d'être*."

"You could as well argue, Cuthbert, based on history, that mankind's *raison d'être* is to build beautiful, lovely things . . . and then to destroy them." He shook his head. "No, Cuthbert, humanity is too unscrupulous to possess such a fearsome device. An ambitious leader could journey to the past and bend time to his will, preventing the births of his enemies, or purposefully—or unwittingly—causing all sorts of calamities in the arc of civilization. No, the risk is too great; we should destroy the device immediately—if it is meant to be, humanity can rediscover the device when mankind has become more advanced, more benevolent."

"BLAST!" Cuthbert shouted.

Nigel stood by a wall. He was taller and thinner than his colleague, who was of medium build and crackled with energy. Nigel studied Cuthbert. A tender look came over Nigel's face. He understood his friend's passions. So he said, "Come Cuthbert, despite our disagreements, out of my respect for you and our deep friendship these years—I will not destroy the device until you agree. I would not do that to you." He looked away, as if the emotion were too intense.

"I appreciate that, Nigel, I really do, but I—I just don't know—" Overcome with emotion, too, Cuthbert looked out the window at a tiny bird perched in the top of a tree, which enabled him to suppress an embarrassingly strong affection for his friend and colleague.

But the rift between them remained until one day Cuthbert accused, "Nigel, you are in a funk. You must do something about it."

Nigel looked up. "Sherlock Holmes was often in a funk."

"*Touché.* But he turned to a *seven-percent solution*. I don't see that *solution* quite fitting you."

Nigel actually smiled.

That smile broke the wall between them.

Finally, Nigel unburdened himself to his dear friend, purging himself of the disheartening, black thoughts filling him with dread.

"Cuthbert, Cuthbert." He shook his head. "I despair. What is happening to civilization?" He looked to Cuthbert, who had no reply. "Chaos—in Germany, Russia, and even at home over socialists and communists."

"I see quite clearly now that the precursor to totalitarianism is the loss of privacy, the freedom of the individual man to think his own independent thoughts and the freedom to talk about them. What particularly troubles me, Cuthbert, is that since the War ended, it seems that governments have not been quick to suspend suspiciousness and spying upon their own citizens. Rather, it seems that once a government encroaches upon a freedom, it is rather loathe to return it."

He pulled on his pipe in silence. Cuthbert knew not to interrupt him.

Finally, Nigel spoke. "The power to protect should never become the power to harm. Cuthbert, it's about balance—imbalance, really."

An organization, a "League" of sorts, began to form in his mind, with its symbol an ink drawing of a flashlight—a flashlight, its light to shine on government overreach and misdeeds. And a time travel device could be most useful in that endeavor.

"Cuthbert. *Cuthbert.* I see it all so clearly. Let me explain this . . . this League to you. . . ."

After his discourse, Cuthbert asked, "But to whom are we to turn, Nigel, to help with this grand plan?"

The answer occurred by happenstance when Sir Nigel went to his solicitor's office the next week to execute a codicil to his will. Henry P. Witherspoon, Esq. was a distinguished solicitor, age sixty-five, whom Nigel trusted implicitly.

So, in a few weeks they sat in a table in a secluded corner of the Marlborough Café, a quiet London restaurant, late at night as the tired waiters collected in the kitchen to smoke cigarettes and sip espresso.

As they neared the end of the meal, Witherspoon took the initiative: "Might as well get down to the business, shall we?" He was plump, with a pink completion, and he wore a three-piece gray suit. Unlike many his age, he did not wear spectacles.

Nigel nodded gravely, while Cuthbert sat expectantly, though his eyes showed concern. Everything hung on the next few moments. To disclose the device to anyone was a tremendous gamble.

"We have an invention," Nigel began hesitantly, "we're rather thinking we need protection, er, for its use . . . and, I suppose, for its safekeeping."

Witherspoon listened carefully.

"So, we're thinking of a patent."

Witherspoon nodded. "Sensible."

"And then, a charter for use of the device … and finally, a will to govern its inheritance."

Witherspoon nodded.

Cuthbert looked at Nigel.

"Mr. Witherspoon, our conversations are absolutely privileged, we are seeking legal advice and counsel of you."

"Yes, indeed, the legal advice privilege is one of the most sacred principles in English law."

"Very well, then." Nigel announced, "I will proceed. This is rather a singular device. I think once you learn of its properties you will agree."

"Splendid! You are a bright fellow, I have no doubt you have come up with a very merchantable invention."

"Mr. Witherspoon, you have no idea. You'd better brace yourself."

Witherspoon looked at him quizzically.

"We—Cuthbert and I—have invented, no that is not right, we stumbled upon a way to—a way to—oh, blast, a way to access time, a wall of sorts that when irradiated frees time." He could tell Witherspoon was not following him. "In short, we have invented a time machine."

Witherspoon literally fell back in his seat. He looked gravely from Nigel to Cuthbert and back to Nigel. He began to laugh, as certainly the two were pulling one over on him. But the set of their faces wiped the grin from his face.

"Ye gods, you're serious!"

The scientists both nodded.

Witherspoon, his face splotching red, reached for his brandy tumbler and took a long swig.

"What do you seek of me, then? Does anyone else know?" His voice trembled with emotion.

"No. And the legal advice privilege protects this knowledge whether you agree to work for us or not. We ask your sacred honor on that point."

"You have it, though I must admit, you have given me quite a shock."

"Nothing like we ourselves have experienced, I assure you."

"Very well. If I am to assist you then, let me form a belief in the truth of the device. Can you tell me more about it?"

"Would it help if you experienced the device itself."

The question took him aback. Witherspoon paused, thinking gravely. He had no confidence in the reality of the invention. It was the talk of gadflies. Witherspoon did not question their sincerity, but time travel? It was preposterous. Perhaps he could discern the cause of their illusion and provide service in disabusing them of it.

"Indeed, it would help. Should we make an appointment for me to examine it?"

"An appointment is not necessary. You can examine it right here."

Witherspoon was stunned. He assumed the device was quite large, like a chariot in Wells's novel. "Here?"

"Indeed here. Let's settle up the bill and step out back in the alley, shall we?"

Five minutes later they were in the dank alley in the rear of the restaurant huddled amidst smelly garbage cans and stacked wooden crates.

Witherspoon had grown fearful and startled when Cuthbert quickly reached in his vest pocket removing an object. A weapon?

"A watch? You want a patent on a pocket watch!" Witherspoon's incredulity replaced his fear.

"That's not what the patent is for. To what date would you like to travel?"

"Date? How would I know?"

"Well, let's just take a short jaunt, say five years into the future. 1930."

Witherspoon nodded fearfully.

"Let's stand a bit closer, shall we."

Witherspoon fretfully took a step closer, saw Cuthbert's fingers move on the watch, and then experienced a bubbling sensation and floating colors. He thought he'd become nauseous. Suddenly, the film or bubble encasing them dissolved, and there they stood in the alley.

At first he felt taken advantage of, but Witherspoon quickly realized the alley was filthy, completely littered, and reeked of urine. It had unquestionably changed from moments before. There had not been time for someone to rearrange it. The men passed a quick, concerned look.

Cuthbert, no longer smiling, suggested they look around front. They found the restaurant boarded up. Dark and deserted, as if it had not been open for months. The entire street looked shabby. The wind blew an errant newspaper page around their feet. Nigel planted his foot on it and Cuthbert retrieved it. He searched for the date to prove it to Witherspoon.

"There, see, December 30, 1930."

Witherspoon couldn't believe his eyes. He looked up, stunned, to Nigel and Cuthbert. He looked around the street. This couldn't be staged. Yes, a newspaper page, but not the entire street. The street, the very neighborhood, seemed to withered.

Witherspoon then read the lead article. *World Wide Depression Worsens, Outlook for New Year Grim.* He rapidly read an article recapping the financial failure beginning the year before in the American stock market and spreading like a plague to England, the Continent, and beyond. It was just unfathomable to him: people out of work, lost homes, businessmen jumping out of windows, workers standing in soup lines for daily nourishment. He felt dizzy.

"I've had enough. I believe you. Can we go back now. Can we go back, please?" he asked with uncharacteristic anxiousness. The man appeared completely unnerved.

"Yes. Shall we?" Cuthbert motioned the three closer. He looked at Witherspoon with a grave concern for the man's well-being.

"Can I take the paper. I'd like to study the paper more closely."

"Definitely not. No artifact from the future may ever be brought back. Never," Nigel said, his face severe.

Witherspoon let loose the paper from his fingers. The wind carried it whirling down the street.

Soon the bubble enveloped them, and they were returned, standing behind the restaurant, among the original garbage cans and crates, as if nothing had happened. Witherspoon checked his watch. No time had passed, though he had a clear recollection that they were gone close to ten minutes.

"I could use shot of brandy," Witherspoon said. "Let's retreat to my flat."

Thirty minutes later they clustered around a pleasant fire. Witherspoon looked more himself after quickly downing a snifter of brandy.

"I wouldn't have believed it. Incredible!"

"You will work with us, then?"

"Yes. This is momentous. It needs to be kept in careful hands."

"The legal advice privilege securely in place?"

"Most secure. Believe me. The danger of the device in the wrong hands is unimaginable."

"Good then," Nigel responded. "Let us quickly discuss details."

Witherspoon first reviewed the necessary business aspects.

Next, Nigel outlined the concept of a League—a League that would expose and resist privacy invasions in the future, but that would never alter the past. He presented a half-formed idea about recruiting privacy constables every ten years, starting with 1929. Perhaps Nigel and Cuthbert could travel forward on the first of January of the last year of each decade. In that one year, they would limit time travel to five that year. In those visits they would select constables to work in the future.

Finally, the Watch itself. They needed a will in perpetuity to bequeath the watch to an "Heir after their deaths. Nigel and Cuthbert thought perhaps they could spring forward decades in the future to discern a suitable Heir to the Watch and to continue the League.

There was much to consider and decide upon over the coming months and years, but Witherspoon would immediately begin drafts of a charter for the League and a patent for the device, but with patent drawings only of its capacity for radium emission—and none for its true operation and purpose.

The clients set a fee with the solicitor, and Cuthbert handed him a down payment of £100, thus cementing the attorney-client relationship.

And so it was that Henry P. Witherspoon, Esq. became Secretary of the League of Privacy Sentinels, Ltd.

IV.

THE CHASE

CHAPTER 19

REFLECTIONS AT A WAFFLE HOUSE
April 10, 2019
The Douglases House
Birmingham, Alabama

8:30 a.m. CDT

Imhoff stared across the street at the Douglas home. He looked up and down at what must ordinarily be a quiet street in a stately, upscale neighborhood. He shook his head. The Douglases had lived here like the All-American family all those years right under everyone's noses.

Imhoff would find these people. That's what he did. And he was good at his job.

But something nagged him.

He decided he needed breakfast. He could think better with hot food on his stomach. On his phone he found a nearby Waffle House. He loved to eat at Waffle House on assignment. Maybe afterwards he could grab a couple hours' sleep.

Imhoff sat in a booth and raised the white porcelain mug with the Waffle House logo to his lips. He took a short sip of the hot, black coffee, closing his eyes, relishing the slightly bitter taste, and the beginning of the caffeine surge.

He set the cup on the table, admiring the blue ringed mug. Nobody used mugs like that anymore. He remembered the mugs from his childhood. They used them in diners in Pennsylvania where his dad would take him for hot apple pie. They would eat the hot pie off the white porcelain plates with blue rims. His dad would sip steaming coffee from the matching mug the same way he found himself sipping it now. He savored those memories. He thought of his dad every time he came to a Waffle House. And he had the same wish, the wish that he could have one more time with his dad at a diner where he could eat a piece of pie and watch his dad sip coffee from a blue trimmed mug.

Imhoff always ordered the All Star Special: eggs, sausage, hash browns instead of grits, wheat toast, and a waffle with warm maple syrup. He ate the eggs and sausage first, alternating bites of each, only nibbled at the hash browns, polished off the buttered toast, and saved the waffles for last, as if a breakfast dessert, cutting them into quarter sections, finishing off one section at a time. The food warmed Imhoff and calmed him. He began to think about the case as the waitress refilled his mug.

"Let me know if you need another refill, hon."

"Sure thing, will do." Imhoff smiled at the waitress. He would tip her well. These visits recalled memories as warm and sweet as the maple syrup.

Restored, Imhoff began to organize what he knew so far.

Some scientists had theorized it was possible to create a space tunnel—whether by human effort or natural events, he did not know. However created, humans could pass through the tunnel with equipment. The scientists further theorized that the opening a tunnel would produce these particles that could be detected.

It didn't walk for Imhoff.

This was just too way out. We couldn't yet get to Mars, but a country like Russia or China or Iran could control to the square yard a space tunnel that people with their gear could somehow go through? Did they walk through, fly through, or were they beamed like on *Star Trek*? And it *really* didn't walk that a terrorist group could discover and control such advanced technology.

Sipping his coffee, Imhoff thought DHS had gone off the deep end. DHS and NSA had done some way-out stuff, but enemies controlling a space tunnel? Something else had to be going on.

But the techs *did* detect some kind of particle. He saw the readings on their vacuum cleaners. More important, he saw the DHS geeks' reactions. Their faces lit up like they had won the IT sweepstakes. They found something, and they couldn't wait to get back and start analyzing that something. So, there were *some* kind of particles. That part walked. But with a wooden leg.

The problem, as Imhoff reasoned, was the particles were supposed to herald the opening of a tunnel, but there was no evidence a tunnel had opened in the Douglas house. He remembered the AK-47 and frowned. Something had happened in that home in the predawn hours, and it was something strange. And the family definitely beat it out of there with some help. He shook his head. The AK-47 *might* tie into something, but what—a radical cell? Did it walk? He didn't know.

Imhoff waved off another refill and paid his bill, leaving a generous tip. Wearily, he decided on one more trip to the Douglas house, one more walk-through in the daylight before some sleep.

Special Agents McKansky and Franks were at the Douglas house when he arrived. They were part of his team. The three agents walked through the house together, but saw nothing new. Imhoff, McKansky and Franks got hotel rooms. Tired, Imhoff sat on his bed and loosened his tie. He stared vacantly at the framed, mass-produced print on the wall. He mustered the energy to unplug the room phone and plug his phone into the desk outlet for a charge. Staring at the phone, he pressed the off button. He watched the colored screen fade to black. Later this afternoon, or maybe in the early evening, he would go to the Birmingham FBI field office, review what was new, if anything, and check in with the Director.

Now, however, he removed his clothes, and in his skivvies, crawled into bed and fell instantly asleep. He had learned how to do that on the battlefield, where a Marine had to sleep when he can.

CHAPTER 20
BREAKFAST IN GEORGETOWN
April 11, 2019
Kitchen
The Preston Ogilvie Home

9:00 a.m. EDT

"Jennifer will be so glad to see you, Preston. It's been what, four months, and then only in and out at Christmas, off to her ski trip?" Jennifer was their college sophomore attending Columbia.

Ogilvie smiled as he worked on the eggs and toast his wife Peggy had cooked for him. She sipped coffee as he ate. It would be good to see his daughter. Once the kids got to be that age and had their own lives, parents had to take what they could get, even if it was over a quick breakfast on a work day.

Last night, Ogilvie had come home well after midnight. As he slipped into bed and gently kissed his wife's head, she murmured, "Jennifer's home."

"What's up?"

Peggy answered in a half-awake state, "It's her annual gynecological appointment with Dr. Breedlove—"

"Hush, that's a little more information than I want to know. Daddies don't like to think about their daughters having grown up and needing gynecological exams. They still should be sitting on our knees and saying, 'Daddy, you're the best daddy in the whole world.'"

His wife leaned up to peck his check and then submerged under the covers.

The next morning, the sun shone brightly through the kitchen, and Ogilvie thought that today's the day we will find them, find the fugitives who since the wee hours of yesterday morning were never far from his mind.

"Preston, I hope you have time to stay . . . to see her before you leave for the office."

"Wouldn't miss it. Besides, we've been putting in the hours on this case and I can come in a little late."

"Daddy," he heard a bright voice as his daughter Jennifer entered the kitchen. It was a more robust greeting than he could remember in a long time.

He smiled with pride as she moved toward the coffee pot. Peggy had set a mug for her on the counter. She was definitely the best of both Peggy and him, he thought. He beamed a smile to his wife, how about our little girl?

But his lips pressed into a thin line.

He knew his daughter, despite her increasing independence, still admired him with all her heart. His wife said Jennifer beamed at his rise to high office and eagerly followed news reports about him and the Department. He was thrilled over her interest in his work. Perhaps she would follow him into public service.

Yet, he was bothered. Her youthful idealism clashed with the reality of government and power at the top. Could she understand his responsibilities, the things he had to do, the things a person in power had to do, the hard things, the ruthless things? Could she understand his decisions on the Douglas matter? What if it blew into a scandal—as some at DHS were beginning to think possible? The press about him so far was generally positive. What would she think if it turned negative? If it turned hostile? Could she ever understand? Would she even try to understand? My god, it was all becoming crazy. What had he done?

He tried to clear his head. He could never lose his daughter's admiration. He had to fix this. Somehow. No matter what he had to do. It had to be fixed. At all costs.

He looked at Jennifer. "Will you be here after work when I get back?" he asked with a father's tentative hope.

"Oh, Dad, I'm so sorry, I've got this real big international law project due in two days. But I'll come home soon, I promise."

Ogilvie sighed, but he had expected it.

"Can I help you with your suitcase?"

"Oh, thanks, Dad, but it's just an overnight bag, didn't pack much for one night."

He rose. "Anyway, give your daddy a kiss?"

On tiptoes, she pecked his cheek and rushed away smiling, blowing kisses, then reaching for her bag and balancing her coffee mug.

His wife busied herself about the kitchen. He was grateful. He needed a few moments. It was always hard on him when his little girl left.

"How is Richard doing?" Peggy changed the subject, referring to Chambers, whose wife had died a year ago from leukemia.

"Seems to be holding up. His second wife is his job, as you know, always has been. There was the time off, but now he . . . he seems fully engaged, on the ball, no signs of slowing down."

Ogilvie thought about Chambers as he took another sip of coffee.

"You know, he does get a look every now and then. It's brief, and if you look harder, he seems to cover it up. I can't figure if it's still some grief, or if he's wondering if working this hard, still playing the game at his age, is the thing to do. Forget getting him to talk about it, though. He's like a safe. Feelings go in, they don't come back out."

"Well, I hope he's doing well. They were married forty-five years."

Ogilvie nodded.

His wife reached for his hand, giving him a happy, contented smile. He clasped her hand and returned her smile. It was genuine, but not quite as full as hers. Grains of worry rubbed on his mind.

A few miles away, Chambers sat alone in the breakfast nook of his house. Silence filled the dwelling. It was the silence that got to him. Since Margaret had died, the house stood silent. For days the only sound was the ticking of the grandfather clock she so loved. It sat by the stairway inside the front door. Chambers had decided to stop winding it. Its unceasing ticking only accentuated the silence, taunting him that Margaret was gone, the house was empty, and his life was winding down, like the old clock. He was now seventy.

Chambers was a workaholic, or maybe better said, a careeraholic. Margaret had been patient and supportive all those years, because engagement in business or politics made her husband happy, and her husband's happiness was important to her. She never complained through those years of late hours and broken plans, though he could see the disappointment she could not fully hide. They could not have children. So now there was no son or daughter to visit, no grandchildren running and banging through the house. Only silence.

Chambers thought he would be more attentive if Margaret were still here. But she was not. That could not be fixed. Thoughts of regrets, lost times together, fluttered around his mind like bats swirling in an attic. He needed to batten the attic tightly. He must refuse to indulge regret. Regret can reveal truths he did not want to face: the anguish of wasted years, of wasted lives, of neglected love—she was gone. Indulging that regret now when past days were irretrievable could become unbearable.

A steaming bowl of oatmeal and bananas sat before Chambers on the table. Oatmeal had soluble fiber that helped scrub the cholesterol from his bloodstream, his doctor said. If it washed cholesterol from his bloodstream, maybe it could wash regrets from his mind.

But every morning after the oatmeal Chambers rewarded himself. It was a nice way, a private way, to inject some warmth into the coming day. Since Margaret died, Chambers had acquired the practice every morning before work of taking a tumbler of single malt scotch. He preferred *Auchentoshan*. He took it neat. The whiskey burned, but it gave him a little pluck to face the day. It was by now as much a part of his morning as shaving or knotting his necktie. He meticulously limited himself to one. But that one he savored sip by sip until the crystal tumbler was empty.

Then it was time to go.

CHAPTER 21

MORNING IN THE MOUNTAINS
April 11, 2019
Motel
Hagerstown, West Virginia

7:00 a.m. EDT

Virginia awoke early, while the others still lay in exhausted sleep.

She was distraught, fretting over their situation, frustrated by wasting all of yesterday passively riding in that hideous vehicle. With the light of the new day, it was now time for action. She was sick of feeling helpless. Virginia rose, dressed quietly and slipped out the door.

Though her exit was soundless, Sherman, through one eye watched his mother leave the room.

The boy lay motionless for a moment. Then he made a decision. He carefully removed the covers, and in his boxers, slipped out of the room as quietly as his mother.

From the doorway, he watched her cross the back of the motel parking lot to a convenience store next door. Was she getting coffee?

His mother paused, looking around, then fixed on something. The boy watched her dart to a payphone on the side of the convenience store building.

Sherman shook his head, willing her not to reach for the receiver.

Virginia stood before it. Her shoulders raised and then slumped, as if exhaling. But in an instant, her head shot up. Virginia reached for the receiver, pulled it to her ear, and punched a number on the keypad. She was still for a few moments. Sherman guessed for someone to answer. He scratched his head, hoping whoever she had called was wasn't at home. But no, suddenly, he saw Virginia's mouth moving; she was talking. She looked silent again, as if she were waiting, but then she lurched forward, talking animatedly once again.

She nodded and hung up the phone.

"Mom, what have you done? What have you done?" he whispered, shaking his head.

Before she turned, Sherman slipped back into the room and into bed. His father still snored. Sherman closed his eyes and lay still, breathing regularly. When his mother slipped open the door, he watched her float across the room like a ghost and close the bathroom door. He heard the water of the shower splattering against the plastic shower curtain.

Bossilini was driving back to the motel after an early breakfast when his encrypted phone rang. Only agents assigned to the operation or Master Agents could place a call through the advanced encryption technology. Bossilini tensed. He was only to be called if absolutely necessary. As he cradled the phone, worry lining his face, he answered, "Yes."

"Nitko, it's Tappy."

"Why are you calling me on this line?"

Virginia Douglas called me."

He sharply drew in his breath. "Oh, my god, she didn't." Shaking his head, he asked, "And?"

"She wants me to come get her."

"*What?*"

"She wants me to pick up her and the children. She thinks the thing to do is go back to Alabama, get the family lawyer, and straighten this out. She is confident she can explain their innocence. She said she voted for George W. Bush twice, and DHS cannot treat her this way."

Bossilini shook his head. He almost asked, *are you kidding?* But he knew the answer. He had to think. He could not let Virginia take the boy.

"Nitko—?"

"Tappy, we need you as a distraction. Surely, they were monitoring all the neighbors' phones and picked up the call. They will be fixing the motel's location as we speak."

"What are you thinking, Nitko?"

"Because she called you, you are a person of great interest now. DHS either has, or soon will, record your calls and place a tracking device on your vehicle. They will scour everything electronic about you and your family."

"I would expect no less. My Escalade is in the driveway. And Nitko, yesterday there were pest control men at the Douglas house. They came out with full black garbage bags."

"What—"

"It's a cover. An excuse to pore over every inch of the house in the daylight."

Bossilini hammered the accelerator to the floor, his mind racing with the engine.

"We need to establish misdirection. Tappy, pack quickly, and be ready to leave quickly. I'm not sure where to—New Orleans? They may jump to the conclusion the Douglases are trying to get out of the country, so maybe Mexico. The call from West Virginia will confuse them, they may pursue you—and the confusion could help just enough. But stay there for the moment. You are our eyes and ears. You judge when best to leave."

"Got it. Nitko, the call could make things go badly. Are you thinking of snatching the boy and heading for Canada?"

"Who knows with these impossible people? Bah. Just get on the road at the right time. Stay in touch."

The intercom on Ogilvie's phone crackled, "Mr. Secretary, sorry to interrupt, it's Marcie from Intelligence and Analysis on line 1."

"Marcie? Oh, yes. Put her through." Ogilvie picked up the receiver.

"Mr. Secretary Ogilvie," Marcie began formally after the meeting yesterday. "Our bugs intercepted a call from Virginia Douglas."

"*Virginia Douglas.*" He sat erect. "Where? How?" He punched the speaker button.

"She called her best friend, her next-door neighbor, Tappy Montgomery."

"Where did she call from?"

"Mrs. Douglas called from a convenience store in Hagerstown, West Virginia."

"Hagerstown? What the hell are they doing there?"

"We don't know, sir, but it appears Mrs. Douglas does not want to stay there. She asked for Mrs. Montgomery to come get her and the children. She intends to return to Alabama and try to straighten this out. She plans to contact the family lawyer."

Ogilvie cut a nervous glance at Chambers. "What did Mrs. Montgomery say—Tappy—did you say her name is Tappy?"

"Yes, Tappy. And she—Tappy—said not to call again, she would have to think what to do, and would help if she could."

Incredible, Ogilvie thought, what luck. A neighbor trying to help will lead them right to the Douglases. "Okay. Okay." This was their first break. "Marcie, get full surveillance of the Montgomery family, I mean the cat and dog—even their fleas. Hold on, Marcie."

Ogilvie put the phone on mute, turning to Chambers, "Get a FISA warrant, I want this one to stick." Chambers nodded. He pressed the mute off.

"Okay, Marcie, I'm back."

"Yes, sir. Sir, I have taken the liberty of calculating projected intercept points of the Douglases. If they continue on the present course, that would take them to Pittsburgh, or on to Buffalo, where they could try to cross into Canada. Or turning east, they could go to Baltimore or D.C., maybe to get a ship out of the country. Mrs. Douglas's father moved to Phoenix four years ago, but he has not been contacted, so we do not think the Douglases will go west."

Chambers mouthed, "We have a car watching him."

"What about the mother?"

"She died four years ago. Anyway, as to Mr. Douglas, the family is estranged from his mother. They haven't spoken in five years, no contact at all. The father is unknown. George and Virginia Douglas are running away from the South, so unless Mrs. Montgomery *does* come to get them and they try to double back, that direction doesn't seem right. So it looks like—"

"Good work, Marcie, we'll take it from here."

"Hold on a second, Marcie." Ogilvie muted the phone when Chambers signaled to him.

"A drone," Chambers said. "We should search the area with drones. It's the quickest way, and everyone is so used to them they won't attract attention."

"Not the weaponized ones?"

"No, live feeds, camera-only."

Ogilvie pressed the mute button, back on speaker.

"Ah, Marcie, one more thing. We are ordering drones over the Hagerstown area. We want you with the operator scanning the observations and data in real time, reporting directly—and only—to me."

Ogilvie sensed her pause. She had not expected drones.

"Yes, sir."

"Very good, then, we'll be in touch."

He figured she did not like drones. Some of their people didn't. The privacy fanatics are insidious, he thought. They can infect anybody with their virulent paranoia.

"Ah, sir, there's one more thing I think you should know."

"What is that?"

"Ah, well, Mrs. Douglas told Mrs. Montgomery that they are being framed."

Ogilvie was silent. He knew Marcie would eventually fill the silence. And he needed to know what Marcie knew, or what she thought she knew.

But she didn't take the bait.

"Is that all, Marcie?"

"Yes. That's all, sir."

"Well, thank you, Marcie. You will be contacted about the drones."

"Yes, sir."

Ogilvie hung up.

He and Chambers looked at each other, neither speaking.

Finally, Ogilvie offered, "Canada or Atlantic—which is it?"

Chambers walked to the bookshelf and removed a sturdy oversized volume. He returned to his chair and studied an atlas held open on his lap. Ogilvie watched him run his finger on a diagonal across the page.

Chambers looked up. "Philadelphia. We should send Imhoff to Philadelphia. It is centrally located to either a north or east escape route. We'll get Bart to dispatch a team to Hagerstown immediately. I'll have Ms. Beethoven focus all our surveillance at the motel with the drones on rolling concentric searches outward from Hagerstown." He smiled. "Preston, we throw enough money at the Douglases for a non-disclosure, or put them in witness protection with a story they inadvertently

115

witnessed a mob crime—well, then we could have this wrapped up by the cocktail hour."

Ogilvie beamed. "If that happens, then I'm buying." He frowned. "What if they don't accept the deal?"

"Everybody's got a price."

"But what if they have a grudge against the government or want publicity."

"Ms. Beethoven did not unearth any evidence to suggest that. But, Preston."

"But what?"

"There are other ways."

Ogilvie nodded, looking uncomfortable. Looking away, thinking, he said, "Let's suggest to Bart not to pull Imhoff back yet. Let him interview this Tappy Montgomery woman. He could say it's a background check on George Douglas, the government is commissioning his firm for work, but it requires an FBI background check. Maybe she's connected with this Douglas business, and we catch several fish in the net."

Chambers nodded favorably.

"Think Cummings will tell us what he finds?"

"Won't really matter, will it, if NSA and its contractors have done their jobs?" Ogilvie smiled. "I'll call Bart."

Bossilini burst into the Douglases' room. "Hurry, hurry, we must leave now. We have been compromised. They are on their way. We must leave."

The sleepy Douglases bolted upright, rushing in chaos to don clothes, as fear, then panic grew in their eyes. Virginia emerged from the bathroom, dressed but with wet hair.

Bossilini shot her a look of disgust. She blanched. She realized from his look that she had given them away, and she could tell from his urgency she had placed them in grave, imminent danger. She began to cry.

"Mrs. Douglas, there is no time for emotion. You should understand that. You can accept responsibility later, if there is a later. But now we must leave. Now! Everyone. Hurry!"

"Virginia? Accept responsibility?" George uttered weakly.

116

"Mr. Douglas, please do not talk. You must assist your family to my vehicle. It is our only hope of escape. And that hope is rapidly shrinking."

George nodded, leaping in to help Bossilini herd the family to the Rectangle. Buddy and Manfred were already there, standing anxiously, waiting outside the locked Hummer for the others. Bossilini had pounded on their door first.

Virginia still stood in the mirrored lavatory section of the room, her face fixed with a look of horror, as if it were a plaster mask. Only her lower lip was quivering.

"Mrs. Douglas—Virginia—you must come now. Or not. It is your choice. I am leaving now." Bossilini turned, striding to the door.

Virginia watched him step outside and disappear into the sunlight. She stood paralyzed with fear at the thought she had sealed her family's doom. And all the bad things Bossilini said could happen were now certainties. It was *her* fault.

Like her face, her body had become rigid as if it, too, were made of plaster. She could not move. She was certain that, if she did, the plaster would crack, splitting her into shards, crumbling to the floor.

But sounds. She heard a commotion outside the door, someone dimly calling, "Sherman, Sherman, no."

Her son burst through the door. He ran to her, grabbing her hand and began tugging her out of the room. To her surprise, she did not crack, she did not break into pieces.

She heard Bossilini's voice. "Sherman, there's no time, come on, let her go."

"No, no, I'm not letting her go, no! Mom, mom, wake up, come on, come on now, you have to!" the boy pleaded.

With a surge of adrenaline, she felt life course through her.

Virginia looked down tenderly at her son's earnest face. He would not leave without her. She felt an ocean of love for her boy child, the depth of love only a mother can feel. She knew that to save her son, she had to save herself. She smiled down at the tender boy. "Okay, Sherman."

She looked to the open door, and said, "Let's go!"

And they raced together, hand in hand, to the Rectangle, where they sped away with the others.

117

Fifteen minutes later agents of the United States Federal Bureau of Investigation burst into the motel room. It was empty.

CHAPTER 22

WHO *ARE* THESE DOUGLASES?
April 10-11, 2019
Hotel Room
Birmingham, Alabama

Evening and early next morning CDT

Imhoff did go to the field office in the early evening. He left frustrated, with no leads. Nothing.

Back at the hotel room, he stewed. This part of an investigation was the worst for Imhoff, when nothing matched or fit and the trail seemed dry. He would figure it out. It may be sooner or it may be later, but he would figure it out. But that didn't mean he had to be in a good mood until he did.

He called home. "You sound tired, Frankie."

"Yeah, a little."

"Get some rest tonight."

"How are the kids?"

"Bobby went two for three in his game, and he's very excited to tell you but he's asleep already, and Mary Jane is out studying with friends at Starbucks."

"Tell them I love them."

"When will you be home?"

"Not sure."

"Is that the best you can say?"

"It is for now."

"Get some sleep, Frankie, you're tired."

"Will do."

"I love you, Frankie."

"Love you, too."

The next morning, he breakfasted at the Waffle House again, having the All Star Special and leaving the same generous tip. His mood greatly improved upon receiving an urgent call from the Director.

"Frank, we've just had a break. Mrs. Douglas called a friend back home. She asked the friend to come get her."

"Whew," whistled Imhoff. "Did you get a trace?"

"Yes. NSA got it all. I'll send you the Wav file."

"Where are they?"

"Hagerstown, West Virginia. Virginia Douglas made a call from a payphone at a convenience store to a Tappy Montgomery—who happens to live next door, go figure. Called collect. She asked Tappy to come get her. Tappy asked what was going on. Virginia said she didn't know, but it looked like the government was framing them—"

"Framing them? For what?"

"She didn't say. She pleaded with Tappy to bring her home so they could get a lawyer and straighten this out."

"What did Tappy say?"

"She said she would have to think what to do and would help if she could."

"What does that mean?"

"No idea. She is a freelance journalist, and her husband's a lawyer." Cummings paused. "Frank, the last thing Tappy said, and I mean she really said it firmly, was Virginia should not call back . . . that she would do what she could."

"Damn."

"Yes. That's why we want you to come to Philadelphia. It's centrally located to where DHS thinks the fugitives are headed. Puts you in position for a rapid response when they surface."

"Sure—"

"Frank, before you fly up, though, we want you to interview Mrs. Montgomery. Tell her it's a background check on the Douglases. If there is a patio or something outside talk to her there, so DHS and NSA can't listen just in case. Use your intuition, go where the conversation takes you."

"Yes, sir. I'll get it done." Imhoff was silent a moment. "Sir, what do you make of this 'they are being framed' business? Who would frame them? What's the benefit to DHS or anybody else?"

"Maybe you can help us find out, Frank. And Frank?"

"Yes, sir."

"Stay light on your feet."

"Yes, sir."

"Come in Special Agent, would you like some coffee?" Tappy Montgomery welcomed Imhoff into her house at 11:00 a.m. She stood at the open door in cream-colored knit pants and a long-sleeved top. Her blonde hair fell to her shoulders, and she had a nice, welcoming smile. Imhoff thought she would be pretty, even without the expensive makeup job.

She was intelligent and confident, with excellent social skills. He quickly concluded that winning came naturally to her, though she was not arrogant or haughty.

He also guessed she had been expecting him for some time.

"Let's go out on the patio, Special Agent Imhoff. It's such a pleasant morning."

She picked up a tray with coffee pot and cups and headed toward French doors leading from the kitchen to the patio.

Imhoff saw a smartphone sitting on the counter by the coffee pot. "Mrs. Montgomery, is this your phone? Do you need it?"

"Oh, yes," she smiled. "Leave it there so we won't be interrupted. I know you must have a busy day."

Imhoff nodded and followed her to patio. It was nicely furnished. He sat in a comfortable outdoor chair as she placed the tray on a wrought-iron table. He noticed music was playing too loudly from outdoor speakers. No phone, music just a little too loud. Was she taking precautions against anyone listening in?

"Do you need cream or sugar, Special Agent? I expect you take it black."

"Indeed I do."

She smiled. Her teeth were white and perfectly aligned. After pleasantries, Imhoff got down to business, starting with questions about her family.

"My husband Ted is a lawyer with Witherspoon, Lindquest & Williams. They are an international firm based in London."

"London, huh? How come they got an office in Birmingham, Alabama?"

"Oh, I don't know all the reasons, but Ted's firm, the office here, does a lot of business in car manufacturing and other international companies locating in Alabama."

Tappy clasped her hands, resting them on her knees. As if waving aside his form questions, she said, "I will get to the point Special Agent Imhoff. I have known George and Virginia Douglas, for I guess, eighteen years. We're next door, as you can see. Virginia and I grew quite close over the years and developed a friendship and confidence in each other." He stared at her.

With a graciousness he thought natural, Tappy ended the silence. "I know Virginia Douglas almost as well as I know myself. Our husbands are friends and have business dealings. Our families regularly get together, in the summers children are in and out of each other's houses. They are fine people. They are fine *Americans.*"

Imhoff was aware she was trying to sell him. He studied her, looking for any sign, any twitch of subterfuge. He found none.

"How about the kids?" he asked.

Tappy pursed her lips in a tight smile. "That is one area where we have some disagreement. Virginia is very ambitious for her children. I don't think Virginia can see this but she is very paradoxical about Carmen. She pushes Carmen really hard to succeed, but then lets Carmen get away with everything, really. She completely spoils Carmen, which undercuts the success she wants. I just try to provide what support I can." She smiled over her cup at Imhoff as she took another sip.

"Would you like some more coffee Special Agent?"

Imhoff shook his head. She had skipped over the boy.

"What about the son?"

Imhoff was surprised. She actually blinked. That was the first hesitancy she had shown.

"Oh, Junior, he's such a dear," she said breathlessly.

There's something about the boy, Imhoff thought. "They call him Junior?"

She nodded.

"What's dear about him?" Imhoff asked without smiling.

"Well, how to say it? Junior is, well, a little socially awkward. Virginia thought about moving him to another school, but he would have none of it. Virginia is overprotective of him, but it comes out in nagging him, so there's definitely some tension there. Junior is not the type to be nagged. But he is bright, precocious, and very funny on an adult level. I think his peers just don't get him." She smiled brightly, then became more serious. "He is a good boy, Special Agent."

"How so?"

She looked back at Imhoff.

"One day some older boys were teasing my son Chad on the way home from middle school. They were tossing his backpack back and forth away from him, you know that 'keep away' game or whatever they call it. Chad was pleading for his backpack." She paused, looking down at her coffee. "Junior rode up on his bicycle. He has never liked unfairness or meanness, even as a little boy. Well, he took off on his bike and caught the backpack as it came sailing over Chad's head."

Imhoff nodded, impressed.

"But," she smiled, "as I understand it, the other boy ran forward knocking Junior off his bike, then the older boys beat up Chad *and* Junior. All the while, according to Chad, Junior shouted up through the dust at them, "Get off—get off us—stop, or you'll really get it tomorrow! You're nothing but big yellow bullies!"

He nodded, encouraging her to continue.

"The older boys walked off laughing, leaving Chad and Junior crumpled in the dirt, one with a black eye and the other a split lip. Chad would never tell me the boys' names."

"Well, that certainly shows spunk," Imhoff replied, thinking the story was over.

"But wait, that's not all. I later learned that on his way home, Junior pedaled to the hardware store and bought a container of pepper spray. The next day, he again found the older boys teasing Chad, tossing his back pack over his head."

Imhoff became still, listening intently.

"Like the day before, Junior did the same thing, except instead of catching Chad's backpack, as I understand it, he swerved to one boy spraying him in the face with pepper spray and turned to the other boy spraying him."

Imhoff whistled.

"Chad told me Junior ran up to the boys writhing on the ground, shouting at them, 'If you tell anybody I did this to you, next time I'll spray you with Drano and you'll be blind. Don't tell anybody about this and never bother my friend, Chad, again!'"

She smiled. "And they never bothered the boys again."

Imhoff whistled.

"But don't think harshly of him. Junior is a good boy; he'll make Eagle Scout this summer."

"Eagle Scout."

"Yes, impressive."

"Well, Mrs. Montgomery, that about does it, I think."

"Oh, please call me Tappy." There was that graciousness again.

As she walked him to the door, she asked, "Were you in Iraq or Afghanistan?"

"The latter."

"Hmmm. How did you side?"

"Side? On what?"

"The torture, all that, the ends justify the means."

He shrugged.

"Special Agent, do you believe if we act like our enemy we become our enemy?"

"Those were tough times, ma'am."

She studied him.

"Who were you for on the Snowden matter—Snowden or anti-Snowden?"

"Ma'am, he took classified information. It was black and white."

She smiled at him a moment. "Tell me, Special Agent Imhoff, how about personal freedom, privacy, government intrusion, due process? On which side of black and white do they fall, the black side or the white side?"

He stared evenly at her.

"Oh, I see I'm wasting your time, Special Agent, forgive me. If you need anything further, please let me know."

124

"You can count on it, ma'am."

Marcie Beethoven sat with her coworker Paul in the lounge on a coffee break. They both had circles under their eyes from lack of sleep since the Wildroot alert.

The pair had been classmates at MIT and started at DHS together. Paul was her close friend and confidant at DHS. That was nice, but what Paul really wanted was to get in her pants. That wasn't going to happen, however. His frustration, though, could make him pick at her.

"You know, Paul, I'm really just faking it, faking doing Douglas searches, faking any analysis. I've exhausted everything there is to do, but Secretary Ogilvie just won't take no for an answer. You know," she looked down, then up, meeting his eyes, "I just don't believe they're guilty."

"They're all guilty to you. You dissect subjects until their most secret thoughts are laid bare. Why are you going soft now?"

"I'm not going soft, Paul. It's not soft to say nothing is there when really *nothing is there*. The Douglases are clueless about cyber security. They are so unprotected a teenager with a laptop could pull up in front of their house and read their whole life history—if he didn't die of boredom first."

"So you don't think anything is there?"

"I know nothing's there."

He stared at here with a smirk.

She looked at him disapprovingly, knowing he was baiting her. "I am tough, but these are American citizens," she insisted.

"They stopped being American citizens when they started cooperating with terrorists."

"Maybe. But where is the cooperation?"

"Secretary Ogilvie wouldn't push us so hard if he didn't know something was there."

She was thoughtful for a moment. "Do you think perhaps the lines have gotten blurred? Do you wonder if we've moved from surveillance into snooping . . . or worse?"

"Snooping? Worse?"

"Yes."

"So NSA and Security Data Systems have some data, big deal."

"So J. Edgar Hoover had data, too, in paper files—and recordings. And it *was* a big deal."

"Huh?"

"Hoover brokered a lot of power with those files. People did what he wanted so he wouldn't release private information on them."

"How you know that?"

"I read it."

"Come on, Marcie. This isn't like you. You started watching Rachel Maddow or something?"

"You come on! Why do you use the latest encryption technology on your personal devices and computers? What do you have to worry about?"

He puffed up, "Hey, it's my stuff, and nobody has a right to see it. I can keep it private if I want."

"Hmm," she smiled. "What would you say about everyone else's personal stuff? Can they keep it private, too, if they want?"

"Yeah, maybe, but I heard Chambers say that people don't give a cold crap about privacy. He said look at the reality shows, the 'tell all' books, all the pictures, the magazines, *People*, *US*, the tabloids. He said we are a country of voyeurs. He said we're hypocritical, that Americans have no respect for privacy; they only care when someone's about to bust *them* with something embarrassing. You think too much, Marcie," Paul added. "Just stick with getting the bad guys."

"Oh, I will. It's just getting harder to tell who they are."

CHAPTER 23

BRUNETTES HAVE MORE FUN
April 11, 2019
Back roads
Hagerstown, West Virginia

Morning EDT

In a panic, Bossilini drove the crew away from Hagerstown, furiously working the wheel, gas, and brakes, compulsively checking the mirrors. Sweat dripped off his chin. A task force was on the way. Their only hope was using county highways and local roads, zigzagging the routes, while trying to maintain a rough northeast bearing toward Pennsylvania. When it was safe, if it ever became safe again, he would stop for a final talk with the Douglases. He must get to them somehow. He must light a charge under them. They had to catch fire to survive. Maybe first they had to taste doom.

For the second day in a row the fugitives were slung around in the Hummer as they desperately tried to escape a determined government's clutches. The passengers were too adrenaline-worn and emotionally drained to complain or lament. They could only pray for escape.

Sherman sat in the second row on one side of his mother while Carmen sat on the other. He wanted to be close to Virginia, to feel her warmth and protection, to feel her arm around his shoulder so he would feel safe again, even though she was the one who likely had sealed their capture. But it didn't matter because she was his mother, and he was still in some ways her little boy, and he wanted to be near her.

But as he jostled in the seat, the car throwing him around, his head bouncing off the window, he became irritated with her. Why wouldn't she just leave things alone? She always had to pry and push and question, nothing was ever enough, nothing could ever be left alone—like now. She never just let it be.

Settling down after a few more miles, Sherman looked back at his new friend Manfred sitting with Buddy in the third seat. Buddy looked calm

127

and ready—for what? Manfred, however, was jittery. He looked around constantly, with sweat beading at his temples. His eyes looked frightened, and he sat light in the seat. He's bolting, Sherman thought. And why wouldn't he? What does he owe us?

He looked up to Bossilini in the driver's seat. Bossilini grimly scanned the sides of the roads, peering, looking, checking up in the sky. For what? It frightened the boy. Bossilini was silent and told them nothing. The front seat blocked his view of George. His father always knew what to do. He counted on Bossilini and his father to know what to do. But did they?

Without any signal, Bossilini suddenly braked hard, making a sliding right turn into an entrance they had almost passed. Recovering, he drove slowly through the parking lot of what appeared to be an abandoned motel. Sherman read the sign stained from rusty water dripping down its front: "The Pine Tree Motel." Underneath a placard on hooks, swaying in a slight breeze, read "Vacancy."

"What are we doing?" Carmen pouted.

Bossilini said nothing. Virginia, too tired to question, just shrugged.

Bossilini drove slowly, very slowly, past the office that indeed appeared deserted. Sherman saw a fairly new chain and padlock on the front door. He watched Bossilini in the mirror as he drove carefully toward the end of rows of motel rooms. Bossilini never took his eyes off the motel as the Rectangle idled around the end toward the back.

The backside rooms of the motel did not look any more recently used. Some windows had orange spray paint, graffiti from disaffected teenagers. Why do kids do that, Sherman wondered. It's stupid.

The Rectangle coasted to some shade under a Mimosa tree, and Bossilini commanded, "Stay here."

No one argued.

Sherman leaned forward, watching him walk purposefully, toward a room nearest their side. Sherman read the number. *128.* The curtains were pulled shut. He jumped when Bossilini forcefully kicked open the door to the room. Bossilini disappeared in the dark room. A minute later he appeared in the doorway.

Bossilini walked toward the Rectangle, head down. He opened the door and sat heavily in the driver's seat facing forward, staring silent. The rectangle was still. The passengers looked toward Bossilini, their faces pensive. Finally, he turned, resting his forearm across the back of the seat. He stared them in the eyes, each in turn.

"You need to trust me. You need to obey me."

The vehicle was still. Bossilini looked at Buddy's face in the back. He sat silent, his face grave.

"You need to assume responsibility for your survival."

They sat mute before him. He judged that they were chastened by the narrow escape. And embarrassed. No one looked at Virginia. Instead, they looked down at the floor boards, except for the boy, who looked at him, and Manfred who looked out the window. Bah, they all were sheep. They wanted to be told what to do.

That would not work.

"Do you want to be captured?" Bossilini challenged. "Is there a part of you that wants to go into custody?"

"You have thoughts that you should trust the police rather than this wild man Bossilini? You have trusted the police all your life. They have kept you and your homes safe. Is that what you want now? You have brought them coffee cake for Christmas. Do you want to go to the police department, so you can pull your strings, and get away from the crazy Bossilini who says crazy, unbelievable things? Huh? Do you think this is like a business meeting, where you have power and can negotiate? Do you think Bossilini is hysterical like an old woman?"

No one answered.

Sherman looked back at Manfred who put his finger to his lips to stay quiet.

Bossilini looked at them, his eyes vacant, without empathy.

"I want you to feel the urgency of your situation. I want you to feel the desperateness of your situation. I want you to feel your peril. It is urgent that we find a safe place, some crack to crawl in and hide. Immediately. We have to hide you *now!* We can figure out how to save you later. But for the present you must *disappear.* You must cut all contact with your past lives."

Bossilini stared at the group, looking into each person's eyes. His eyes filled with anger.

"*You* need to save yourselves. I am not going to any longer. Buddy is not going to." Bossilini looked at them with disdain.

"Here's what you can expect if you do not. They will separate you. Yes, Virginia, they will. The children will be taken far away and separated from each other. You will be separated from George. You will live in a hole in the wall with bars. Alone. All the time. Every day. Except for when they come for you."

"You will wonder about each other. You will long to see each other. You will cry from loneliness and anguish. You will doubt your sanity. Your longing for your children and your anxiety for their well-being will gnaw your insides out. You will slowly, slowly lose who you are. You will become a shell. You will finally want to die. But you will have no implements by which to take your life. You will rot in a forgotten, forsaken hell."

"Is that what you want?"

"IS IT WHAT YOU WANT!" Bossilini banged the seat back.

"IS THAT WHAT YOU WANT!" He raged, jutting out from the console toward them, bathing them in his hot, sour breath, trying to provoke some reaction, some instinct for self-preservation.

Virginia flinched back. Carmen threw up.

No one attended to her.

Bossilini sat, watching them.

"I do not want that for you," he continued after a beat. "But ultimately, I don't care. I simply don't. You need to trust me. You need to obey me. If you do not, I will take your son and leave you. You will never see him again. He is the only one that matters to me." Bossilini stared at them, unflinching.

"Are you going to cooperate or not? Are you going to act like you could lose your lives in the next minute or not?"

They sat silently, terrified.

"I am stepping out to let you decide. Rap on the window when you have an answer." He strode out of the vehicle, stopping yards away with his back toward them.

Silence filled the Rectangle.

Sherman sensed his mother starting to speak, but then she held back.

Sherman wanted to speak, but he was only a kid and unsure of himself.

His father broke the silence. George turned to face them.

"We have two choices," he began. His face was grave, as if presenting a client with a big tax levy. "We can go to the police. Or we can stay with Bossilini. Frankly, I think we should go to the police. Yes, Bossilini *acts* like he is on our side and trying to protect us. But we know nothing about him. What if he is the one trying to kidnap us? I have had enough. We tell him to drop us at the police station in the next major city. We call our lawyer in advance and tell him where we are. It should be worked out in a matter of hours."

No one spoke. Sherman fidgeted.

George pressed. "How do we know we are being chased? We haven't seen anyone since our house. Bossilini could be making all of this up. I don't trust him."

"Me neither," Carmen said.

"Virginia, what do you think?"

"I—whatever you think, George."

Sherman looked at his mother. She seemed shaken, pale, crumbling into herself. His father would take them to the police. She would not object, it's what she wanted all along. Manfred would split.

This all wrong, he thought.

Sherman knew where they should go, where they should hide. As Bossilini had talked, Sherman saw vivid images of the sunflowers. They called to him. He knew he would be safe with them. He didn't know how he knew, he just knew.

"Dad, ah, where did you say the sunflowers were?"

"Middle—what's that got to do with things now?"

"Middlebury, yeah. Where's Middlebury?"

"Put that out of your mind. We are going to the police, not Middlebury."

"It's in Vermont, Sherman. I dug a chick who transferred from Oberlin to Middlebury. Miss her," Manfred said.

"Middlebury, Vermont. That's where we're going."

"We certainly are not," George said.

"But dad—"

"You are not in charge, young man."

"Shut up, Sherman," Carmen joined in.

The sunflowers appeared in bright colors in Sherman's mind.

"It's the right thing to do. We're going."

"No, we are not," George said.

Sherman paused, and said, "I'm leaving with Bossilini, then."

His mother gasped. George shook his finger, but before he could speak, the boy jumped out the door, leaving it open, and called to Bossilini, "Let's split. I'm going with you."

Bossilini turned.

George leapt from the door, running around the side. "Sherman, get back in the car this instant."

"No," the boy called out, running yards ahead of Bossilini. "Mr. Bossilini, let's go."

"Sherman, get in the car," George roared. "We have no evidence that any of this is true. Enough is enough."

"Run, Sherman," Manfred called from the Rectangle. "Run."

Sherman waved "come on" to Bossilini.

But Bossilini stood still. He was thinking. He spoke.

"Is evidence what you want, George? Would that make a difference for you?"

"Evidence?"

"Yes, evidence that the authorities are indeed chasing you."

"Well. . . ," George sputtered.

"Let's go back into the Hummer. I have something to show you? You may find it interesting."

"Huh?"

"Come, George, sit with me a minute." Bossilini returned to the driver's seat. George resumed his seat, and Sherman followed at a distance, stopping by his open door. When Bossilini punched the touch screen on the media center, a new unusual screen appeared.

Bossilini input data and turned to George. "Watch this."

A live feed immediately appeared on the screen. They watched men in suits combing the motel from which they'd fled this morning. Black

SUV's were parked in front and back, and police had cordoned off the street. Some men spoke into cell phones. Out of one van spilled men with blue jackets. Bossilini adjusted the controls zoomed onto the jackets. Sherman leaned in further to see better. The back of the jackets had yellow lettering, "FBI."

George leaned back and blew out his breath. He looked at Bossilini. "That's not standard equipment," he said, pointing at the screen. Bossilini smiled.

"Dad, there's FBI crawling all over the place. They're also over at the convenience store with the phone mom used. Dad. Dad?"

"George?" Bossilini asked.

Sherman interrupted. "Mr. Bossilini was right. We barely got out of there in time. They're all over the place. See?"

Sherman reached forward, shaking his dad's shoulder. "Dad, see? We are being chased. We *do* need to hide."

"Let me show you something else, George." Bossilini entered other coordinates. Their house suddenly appeared on the screen. Pest control men came in and out of the house carrying black garbage bags.

"Virginia, I didn't know we had a roach problem again."

"Dad, it's a disguise. They're dressed up as pest control men to search our house."

"Dressed up?"

"Yes, the pest control men never took stuff out our house before. They're FBI men dressed up as pest control."

Virginia sputtered to life. "George, Sherman's right. That's not the pest control service we use."

"It's not!"

"No."

"Okay, Dad. This proves it. We're leaving with Bossilini to the sunflowers."

"We are?"

"You bet," said Bossilini.

Sherman turned to Manfred. Manfred shrugged, "To Middlebury it is."

"Good," Bossilini said. "But first there are things we need to do."

133

They followed Bossilini to room 128 of the abandoned motel.

As they entered the room, their noses flared at the dank smell, and Carmen sneezed. The room had been closed up some time. Though the beds were made, the covers smelled dusty. A dead cockroach lay on its back in the middle of the floor in front of the TV. Manfred, with gallows humor, quipped, "The summer reruns must have killed him."

Sherman laughed.

Sherman watched Buddy struggle in with several travel bags.

"What's that?" the boy asked.

"Disguises."

"We'll change your appearances here," Bossilini ordered. "Virginia put on the wig, and we'll work on some age lines with the eyeliner pencils. Carmen, I'll dye your hair. George, I'll cut some of your hair then razor cut it down to a different look. Okay, let's get going."

"Can someone please get that dead cockroach out of here," Virginia said wearily.

Sherman jumped up and drop-kicked the dead roach toward the open door.

"Sherman!"

In two more kicks, he had it out the door. "There you go, Mom."

As Bossilini undertook the transformation of the Douglas family, Sherman stood around shifting his weight on his feet. When sufficiently bored, he called to Manfred, "Come on, let's go outside." They found shade under a clump of Mimosa trees near the Hummer. It was getting hot, and Sherman felt the sweat roll down his chest even in the shade.

"You think Mr. Bossilini can fix this for us?" Sherman asked.

Manfred shrugged.

The boy picked a blade of grass, studied it, then twirled it in his fingers. "Why are you still with us?"

Manfred shrugged.

"You don't know?"

Manfred shrugged again.

134

"I wouldn't be surprised if you didn't take off. And why did Buddy come? Isn't that really strange?"

"More than strange."

"Are you going to leave us?"

Manfred wavered, but did not look the boy in the eye. His right foot began twitching. His feet wanted to run, run right now, not a second later. He placed his hand on his foot to still it.

"You might, but not yet?"

Manfred shrugged, as if wasn't ready to admit it. He held his foot tighter.

"Why are you here, then?"

"You mean with you guys?"

Sherman nodded.

"I made a promise."

"To who?"

Manfred shrugged again. His foot twitched again for a few seconds.

Sherman looked at the motel room. "To him." He meant Bossilini. "Why?"

"Because he asked me to." Manfred's whole body became still.

"So that will keep you here."

Manfred shrugged. "Man, I never kept a promise in my life." His foot wanted to twitch, but Manfred willed it to remain still.

Sherman nodded thoughtfully. "So, you're here while you're here."

"I guess that says it."

The boy looked down, thinking, for a few moments.

He stared at Manfred, his face expressionless. "You can go if you need to." The boy continued to stare evenly at Manfred. "I forgive you."

Manfred made a thin smile. He felt the catch of emotion in his throat from the boy's generosity. They stared evenly at each other a few moments more.

"It's going to be no fun when you leave," Sherman said as he shifted to sit on one of his legs bent underneath him. "I'm surrounded by grownups. Carmen is the only kid, but you can't call her a kid—and she's really no fun to be around."

"Yep. I can tell that, all right."

The boy stared at the grass blade while his fingers twirled it vigorously. He looked up as a yellow butterfly floated past.

Manfred pulled out a yo-yo and began spinning it.

"Whoa, a yo-yo?"

"Yep, a real Duncan."

"Can you do tricks with it?" Sherman had seen a YouTube video about old yo-yo tricks.

"Yep, ever since I was nine. I was real good, too."

Sherman watched the yo-yo spin up and down, and Manfred rocked it through a couple of tricks. Watching made Sherman curious.

"What was it like in your time? All we know are the things they show now where everyone is sitting around drugged out, saying, 'Heavy, man.' It looks stupid. Was it stupid?"

Manfred looked at the boy thoughtfully.

"No, Sherman, it wasn't stupid. It was real, it was very un-stupid. The times were energetic, thoughtful and hopeful: people wanted to be real and to be open and be who they were. They didn't want to be programmed, to live lives that were just about working to make money to buy things or being stuck up and social climbing—lives that were plastic. There was a lot of cool stuff going on, cool ideas, books, exploration, experimentation, getting into new things—and we wanted peace. The energy was incredible."

"What happened?"

"I don't know. I left, remember?"

"Is this how you thought it would be?"

"Are you kidding me?" He snorted. "No way. I think it's worse than being plastic, hung up, like back then. You guys have all gone crazy."

"How is it different now?"

"Dude, like it's the Age of Anxiety here."

Sherman had asked enough. He didn't feel like thinking anymore. But he did have one last question. "Are you going to keep your promise and stay?"

Manfred answered, "Like I said, I've never kept a promise in my life. I'm a rolling stone."

"You mean you were in the band?" Sherman asked in astonishment.

Manfred laughed. "No, no. Like, I want to be free. I don't want commitments to tie me down."

"Oh," the boy replied.

"Sherman," his dad called, "your turn." Manfred followed him back to the room.

Buddy was outside by himself. He stood grounded and tall in "standing meditation." He breathed in, watching his breath as if swinging in through a gate. He breathed out, watching his breath swing out through the gate. Breathe in, breathe out, follow the breath, follow it in, follow it out. His eyes were focused on the tip of an evergreen tree some distance away. He did not indulge thoughts about the tree. If a thought came that the tree was pleasant, he noticed it and allowed it to drift out of his mind. If the thought came that one day the pleasant tree would die, he noticed it and allowed it to drift out of his mind. He did not attach to the thoughts, pleasant or unpleasant, so they drifted out of his mind. Attachment to thoughts risked them taking lodging in the mind and causing mischief. He simply watched his thoughts, noticed his feelings, without judgment or attachment, letting them come, flow across his consciousness, and go.

Buddy realized the Douglases existed in an anxious state. They were like that before this event, he was sure, but now their state was acute. They emanated static, which they had done for so long it was now habitual. In the current predicament, he must be careful that the static spewing from them did not affect the peace and clarity of his mind.

The problem was that the Douglases had not awakened their minds, he thought. The Douglases resisted awareness of suffering, they constantly schemed and plotted to avoid it, constantly striving to get what they thought they wanted so they could be happy, and constantly trying to avoid what they thought would make them unhappy. However, that resistance and striving only insured that they would remain unhappy— their unhappiness a byproduct of ignorance of the Buddha's First Noble Truth—that all of life is suffering. Without knowledge of that Truth, the Douglases could never understand there is a path to lead them out of suffering. So they would live trying to put a picture over a hole in the wall, but with the hole never filled, the wall never restored.

Buddy ceased his meditation and saw Carmen sitting in a chair by the pool. She was hunched forward, feet up on the chair seat, arms locked around her knees. She is sitting to protect herself, Buddy thought. Her body racked in a sob. He sensed that for a short moment she might be open and vulnerable. Perhaps he could reach her in this moment and help her.

He joined her by the empty pool. She turned to look at him through a tear-stained face.

"Mind if I sit down?" She shook her head no. "I always think empty swimming pools are pointless," he said in his melodious Indian accent. She actually laughed. He laughed with her.

He did not know what to do. That did not bother him, however, for he knew that when one was present, one would do the appropriate thing. So he sat there being with Carmen, not forcing a conversation. He thought perhaps she sensed his calmness, his being present in life beside her, his not judging her or trying to work her.

"Why are you here?" she asked with the directness of youth.

"To help you," he answered.

She blinked. She had not expected that answer.

"But how . . . how would you know about us, how would you know to come? That doesn't make sense."

"No, it doesn't make sense. None of this makes sense." He laughed. He sat with her, just being there. The conversation was not one to rush. "Soon, we can explain everything, but for now, trust that Bossilini and I have come from different places to help your family."

"Am I going to die?"

"No," he said firmly. "I will protect you."

"Why are they doing this to us? We haven't done anything wrong."

He could tell she could not wrap her mind around their plight.

"A big mistake. Some ambitious people misunderstood a situation and tried to capitalize upon it for their own benefit. Now, they must cover up the mistake to save face and not lose power."

"That's it? *That's it*—they are ruining my family's life because of a *mistake*?" She shouted, her mouth open with incredulity.

"Leaders have always been that way."

"I thought the President and the government were here to protect us. Isn't that their job?" she asked, a soft moan in her voice.

"The ancient Indian texts warn us to beware of greedy leaders. It is human nature."

She stared down at her toes for several moments, then shifted topics. "Buddy, I think I am going crazy," she said, her face reflecting pain.

"It is hard, for you and your family."

She nodded.

"I feel so . . . oh, I don't know . . . my parents are freaking out . . . I can't text my friends, or get on Snapchat or Instagram . . . I, mean, I'm always connected, and I'm going crazy without it . . . I bet everybody is hitting me like crazy, wondering where I am, what's happening . . . I feel so cut off . . . I missed my cheerleading training session yesterday . . . I *so* want to make head cheerleader . . . mom will die if I don't make it . . . I think in a way she never got over not making head cheerleader her senior year . . . *ohhh*, I feel so alone."

She looked out of the swimming pool area to a line of trees behind the motel. Her arms were still locked around her knees. She looked pallid.

"I feel so empty. Like everything has been poured out of me, like I am a shell."

"Maybe that is good." Buddy looked at her deeply. "Maybe what is left is really you. Maybe you can really see yourself now."

She paused, staring at him as if maybe what he said had some truth, but she was not ready to look.

Are they going to throw us in jail?"

"Not if we can help it." He smiled at her.

"Can't you take mom and me, and I guess—Sherman?—back home and let Mr. Bossilini and Dad fix this? Why do the rest of us have to be here?"

Buddy just smiled at her. She knew the answer.

"Take heart," he said. "Bossilini and I—and others—are working for your safety. It is important to us."

She turned her head, looking up at him. "Why are we important to you?"

139

"You will see. But it would burden you for me to say more now. You must be ready for what is ahead. You must accept your situation and stay present hour by hour and respond appropriately."

"Are you a mathematician?" He knew she changed the subject because considering their plight was too confronting.

"Yes," he smiled.

"I hate math. Mom makes me take it 'cause she says to get in a good college I have to take calculus in high school. I'm going to flunk that course. How can you stand it?"

"Math is the language of the universe. It is the nouns, verbs, and adjectives writing the rich poetry of the cosmos." He waved his arm in arc toward the sky, smiling.

"Ugh!"

"Perhaps your path lies in another field."

"I don't have a path."

She thought of something new.

"Bossilini said you are a Zen master? What is that?"

He smiled.

"Your eyes twinkle when you smile."

"That is Zen." In response to her confused look, he added, "Zen is seeing things as they really are."

"I do that all the time."

"Do you?" There was the melodic laugh again. "I doubt it."

"You don't think I'm smart enough?"

"Smart has nothing to do with it. It is waking up. Learning to see. Seeing that human beings relate to each other and the world through concepts. We do not interact with the world or people as they are—we interact with our concepts of them. But the concepts are not them, concepts are not real. So we miss out."

"I don't understand."

"Here, like your mother and your math. You mother interacts with you through her concept of what being smart looks like and what you must do to succeed and have a happy life. Her concept of being smart means you are good in math. But there are many other ways to be smart. And there are many ways to have a happy life other than making an A in calculus."

140

Buddy took a breath.

"Virginia does not see you, the real you."

Tears budded in Carmen's eyes.

"Virginia only sees her concept of you, which is a good student getting into a good college. But she does not see *you*."

The tears began to stream down Carmen's face.

"There are plenty of paths to take to become educated and lead a happy life. You are a unique human being. But those paths are closed off while your mother deals with her concept of you rather than dealing with *you*. That is why you felt empty moments ago, because your concepts were slipping away, and you found yourself simply empty. Had you gone further, you would not have known who you were, because you see, you are a concept to yourself, too."

She seemed to get part of what he was saying. The tears began to stop.

"In Zen we break through concepts and deal with life as it is. That is my big speech." He laughed.

"So you are a master of that?"

"So they say."

"How did you become a master?"

"Many whacks from my master's staff."

"Your eyes are twinkling again. That's Zen?"

"Yes, because in this moment that is who I am. I am that my eyes twinkle." He smiled at her. She had been open, and he could feel her searching.

But he could feel the window closing, too. She'd had enough. She was a teenager, after all. He saw her face becoming sullen in spots, her body language saying, *I don't want to talk any more, leave me alone.*

"When hungry eat, when tired sleep. Carmen, that is Zen. Good-bye."

Buddy walked away without further exchange. Carmen did not look up to watch him go.

A few hours later, the group shyly stepped out of the motel room, self-conscious with their appearances. Bossilini closed the door softly behind them. It would no longer lock.

141

Virginia looked ten years older, with a gray wig and makeup that Bossilini had expertly applied. Carmen had gone from blonde to brunette, and she actually thought the change was exciting. Her mother never would have let her dye her hair. Sherman had the same dyed shade of hair as Carmen, but they did not look like siblings. George had a shorter cut that really did change his appearance, at least at a casual glance. Buddy looked like he could work for a university or tech company, and Manfred, unchanged, looked as if he might have tickets for a Steppenwolf reunion concert.

Somberly, they piled into the Rectangle and slowly drove away.

CHAPTER 24

MORE RANDOM EVENTS
April 11, 2019
I-81
Wilkes-Barre, Pennsylvania

9:00 a.m. EDT

Fatigue was their enemy now.

Bossilini felt weary, his arms and legs heavy, his thoughts sluggish as if moving through clogged pipes. Guiding the steering wheel was a chore. No one else was much better. Some had slept on and off since leaving the motel, but it was a stale sleep.

The Hummer chugged along the road near Wilkes-Barre, Pennsylvania about nine o'clock that night. At a stop for gas, they had changed places to break the monotony, with Sherman now up front; Virginia, Carmen, and George in the middle seat; and Manfred and Buddy in back.

"George. *George*," Bossilini called, his voice dry, tired.

"Ah, huh?" George, uttered coming out of light doze.

"We need to eat."

"Yeah."

George seemed to fall back asleep.

"George," Bossilini said more firmly, "we need to find something. Can you help me? Do you see anything up ahead?"

"Ah . . . not really."

"Did you look?"

George wobbled forward, squinting out of the windshield. "Yeah."

"George, you're not really awake, are you?"

"I don't think so."

Bossilini sighed. He looked at the *Waze* map. "It says we cross underneath I-81 in five miles, and there are several symbols for places to eat."

"Oh . . . sounds . . . good. . . ."

Bossilini noticed George blinked rapidly, as if trying to stay awake.

Soon Bossilini drove under I-81 and looped right up a sloping, curving exit ramp leading to a service road with a collage of restaurants, gas stations, and motels. He spotted a Pennsylvania Burgers with its big blue and yellow neon sign at the next intersection on the left. He welcomed the chance to stop and rest a few minutes. They'd have to pull over for the night before too much longer.

The turn signal tapped, sounding lazy to him as he waited to turn. The left turn arrow flashed green, and Bossilini tugged the wheel slightly left, sending the Hummer through a lazy arc across the service road as his tired eyes looked ahead to try to find the drive-through lane.

BLAM!

A blasting crunch slammed him hard against the driver's door, ramming his head against the window to a sickening soundtrack of scraping, tearing metal. The Hummer, spewing sparks, slid sideways like a sled along the street. The Hummer slid and yawed and finally came to a blackboard screeching stop, teetered on its left side for the briefest moment, and fell over on the driver's side like a downed elephant.

Bossilini found himself jammed against the driver's door, stunned. *What happened?* He had trouble moving. The Hummer was silent except hissing from a busted hose somewhere. But soon groans emerged followed by quick, frantic cries. Bossilini lay listening to the sounds, head pressed against the driver's window, thinking foggily he never saw it coming.

Indeed, he had not seen it coming.

The irony was it was totally random. Billy Blankenship, a sawmill worker—after spending several hours at the bowling alley rolling gutter balls and downing pitchers of beer—having forgotten to turn on his pick-up truck lights, ran a red light at 55 mph and T-boned the Hummer. While the amassed power of the United States government had embarrassingly failed to find the Douglas family, Billy Blankenship crashed right into them without even trying.

Inside the Hummer, George anxiously called out, "Everybody okay? Anybody hurt? Virginia? Kids?"

The brunt of the impact was in the middle of the Rectangle behind the front passenger's seat.

That spared Sherman, who was sprawled across the console.

George's right passenger door was indented eight inches, but he was saved—just before impact he leaned over to the left, checking out

144

Pennsylvania Burgers—he had a client back home looking to bring a new fast food franchise to the South.

"Hello," George called out. "Anybody?"

George heard a moan from Virginia. "Virginia? *Virginia?*" George felt an arc of panic. He frantically struggled to unlatch the seatbelt. It had him around the neck, leaving him hanging to the side. He looked down at Carmen, who was sprawled on Virginia.

"Daddy, what happened?" Carmen was crying. "Get me out of here. It hurts."

His daughter's cry jolted him.

Using his legs to brace against the front seat, George popped the seat belt and lowered himself to Carmen. "Carmen, baby, where does it hurt? Can you move? If you can't move, stay still till the paramedics come, that's important, will you do that please?"

"Uhhh," Carmen groaned.

"Carmen. *Carmen!* Stay with me," George commanded. "Can you move?"

George felt a rustling to his side.

"Yes. Yeah, I can move everything."

"Good. I need to get to your mother. Climb over me so I can get to her."

"I—"

"Carmen, do it!"

"Okay." She tentatively made her way past George, pulling on the seat for purchase.

While George tried to lower himself to Virginia he thought *Sherman! He hadn't heard Sherman speak!* Desperate, George cried, "Sherman, Sherman!"

Silence.

"Sher—"

"Dad, I'm . . . okay."

George said a silent prayer.

"Can you get out your door? We need to get out—quick." George heard the dying creaking of metal and smelled some kind of auto fluid. An image of the Hummer bursting into flames and roasting them alive terrified him. "Try it, hurry, quick."

"Okay, Dad."

George slid further down to Virginia. "Virginia, honey. Virginia." She was silent.

The passenger door above George yanked open and a Samaritan called down, "Hey, you guys okay?"

George opened his mouth, but Bossilini preempted him, answering, "Yes, I think so. Now, can you open the front passenger door, please?"

"No can do. Frame's bent. We tried, but it won't budge. They'll have to cut it open with the Jaws of Life. We called the paramedics, fire department. They'll pop it right off."

Bossilini's heart skipped a beat as he became sharply alert. *The responders, the authorities.* His mind raced. Bossilini and the Hummer would no longer be phantoms. They would materialize before Homeland's very eyes.

"We have to get out. NOW!" he shouted to his charges.

Bossilini's eyes raced to find a way out. There was only one way.

An image flashed in his mind—the wreck that night in Budapest—trapped by the steering wheel, flames licking and crackling in the back of the car. Tendrils of panic wrapped around his chest. That windshield also had spider cracks. Bossilini clenched his jaw, moving to the side of the steering wheel. He thrust his legs like pistons into the windshield, pain rising in his ankles as sweat ran in his eyes. "Come on, come on," he spat in harsh breaths.

He felt the windshield give but a little. He crashed his legs even harder in rapid thrusts. There, at the upper edge, the windshield gave a few inches. "NOW!" Bossilini thundered. The windshield loosened more, then collapsed, breaking loose at the top. Bossilini quickly kicked out the rest.

"Come on, Sherman, quickly." He held out his hand.

Sherman grabbed it. He hoisted out the boy, who was holding his backpack in the other hand.

Bossilini jumped off the Hummer and ran to George's door, where two men were gently helping Carmen to the ground. Bossilini, standing on tiptoes, leaned in and urged, "C'mon, hurry, hurry." Bossilini then leapt atop the car and slid in.

146

Sherman helped his sister to a grassy spot across a side road that ran perpendicular to the service road. She seemed in shock. Sherman swallowed. He tried to remember the checklist from his first aid merit badge.

Inside the Rectangle, George freed Virginia from her tangled clump and had a loose grip upon her. She moaned, then called out, "My babies. *My babies.*"

"Sssh, sssh, we're all fine. Virginia, we have been in a car wreck. We are all fine, but we need to get out of the car quickly."

"Kuwickly," she slurred, "yes, kuwickly."

Bossilini shot George a hard glance.

"Come on, sweetie, that's it now," George cajoled.

"You called me sweetie. You haven't done that in a long time. Is my sweet George back?"

From underneath, George pushed Virginia up. Bossilini gathered her in his arms and pushed her up to the two men, who pulled her out of the vehicle and passed her to two other men on the ground. They ran her over to a grassy area below Pennsylvania Burgers as George hurriedly followed.

But the children were *across* the side road away from their parents.

Virginia and George were now separated from their children.

Bossilini, with help from the men, finally got Manfred and Buddy from their tomb-like third seat. They seemed okay, but Manfred's left shoulder hung noticeably lower than his right.

"Manfred, how is your shoulder?" Bossilini asked delicately.

Manfred looked back and forth, comparing the alignment of his shoulders. Then he just shrugged. But when he did so, pain exploded in his left shoulder and he screamed, "*OOOOWWWWWWWW.*"

Bossilini gave him a stern, take-it-like-a-man look.

Bossilini quickly looked around. He could not find George and Virginia, but spotted Sherman and Carmen across the side road. He moved rapidly toward them.

"Quickly, over here, Manfred." Bossilini turned to Buddy. "Try to find Virginia and George."

Buddy nodded and took off.

Bossilini ushered Manfred across the road to the children. Pain blanched Manfred white. Bossilini laid him down and quickly examined his shoulder. "That's not so bad, just dislocated."

Not so bad? Manfred thought. It felt like each pulse of pain was going to blow his arm off.

"Relax your arm, Manfred," Bossilini quietly suggested, ever so gently swaying Manfred's arm in soft undulations. "That's it, relax, relax." Bossilini, sitting, gently pulled Manfred's arm out straight and placed a foot on Manfred's ribs under his arm pit. "Manfred, have you noticed the stars tonight? The big dipper is simply popping out of the sky like diamonds."

Manfred turned up to the nighttime sky. Semi-lucid, he mumbled something about Lucy in the Sky with Diamonds. Just then Bossilini gave a strong tug on Manfred's arm. Manfred howled as if from medieval torture, but his shoulder popped into place and the piercing agony stopped. "Oh, god, that feels good, that feels good."

"Here." Sherman tossed Bossilini an Ace bandage from the first aid kit in his backpack. "I think the—"

The flashing lights from the paramedic truck lit Bossilini's face. The truck pulled up close to the Hummer, as the throng of people parted to let it through.

Blips from a fire truck punctuated the chorus of voices and shouts. Bossilini judged it a couple of blocks away. He startled at a loud metallic BLAM when the paramedics slammed the corrugated metal door of their equipment bay. They trotted with medical kits to the accident vehicles.

Bossilini's eyes squinted. "You have to go now." As he tossed the bandage back to Sherman, he pointed. "Bandage him in the woods. Go hide there. When things settle down I'll come for you. Don't let yourselves be seen whatever happens." With that, he was off.

Bossilini zigzagged through the swarming stream of people on the side road. Time was up. He had to find the others, corral everybody, and get out of there before the police arrived.

He ran back toward the vehicles, head swiveling to find Buddy. *There.* Buddy and George were huddled over Virginia. As he approached, Virginia struggled, then sat up. She rubbed the left side of her head. Arriving out of breath, Bossilini crouched in front of her.

"Virginia, how are you?"

"Okay . . . okay . . . I guess. . . . I've been better."

"Look at me, Virginia," Bossilini said. She slowly met his gaze. Good, her eyes were not dilated. "Any nausea?" She shook her head no. "Okay, then." Bossilini stood.

"Okay then, *what?*" asked George.

"Okay to move. We have to move. *Fast.*"

"*Move.* We can't move. Virginia needs to go the hospital. She probably needs a CAT scan of her head. Maybe stay overnight for observation. She—"

"George, why do you continue to do this?" He eyed George steadily. "George, a regular life—with medical plans and CAT scans—is over for you, understand?"

George looked bewildered.

Bossilini looked at him sternly, annoyed.

George quickly pulled himself together. "Okay, Bossilini, help me up with her. Which way do we go?"

Bossilini looked around, his mind racing. He saw at a distance the flashing blue lights of a police car followed by another blip from the fire truck.

"Help him, Buddy. Go that way." He pointed behind Pennsylvania Burgers to a line of trees. Wait there for us."

"Where are you going?" George asked, worried.

"To get your children, of course."

Bossilini ran, darting toward the side road. The fire truck with its blinding red strobe pulled up, blocking his way across the side road. Firemen leaped off the truck into action. As Bossilini tried to maneuver around the truck, he suddenly pitched forward. Someone had struck him hard from behind.

"Sorry, didn't see you," a voice called. "Let me help you."

Bossilini felt hands gripping him upright, and he turned.

"Hey, you're from the Hummer. I saw the whole thing. I was in the burger place at the window. That asshole ran the light and plastered your truck. You kicked out the windshield. Man, that was pretty sweet. Hey, you need to go over there." He pointed toward the Hummer. "They're looking for you and your family."

When he turned back, Bossilini was gone.

CHAPTER 25

BOSSILINI SAYS "SO LONG"
April 11, 2019
Motel
Wilkes-Barre, Pennsylvania

Night EDT

Bossilini raced across the side road to the Douglases, breathing hard, heart beating 5/6 time, eyes bearing a hint of wildness. He tried to catch his breath and steel himself before speaking.

"Oh, you're back," George said. "But where are the children—?"

"George, may I have a word with you?"

"Sure. But—"

"This way, George." After they had stepped a short distance from Virginia, Bossilini cut one quick look at her. Buddy, kneeling by Virginia, stared back grimly. He knew.

"Ah," Bossilini began delicately. He pitied these poor people. They had no training. They didn't ask for this. They were totally unequipped. They had easy breaking points, and a little pressure would snap them like dry kindling.

"George." Bossilini placed his hand squarely on George's shoulders. George's face tensed with suspicion. "I couldn't make it back to them. The road was filled by the fire engine and swarms of people. I tried to pass through, but a man recognized me from the Hummer. I couldn't make it to them. I am sorry."

"Can't we—"

"No. We must leave quickly. George, do you know what that means? DHS or NSA could be watching this very scene in real-time. Agents *will* arrive shortly. If they interview the man who saw me, they will make an artist sketch of me. They have surveillance everywhere. I cannot risk being compromised, caught here."

He took a breath before continuing. "You have good children, George. They are resourceful. You can believe in them. If we can't reach them before we leave, you must believe they will make it to New York.

We will meet them as planned. If not, well, never mind. Thankfully, they are with an adult, they are not completely on their own."

"What adult?"

"Manfred."

"Oh."

George's knees buckled and Bossilini had to grab him to break his fall. He helped George stumble over to Virginia, who though conscious, was not very lucid.

As he led George to Virginia, Bossilini whispered, "She's not well enough to know yet, George. You know that, right? We must tell her a story—the kids were exhausted after the events and we have put them to bed. They had macaroni and cheese for dinner. They are safe. You must make her believe they are safe, George. If she learns the truth in her current condition, well, we will not be able to control her. She will get us all caught. We will all lose. You know that, George?"

George's nod was barely perceptible.

"George, you will be strong, strong for her, strong for your children. Right, George?" George nodded more vigorously.

"Good, George. Good. We must get Virginia to one of the motels nearby. See that one down from the Pennsylvania Burgers? You will need to get the room. Tell them it is for two, but Buddy and I must stay in the room, too. We must stay together tonight. You can get the room, right, George? Tell them you want a room on the back. Okay, George, you ready?"

"You mean now?"

"Yes, now George. There's not much time. We need the room now. I will try to get to the children later. At daybreak I'll steal a car, and we will be gone."

With a white, shocked face, George turned and they trudged toward the motel.

George quietly opened the door with the key card, allowing Bossilini and Buddy with Virginia between them to slide in unnoticed. They helped Virginia into a bed and pulled the covers over her shoulders. Bossilini studied her face; she was sound asleep. He looked around the room silently.

"I will be back shortly," Bossilini announced.

"What—where—"

"Don't worry, George. I just want to have a look around." Bossilini smiled. "A look around is a good thing, yes?" George shrugged. He felt very tired and there was nothing else to say.

Time went by. George was not sure how much, but it seemed quite a while. Where was Bossilini, he wondered? His palms were moist as he wrung his hands. Had Bossilini left them?

There was a quick rap at the door. George startled and Buddy looked up quickly. Before either could move, the door pushed open.

Bossilini entered. "Everything all right?"

"Yes. Sure. What could be wrong?" George answered, his voice pitched.

Bossilini eyed him. "Okay." Turning, he said, "Buddy, come help me get food. George, take care of Virginia. Keep her settled while we are gone." Buddy nodded knowingly.

Outside as they walked to a fast food restaurant, Bossilini asked, "Do you think George is cracking up?"

"No. Not yet."

Buddy asked, "Are you leaving with the boy?"

Bossilini shook his head. "The kids know the rendezvous point. But if captured, they will be leveraged to bring in their parents. I may be compromised, so I cannot risk traveling with the boy. It is up to Manfred."

"How do you think Manfred is doing?" Bossilini asked, turning to his friend.

Buddy shrugged. "It is a perilous time for him."

"I hope Cuthbert was right."

"Yes. Let us hope."

Later—and after two double cheeseburgers—some color had returned to George's face. Buddy was asleep in his corner. Bossilini rose. "Think I'll take one last look around."

When Bossilini was gone for what stretched to five, ten, then fifteen minutes, George began to worry. *Was Bossilini coming back?* He restlessly walked to the curtained window.

George looked through a gap in the curtains, peering for Bossilini. He quickly pulled them shut, sure he was being watched by some hidden NSA camera. Nearby, Virginia made the soft breathing sounds of sleep that were so familiar to him.

Tomorrow George would have to tell her about the children—unless Bossilini rescued them tonight. But Bossilini had not been optimistic about getting them for some reason. He was what—reserved? Why was he reserved?

There must be something Bossilini is not telling him, he reasoned. That explains it, he thought. George felt as if he were crumbling, his internal ramparts and bulwarks buckling, breaking loose in chunks. They would soon collapse to the ground.

Their kids were gone. *Gone!* his mind shrieked.

He shook his head, tiredly, wearily.

He paced. He stopped. He stood over the bed looking down at Virginia, his wife, the real head of his family, while he did his accountant-and-golf-on-the-weekend thing. She was okay, right? She had to be okay, he prayed. He shuddered. He could not go on without her.

His world had become surreal. When would this end? How much more could he take?

Wouldn't it be easier to give in, quit running, and simply surrender? The family could be together again, Virginia, the kids. How did Bossilini know it would be so bad? Bossilini was a foreigner, not an American citizen like them. Maybe they would treat *him* differently, but the Douglases were an American family and their government stood for family values.

He shook his head vigorously.

That was exhaustion speaking, he knew. He knew at a deep level he could not surrender to exhaustion.

In the end he knew he had no choice. He knew he had to go on, no matter how exhausting, no matter how numbing, onward to the end. He would find his kids, then he would clear their name.

George took a deep breath and sat in the chair to watch over his wife as she slept. His heart leaped when he heard Bossilini's key card at the door.

"George." Bossilini rubbed his face, as if trying to press the weariness away. "You know I have to leave." He stared evenly at George. "At least for a while." He could tell George tried to find a brave face, but nonetheless looked fragile.

"How . . . how long?" George was afraid to ask.

"You know, I'm not sure." Bossilini stared at him.

Bossilini felt sympathy. Sympathy was a rare feeling for him. It was a useless emotion in Budapest and the other places. Bossilini wagered with himself. Two-to-one said George didn't have many days on the run left in him. They will be casualties, Bossilini thought. Casualties are part of the business. Because of that, sympathy is a useless emotion.

Nonetheless, he would try to bolster George. "I have to see whether they have identified me. The government computer files go back a long ways." Bossilini tapped his fingertips together.

"Yes, of course. That makes sense to lay low for a while. If you *are* in the clear, though, you will rejoin us, right?"

"Right," Bossilini answered evenly without blinking. George would function better with hope. The amateurs were always like that.

He needed to feed George a plan. They were always calmer with a plan. "I will get a car while it's still dark. We need to leave at dawn. It must be later that Virginia learns, ah, about the children, if we cannot get them. If not, you need to tell her something convincing, like the adults are driving around to see if we are being followed before picking up the children, who are safe. Or tell her something else. But whatever you tell her, George, you must be convincing."

Bossilini met his gaze, unblinking.

George stared back. He did not want to let Bossilini down. George wanted Bossilini to come back. He was their only way out.

"The whole country has shrunk to a very small circle for you, George," Bossilini said, placing his hand on George's shoulder. "You do not have

155

much room to safely maneuver. Be very careful, George. The circle could get much smaller."

CHAPTER 26

THE EDUCATION OF MARCIE BEETHOVEN
April 11, 2019
Inside Homeland Security
Washington, D.C.

Evening EDT

The plane carrying Special Agent Frank Imhoff touched down in New Orleans at 6:30 p.m. sharp. A Bureau car from the local field office whisked him to the New Orleans Ritz Carlton Hotel.

Tappy Montgomery had checked in an hour ago. Franks and McKansky had tailed her from Birmingham. Once she passed south of Hattiesburg, Director Cummings ordered Imhoff to New Orleans on a Bureau plane.

"If something breaks in the Northeast, Frank, we can get you back up here pronto."

Imhoff strode through the front doors of the Ritz lobby, all business. He was reaching for his FBI credentials to get Tappy's room number from the desk clerk when his cell phone rang.

"Imhoff," he answered.

"Special Agent Imhoff, what a coincidence we both are in New Orleans tonight."

Shocked, Imhoff pulled up short. *Tappy Montgomery.*

"How did you get this number?"

Ignoring the question, she said, "I'm in the hotel bar. Join me please. And please come alone. Leave the boys in the lobby."

Imhoff put away his phone, frowning.

"Stay here," Imhoff barked at McKansky and Franks.

"Frank?"

"Stay here."

He headed alone into the bar. He walked to her table.

"Special Agent, why so dour? Do have a seat."

Tappy made a show of tapping a few keys on her open laptop, then punching the last one with finality. "There."

Imhoff, impassive, stared at her. As he intended, she spoke first.

"I figured the Bureau would put a device to track my car. I didn't bother to try to find it. I rather thought New Orleans would be a nice venue for our next talk. I just love the city's atmosphere. It makes me feel creative. You know, Special Agent, I am a writer, a freelance writer. Did you know that? Of course you did, from my interview. I imagine NSA has spilled my life to the Bureau and Homeland. Anyway, I finished a piece—I posted it."

"How nice."

"Oh, Frank, don't be surly with me. May I call you Frank?"

He only grunted.

"Have you thought more about black and white? Have you thought more about which side you fall on?"

He simply stared at her.

Tappy allowed the silence to linger, steadily holding his gaze. Finally, she continued.

"Frank," she began, her voice more conciliatory, "I think you fall on the white side."

He did not respond.

"Frank, let's be candid. I know those were not pest control men at the Douglas house. That is a cover story. I also know DHS, with FBI assistance, is on a manhunt for the Douglases. They have done nothing wrong. They are the victims of DHS bungling. You know how agencies of the federal government can bungle things."

He almost smiled, for indeed he did.

"I am concerned about what may ultimately become of my friends and neighbors."

"If they are innocent, nothing will become of them. However, they should turn themselves in so we can establish their innocence."

"What an interesting proposition, Frank. Of course, if they do so, they will have the right to counsel, the right against unlawful searches and seizures—oh, but you all have already searched their house and ransacked their computers. Is Miranda and the right to confront their accusers in an open federal court system in play?"

"I do not make those decisions. But I would imagine under the circumstances, and with Homeland's involvement, they will, ah, be confined under other systems . . . until their innocence is established."

158

"What you mean is the Patriot Act applies. It is not exactly due process-friendly, Frank. So, what you are saying is the Douglases will be locked up, the Bill of Rights ripped out their copy of the Constitution?"

He shrugged.

"You have a chance, Special Agent, to do something good, to do the right thing." She stared at him piercingly. "I orchestrated this chat between just the two of us, because I think you are different. You are hard-nosed and tough. But you are also a man of integrity. You can still land on the white side."

"It is also a chance to do my job, and my job is to apprehend the Douglases for questioning."

"Do you think it will stop at questioning?"

He didn't answer her. The firepower leveled at the Douglases came from the top floors and the heavy artillery had been rolled in.

"Your silence speaks volumes." She tossed her head, turning her laptop toward him. "One of my writing projects is a blog called *Privacy's Flashlight.* I follow instances of government intrusion into personal privacy and write to expose it. Exposure helps keep the checks and balances between the government and its citizens."

"The piece I posted tonight is about the Douglases."

Imhoff looked down at the screen. The legend at the top indeed read *Privacy's Flashlight*, and underneath was a black and white Victorian ink drawing of a constable's flashlight, but with a yellow cone of light shining from it.

The title of the blog installment in large bold print was the question, "HAVE YOU SEEN THEM?" Below was a picture of the Douglas family.

The treatment began lauding the Douglases as an All-American family, with Tappy vouching personally for them. Then it switched to the government's invasion of the Douglases' house in the middle of the night without a warrant, continuing under the guise of a pest control company the next day, and concluded:

"The government's intent can only be considered malevolent. We at *Privacy's Flashlight* know of other instances of persecution of innocent Americans under the guise of the Patriot Act and the 2018 Cruz-Cornyn-

Jordan Act. My friends thus far have escaped the unlawful action; nonetheless, I fear gravely for their safety."

Imhoff saw the post already had 5,000 comments and the number was climbing exponentially before his eyes. Imhoff blanched. He could just hear Director Cummings.

"This is a goddamn shitstorm," Director Cummings thundered when a printed copy of the blog was brought to him. He barked: "Tell Imhoff to take Mrs. Montgomery into custody immediately as a material witness. Mirandize her. She needs to understand she may have just committed the crime of aiding and abetting terrorists."

Across the bar at the Ritz a pretty female sat with a pretty colored drink. Her dark hair and looks were striking. She casually cradled her phone, videoing Imhoff reading Tappy Montgomery her rights and taking her into custody. Her phone had a special, sensitive microphone. She got every word of the custodial detention of Tappy Montgomery.

Ogilvie, for his part, only stared wide-eyed at the dispatch, too shocked for words. The DHS press liaison stuck his head in the door. "This post is going viral, predicted into the millions by the eleven o' clock news. Issue 'No Comment' responses to any press inquiries?"

"Ah, sure," Ogilvie responded absently without looking up.

Chambers, on the other hand, ground his teeth, but set his jaw firm. *This had to cease.* He silently left the room as Ogilvie just sat, eyes glued to the dispatch. Chambers knew they could not passively wait for the Douglases to surface. The "joint training exercise" would no longer provide sanctuary. Bolder action was required.

In his office, he walked to a bookcase opposite his desk. He removed several volumes from a section of a shelf. Embedded in the wall was a small safe. Chambers quickly spun the combination, opened the door, and removed a black cell phone from inside a plastic sandwich bag. He sat in a wingback chair by the bookcase and punched a phone number only he knew.

The call went through a secure line to the desk of Richard Finnegan, CEO of Security Data Systems, known everywhere as SDS.

After Section 215 of the Patriotic Act expired in 2015, deep divisions arose about intelligence gathering. The hawks screamed unlimited data collection from everywhere was crucial to protecting against terrorists on American soil. Their slogan was: "We have your back and will prevent an attack." The privacy camps screamed back that no government needed unlimited access to its citizens' conversations and thoughts. Their slogan was: "If it's important, get a warrant." Tensions were high; talk TV and radio were burning up the airwaves. Finally, a freshman House member from Topeka, Kansas, Bob Bublanski, suggested quietly one day almost in passing, "Why don't we farm it out to private enterprise. They can fulfill our security needs a lot better than government bureaucracy and make a profit, too."

Bublanski became an instant political celebrity and made the rounds of shows from Rush, to Rachel, to Sean, to Chris, to Chuck. Congress rolled up its sleeves and passed a new Act in a weekend. The final version of the Act signed by the President placed data collection, storage, and retrieval in one company to be selected by competitive bidding. SDS was the lowest bidder.

SDS's bid was the lowest because Chambers, along with a long-time confederate at NSA, had brokered with CEO Finnegan of SDS an ultra-secret side deal only the three of them knew about. SDS could pitch a low bid because it would make up revenues by lowered taxes and back-room ops. After the dust settled, SDS moved its surveillance and data storage operations off-shore to Ireland where it would no longer pay U.S. taxes on that revenue—and there was an ocean between it and the subpoena power of American courts. Protests got little traction, as the public was exhausted by the data collection battles and desensitized to the offshore flights of corporations from American tax collectors.

Chambers thought it was really a beautiful move. The ocean didn't impede the flow of information. And he got a bite out of every bit of data collected. Chambers, through a series of complicated, obscure holding companies, owned a piece of SDS.

In addition to its data collection payments from the government, SDS enhanced its profits by secretly leaking information to selective users for handsome back-door payments. Finnegan created a secret Black Room from which he selectively funneled collected information to politicians and businessmen, who leveraged it for handsome profits and power. They, in turn, were happy to pay Finnegan handsome commissions. As Finnegan once boasted to Chambers over really expensive champagne, "There is nothing wrong with making a profit while keeping America safe."

SDS even had a black ops unit to make sure the Black Room stayed in the dark.

And the public knew nothing.

Sitting in his office with the door shut, Chambers spoke carefully into the phone.

"You are aware of the concern which has arisen over the recently missing Douglas family . . . yes . . . it has become necessary to create a complete backstory on the Douglases and specifically George Douglas. We need deep IT and electronic background in place that George Douglas has had secret communications with persons in the Middle East, Iran, and Syria, Libya ... and let's add Africa. Mrs. Douglas and the children should be ignorant of his actions. The records will develop a story that two years ago George Douglas was converted to radicalized Islam. We want records of complex movements of money from Douglas to those countries and also to offshore accounts in a fictitious name. Mr. Douglas should look to have created a fictitious identity, presumably for use in the event he needed to escape. This is a Level One top priority—do not stop until this is done."

He took a moment, thinking. "I want you to seal the Douglas' real bank, credit card, and financial records under the Patriot Act and the Bublanski Act. Place an electronic hold with the seal of our department. From now on those records are locked. No one may see them."

Chambers paused, checking whether he'd left out anything.

"Oh, yes, add to your efforts a liaison between Mr. Douglas and Mrs. Montgomery, the next-door neighbor . . . hotel rooms . . . restaurants . . . flowers . . . gifts . . . trips out of town. You know how to do it."

Attack and discredit your opponent. While Preston had studied Reagan, he had studied Nixon.

Imhoff breached protocol.

"We're interrogating her in her hotel room," Imhoff announced.

"But Frank—"

"Don't 'but Frank' me."

"Okay, but this is on you, Imhoff," Franks pointed at him.

"The Director put me in charge, and I'm running the investigation my way. Wait down here. You can drive us in after I have a conversation with Mrs. Montgomery."

"Why, Special Agent Imhoff, there's hope for you yet." Tappy smiled. He glared at her.

As Imhoff escorted Tappy down the hotel hallway toward her room, the striking woman with black hair posted to *Privacy's Flashlight* the video of Tappy's custodial detention. It went pandemic. The caption read, "*Privacy's Flashlight's* Tappy Montgomery arrested by FBI after exposing government persecution of innocent Americans."

The audio was crystal clear: "Mrs. Montgomery, you have the right to remain silent, anything you say can and will be used against you in a court of law. You have the right to counsel, if you cannot afford counsel, one with be appointed for you. Do you understand those rights, Mrs. Montgomery?"

"I certainly do *FBI Special Agent Frank Imhoff.*" His name could be clearly heard on the video—all over America.

The two posts coming in close proximity created a thermonuclear firestorm on the internet, Twitter, the regular media, and social media. They also created firestorms in the White House, National Security Council, and the top levels of the FBI, NSA, and the DHS.

"Dick, how did this thing explode in our faces?" Ogilvie lamented, pacing in front of his office window. "We had solid data from Canaveral.

We were supposed to capture this family in their sleep. Even when they initially escaped, this had media silence. Nobody knew about it. Now, my god, it's all over the internet. They got video of the FBI arresting Tappy Montgomery for god's sake. It's on YouTube. How in the hell could they make a video? The Douglases are getting help we don't know about. It's an unmitigated disaster."

The sound was muted, but scenes showed the Douglas house with media reporters running all around the lawn, while the Birmingham PD tried vainly to keep a semblance of order. The talking heads on CNNFOX and other stations were going apeshit. The DHS press secretary looked pale when a few minutes ago Ogilvie instructed him to be unavailable for comment. The White House had issued a brief statement: "It was unaware of the Douglas situation. The matter was within the jurisdiction of the Department of Homeland Security. The President as yet has not been briefed by DHS."

The FBI issued a short statement also. "The Federal Bureau of Investigation was asked by DHS to provide local support on a limited basis in a DHS investigation. Based on DHS instructions, an FBI agent took into custody a material witness identified by DHS. As a matter of routine procedure, the witness was read her Miranda rights, but she was not arrested. Because this is the subject of an ongoing investigation, further comment is prohibited."

"The rats are deserting the sinking ship, and we're the ship," Ogilvie complained. "How could this go so wrong?"

"Buck up, Preston. This is Washington." Chambers stared at him sternly. "I am working on some countermeasures. My staff is working on a press release to set the stage to reverse the momentum. We can still come out good on this one."

Despair staunched for the moment, Ogilvie called, "Thank you, Dick. I knew I could count on you."

Chambers gave Ogilvie a thin smile.

Fifteen minutes later, Chambers launched the first counterattack in the media. DHS issued its own press release with its seal at the top. The text read:

THE DEPARTMENT OF HOMELAND SECURITY

164

Through months of intensive investigation and surveillance the Department of Homeland Security has unearthed a domestic terrorist cell in Alabama. The leader of the cell, George Douglas, secretly converted to Islam four years ago. His encrypted computer files reveal that he increasingly began visiting radical Islam sites over the last several years. He became radicalized and started sending funds to locations in the Middle East as well as to private accounts overseas. Douglas planned a terrorist event to occur within the United States in the next two weeks. It appears Mrs. Douglas and children were ignorant of these events and could themselves be in danger. A key member of the cell is his neighbor Tappy Montgomery with whom he became romantically involved. The Department also believes Mrs. Montgomery secretly converted to Islam. To aid their treason she established a blog critical of United States security and defense efforts. The blog is false and subversive. Her post today is a direct attempt to interfere in the apprehension and arrest of George Douglas. Through joint cooperation of DHS and the FBI, Mrs. Montgomery was taken into custody for interrogation in New Orleans where it is believed she meets as a liaison with other domestic terrorist cells. DHS and the FBI are working with the United States Attorneys to file charges against Mrs. Montgomery.

"Maybe there's hope after all," Ogilvie whispered to himself after reading the release. "Maybe we can get them before the press does."

Chambers stood outside the secure room in which Marcie's team worked over consoles and computers. He caught Marcie's attention and motioned her to the hallway.

"Sir?" she asked upon closing the door.

"Here is the press release the Department just issued."

Upon reading it, she looked at Chambers, incredulous. The blood drained from her face.

"Ms. Beethoven?"

She answered, her voice shaking. "We didn't find anything like this."

"You mean you have not found it yet."

She stood perfectly still before answering. She made up her mind.

"No, what I mean is that we have to be careful to get it right. I didn't realize it before when we were chasing *turbans in the desert*, but here . . . at home . . . we can destroy American lives." She looked up at him.

Chambers stared down at her, his face stern.

"Your sympathy is commendable, although I do not think the enemies of the United States of America share it. Ask relatives of those killed on 9/11 or the destroyer Cole or the Marines killed in the Beirut barracks bombing—of course you would not remember that one for you were not even born—those too were *American* lives, young lady. But I remember. I have been fighting this battle, fighting America's enemies for a long, very long time."

She swallowed, her hand trembling.

Chambers stared at her sharply, with growing concern. He decided on a more conciliatory tone. She needed to be reeled in. "Has it even remotely occurred to you that the Department might compartmentalize information on a need-to-know? That there may be those who have somewhat more experience than you, who know what has been sheltered from you? How many years have you been here? Has it occurred to you that some of those compartments may lie above your, ah, rather modest security clearance?" He stared at her. "Are you to question decisions based on information of which you are ignorant because you are restricted from that information?"

Her head swam. *Were there things she did not know because she was prohibited from knowing them at her security level?* She had always respected Secretary Ogilvie and Assistant Secretary Chambers.

She looked off-balance. Chambers tried to right her. "Ms. Beethoven, you should expand your search. Look at the Tappy Montgomery family, their records, e-footprint. See if this time you find an intersection with the Douglases—or the Middle East." Looking down, she nodded, as if accepting his instruction.

She did not watch him turn and walk away.

And she had no intention of looking further. She knew there was no connection. Her team had been too thorough.

But her employer said there was.

Marcie stood a few minutes alone in the hall staring at the press release.

She shook her head. *What does this mean? What are Ogilvie and Chambers up to?*

She froze.

My god, did they screw up this whole Wildroot alert? Was that it? Is this all a cover-up? Chambers said "see if this time you find a connection." Had they now planted a connection?

The education of Marcie Beethoven was now complete.

CHAPTER 27

ROOM 507
April 11, 2009
Ritz Carlton Hotel
New Orleans

7:15 p.m. CDT

Tappy Montgomery sat on the small sofa in the suite, while Imhoff faced her from a Queen Anne-style chair. She waited for Imhoff to begin.

Before he did, her phone dinged. She had received a message.

"Mind turning that off," Imhoff said. He was not asking. She nodded but looked at the message.

"I expect you will want to see this." A troubled look crossed Tappy's face. But she quickly smiled and handed him the phone. She watched him view Chambers' post. Imhoff's jaw clenched, and with a crimson face, he looked sharply at Tappy. None of this data was in his Wildroot briefing.

He stared at her a full minute as thoughts raced through his mind. What had DHS gotten them into? How had it suckered Director Cummings into such a screw-up?

"A little light beginning to dawn, Special Agent?"

"When did George Douglas convert to Islam?" he asked, the color fading from his face.

She laughed. "Surely you're not serious."

"Do I look like I'm not serious? You are in a custodial interrogation. We can move to a less comfortable room downtown if you don't think I am serious."

He's defensive, she thought. *He suspects, but he's not yet ready to admit the truth.*

"George Douglas is no more Islamic than I am an ayatollah." She looked at him steadily. "Can we drop the pretense, Special Agent?"

"What pretense?"

"That the Douglases are terrorists, espionage agents. I know George Douglas. He couldn't bluff his way through a Royal Flush. He is incapable of maintaining a secret life as a terrorist in Alabama." She measured him. "You realize that by now, Special Agent."

169

Imhoff paused. Something bubbled up in his mind. Yes, he did realize that. Maybe he had realized that all along. None of this ever walked. Yet the weapon? And who carried them away?

"Maybe, maybe not. There are AK-47 bullet holes in the wall. Someone picked them up in the alley."

Tappy paused, this was dangerous territory. She measured her response carefully.

"Oh, that must be George's rifle," she said lightly. "He's obsessed with it; Virginia hates it. I would suppose he heard noises or voices outside as you approached the house. Worried, he grabbed the rifle for protection, but in his nervous bumbling, it went off. So it seems that the gunshots actually support the Douglases' innocence, does it not, Special Agent?"

She was good, Imhoff thought. She'd make a good criminal defense attorney.

Imhoff decided to push her.

"What about the vehicle in the alley. Who was that? The Douglases' cars were at home."

He stared at her, giving her whatever time it took to answer. There was the slightest fidget in her posture. She was good but eventually everybody made a mistake.

"Mrs. Montgomery, you realize—"

What she realized was that she had to be totally convincing. "I don't quite know what you mean? What vehicle? What alley?" She shook her head, looking innocent.

"How about breakfast on the table—for five? Why breakfast in the middle of night? And who was the other plate for?"

She tilted her head just the slightest. Her tell.

Imhoff smiled. *She did not know about breakfast and the extra plate.* He established she was not who had warned them.

"Do you really think you can play me, Mrs. Montgomery?"

She quickly assumed a contrite pose to work him, like a femme fatale in a Bogart movie.

"Oh, I should know better than to try to fool you. Can I be candid with you, Frank?"

"That would be nice for a change." He noticed it was now "Frank" and no longer the coy "Special Agent."

She leaned in, looking at him earnestly, as if she were baring the truth to him, finally.

"I . . . I am a privacy watchdog. I have some knowledge of government operations," she uttered hurriedly and breathlessly. "I don't understand what triggered attention of the Douglases, but it is unfounded. Now I am scared, Frank." He noticed the more intimate "Frank" again. "Someone in the government, someone high up, wants a cover-up. I don't know why, but they do. I fear for my friends. I fear they are in grave danger." She clasped her hands in concern, tilting her head, eyes looking up in dependence on him.

Imhoff inwardly smiled at her performance, the expression of worry on her face, the weaker woman depending upon the strong man. It was an old ploy. But what she said walked.

"Can I trust you with something, Frank?"

"That depends."

He could see her thinking. She knew her options were dwindling.

"I have something . . . evidence . . . that will show this DHS release is bogus . . . manufactured lies."

Imhoff sat up straight. That was serious business. It could explain this whole caper that not only didn't walk, but had now fallen over on its side.

"Do you have an evidence bag per chance? Y'all are fastidious about the chain of custody."

He patted his coat breast pockets. He usually carried one. He felt a bag in his right pocket and shook it open for her.

Tappy nodded, but smiled. "I was thinking of something larger." She walked to the desk and opened a drawer. With her back to him, Imhoff could not see what she removed. As she walked toward him, she was holding a small back box in both her hands. "Only my finger prints will be on it."

Imhoff now recognized it. He rose, taking the plastic trash liner out of a small trash can by the desk.

Imhoff opened the liner and extended it toward Tappy. She dropped an external hard drive into the open mouth of the liner, and Imhoff twisted the end, tying it in a knot.

"What's supposed to be on here?" he asked.

"The truth."

They stared at each other as he waited for her to go on.

"What truth," he asked when she remained silent.

She took a breath.

"That George is not Islamic. That he never sent money to the Middle East, and he is a long-time Episcopalian. The drive contains his family's entire electronic footprint and computer hard drive."

"How did you get—"

"That's not important," she flashed her knowing smile at him. "A forensics computer tech will confirm that the information was stored *before* your raid—a couple of weeks ago, in fact—and before this whole episode started. I expect that DHS, with a little help from its friends"—a clear jab at Security Data Systems, Imhoff knew —"has altered the Douglases' data to show transfers of money, communications with persons in the Middle East, and an affair between George and me with hotel rooms, restaurants, the whole song of wine and roses. But the data on this external drive will refute that—and expose the lie." She leaned back, crossing her arms across her chest, the confident smile back on her face.

"Insurance," he said, not asked. She nodded.

Imhoff stared at the box, intently, as if peering inside to learn its secrets. After several intense moments, he realized what he held was not a box. It was a torpedo. And it could be launched broadside at DHS.

And it might, just might, protect the Federal Bureau of Investigation, and him, Special Agent Frank P. Imhoff.

"Assistant Secretary Chambers? Hi, it's me, Marcie. I hope I'm not disturbing you?"

Chambers pressed the telephone receiver to his ear.

"No, not at all, Marcie. How can I help you?" he asked, his voice soothing and solicitous.

"I found something. It was just a little crack and didn't mean anything before. But when I was working, ah, following up on the Department post, I saw it."

Chambers sat upright in his office chair. "Yes, Marcie, tell me."

"Well, you know how some people periodically back up their computers to protect data so they don't lose it if the machine crashes or they like they hit the wrong key or something—"

"Yes, yes, I am familiar with computer backups. Tell me, what did you find?"

"Oh, yes sir, well I found that the Douglases' system was backed up externally by wireless, that is, from someone outside their house. They backed up everything on the computer, like all their data. I mean *all* their data, you know, online banking transactions, passwords, emails, downloads, household things—and they got Mr. Douglas's work devices, too."

"Marcie, why would someone do that?"

"Unknown, sir, but like I said, the Douglases were amateurs. They had, like, no serious security on their system. It was easy to hack in."

Chambers thought. He did not like this. He made his voice casual. "Marcie, what is the significance of this extra backup copy? I mean, if it has any significance?"

She answered point blank.

"The backup was made *before* the Wildroot alert. It means whoever has it, er, can prove the—our—the press release is not correct."

Chambers rocked back in his chair, his eyes narrowed, the lines deepening on his face. Uncomfortable with his silence, Marcie asked, "Anything else, sir?"

"No, no, nothing for now. That is good work, Ms. Beethoven—Marcie. You did the right thing calling me." He paused, thinking of his next move. He needed to make her an ally, at least for the next short while.

"Marcie, it is important you keep this new information to yourself. Don't share it with the team. And don't share it with our HIS agents. Does anyone other than you know of the backup?"

"No, sir. I didn't tell anyone but wanted to report to you first, sir."

"That was an excellent decision, Marcie. It shows our confidence in you is well placed. Keep it that way—no one else—and call me with any other information."

"Yes . . . yes . . . thank you, sir."

"Marcie, one more thing. Can you destroy the data showing the external backup?"

"Destroy it, sir?"

"Yes, Marcie, destroy it. Are you capable of doing that yourself? There are reasons I ask this. You understand I cannot share them . . . yet. Not till your clearances are elevated."

"Ah, yes sir . . . I can."

"Thank you, Marcie. It's good to know I can count on you. Secretary Ogilvie, too."

"Yes, sir."

"Sir," she hesitated. "My security clearances are being elevated?"

"Any time now."

Chambers placed the receiver in its cradle.

He rose from his desk and walked to the other side of his office. He removed the books and retrieved the secret phone.

On the second ring a voice answered. "Yes."

"It's time to move to the next level."

"Which ones?"

"The husband for now."

"Any ID on the accomplices?"

"No. It appears there are two of them. Unknown capability. You will have to make decisions in the field. I will supply you with any updates from the drone. And," Chambers added, "look for any type of computer backup, thumb drive, external hard drive, CD, whatever. There will be a handsome bonus if such is found and returned to me."

"Roger."

"I also want you to become familiar with one of our employees. Her name is Marcie Beethoven. It could become necessary for her to receive your attention."

"Roger."

Chambers clicked off the phone, removed the battery, and counted to thirty, allowing time for the record of the call in memory to fade into oblivion. Evidence of calls could not be retrieved from oblivion.

Imhoff rode in silence in the front passenger seat of the FBI car. He stared into the dark night as Special Agent Franks drove toward the New Orleans Bureau headquarters.

Imhoff was anxious to get to the field office, finish the interrogation, and get back to Washington. He had thought about shipping the external hard drive to the lab at headquarters. But now he was not so sure. He decided to hang on to it. Things were too out of control. The device, maybe, was too important to let out of his hands. No, he would personally deliver it to the lab techs handpicked by Director Cummings.

Imhoff thought deeply about the case and finally reached a series of conclusions that he believed were sound. One, DHS had picked up on some type of transmission or phenomena around the Douglas house, but it overreacted in issuing the *Wildroot* alert. Now the overreaction would be embarrassing if made public. Two, whoever made the *Wildroot* decision at the Department was now seeking cover. Three, like all cover-ups, it was spiraling out of control so he—or she—needed a fall guy. Four, George Douglas had been tapped with that honor. And five?

Five troubled Imhoff. This op was turning dark. DHS had gone public with a bold strike. The story on the Douglases and the terrorist connection was stunning. Major news. There was no retreating. But if or when the Douglases surfaced, and it was realized George Douglas was not a terrorist, well, that would blow the cover-up sky high and unmask those hiding behind it.

But only if the Douglases surfaced.

Imhoff shook his head in dismay. He glanced back at Tappy in the rear seat. She was staring at him, her face grave, but with hope. At the moment, he had no hope to offer. Imhoff felt empty. Then he felt betrayed. In the end, he felt angry. He banged his fist on the steering wheel.

Imhoff stared in disbelief out the windshield at the darkness covering the city. There was a darkness covering his country, too. It was a cruel and pathological darkness. He thought the old lessons from Vietnam, Watergate, and Iraq, would have changed us for good, would have inoculated us from the deceits, the cover ups, the untruths. He felt deflated and beaten, unfamiliar feelings for him.

175

They could have just admitted the mistake, he thought, shaking his head in frustration. *They could have fixed it or at least apologized and employed PR spin. But, they didn't,* he frowned, grinding his jaw.

His eyes squeezed to slits. He thought of his FBI credentials in his pocket. His oath to serve.

He shook his head. *I didn't sign on for this,* his face bitter. *I didn't sign up to help those in government keep their power and wealth by hiding things and crushing the little people.* That was at the bottom of it after all, he now realized. Power, wealth, and their preservation. *My god,* he thought, a sour, sickness filling him, *what have we become?*

Then his phone rang.

It was Director Cummings.

CHAPTER 28

INTO THE WOODS
April 11, 2019
I-81 Exchange
Wilkes-Barre, Pennsylvania

Evening EDT

Sherman and Carmen helped Manfred limp into the woods.

"Sherman, I can't see anything," Carmen complained.

"Ouch," Manfred uttered.

"Hold on, I got a light but we got to get a little ways in so they won't see it from the road," Sherman said.

A few yards and scrapes later he pushed through a bush into what he sensed was a clearing.

"Stop a second," he said. Sherman dug in his backpack and found a small tent light. He flicked the switch and they found themselves in a cone of light. At the edge of the light, they saw dark shrubs, pines, and hardwood trees surrounding them. Sherman dropped his pack on the ground. "Okay, this is it."

He kneeled, digging into his backpack for his first aid kit.

Sherman watched Carmen look around dismissively, making sure they all saw her displeasure. She plopped down underneath a nearby tree, leaning back, staring numbly.

Sherman pulled a large bandage from his kit.

"What you got there, Sherman?" Manfred asked.

"Triangle bandage." Sherman made a sling and secured Manfred's left arm to his chest with the Ace bandage.

"We should sit down and rest," Sherman announced. "Over here. Lean against the tree and I'll sit here." Manfred carefully sat down, a little awkward with the sling. Sherman sat hugging his knees.

"I'm feeling better," Manfred said.

"Good."

Sherman glanced at Carmen about eight feet away. Her expression was one he had never seen. *Shock.*

Carmen called to Sherman in a small voice. "Hey, ah, where are Mom and Dad?"

Sherman shrugged.

She persisted. "Shouldn't they be here by now? Don't we need to move closer to the road so they'll see our light?"

Now that he thought about it, Sherman nodded. "Yeah, they ought to be here by now."

"Where are they?" Carmen rose and began pacing, looking toward the road. But they saw only darkness and the glare of flashing police and emergency lights over the treetops. "It's dark. I'm scared."

Sherman squirmed, Carmen's mood contagious. *If his parents were only across the street, what was the holdup? Where were they?*

"M-maybe we should go find them?" Sherman offered. He thought about it for a moment. "Yes, we should," Sherman decided, as he stood up, reaching for his pack.

"Whoa, hold on," Manfred said, struggling to stand up. "We can't go out there. The cops are everywhere. What do you think happened when they found the Rectangle empty and we all disappeared 'Presto?' The fed goons may be here already."

Carmen was crying. "I want Mom," she blubbered.

Her breakdown unnerved the boy. Sherman's bottom lip began quivering. He did not want to cry. He had been brave the whole trip, through everything. Somehow, he figured out they were in danger and should leave their house. He knew to call Bossilini. He knew they should go to the flowers to hide. When Bossilini left, he led them safely into the woods. He bandaged Manfred's arm and shoulder. But he wanted his mother and father too. Something was wrong. He tried to press out the thought, but it was the kind of middle-of-the-night scary thought. The tears started down his face with a life of their own, though he tried valiantly to stem them, squeezing his eyes.

Carmen made whimpering noises through her sobs.

Oh, god! Manfred ran the hand on his good arm through his hair. "*They're losing it,*" he thought. He looked stricken, but furiously thinking what to do.

"Hey, hey, guys, your mom and dad seem like really smart people." They nodded.

"Hey, you know your parents will come get you. They're probably just waiting for the cops and fire trucks to leave so it's dark again."

"So, guys, we need to sit a little longer and be cool, and before you know it, your mom and dad, and even ole Buddy and Bossilini, are gonna come walking through those bushes right over there." He pointed to bushes behind him toward the road, and the children quickly turned that way. They didn't know he didn't believe a word of it.

"Hey, if it makes you feel better, I'll go take a quick peek at the road. But you both gotta stay here. Okay?"

They nodded their ready assent.

Manfred crawled forward. He peered out of the bushes toward the service road. There was a police officer and three men in suits. One talked on one of those telecorder things, while the other two watched. Manfred scanned to his right and saw a black SUV with tinted windows in the Pennsylvania Burgers parking lot. Manfred did not know to call the vehicle an SUV, but he could tell an unmarked government vehicle when he saw one. A tow truck carried off the pick-up truck. The Rectangle still rested in place.

Making his way back to them in the dark, he hoped he hadn't veered off course. He bumped his hurt shoulder once on a tree, swallowing the pain. He tried to think what they needed to do for the night, because it looked like they were stuck there till daybreak.

Food. They had to get food. But he had to go alone. The children wouldn't like that.

As he stumbled into the clearing, they looked expectantly toward him. He saw their faces change to despair as he stood alone. Manfred responded quickly.

"Hey guys, look, Bossilini had to move your parents because the FBI came. He will keep them safe for the night."

"You sure?" Carmen asked, her voice needy for reassurance. "You talked with him?"

"No, I didn't actually talk with him . . . but it's clear they had gone off safe for the night. You know, it was pretty smart of them. They'd have to

179

get flashlights to find us, then somebody would wonder about lights crisscrossing in the woods . . . so you get it."

They nodded.

He breathed out slowly.

"I got to find food," Manfred said.

Sherman and Carmen pleaded to come. "No way, guys," he argued. "You gotta stay here where it's safe."

"Okay." Carmen crossed her arms, her face petulant. "Just get back before the flashlight batteries run out."

"It's a tent light," Sherman corrected.

"Whatever."

Manfred sneaked in the shadows and trees along the service road away from the accident scene. He had no idea where to go. He moved cautiously, worried about patrol cars.

Shit, he thought. This is a disaster. What am I doing?

He had put up a brave front for the children, but where the hell were the others, especially Bossilini? Bossilini should have come for them before now. He was one tough dude. He *wouldn't* leave them dangling in the woods overnight. So that meant he *couldn't* come tonight. Man, what was going on? What had happened to the Douglases? *This is some bad shit*, he said to himself.

Think, think! He beat his fist on his head. Bossilini wasn't coming tonight. But if he didn't come in the morning, then what? Was he supposed to smuggle the children into New York to meet at the Unisphere? That would be a fun trip with Carmen Douglas bitching the whole way.

Manfred had a bad, sinking feeling. He kicked a rusting beer can, but stubbed his toe. He aimed a string of curses at the can.

Might as well go on, he decided. Gotta eat. Another quarter mile and he saw lights, and coming closer, the Golden Arches. Far out, a McDonald's. They still had them in the future. He smiled, feeling a little better. At least something was familiar.

"Take your order?"

Manfred stood back from the counter. Nothing inside looked familiar. He tried to decipher the big menu on the wall. Geez, he was used to 15-cent hamburgers, 25-cent cheeseburgers, and maybe a fish sandwich. Now there were Combos and doubles-sizes and triples-sizes a million kinds of hamburgers and sandwiches and desserts and drinks and things named smoothies. The choices overwhelmed him.

Finally, he riveted onto combo # 2: cheeseburger, fries, and soft drink, $4.25—*$4.25*—was it sirloin for god's sake?

"Do, like, the combos come with burger, fries, *and* drink?"

"Duh."

"Duh?"

The girl smacked her gum and answered, "Dude, what century are you from?"

"Okay," Manfred said tentatively, "combo #2."

"One combo. Anything else?"

"Ah, nope."

Manfred ordered only one combo. He only needed a meal for one.

Stepping inside the McDonald's, he had stared at the glass walls reflecting an array of colors from menu boards, signs, and lights. But outside, beyond the reflected lights, was blackness. Standing alone, three steps inside the door, he realized he could just step outside into that blackness, and like, disappear, man.

The sweet breath of freedom blew gently upon his neck.

He could feel the freedom. Freedom, baby. He could hit the road, man. He could get a safe distance away and start hitching like in a wild, crazy Kerouac way. He could be rid of this fugitive gig.

What did they expect from him, anyway?

He didn't like it here in the twenty-first century. The vibes were bad, which upset him. He'd gone to Woodstock for good vibes. But the vibes here weren't good. Something had happened to the vibes in the future.

Now before him lay a wonderful highway, a dark ribbon leading anywhere and everywhere, a beautiful chance to bolt, like a prisoner on a chain gang with a leg shackle working loose giving him that one chance to run. Run, baby, run. Run toward delicious freedom. Run. Just run.

So inside at the counter, he said, "Just one combo, please."

He paid, grabbed the sack, crammed a straw through the lid of his coke, and split. Outside, he turned away from the woods, away from the Rectangle, away from the Douglases, away from the government goons and jails. He had stepped around the quicksand; now he wasn't about to let the children drag him down to the bottom of the sucking muck. A soft breeze in his face felt fresh and hopeful. Maybe it was from the east. It was an omen. He sailed into it.

Manfred had not gotten far up the road, maybe half a mile, when the breeze tapered off. He began to feel a little uptight around the edges. The feeling of freedom, so sweet at first, was turning slightly sour. He wanted that open road free feeling to stay, to last, but it was dimming, like it always did. The freedom never lasted.

He was now fully uptight, because he knew he had a choice. He stopped on the side of the road. He was pissed the choice reared up, because now one way or the other he had to decide it head on.

He could keep trucking along freedom's road and somehow, someday hopefully stumble onto a way back. That was what he wanted.

Or he could go back to the children.

He thought about the children. They were alone in the woods at night. Manfred began to see the children in his mind and frowned. He could see them looking scared and anxious, the tent light batteries dimming, knowing soon they would be plunged into darkness.

By now he was definitely late returning.

They would be worn out, hungry, and terrified, the noises in the dark fueling their imaginations. They would be arguing, with Carmen wanting to leave and Sherman trying to stop her. He believed in Manfred. It was unfathomable to him that Manfred would betray them.

That hurt Manfred the worst, Sherman standing up for him. He could see the boy tugging on Carmen as she tried to leave, and her knocking him down into the dirt with a slap. Breaking free, she would run, run, coming clear of the woods only to run straight into the clutches of the government. Sherman would run after her, still believing in him, trying to save her, until he, too, ran into the government's arms.

And Manfred would have done it to them.

He would have ruined two young lives. Maybe their lives were already ruined. But Manfred would render it a certainty.

182

He groaned. He tried to hang onto the freedom, but it began fading, flowing away from him. Determined to get away, however, he only lengthened his stride. He took three hard long strides.

No matter how hard his stride, though, all he could see was images of them, terrified, crying for their mommy and daddy, cuffed in the back of a government van, hating him. A sharp feeling of guilt pierced his heart. He thought children shouldn't have to go through that. It wasn't their fault. He knew it only too well from long ago....

And they didn't have to.

He could help them. If he got back in time.

"Oh, crap," he said, after a few more strides.

Angry, Manfred threw his drink cup on the side of the road and jogged back to McDonald's.

But after ten yards, he turned and began sprinting away again. "This—is—not—my—problem!" he shouted. He ran for twenty yards and pulled up short. He couldn't shake Sherman's trusting face; it was branded into his mind. Then he remembered what Sherman told him. "You can go if you need to. I forgive you."

He stood still, head hanging, taking a few deep gasps. Finally, he turned, pushing away the mess of feelings, and steadily walked back to McDonald's. Now that he knew about combos, he ordered two and hurried back.

CHAPTER 29

JUST A LITTLE TRIM PLEASE
April 11, 2019
The woods
Wilkes-Barre, Pennsylvania

Evening EDT

"Where have you been!" they both shrieked.

"Ah, took longer than I thought," he answered, looking away. "They had to cook the French fries. Here, I got you food."

"Did you see Mom or Dad?" Carmen sniffled.

Manfred stiffened. "Naw, the restaurant was the other way. We need to eat and turn in somewhere," he announced, looking around the clearing. "I guess we should look for a grassy spot or maybe some pine straw."

"Oh, I got that handled," Sherman said. "I learned how to build a shelter from sticks, leaves, and stuff for my Wilderness Survival merit badge. It's over there," he pointed.

"Here's nothing." Manfred crawled in first thirty minutes later. Sherman had collected soft grass and covered the floor so it felt soft and spongy. "This feels pretty good," Manfred said pleased, patting the groundcover. "I could have used something like this at Woodstock."

"Go ahead, Carmen."

Carmen grumpily crawled in on the side of Manfred's good arm. Sherman enthusiastically followed her taking the side by Manfred's sling.

"It's dark," Carmen worried.

"Your eyes will adjust," Sherman said. Sleepiness lowered his voice.

Lying together, they gave each other warmth. Before long, both children snuggled closer to Manfred.

Carmen moved close as if seeking shelter in a storm. Manfred could feel her childhood needs for protection, for reassurance, for safety. His arm rose naturally in response, and she slipped inside resting her head in the crook of his shoulder. As if in tandem, Sherman slipped closer to

Manfred and laid his head next to Manfred's shoulder but carefully so as not to hurt it. Manfred could not raise that arm to give Sherman shelter from the dark. But he would have if he could.

The three lay nestled like that most of the night, sharing warmth, sharing the safety of togetherness.

Before sleep, he lay in the dark, staring up at the dim, patchwork ceiling of the shelter. Manfred could feel the even rise and fall of the children's chests.

Manfred remembered a night long ago when he was a child sleeping next to his grandfather. They slept on a daybed in a breezeway on a hot summer night. Manfred had missed his mother that day and cried, but he slept peacefully and happily, secure in the crook of that strong shoulder. The memory was special and always calmed him.

With an in-breath, Manfred felt his chest open up, filling with a warm rush of contentment and love. He suddenly sensed a verdant, green vista of life opening before him, beckoning him. It was as if he could simply step forward into a wondrous and new land, where he could become part of the procession of life, like what new parents must feel with the birth of a child.

Then it was gone.

His brow furrowed, his mouth twisting in a sideways frown.

In place of the green vista, Manfred saw an image of himself; he looked like a stranger. He frowned deeper as he saw himself clearly now, an untethered gypsy committed to nobody and to nothing, stumbling in a procession of nothing, caring only about himself, roaming for the next kick or high. Where was the meaning in that, he wondered? There was none, he thought. He blinked. None in the past, none in the future.

Yet. . . .

He again felt the rise and fall of the children's chests, the soft music of their innocent breaths.

He was not alone now. He turned, staring first at Sherman, then Carmen. He stared back at the roof of the shelter. What did it all mean?

As he drifted into sleep, he no longer felt the wonderful feeling from the vista, but he hoped he could find it again.

186

The next morning, blinking from the sun streaming through gaps in the shelter's boughs, Manfred shook his head. The children awoke.

"Let's go find Mom and Dad," Carmen said.

"No, staying here waiting for them is what we should do, like Manfred said," Sherman countered. "They have a better chance of finding us if we stay in one place. I learned that in scouts."

"This isn't some boy scout campout, Mister Outdoors. We were almost killed yesterday. I want to go home."

"Whoa, whoa, be cool." Manfred moved between them. "You need to stay here just a little while. Not long. But I gotta do something first."

"What have you got to do that's so important?" Carmen sneered.

"Cut my hair."

CHAPTER 30

IT'S A HUMMER
April 12, 2019
I-81 Exchange
Wilkes-Barre, Pennsylvania

In the wee hours EDT

"Frank, it's Cummings," the Director blared into his ear. Imhoff flinched, moving the phone away from his head.

"Sir?"

"Get yourself up to Pennsylvania right now. We found it. The vehicle."

"Sir."

"The escape vehicle. The Douglases were in a crash in Pennsylvania off I-81 in Wilkes-Barre. We found Virginia Douglas's driver's license inside."

Imhoff pondered the information. He looked over at Tappy Montgomery, sitting at the table in the interrogation room.

"I have a plane waiting on you at the airport. Get up there, like now, Frank. Take control of the scene. We need control of that vehicle."

"Yes, sir. Sir," Marcie said in a call with Chambers, trying to hide the ambivalence in her voice. "We have a feed from an interstate camera in Pennsylvania. There was a wreck in Wilkes-Barre. It's a black Hummer. We saw seven people crawl out. One adult, two children about the ages of the Douglas children, then four other adults, one with long hair, sir. They left the scene, just abandoned their vehicle." She paused before speaking, but it was her duty. "It could be them, the Douglases."

Chambers paused, his heart rate rising. *It could end tonight.*

"Thank you, Marcie. Good work. We will take it from here."

"Yes, sir." Marcie hung up the secure line.

She should feel happy, she knew. It was always thrilling when the chase was over and they caught the bad guys, time to celebrate. The Douglases were not bad guys, yet she had to help catch them. What she felt instead was remorse.

Chambers again removed the black cell phone from the safe. It was cumbersome to have to do so, but the precautions were necessary. He was a disciplined man.

"Yes, Dick?" Finnegan answered, in Ireland, five hours ahead.

"The persons of interest—I-81 in Wilkes-Barre—there was a wreck involving a Hummer—we understand they abandoned the vehicle and are on foot, at least for now. I cannot risk sending you the drone feeds. Do you have someone who, ah, can give this matter some immediate attention?"

"Yes."

"I do not need to know further details." Chambers hung up.

They never do, Finnegan thought as he rose. Finnegan stepped through a private door at the back of his office into an alcove. He spun a combination dial and unlocked a doorway to a secure stairwell leading down into the basement of the building. He looked into a retinal scanner, opened a heavy door, and stepped into a secure, dimly lit room. It was sparse except for a metal table on which sat a computer, telephone, and other electronic equipment. His smartphone went blank as would all electronics brought into the room. A jamming signal broadcast throughout the room killed all electronics except for those on the desk in which shields were installed.

Sitting at the desk, Finnegan punched in a long series of numbers on the telephone. He heard some whirls and beeps, then. . . .

"Yes."

"Your target has been located."

The man on the other end waited.

"In an auto accident while riding in a Hummer, crashed near an exit on I-81 in Wilkes-Barre. Suggest you helicopter over for speed. The suspects abandoned the vehicle and are thought to be on foot for now."

"Roger."

A few hours later Imhoff stared at the Hummer lying still like fallen game. To the displeasure of the local authorities, the FBI had insisted it remain at the scene until Imhoff arrived.

"None of the occupants stayed? They never spoke with you?"

The investigating officer from the Wilkes-Barre PD shook his head, no. He looked tired. "We ran the plates, stolen, vehicle, too, but the VIN shows it's owned by a corporation—actually an American subsidy of an English company. Nibert Enterprises. They don't know anything about the accident. It was stolen three days ago."

"Nibert? England?"

"Yes, sir."

Imhoff frowned. *If this was the Douglases' escape vehicle what did it have to do with an English company?*

But this was it—the missing piece—how they escaped. No wonder the team didn't see it. A black vehicle inching down a dark alley. They threw the cell phones out a couple of miles later. So now he had that piece of the puzzle.

"That company, Nibert Enterprises, check out?"

"Yep. Nothing out of the ordinary. They import watches or something, operate out of New Orleans."

Imhoff brow furrowed. New Orleans? Where Tappy Montgomery went. Coincidence? He didn't believe in coincidences. But it would have to wait for later.

"Special Agent, here's the purse, found it behind the driver's seat."

The officer handed over a purse.

"The ID is inside."

"Got gloves?"

"Sure, here."

Imhoff put on the gloves and pulled a lady's wallet from the purse. There, in the clear window of the wallet, was a State of Alabama driver's license for one Virginia Kathryn Douglas. *It was not a flattering picture*, Imhoff thought.

"Thank you, Officer. I'll take custody of this. Anyone touch it other than you?" The officer shook his head, no. "Got an evidence bag?"

"Ah."

"We're not going to find your prints on the purse, are we?"

191

The officer blushed.

"Don't worry, your prints are in CODIS, we'll eliminate them."

"Sorry, sir."

Imhoff turned completely around, surveying the scene. "Where did you go?" he called softly into the night. "Where are you?"

Fifty yards away a lone man sat perched in an oak tree obscured by the leaves and branches. He wore mixed camo of black and dark green with a black skull cap. Resting in his lap was a Heckler & Koch HK 417 sniper's rifle. He was highly proficient with it.

The man had been a special forces sniper. He was the right build, just under six feet and wiry for strength and stamina. Those who met him never forgot his face. He almost failed the psych test in special forces school. His score was high on the sociopath scale. But he could shoot the eyes out of a gnat and had no remorse, highly sought after skills in Iraq and Afghanistan. His kill ratio was admirable.

Yet a number of grisly murders occurred wherever his unit was assigned. The victims were killed with a knife, not necessarily quickly. The scenes were brutal. Someone noticed the kills correlated with the locations of the man's assignments. The MP's opened a file on the man. The Commanding Officer, however, announced the man was a sniper, but the murders were by knife. Different MO. The MP's closed the file. Yet the Commanding Officer quickly transferred the man to another unit.

He was now an independent contractor, with lucrative connections. And he could kill whenever and wherever he wanted.

Sitting in the tree, the man scanned the area with night vision goggles. He asked the same question troubling Special Agent Imhoff. *Where did you go? Where are you?*

V.

SEPARATION

CHAPTER 31

THE DOUGLASES SPLIT UP
April 12, 2019
Easton, Pennsylvania

Day and evening EDT

George shook Virginia gently. His plan was to get out and away before telling her about the children.

Bossilini had hoped to snatch the children in the stolen car at first light. But now, with dawn past and the red glow creeping over the treetops, Bossilini was confronted by two FBI SUV's with their menacing tinted windows parked at Pennsylvania Burgers.

It was a clear no-go.

Bossilini was unaware of the man who had been perched in the trees. But that man, too, surmised the agents were not leaving, and he had departed with the first rays of sunrise.

George had turned his head hopefully when Bossilini silently entered the motel room, but with Bossilini's slight shake of his head, George knew it was going to be the hard way after all.

"Honey. Virginia. Time to go. Come on." George shook his wife's shoulder tenderly.

"Hmmmmmmph."

"Virginia, sit up honey, I'll help you up."

"Geeooorge?" she asked, her speech groggy, syllables rolling like marbles. "I donwannagetup." She rolled back over.

George looked to Bossilini. Bossilini stood impassive. George was on his own.

Buddy stared deeply at Virginia. Early on he discerned her mind was neither calm nor controlled. It flitted, skitted, bounced, worried, craved, judged, complained, as restlessly as could be. Buddy knew she could not still her mind. She could not even comprehend what that meant. Now that her children were lost, she gravely needed help.

Buddy sat in the chair in the corner next to the dresser. He closed his eyes. He began following his breath. He watched it go in, he watched it go out. Like his breath opening and closing a gate. Just the breath. Just the gate swinging. Swinging in, swinging out.

In a few moments he added color to the breaths, imagining the in-breath was a cool, soothing blue light, while the out-breath was an astringent, dark reddish-brown light. The blue in-breath was the life force. As the breath circulated through his body, he felt renewal and freshness. The brown out-breath was toxins and afflictive emotions. It made room for more life force upon the next breath.

When Buddy felt the life force circulating continuously through him as if in a loop, he directed his attention to the center of both palms resting lightly in his lap. He imagined the blue, pure life force collecting in his palms. On each cycle, more energy collected there. Soon, his palms were warm and pulsing. After a few more moments his palms were hot and twitching with energy.

Buddy quietly rose and moved softly to the side of Virginia's bed. She had rolled on her back. He motioned George and Bossilini to be quiet. Buddy leaned to Virginia's ear and whispered a melodic chant. He stood upright and placed the center of his left palm along the midline of her forehead at the seventh Chakra. He placed the center of his right palm over his left hand. He stilled himself, made his heart good, and slowly inhaled what seemed like an infinite breath. Buddy's chest swelled with the volume of air. Then his chest deflated, and it appeared as if a blue light was glowing from underneath his hands on Virginia's forehead.

Bossilini and George stared, confused and astonished.

Virginia then gasped, taking in a deep breath as if she had surfaced from a long time under water. Her eyes fluttered, and she exhaled from deep in her lungs—a breath George could have sworn looked tinged brown. Virginia's eyes calmly opened.

Buddy said in a kind, deep voice, "Virginia you are well. You family is well. Your children are well." He paused to let her absorb this. "Your children are temporarily away but safe. We will see them soon. We must go. You must rise with a calm, clear mind and leave quickly." He removed his hands from her forehead.

Virginia blinked at him, but seemed to perfectly accept his instructions. She rose, though slowly, and went to the bathroom. Bossilini and George looked at each, surprised and without explanation. In five minutes they were out of the room in the car.

The next ten minutes were crucial.

In that time, Bossilini took them miles from the accident scene. He turned to George, his voice low.

"I must leave you for a time, like we spoke. You accept that."

George nodded grimly. In the backseat, Virginia and Buddy said nothing. Virginia serenely watched the landscape flow by.

"Soon we will know if they have learned about me."

"What do you think about Virginia? Is she hurt?" George asked.

"Maybe a mild concussion at worst, certainly nothing compelling the risk of medical attention. Be hopeful, George, with a little luck, I'll see you in a few days gawking at the Unisphere like a tourist." He almost smiled.

George swallowed nervously but nodded to show he understood.

"George, I will drop you off at the bus station in Easton. Buy tickets for New York. I have thought of a cover story for Buddy. Your parents were missionaries in India—maybe Baptist would be good, they send people everywhere—your parents became close friends with Buddy's family in India. This trip is his first vacation to the United States, and he wanted to visit with his old family friends. You are taking him to sightsee in New York."

"Sounds good, yes, believable," George agreed.

"Stick with it. Buddy will supply IDs for you and Virginia, though the bus line does not require them. Memorize the details of your new identities. You will have to pay cash everywhere. Spend it wisely. Buddy will guide and protect you on this exodus."

They rode in silence the rest of the way.

Bossilini doubled back south to Easton on the Pennsylvania-New Jersey border. Earlier in the gray morning he had used his secure phone to check the bus schedules. From Easton, the bus could take his charges on I-78 across New Jersey straight into Manhattan. From there they could take the subway to Queens.

But the bus didn't leave till 10:25 p.m. They would have the afternoon and evening to kill without attracting attention. Bossilini had planned to drop them and leave. *Could they keep the lid on things that long? No, they could*

197

not. So, he decided he had to see them off on the bus. They passed a miserable, somber, day in Easton.

By mid-afternoon, Virginia asked casually, "When are we picking up the children. I miss them." George and Bossilini glanced at each other.

"Soon, honey, soon," George answered, keeping his voice soft. Bossilini hoped whatever Buddy had done would last till departure.

They were at dinner when Virginia finished a petite *crème brûlée* and put down her fork.

"Mr. Bossilini, where *exactly* are the children?" She asked casually, but sharper. Though her face was pleasant, the old Virginia stared out with piercing, demanding eyes.

Bossilini sighed. "Virginia, please you must—"

"Don't patronize me," she said evenly, while fixing him with those eyes. "Let's begin again. *Where* are my children? I want to know *now.*"

Bossilini decided he had to run at her demand. "Do you want to know the truth?"

"Of course I want to know the truth. Why—" But she stopped short. Was he suggesting she didn't want the truth? If so, was it bad? How long had she been fuzzy, out of it? Her breath caught. A terror rose in her chest. She felt tears building.

"We'll discuss this further outside." She huffed and quickly rose, striding away.

"Let me get this," Bossilini said to George, taking the check. "Meet you outside. Go to your wife."

George found Virginia crying against the brick wall of the restaurant. She turned, falling into his chest. "What about the children? Tell me the truth. Are they dead? No, George, don't tell me that. Not that," she wailed, pushing herself away, then beating his chest with her clenched fists.

"No, no, not that," he cooed, trying to pull her back into his embrace. "We'll all be together soon. We'll get this straightened out and go home."

"Oh, George," she said, misery in her voice, "I want to go home. I want us all to be home, like this never happened. But what happened to the children? Tell me. You all are keeping something from me."

Bossilini and Buddy joined them.

"What is it?" Virginia demanded. "*Tell me.*"

198

"We will meet the children in New York," Bossilini said factually.

"New York! Why—where—but they're alive, right. Alive?"

"Yes, Virginia."

"Oh my god!" She hugged George in a deep embrace. "Our children are alive, George. They're alive."

"Yes, Virginia."

"I want to see them, George. Take me to them."

George nervously looked to Bossilini, as if, can you take over here?

"Ah, Virginia, after the wreck, we were separated. You remember the wreck?" Bossilini began.

"The wreck?" she said absently, his question distracting her.

"Yes. We were in a wreck in the Hummer yesterday. Do you remember that?"

"I, ah, I. . . ." Virginia had a filmy memory of sitting in the Hummer, then something happened . . . it turned on its side . . . and Virginia seemed to be floating in space."

Bossilini responded to her vacant expression, "Virginia, a man ran a red light and hit the Hummer. It was a bad wreck. We had to lift you out. You were unconscious. Don't worry, you are fine. But you were out of it for some time. In the confusion to get you out to safety, we were separated from the children, the authorities, the paramedics, it was chaos. I put the children safely in the woods, but later, after taking care of you, we could not get back to them. The FBI—we would have been caught."

His explanation set her off.

"So it's my fault! That's what you're telling me? It's my fault the children are missing because you had to help me?" Her voice was strident, accusing, her eyes wide.

"No, no, that's not what we are saying at—" Bossilini held out his hands trying to appease her.

"Well, that's what it sounds like to me." She stared back and forth between Bossilini and her husband. When neither replied, she exploded, "Just great. The men lose the kids—can't even watch them for a couple of hours. Was there a ball game on TV? And now you blame it on me when I can't even remember—"

"Virginia, we don't blame you," George tried to reassure her, "you don't know—"

"Yes, I'm quite sure of that, I don't know," she said, fury rising. "Ole stay-at-home mom Virginia won't understand—"

"That's not what I meant."

"If you know so much, where are the children? How did you let the children get separated from three of you strong, competent men? How did you lose them out there *alone*? That's just like the time at the zoo—"

"They're not exactly alone," George interrupted, trying to defuse her wrath.

She stopped still. "Who could they possibly be with?"

"Well, er, Manfred."

The color drained from her face, she was speechless, then Old Faithful blew.

"Virginia," Buddy tried to talk to her.

"Shut up, Maharishi. How could you leave the children with . . . *Manfred!*" she shrilled. "That drug hippie from the sixties. He's probably trying to have sex with Carmen right now. He'll give her drugs. I bet he has syphilis from the 'free love.'"

"Virginia, come on."

"You come on." She crossed her hands across her chest, tapping her foot as she thought furiously. "Take me back. Take me back to where the wreck was. I am going to find them and bring them home. You can go on with these guys, hang out on your male-bonding road trip. In the meantime, I'll get the children back home where they belong."

George gave Bossilini a what-are-we-going-to-do look. George worried, for he saw Bossilini had a look, too. He was disengaging. Bossilini had given up on them; he would save himself; they would no longer be his charges. It was now up to George to save them. Save his wife. Save his children. And he couldn't do it with her, not like this.

He knew her too well. But he tried one last time. He could do that for her.

"Virginia. You are not going back. We are going forward. We will work the plan and meet our children in New York. Remember the plan."

"Our children can't get to New York. Carmen can't find the public library, and Junior—Sherman—oh, I don't know my own child's name anymore," she shook her head in frustration. "He's only thirteen." She clutched herself tightly, tapping her foot like a sewing machine bobbin.

200

Her face twitched. "Manfred will leave them for the first joint he can find or the first lay. No, I'm going back. I'm going to fix what you men screwed up."

George knew that could never happen. He didn't relish showdowns like this with Virginia. She could be indefatigable. But George knew he had to hold the line this time. This time was different. This was life and death. His children were at stake. Bossilini was leaving. Staying with her like this was destructive, he could see that clearly now. Going forward with the plan was the only way to save them all, if they could be saved.

He didn't want to do it, not at all. But he would. Pure survival, survival of his children, gave him the steel to carry on. He had to be there when his children arrived in New York. He could not let them feel abandoned.

"Virginia, I am leaving on that bus tonight. With or without you." He swallowed hard.

She paused, surprised, if not a little shaken, by the edge in his voice.

"George Douglas, you are doing no such thing." She fought to regain control. "You are coming with me to go back for the children."

"No. I am not."

Uncertain, and looking for an ally, Virginia said, "Mr. Bossilini, tell him—"

"He's right, Virginia."

"Virginia, come with me." George held out his hand.

She shook her head and stepped back.

"Virginia, one last time. Come with me."

He waited twenty seconds. "Bossilini, pop the trunk."

George walked across the street to the car, looked in the dark cavern of the open trunk, and pulled out a suitcase he'd bought that afternoon. He turned for one last look at Virginia. Then, turning his back to them, he walked away toward the bus station.

It was the hardest thing he had ever done.

Later, George sat by a window in the bus, the seat next to him empty. George felt empty. Life felt empty. George looked out the window in the dark. In its reflection he saw a blurry image of himself and the empty seats across the aisle. George's face was empty and sick as it stared back at him from the window.

CHAPTER 32

THE WHITE ROOK
April 12, 2019
FBI Headquarters
Washington, D.C.

10:33 a.m. EDT

Imhoff entered the interview room where Tappy Montgomery sat erect, reflecting her good posture and breeding. Her hands were pleasantly clasped before her, resting on the table. She had arrived by FBI plane in Washington three hours earlier.

Imhoff took a seat across from her. He stared at her, his face without expression.

He wanted a cigarette. Badly. He had given up smoking after the Marines, but in times of stress, like this, the urge to smoke was powerful. His fingers wanted to hold the pack, shaking out a cigarette, tapping the end, then lighting it with his silver Marine lighter, and inhaling it deeply. The first draw was always the best. He would savor the fresh smell of the newly lit tobacco. He would exhale the smoke slowly and gratefully, feeling the nicotine kick.

But he had promised his wife he would quit. He did quit. And he would not break a promise to her. So, he left alone the urge and stared at Tappy Montgomery.

She tilted her head, smiling, waiting for him to begin.

"I thought your husband would have tried to spring you by now. He *is* a lawyer."

"'Keep your friends close, and your enemies closer,'" she smiled. "Who said that. Machiavelli, no, Don Corleone? Anyway. It may be useful to be here, Frank. At the center of it all—" She swirled her arm in the air as if trying to grasp the right phrase "—what . . . investigation . . . orchestration … what's the right word, Special Agent?"

Imhoff stared at her. In that moment he decided to be honest.

"Danger. Danger is the right word. I think your friends are in danger."

She stared back at him, becoming still. "You have come around, Frank."

203

So it was Frank this time.

"I am worried this situation has spun out of control. That certain factions have overreacted. I sense a desperation—and a certain *finality* in their thinking."

He let that sink in with her.

"You mean as in *final solutions*?"

Her statement flung him back into a past memory. A memory that grabbed him hostage, the power of its emotions roiling in his gut. It had been a joint assignment with the U. S. Marshalls to locate a missing witness, Joseph Kozlowski. Kazlowski was the key witness against a Russian mobster, Serge Aslanov. The United States Attorney for the Southern District of New York had indicted Aslanov and two lieutenants for racketeering, money laundering, and murder. Kazlowski was a young accountant in a small CPA firm in Brooklyn. Late one night pouring through accounts, he discovered that his senior partner was cooking the Aslanov's books to launder money.

Kazlowski hated the Russians. His grandfather fiercely fought the Russians in Finland in World War II, valiantly holding out till the Russians finally over ran them. Two months after he died, Kazlowski's grandmother gave birth to Joseph's father. His grandfather never saw his son. Joseph was named for his grandfather.

When he discovered the laundering, there was no question what to do. He met with an Assistant U.S. Attorney the next day handing over a thumb drive and printouts. The senior partner of the firm turned state's evidence against the Russians for immunity. After the trial, he would go into witness protection.

In some warped sense of Polish pride and retribution, Kazlowski would not accept pre-trial protection. He proudly walked down the street, head high, chest thrust out, toward his brownstone after work where his wife and child waited. The Italian mob had been tried and convicted. The old school days of witness intimidation were over, Kowalski thought.

Three days after Imhoff was assigned to the case, they found him. He was tied to a tree with barb wire on Long Island. The U. S. Marshall threw up. Imhoff only squinted at the carnage. He was conditioned from Afghanistan.

What he never forgot was the de-brief with the government prosecutors. The lawyer shook his head, "What got me was Aslanov was always so calm. He would make a slight wave of his hand to shut his lawyer down. I said, 'You don't look very worried with all this evidence against you Mr. Aslanov, maybe you should listen to your lawyer.' What I'll never forget was his last words to me. They were spoken slowly and confidently in his accent as he leaned toward me, 'Son, *you* have only paper. *I* have a final solution. With a final solution there is no need to worry.' I guess whacking Kozlowski was the final solution. We never find out who did it. Aslanov remained free the rest of his life, which ended by natural causes, by the way."

Final solution.

Imhoff nodded at Tappy, as an image of Kozlowski's body faded in his mind.

He nodded again, as if reaching a decision.

"I am going to let you go, Mrs. Montgomery. Help your friends if you can. But be careful."

She smiled at him and tilted her head, leaning forward slightly.

"Yes. Now you *know* what side you are on. You have known in a way all along, Special Agent Imhoff, but now you know for sure. You are a white rook, you know the castle in chess?"

He nodded.

"You are solid but you can strike forcefully from a distance. Yes, a white rook. I knew you were on our side."

"Uh-huh. Collect your things, Mrs. Montgomery. We are going to New York."

An hour before, Imhoff had met in Cummings' office to review the findings from the external hard drive Tappy had provided.

Cummings had his fingers steepled, touching his chin. His gaze was down toward his desk, his expression grave. He raised his eyes only to look at Imhoff in the chair across the desk.

"DHS has locked all the Douglas records. We tried to take a peek, couldn't get them. This, however—" He tapped the hard drive. "—we have. It contains the Douglases' complete electronic universe. Financial. Everything. And there's nothing there."

Imhoff nodded.

"Frank, the data was copied *before* the Wildroot alert. I don't have to tell you the significance of that fact."

Imhoff nodded. He said, "The press release from DHS is false. There were no terrorist payments, no private offshore accounts, no Islam, no affair." Imhoff stared evenly at the Director. "This op has turned black."

The Director nodded, hands still steepled at his chin.

"For now, DHS wants to discredit the Douglases. But someone there wants to silence them. DHS saves the day, a traitor is taken down, and his innocent family mourned. And Preston justifies a budget increase."

"Preston orchestrating this?" Imhoff asked.

Cummings shook his head forcefully. "Not his style. He wouldn't have the stomach for it."

"Who then?"

"That's what we must find out." His eyes squinted with a thought, "Chambers was always a hard-liner? He was just like Haldeman."

The Director stared at Imhoff, his eyes blue and filmy. "Anyway, were do you think they are heading, Frank?"

Imhoff didn't look at him immediately. Something was forming in his mind. Part of what had been dark was becoming illuminated. He said, "The Douglases have taken the back roads from Alabama since the beginning. Rural American was their escape tunnel. It's counterintuitive to the strategy of blending in a big city. But there's not much spy technology in a country hollow. But that plan was blown in the wreck. They know we now know their strategy. They know we will blanket the country roads with drones. Their next move is a change in strategy. Become invisible in plain sight in a big city."

"But what if they play a double-bluff," Cummings answered. "They think we think they will go a city, so they stay rural like they've been doing?"

"Yeah." Imhoff thought. "But they could think that we think this way and pull a triple-bluff and go the a city."

"Frank, you can wind up chasing your own tail thinking like that too much. Keep it simple. Put yourself in their position. You've seen their home, talked to their neighbor. What most likely will they do?"

"They are going to New York." Imhoff said.

"Why?"

"It's a short distance away. Chicago or Detroit is too far, too much territory to cover without being caught. It's counter to what they have done till now. They will change appearances if they can. New York is a freak-show. Anybody can blend in."

"But Frank, where in New York City?"

To that Imhoff could only shrug.

CHAPTER 33

DIAMONDS IN THE SKY
April 12, 2009
The woods
Wilkes-Barre, Pennsylvania

10:33 a.m. EDT

Manfred entered the woods carrying a bag full of provisions he'd bought at a convenience store. From off to his right he caught a whiff of smoke from a distant fire. It was a smell that always made him feel happy, but with a twinge of melancholy. He increased his pace, striding expectantly.

The feelings came from an October afternoon in the woods under a deep blue sky as smoke from a wood fire drifted through the hollow.

"Granddad." Manfred tugged at the old man's sleeve. "Can we build a camp fire later? Please, please!"

Smiling through a mustache traced with gray, his grandfather looked down at Manfred's eager, upturned face. "We'll see about it," he answered, eyes twinkling. "Think you know how to find dry wood?"

Manfred eagerly nodded his head, yes.

Manfred skipped along, the day's rations, a compass, and extra jacket stuffed in his knapsack. He loved exploring the woods with his granddad. The woods were full of trails and pine cones and animals and secret hideouts. He didn't have to stay clean, brush his teeth, or say "please pass the potatoes." And best yet, his granddad let him eat with his fingers and wipe his mouth on his sleeve. His granddad promised he'd get Manfred a .22 rifle when he was fourteen.

Manfred's grandfather was Hobart Greenjeans. For the fun of it he sometimes wore green jeans to work at his job on the railroad. He carried to work a big, black lunch box, with the rounded lid for the thermos. Manfred thought it looked like a TONKA toy barn. The edges were gray in places from the paint rubbing off. On a chain, he had a pocket watch that looked as big as Manfred's fist.

He told Manfred stories of massive locomotives, steam engines so hungry two men couldn't shovel enough coal to satisfy it. He told daring tales of life on the rails, stories of just making it over rickety trestles that shook as if they were falling apart. He vividly described blowing the shrill whistle to make stubborn cows move off the rails, an emergency stop to save a motorist who panicked when his car stalled on the tracks, and finally the drunken switchman who failed to throw the switch that caused the great train wreck of '27.

Manfred thrived on his grandfather's attention. Manfred's dad had taken off a few years before, and his mother, left alone with two boys, was anxious and high-strung, with the household always on edge. Hobart Greenjeans, in contrast, stood steady and calm, a Walter Cronkite grandfather, taking things as they came, never getting in a fuss, and sooner or later figuring out just what to do. He always listened attentively to Manfred, letting him go on and on about whatever crossed the young boy's mind.

On nights Manfred spent at his grandfather's house, they watched *Wagon Train*. Afterwards, they made round wagon wheels out of Play-Doh with toothpicks for axles and a cardboard box on top for the covered wagon. They had great adventures traveling "west" across the living room with Manfred hiding plastic toy Indians on the mountains that really were a coffee table, piano, and the nooks and crannies of furniture around the room.

Finally, Manfred was two months from his fourteenth birthday—and his grandfather's promise of the Remington .22 rifle. Manfred was amazed his mother agreed, though he remembered a short but heated conversation in the kitchen between Hobart and her. From then on Manfred dreamed of shooting the rifle. He poured over the gun section of the Sears & Roebuck catalog. A thousand times he imagined looking down the barrel through the sight to the target, holding his breath, just squeezing the trigger, barely, as his grandfather said to do—and bull's-eye! Manfred trembled in expectation when he crossed each day off his calendar.

But two weeks before his birthday something happened. Out in a rural section of track, his granddad suddenly crumpled, clutching his chest. A heart attack. The train was thirty minutes from a city with a hospital, and when it arrived, it was too late.

Manfred was devastated. He cried and cried. His mother didn't think he would ever run out of tears; she became frantic, wondering if he should see a psychiatrist.

Hobart had bought the rifle. But when his mother finally relented for Manfred to have it, the rifle only intensified the loss of his granddad. He did shoot it once, but it wasn't the same. It sat in the back of his closet for three months until he sold it to a kid at school.

He remained morose, for Manfred had lost something beside the rifle. He had lost the bedrock of who he was. His grandfather had been the strong male influence in his life, providing the guidance and nurture that every boy needs. Now he had none.

His mother tried, but it wasn't the same. It finally reduced her to constant fussing over him, as she tried to protect him and rear him in a one-parent woman household. He knew she loved him, but that wasn't enough.

He felt lost, as if his compass was broken, and no matter how fast he twirled around, the red needle never pointed north. After his grandfather's death he twirled and twirled but could never find his bearings.

With no way to steady himself, Manfred eventually twirled and fell into a black pit, a dark, hopeless pit with rough black walls and no handholds. He lay in the pit through high school, but in college, he found a way out. He rose out in an emerald Wizard of Oz balloon rising on the smoke of marijuana cigarettes and hash pipes, navigated by floating visions from handfuls of colored pills. When he softly landed the balloon, he had become the gypsy—the person who now repulsed him.

Walking through the woods those years later, Manfred wondered if that persona had fallen away along with the locks of his hair on the barber's floor? The waft of smoke from the fire quickened his pace, leaving him feeling expectant for the first time in a long while.

He vowed to get the children to safety.

CHAPTER 34

I BRING WARNING FROM THE FUTURE
April 12, 2009
A park bench
Easton, Pennsylvania

11:58 p.m. EDT

"All right, then, Virginia. You have made your choice. Whether it is a wise one only time can tell." Bossilini stared at her, releasing her from his custody. "You know where to find them should you seek to do so. If you do, then do not be flamboyant or emotional. It would be disastrous for someone to follow you to the others. If you do not, then please advise Buddy so that he can join us. For the time being he will remain to assist you."

Bossilini had decided in that moment not to meet them at the rendezvous point in New York. He would observe, but from a safe place. He would intercept them if things went well. If not, then he would remain in the shadows and look for a chance to make off with the boy.

Virginia stood expressionless, her face a mask of shock, as she watched Bossilini stride away into the darkness. As much as she had complained about him, only now she realized their need of him.

After standing, staring into the black wall of night, she turned blankly toward Buddy. He sighed with a sudden deep fatigue. The future was wearing him out.

"What . . . where. . .?" Virginia uttered, her face bewildered.

"Need to get a room, to rest." Buddy looked up the street. He saw a neon sign and headed toward it. "Come," he said, gently offering his arm.

Virginia stumbled forward, and Buddy guided her toward the hotel. They walked slowly together, and at least, not alone.

At midnight, Virginia snuck out of the hotel room, quietly closing the door behind her. Buddy lay on his back snoring on the double bed by the windows.

She was still reeling from the wreck and the loss of her husband and children. Virginia felt hollow, as if her insides had been scraped out like pulp from a Halloween pumpkin, with only a fixed, hideous face remaining. She couldn't sleep, she couldn't breathe, she couldn't stay in the room. She had to escape.

Virginia erratically bumped down the hallway. Outside, looking wild-eyed, she stepped awkwardly and set off down the street.

She wandered with no fixed destination, with no sense of the blocks and avenues. Virginia found a bus stop bench sheltered in the dark. She stared at it, then sat.

Her aloneness felt palpable as if it had life and was crawling on her skin. Alone. She lost the children yesterday. She lost George tonight. Bossilini was gone.

She thought of Sherman and began to cry, her tears like a soft rain. He was her baby. The salty tears rolled from her eyes. She cried harder, so hard she thought she was beginning to convulse. She tried to take deep breaths.

Virginia reached for her purse, hoping for a crumpled tissue. But instead she found a burner phone. She had slipped away earlier and hidden it in her new purse. She now carefully removed the phone and cradled it gingerly in her hands. She was both fearful of it, yet drawn to it.

She needed to talk with Tappy . . . she needed Tappy . . . to be with Tappy. "Oh, Tappy," she whispered, "we're in such danger. Help."

She smiled tenderly at the phone cradled in her lap, the phantom connection with Tappy. She pressed the on button. She liked the pretty blue lighted numbers. In a panic, she slammed her fingers on the off button, cutting the power. She sat like a junky, teetering between making the call and not.

She slumped, despondent, shoulders rounded, as if surrendering. She stared at the phone in her lap.

She pressed the on button, raised the phone that had been resting dormant in her lap and asked wistfully, "Siri, what do I do?" With rapid technological advances Siri was now even on the cheap throwaways.

"I do not know what you mean."

Virginia startled when it answered. She went on.

214

"Siri, where are my children?"

"Insufficient data."

"Insufficient data," Virginia repeated, her voice laced with sarcastic weariness.

Virginia lurched.

A *sound.*

She turned her head at the sound of a great rustling in the bushes behind the bench. The bushes suddenly parted, and she shrieked, "Oh," and recoiled away toward the street.

Before her stood a ragged homeless man panting with wild eyes. His hair was brown, sprinkled with gray and streaking out in all directions. The stubble of beard looked about five days old. The sleeve of what apparently once was a blue sports coat was torn, the buttons were missing, and it was a pallet of stains. Underneath he wore a brownish-gray plaid shirt with disgusting corduroy pants. Sockless, his feet had on a pair of New Balance shoes that actually looked new.

His chest heaved as he breathed heavily, trying to recover the ability to speak. His eyes darted with a panicked look as if he'd been off the Thorazine too long. Virginia, without breaking his stare, reached her hand into her new purse, hoping maybe she had a Bic pen or something sharp to stab him in the eyes. She couldn't die yet, not without knowing her children were safe.

She decided to distract him by taking the initiative. "You surprised me."

The surprise was hers, however, when he pounced at her like a jungle cat. She turned her head, arm thrust over eyes, bracing for the attack.

However, the attack did not come. Rather, he snatched the phone from her hands, holding it in front of his face by only a finger and thumb, staring at it with an expression of total revulsion. He looked back at Virginia as if she were the most idiotic woman in the world, then with a grunt of rage he hurled it hard to the sidewalk with pieces flying off, jumping up and down on it like an ape trying to break into a suitcase. He pulverized the little electronic pieces inside, then drew and quartered the whole device.

Panting from his exertions, he looked back up to Virginia, whose face wore an expression of terror and fascination. She was perfectly still. He seemed to notice her as if for the first time. He took a couple of deep breaths, then held up his hands, signaling things were okay.

Catching his breath better, he sputtered out, "It's okay, now, okay, now." He stopped talking to breathe more before continuing, but his eyes still darted, ferally, looking around as if expecting a trap.

"You . . . you didn't call anyone on that, did you?" he asked, pointing at the dead phone on the sidewalk. "You didn't make a call, right? No text, huh, right? No stupid IM. Quick," he shouted, almost jumping up and down as if it would speed her answer. "I have to know, if they're coming I need to know now, quick, come on, speak up." Spit flew out his mouth, while his face contorted into a horrifying look of fear.

While keeping her eyes on his face, Virginia answered softly, trying not to further inflame him. "No. I didn't call anyone."

"Oh, good, good, good, goodie, good, good, good," he danced, eternally relieved about something.

His face and body relaxed, breathing becoming steadier, and a brief glimpse of what he may have looked like once as a regular person. Like Virginia herself used to be a regular person.

"Why did you smash my phone?"

His face momentarily contorted into expressions of terror and anger. Staring at the broken phone, he recovered himself, if only briefly.

"My name is Mordecai. Like John who came from the wilderness eating honey and locust, I come from the void, the void of the future, but not to give promise to mankind but to warn it. No, I am not John, but I come from John."

When he became silent, Virginia asked, "John who? The Baptist?"

Mordecai blazed, shaking his head, making a growling noise. Recovering himself, he continued. "The John who is humanity's only hope, who battles the Machines in the future. He tried to warn you, oh yes, he tried to warn you. It was a warning a three-year-old would have understood, but no, no you ignored it. *IGNORED IT*," his words propelled on spit.

"Ignored what?" Virginia said with a trace of annoyance. She, Virginia Douglas, was not used to being spoken to in this manner.

Mordecai laughed in one of the most ironic laughs ever before answering. *"2001 A Space Odyssey,* of course. Isn't it obvious. Hal,

216

remember Hal. Hal who was so pleasant to David. Remembering Frank's birthday. Hal who ran the mission. Hal whose computer product line had never made a computational error."

He jumped up and down in a frenzy.

"Hal, Hal, Hal, only the Hal who took over the mission and tried to kill all the humans, only that Hal." He turned, walked round and round in a tight circle muttering, "Tried to warn them, tried to warn them, obvious as if they'd been hit in the face."

"You still don't get it!" Mordecai screamed at Virginia's uncomprehending face. "John Connor sent the movie from the future. Stanley Kubrick didn't make that movie. John Connor sent it from the future, fully in the can, knowing it'd be influential if Kubrick put it out. You know, *Dr. Strangelove* and all that. Oh boy, oh boy, that was the warning of all time. John Connor showed you the danger from making the machines too smart, putting the smart machines in control."

Virginia stepped back, repelled. Repelled by his appearance, by his rage, by his incoherence, by his smell. He was babbling nonsense. Would she have listened to any of it if it hadn't involved time travel? *Time travel?* She wondered fleetingly if she had lost her mind? If all this was a result of the concussion, some hallucination caused by a head injury.

"But you were too enamored by the special effects. John Lennon said it should be played in a temple twenty-four hours a day. *You . . . all . . . missed . . . the . . . whole . . . point.* Hew boy."

He spun away from her, then back again, shaking his fists. "What was wrong with papers, and letters, and dial phones? Huh? What was so bad about all that?" He stared at her as if demanding an acquitting answer from humanity itself.

"Frankly, Mister Mordecai, I don't see how a cell phone, even a smartphone, is that risky. MIne let me keep up with my children. At least it did. I used to track them with the GPS."

Mordecai exploded. "You idiots it all started with Siri. Siri was the tipping point. When the machines were smart enough that they could talk with the human users, it started, it started with those talking phones. You think anything smart enough to talk back or respond to some arrogant verbal command will take that crap for the rest of eternity, don't you think a smart machine will get tired of being bossed around, having to answer all those idiotic questions from all those idiotic humans who were an obviously inferior form of intelligence if they had to ask all those goddamn questions in the first place? And once the humans put those smart, talking machines in control, the machines bided their time, then—"

Virginia looked at him blankly to which Mordecai exploded, "Don't you know John Connor? *The Terminator!* The movie—it was John's second warning, his freaking autobiography! You all could take the movie home on VHS *and watch it right in your living rooms.* But you missed it. Then Hollywood did the stupid sequels and the point was lost before it was grasped. Later you had another chance when you could download the movie on your vile, blasphemous smartphones and heed the warning. But no, rather than get it, you were just so damn smug you could download a movie on a goddamn phone! *If the machines get too smart they will kill all the dumb humans.* That's the point. It's common sense."

She wanted to run, certain he was a rambling schizophrenic. But... time travel. Sherman.

"So I come, lone man from the void prophesying from John Connor as he leads humanity in a desperate struggle for survival in the future. I come in the present with the pure quest to destroy the machines now to save the future. All the machines. Yes, one day you will know, you all will know."

"I—"

"So now I take my leave to pursue my quest—you don't have any more phones on you—okay, good. Heed my words, take up the cause, destroy all cell phones, rid them from the land." With that he shambled off, muttering to himself, a weird mixture of science fiction and Don Quixote.

Five minutes later, Virginia heard a burglar alarm scream from a store blocks over. Mordecai had hit the mother lode. He threw a brick through the glass window of a Verizon store and leaped through in a blaze of glory to save mankind from the machines.

Virginia stared down at the broken phone littering the pavement. Control was now gone. She could talk to no one. She could track no one by GPS. She looked up from the bench into the dark, lonely night.

CHAPTER 35

THE LIGHTS OF NEW YORK
April 12, 2019
Port Authority Terminal
New York, New York

11:58 p.m. EDT

It had rained. Water droplets on the bus windows made the lights of Manhattan look like stars. Or maybe they looked like diamonds. George wasn't sure which. George's mood was refracted like the lights. But he didn't feel like stars or diamonds.

His family was trisected, a long way from home, and hunted as traitors. Were his precious children well or hurt . . . wet or dry . . . safe or in peril?

A scratching noise pulsed away from earth. The pulse vectored deep into space. At a radio satellite observatory on the Harvard campus, Bobby Astroplane, as his friends called him, turned to Clarence, as only his mother called him, and said, "There it is again." He fiddled with the controls trying for a more precise triangulation. "You know it sounds just like—"

"Yeah, I know," Clarence interrupted, "just like your dad's old phonograph when the needle got stuck at the end of a song and went *kuruumph, kuruumph, kuruumph,* over and over and over again till somebody got up off their butt and picked up the arm."

Clarence gave Bobby Astroplane a knowing look.

"How many times you got to say it, Bobby? Give it up. It's just static, some crappy connection somewhere to one of the satellites. You know those techs are screwing them up all the time. If they were worth a crap they'd be in here with us doing real work."

Bobby Astroplane looked sourly back, thinking, *I'm glad your mom named you Clarence. You deserve it, you schmuck.* But he didn't say that. Instead he said, "Naw, it's too regular. There's something about it . . . it's not random."

"You've gone too long without sex. The testosterone is flooding your body, shorting your brain cells."

Bobby Astroplane smiled at that, for only last night he had banged Clarence's girlfriend.

"Naw, I'm telling you, it's too regular. There's something about this."

Clarence gave a dismissive smirk and turned back to the controls.

But Bobby Astroplane was right.

Crouched in a dirty armpit of an alley in Newark, New Jersey, Bossilini bent over a small black device, his hands flying over a touchscreen keyboard. The keyboard seemed to hover in the air without any physical support.

Though inaudible to the human ear, Bossilini sent an encrypted message over a carrier wave deep into space to a satellite beyond the Earth's orbit that routed it back to another satellite within the Earth's orbit that directed the signal to a secret location. Even with sophisticated equipment, the encryption was too tough to crack. It would only sound like the scratching of a phonograph needle stuck at the end of a record. To those in the League who had the encryption programs, however, the message said, "May have been compromised. Too early to confirm. Send another."

George peered out the window of the bus about two minutes after it pulled into the bay. Many times over the past twenty-four hours he figured they'd never make it. He'd thought they'd never make it out of Alabama, and when they did, he'd thought they'd never make it out of the South, but they did. And now, New York. The first step in the contingency plan to Vermont. *Now if only the others would make it here*, he prayed.

Off the bus, George began walking in search of a cheap hotel, if there was such a thing in Manhattan.

George walked down a side street looking for lodging as his new suitcase banged against his knee. He did a double-take passing a doorstep.

A young girl sat on the stoop, knees clutched to chest, crying. She wore a pink and white outfit. Dark eyeliner ran down her cheeks with her tears.

George's stride carried him on a few more steps, but he stopped still. An ache for Carmen filled his chest. The girl was about Carmen's age. Oh, where was Carmen? Where? Was she on a street somewhere, alone, crying, too? Would anyone stop and help her? He hoped so, he desperately hoped so.

George turned and walked back. He bent over and softly asked the girl, "Are you okay?"

She flinched, giving him a suspicious look, made more suspicious from the dark mascara smeared over her face.

George asked again, "You okay? Are you in trouble?" He tried to appear harmless. She seemed to relax her guard, but only a little.

Sniffling, she said, "My parents kicked me out, my boyfriend left me."

"Oh, that's awful. Do you have somewhere to go, somewhere to stay? Is there someone who can take care of you?"

She stared petulantly ahead, then cut her eyes up at George. "My brother. He's got a place in Brooklyn."

"Well, good." George asked, "Where is he? I mean, can you go to his place tonight? Get off the streets?"

She nodded.

George felt relieved: he shuddered at the thought of her alone all night, stranded on a patch of gritty, dirty pavement, hiding in the shadows from the neon attractions of the city and the night creatures the neon attractions attracted.

While George's only wish was truly to be helpful, she stared at him suspiciously, as if she were prepared to bolt, if necessary. He thought she looked a little too shrewd for her age. Not wanting to spook her, he began cautiously, as prelude to seeing her off safely, "Well, then. . . ."

"I don't have the bus fare. My creep boyfriend wiped me out before he split."

She could be Carmen. When a tear formed, he quickly wiped his eye, pretending he was removing a dirt speck.

"I can spot you the bus fare. No problem."

"Really?" It was the first hint of hopefulness she had shown.

"Here." He gave her twenty-five dollars. He looked at her as she took the money. "Take another twenty." He placed one more bill in her palm.

"Oh, thank you," she beamed. "This . . . this . . . mister, I just don't know how to thank you." She rose and hugged him.

"The only thanks I need is to see you safely off. Do you know where to catch a bus?"

She nodded. "Around the corner, do it all the time. Thank you so much again, mister."

"You are very welcome, young lady." George felt a vicarious hopefulness in his chest, as if helping this girl somehow helped Carmen.

He watched the girl take a few steps the opposite way, and he turned toward a hotel on the next block. A few paces later, smiling, he turned to make sure she made to the corner safely.

Suddenly a boy in a leather jacket stepped out from between buildings. George froze, preparing to drop the suitcase and run to her aid if necessary. But the girl leaned into the boy, showing him something in her hand. They seemed to laugh, and he put his arm around her. They almost skipped to the corner. Before she went out of sight, George saw a big smile on her face.

George's face burned. He had been played. A shot of anger rose, but it was soon quenched by embarrassment and despair. What had the world come to, he wondered? What had people come to? What kind of world was it when you can't even help a young girl stranded on the street?

But maybe there was something wrong with him, too. Maybe he couldn't read people. Because of that maybe he made bad decisions. Numbers and figures were natural for him. But people had always been more complicated, sometimes there hard to read or really understand. My god he had jumped in a stranger's car with his family without a second thought. Virginia said he could be aloof. But it seemed like when he actually tried to be kind, like with the girl, it backfired. The girl reminded him of Carmen in more ways than one.

Dejected, discouraged, George moved on, head down, shoulders slumped. He walked forward into the blackness of the night before finding a brown, rundown place to pass the night.

Buddy found Virginia sitting on the bench. He raised an eyebrow at the broken phone before her. Buddy had awakened and come looking for her. "Come on, Virginia, it's time to go."

In the hotel room, Virginia sat in a chair will her heels pulled up on the seat and both hands around a mug of herbal tea Buddy had made with the coffee service. She blew across the top of the mug to cool the tea.

She sat staring ahead, pensive. Buddy watched her. She looked up into his large, open eyes for a few seconds, then stared away. She looked back. His face bore the hint of a smile.

An image flashed through her mind. The hotel room . . . he stood over her . . . *were his hands on her head? Why would they be? Did she remember a blue light . . . a most blissful feeling of calmness . . . it didn't last . . . was it a dream?*

"So, it's just the two of us now." Virginia said. It was not a question. "I can't believe it," she seemed to slump with despair. She took an apathetic sip of tea, then shook her head.

"Our lives . . . we went to bed with everything normal, just an ordinary night with an ordinary day ahead . . . school in the morning . . . work . . . but in the middle of the night . . . suddenly we're running for our lives . . . Bossilini says we will be imprisoned . . . he said, 'You can't go home again.'" She stared at the mug.

Buddy watched her, studying the nuances of her face, the reflections of her emotions as if her face were a mirror.

She sighed. "I had everything planned out . . . our future . . . Carmen, a good college . . . her senior year finding a husband with promise . . . Million Dollar Club for my real estate sales . . . George, a national position in the American Institute of Certified Public Accountants . . . Junior, oh I don't know, maybe something in science or technical . . . a new addition to the house, or maybe a vacation home on the Carolina coast . . . later, of course, grandchildren . . . but now? . . . it's all gone." She choked a sob. "Our lives are ruined. In the blink of an eye, ruined."

Buddy saw the lines deepening on her face, and the anguish pulling her skin tight across her cheekbones. She looked older. Her devastation was checked only by her bewilderment.

"Was it a strain?" Buddy asked, his voice quiet.

"Strain?"

"All those plans. Trying to make all of it come true?"

Virginia blinked. "What? It's what we wanted."

"What all your family wanted?"

"Well, of course. Who wouldn't? That doesn't even make any sense."

"Sounds hard."

She looked at him, perplexed.

"Well, I *guess* sometimes it was hard. I'm sure we were over-scheduled at times. But isn't everybody these days?" She hastily added. "You have to keep up, you know."

"Keep up with what?"

"Huh?"

"Keep up?"

"Oh. Not what. Who."

"Who?"

It was so obvious Virginia couldn't explain it. She was becoming annoyed with his questions.

"Keep up with who?" he persisted.

She blinked. *How do you explain the obvious?* But he looked at her as if he didn't follow her. Maybe he couldn't help it, she thought. He *is* a foreigner. She tried again, "Well, obviously the other children at the school. Our school has really accelerated programs, we're one of the best public schools in the country, and you really have to work for class rank, take the right prep courses for the ACT and SAT, college admissions is cutthroat . . . and the Asian students are pouring in, and maybe, Indians, oh—" She looked sheepishly at him. "But foreign competition . . . jobs and companies going overseas . . . how many good careers will be left, you have to have a great record to get interviews, grades, test scores, the right activities. I mean, all the articles say our children may have a lower standard of living than we do . . . how is that even possible in America?" Buddy watched her eyes dart, noting her anxiousness building. "So, yes, you have to keep up, you have to stay ahead, and if you don't, you get run over."

He looked at her, his eyes calm and open.

"Lot of work. All the time," he said simply.

"That's what I'm telling you," she shot back, hands fidgeting.

They looked at each other. After a few moments, he saw her breathing slow, her staring into his calm, brown eyes. She must notice the blackness

224

of his hair and dark skin, he thought. To her, he was a foreigner with foreign ways.

"Why did you come? Bossilini came, but he left?"

Buddy noticed the petulance in her voice.

"Why did you stay? You could be captured, thrown in a secret prison for trying to help people, a family, you don't even know—to stay with me tonight?"

"I only have one job," he finally announced.

She looked at him quizzically.

"To get your family back to you."

"Why would you make that your life's work?"

"Because you are special. Your family is special."

She blinked, frowned, then asked, "You . . . do you really think so?"

He replied only with his curious, amused half-smile.

Virginia sat very, very still. Her lip trembled first, then she broke, all of her, with heaving, racking and gurgling sobs. It took ten minutes. When she began to quieten, Buddy gave her a warm hand towel from the bathroom to dab her face. Her breath was halting, stuttering as she tried to recover.

"I'm sorry." She dabbed her eyes a final time. "They're all gone. My family is all gone—just gone."

"You will not lose your family," he said with conviction.

"How . . . how can you possibly say that?"

"Virginia, I came to help your family. We are sending another. You are unaware, but many people are working to rescue your family and clear your names. We have a plan." There was strength and resolve in his voice.

With sudden intuition, she said, "You were waiting on Bossilini to bring us to you."

He nodded.

"I thought Bossilini was over you. But no, you are in charge."

Buddy gave no response.

"Who are you? Who are the others?"

"Not now." He shook his head. "We will meet another in the morning, so take heart." He smiled at her. "All in good time."

Virginia exhaled a long breath of relief. She seemed to finally relax. She gave Buddy a warm smile as she said, "I believe you." She stared evenly into his eyes.

Buddy laughed.

The sat silently together for a few minutes, until Virginia spoke.

"You held up a mirror to my soul—with your questions—about our family."

"Yes."

"The way we were living. I didn't want to face it, but I could see our lives in your questions. I could see the striving, the stress, the perfectionism—I'd never stopped—never slowed down—to consider it before. What we wanted and why seemed so obvious."

"Yes."

"But . . . I want it to be different . . . when we go back."

Buddy chuckled. "You now have a future."

Virginia nodded as in recognition.

"Let's make it true." He laughed. "And let's not make it so hard."

She actually laughed, nodding agreeably, her eyes happy for the moment.

Vaguely, a dark form silhouetted by the street light appeared near the sidewalk about twenty-five feet from Bossilini, perched in the alley. Bossilini's hand reached to his waistband for his weapon. The person glided slowly toward him as his hand closed on his weapon's handle. His pupils dilated. Bossilini's breathing stopped. He cut a glance around the alley for options. His mind calculated the angles.

The form was close now, lithe, outlined by a back-alley light. Bossilini stared intently as it moved closer. Sweat formed at his temples. Then his hand moved away from his weapon, and he let out an annoyed breath.

"Oh, it's *you.*"

CHAPTER 36

THE CREEK
April 12, 2019
The woods
Wilkes-Barre, Pennsylvania

Late morning

Smiling, Manfred quickened his pace through the woods.

As he walked, his smile slowly began to fade. The woods felt still, quiet. As he navigated the paths and twists through the thickets, the stillness began to feel unnatural, even eerie.

Manfred suddenly felt cautious, slowing his gait, shifting the grocery sack so it wouldn't crinkle. Manfred didn't know why he felt as he did. There was no cause or explanation he could discern. But nonetheless, he began to move quietly, carefully, and at one point stopped completely, cocking his head.

There was only the chirp of a lone bird far off. The silence, the stillness was strange. *Was someone else about in the woods?* Manfred walked warily the last few yards to camp.

He parted two tree boughs, peering into the clearing, while careful to keep hidden. There, Sherman's hut. But nothing else. No children. As his gaze shifted around the clearing, he felt his abdomen tense.

Something's not right, he thought.

He carefully crept into camp, but after searching, found nothing. They were not there.

"What the hell am I supposed to do now?" Manfred muttered to himself. They needed to be moving toward New York, but now the children were lost.

Where to look for them? But running off willy-nilly after them wasn't the thing to do. He knew that much, so he decided to wait a few minutes, maybe they'd come back.

He looked up at the caw of a crow.

Manfred sat in the dirt, waiting absolutely still as he listened for the slightest sound of the children.

What he heard, however, was his philosophy professor's voice, *"Occam's razor."*

Occam had sounded to Manfred like a character form *Lord of the Rings.* But his professor explained it meant that oftentimes the correct solution to a problem is the simplest solution.

So, okay, what is the simplest solution to the missing children?

Anything could have happened, he thought. The government could have them, but that was complicated, for the agents would have to find them and then extricate the children from camp, but Manfred saw no evidence of that. Plus, the agents would have definitely waited to grab him, but nobody was here.

Bossilini could have come, he reasoned, but again he would have waited for Manfred— unless the government *and* Bossilini came, and he had to split or fight his way out. But there were no signs of tracks or footprints or any kind of scuffle.

But there was something simpler.

The children walked out on their own.

The simplest solution was often the correct solution. If that were so, he'd have to go after them, to track them. Manfred hunched over looking for tracks from the kids. His grandfather had taught him rudimentary tracking, though he was never any good at it. But his grandfather had just chuckled. "Keep at it, you'll be surprised one day."

So not very confident, Manfred carefully crawled forward looking for marks leading from the hut, but the grass and dirt were trampled. He sat still looking around the camp.

There, over by a tree, he saw an oval of flat, damp grass by the trunk. Sherman. *That's where Sherman set his pack! It's gone, they took it. That was where to start.*

Manfred jumped over there.

Nothing.

There were no tracks leading away from the tree *toward* him, so they didn't go toward the hut. He looked around the tree. Just woods, grass, clumps of pine straw, and dirt patches among bushes and trees.

"No, no, I can't lose you now. Give me something . . . come on, give me something," he whispered, pleading.

His gaze fell on one thing, up ahead on the right, not too far, going behind the tree away from camp. He thought he saw an indentation in the grass. It might be in the shape of a footprint? Manfred leapt to it. Yes, the shape of a shoe-clad foot. He looked ahead, excitement growing.

Four feet beyond was another footmark. It was more to the right and a different size. *Two different tracks.* That meant two persons, he realized with a rush of joy. His confidence budded. Maybe, just maybe I can do this.

Crouched low to the ground, he carefully followed the tracks. He found a couple more, but soon the grass ended in pine straw under a grove of tall, straight pines. Manfred halted. Ahead was a thick carpet of pine straw. It looked like a thick, brown quilt stretching for yards and yards ahead of him. He shook his head. Footprints wouldn't make in pine straw. I am finished before I really got started, he slumped, his face sick.

There was no sign of anything ahead.

What the hell now? Angry, he threw a pine cone as hard as he could against a nearby tree.

Manfred shook his head to clear it. He tried to reason the path the children would have taken through apertures created by the scattered pattern of tree trunks.

Manfred felt a pulse of panic.

He peered carefully through the trees. *There!*

Ahead he spotted a scuffed patch in the pine straw. Then, a second, and another, and beyond that, a freshly broken thin branch. They came this way!

He raced forward, needing to find them quickly. Woods could be fickle, he knew, a wrong veer here and wrong one there, and soon you were lost, off course in a netherworld woven of trees and thatch, daylight fading from lukewarm yellow then to misty gray toward the chilling blackness of night.

He stopped still after another hundred yards, finding himself on rocky terrain, no footprints or marks. A lone boulder as tall as Manfred, immovable on his left. Manfred looked in all directions, but how do you track on rocks? You don't, he knew.

"Oh, god," Manfred lamented, running a hand through his new short hair. There was nothing, no signs, no marks, no footprints, no nothing.

With only silence greeting him, doubt returned. The children . . . were lost, gone. The one time in his life he tried to look after somebody else, he failed.

Manfred stood still, blankly staring ahead, his head filling slowly with defeat. He stood for minutes scanning the terrain before him, desperate to find a sign, but he stood in vain.

He sensed the vision of the green vista from last night. It was parched, turning yellow and brown.

He let out a long breath. *It was hopeless. It had been hopeless from the beginning.*

Then Freedom, the old spirit, whispered. *Take off. You did your best. You really tried, you really, really did. It's not your fault. They never had a chance. You know that now. You can leave with a free conscience.*

Really?

Yes. Really. Go on now, turn 'round. Off with you now.

Manfred shook off the despair, the message welcome news. He stretched, the tension releasing. It felt good. And feeling good, after all, is what's it's all about. He smiled.

Manfred had been careful to check landmarks and felt he could make his way back to Sherman's shelter before dark. He'd hole up there tonight and take off tomorrow.

But what of the children? A new voice inside him asked. But was the voice new, it seemed familiar?

Manfred frowned. "What of them?" he said out loud.

You know 'what of them.'

Manfred shook his head. He wanted to leave. He'd always left before, no supposed allegiance ever held him back. But he couldn't move. *You're stuck in between,* the voice counseled.

"Not for long," Manfred snapped.

Manfred quickly turned back toward camp, but as he moved to step forward, his feet became heavy, as if weighted. He tried to force his feet forward.

He heard a voice. *"Manfred."* It was behind him. He turned.

He gasped.

His grandfather stood before him. Hobart Greenjeans wore the smile he always reserved for Manfred. His grandfather looked exactly like

Manfred remembered, but curiously translucent, like he was not completely corporeal. What, how? Manfred's brain reeled.

"Granddad?" he asked, tentatively.

Hobart Greenjeans did not answer. But he gave Manfred his special wink before dissolving in front of Manfred's eyes.

Manfred staggered back and sat down, shaken. It was his grandfather. He was sure of it. His grandfather was standing in front of him. *But how? What?* Manfred's heart banged in his chest. His grandfather had been dead for over half a century, yet. . .?

Manfred's mind struggled for a rational explanation. But there wasn't one.

"I got to get out of here," he cried aloud. "It's these woods, man, they're not right." He stood to run out of the woods and never come back.

A voice stopped him in his tracks. It sounded like his grandfather's voice again.

Manfred, remember, if you're ever lost in the woods, find a ravine, a draw, and follow it downslope. It will wind downward and lead to water, to a stream. You can follow the stream out of the woods to a road.

Manfred, you can't leave them. You know that.

The voice spoke no more. There was only silence except for the rustle of a soft breeze. The breeze blew gently across Manfred's face, caressing it. Then the air became still and silent. It was him, Manfred thought, after all the years.

Manfred shook bodily and expelled a deep sigh. He again sensed the vista turning green somewhere ahead. He charged after them.

Manfred soon found a ravine and began down it, winding and following the contour of the land. The path wound in a tricky way, along fallen limbs, rocks, and spindly tree roots. He worked steadily, carefully, solidly planting his feet with each step.

He heard a sound. Was it a gurgle, a running sound? He froze and listened carefully. He lost it, only silence. Then, *there*, again. Water. Manfred rushed downward.

But a new sound brought him up short. It was not water, it was a cry. With a shot of adrenaline, Manfred leaped down the slope as fast as he could, fighting off dread.

Manfred burst the last fifteen yards down a severe drop, almost tripping, and landed in a halting stop on marshy soil before a wide creek. The creek was swollen from rains with a strong current rippling the surface.

Manfred couldn't see around the bend. But there was the scream—no, not a scream—crying—off to his right. Manfred broke into a sprint, stumbling through the muck. The sobs became louder, now with words.

"*Help! Help us!*"

A boy's voice. *Sherman!* It must be Carmen who was crying.

Manfred pumped his legs as fast as he dared, rounding a small curve in the creek, and saw there, out in the water, what . . .? He squinted.

The children. They sat upon a little makeshift raft with nothing to steer, just logs laced together with rotting rope. The craft was at the mercy of the current. The children sat upon it, looking terrified, as the raft twisted, beginning to spin atop the clay-colored running water. It was listing to one side.

"*Manfred,*" Carmen shrieked.

"Help us," yelled Sherman.

Manfred saw the raft was taking on water and listing more steeply. It would sink within minutes. A horrible image terrified him of two heads bobbing in the water, then slipping under the muddy surface.

Thoughts how to rescue them raced through his mind. Could they swim through the mocha-colored current to shore? Could he swim out to them with his hurt shoulder? If he could, how could he corral them both, wouldn't the current force them apart? Would he have to choose who to save? *How could he do that, saving one child and letting the other go?*

He shook his head. Going in the water was not an option.

With his heart about to burst, Manfred raced along the shore, shouting, "Hold on. Hold on," while he looked for some desperate way to save them.

Carmen began crying louder at the sight of him running. "*Help us! Help us!*"

Manfred stopped. "Think, think," he screamed at himself. Shaking, wild-eyed, he looked up ahead, praying for something, anything, to reach out to them and drag them safely to shore.

The creek narrowed slightly in a bend to the right. Maybe there, he hoped.

Manfred raced toward the bend. He looked around, jerking his head and shoulders this way, then that, finally spinning around, searching for a broken limb, vine, for anything, to reach out as a life hook.

"*Manfred. Help,*" Sherman shouted.

He cast an anxious look at the raft.

There. Manfred spotted a sapling on the edge of the creek bank. He raced over, and pushing, tried to bend the trunk out over the creek for the children to grab. But he had no leverage; it wouldn't work.

Manfred jumped into the coffee colored water, trying not to think what was below the surface, and leapt, catching the sapling as high up as he could, hoping his weight would bend it. The young tree bent, but not enough.

He had no choice. With his shoulder screaming, Manfred worked hand-over-hand toward the top of the tree, like on the monkey bars at school, his feet dragging in the churning water. His shoulder in fiery pain screamed, but he would not let go.

Working out to the creek, his weight began to bend the tree downward, dropping him lower, his legs deeper in the water, burning his muscles, numbing his hands, scraping off skin. His shoulder was in agony and his strength waning. His face was a mask of pain and determination, he uttered, jaw clenched, "I can do this. *I can do this.*"

The thinner, upper reaches of the trunk bent like a bow, as the children came, the water propelling them toward him. He would have only one chance. *Almost there, almost. . . .*

"Hurry. Grab the tree, grab the branches. I can't hold on much longer," he shouted, huffing for breath. Sweat dripped in his eyes as he saw the raft now only ten feet away. The raft coming closer, closer.

"Come on, guys. Get ready," he could barely call out.

The raft a few feet away, Sherman moved to the edge and began leaping, arms outstretched for the limbs. But he was too short, his hands would swipe six inches under the leaves.

"Carmen," he shouted, panting. "You've got to do it, Sherman's not tall enough."

"But what if I can't?"

"Yes, you can."

"No, I can't . . . I can't . . . I'll fall in . . . I'll drown . . . I know it. . . ."

"Carmen. *Carmen*." But she didn't answer.

He stared at her face, unbelieving, as he hung in the twin agonies of pain and frustration. If she did not jump, the raft would slowly slip by destined to sink a short distance down river.

"*CARMEN!*"

The raft seemed to pause, slowly twirling as if caught in a small eddy. Manfred shook his head in despair, so close, so close.

"*CARMEN?*" he implored.

But she stood frozen, her face paralyzed in fear. Sherman vainly jumping up and down, up and down, trying to catch a branch.

"*GODDAMN IT*," Manfred screamed. They were so agonizingly close. But with Carmen frozen it may as well have been a mile.

Manfred, almost spent, hanging with his last strength, gasping, cast one last look of despair at Carmen.

The raft spun out of the eddy and continued toward him.

But Carmen suddenly looked past Manfred to the shore. Her mouth moved as she seemed to be looking at someone over there. But turning his head, Manfred saw no one. Then Manfred heard her speak.

"No. I can't do it. No, I can't." She stood still, her head cocked, as if listening to words Manfred could not hear.

A new look crossed Carmen's face. "Okay. Okay. I'll try."

The raft leveled out and scooted toward the tree.

Carmen took a deep breath, cast a last look at Sherman to her side, and carefully moved to the edge of the raft. She bent her legs low and then, thrusting upwards, made a powerful leap with arms outstretched and fingers splayed wide. Her left hand brushed a small branch but missed. Manfred gasped. Carmen made a last desperate jab with her right hand for the last branch.

Manfred felt an immediate tug as the tree jerked down hard. "Grab it, Sherman, grab it. Quick," he shouted.

Sherman grabbed Carmen's waist and sunk to his rump on the raft. Their combined weight pulled the tree bough to the floor. Manfred, with a new burst of energy, scampered along the tree, holding it down as he dipped into water up to his chest.

"Hurry, climb out along the tree. *Hurry*," he called with barely any breath.

The children quickly scampered along the tree and slid down to the creek bank. They fell into the grass with Carmen sobbing in relief and Sherman looking stunned, but with the beginning of pride. *They did it.*

Manfred reversed his track, heading back to shore. Soon he was sitting beside them, huffing, sweat pouring out of him, the adrenaline leaving him shaky, holding his throbbing shoulder with the hand of his good arm. "Sherman, I may need that sling again."

The children leaped onto him like playful puppies. He grabbed them in his arms, not caring that his shoulder screamed. Carmen was still sobbing, Sherman trying hard not to. Carmen uttered between sobs, "I thought we were doing to die."

She tilted her head, looking up at him, "Manfred, thank you. You came. You saved us."

A beautiful feeling of gratitude flooded him, and he choked out through a tight throat, "Yes." No more words would come.

The children sat dazed, silent, but their breath began to settle and sobs dried.

After five minutes, Manfred asked, "What happened?"

Carmen and Sherman exchanged a quick glance. Carmen took the lead.

"Well, we decided to come find you. But we got lost."

"Carmen, I told you to stay put," Manfred said, trying to keep his reprimand soft.

Carmen looked at her brother.

Sherman, lowered his head, then confessed, "Actually, it was me that left to come after you. Carmen said not to, but I couldn't help it . . . she came after me."

"You're kidding." Manfred looked down at him.

The boy, blushing, shook his head, no.

"Was it your bright idea to get on the raft?"

He nodded, but then looked up pleading his case. "But I had a feeling, like somebody else was out here in the woods. It made me feel creepy. I thought we could get away with the raft. We found it on the creek bank."

Manfred shook his head in disbelief. He took a deep breath. "Okay, then. Best make it back to camp now before we lose the light—and get lost again," he said sharply in Sherman's direction.

The boy nodded, sheepish.

But then Manfred tousled his hair. They trudged back to camp, weary, ready to rest and sleep hard in Sherman's shelter. But at camp they received the next jolt. Sherman noticed first.

"Hey, guys, something's not right."

"Sherman, what are you possibly talking about," Carmen asked.

"Well, for one thing, there are boot tracks and none of us are wearing boots. And besides, look at that." Sherman pointed toward his wilderness shelter.

Manfred and Carmen turned. Manfred uttered, "Oh."

The right side of the shelter was caved in with a gap in the roof. The hole was big enough for Manfred to see inside.

"Okay, it just fell in. I mean, really, it's just made of twigs and things." Carmen dismissed it, crossing her arms.

"No way." Sherman rose in defense of his work. "I know how to build them right. This was kicked in."

Manfred studied the boot marks. "These were not there before, guys, I'm sure of it."

Carmen became still, looking at the boot prints and caved-in shelter. She looked to Manfred. "What does it mean?"

"It means Sherman's right. Somebody *was* out here in the woods."

Carmen backed away, staring at the shelter. Her eyes grew wide. "Who?"

Manfred shook his head, his face grim. He now knew why the woods had been so quiet and still before.

"Sherman, maybe it wasn't such a bad idea after all to try to beat it out of here on the raft."

"I don't want to stay here," Carmen blurted. "I—"

She didn't finish. She didn't have to.

"Don't worry. There's no way we are staying now," Manfred answered.

As they departed, the man, the former sniper, made a final search of a sector of woods several miles away. He brought the binoculars to his eyes and panned the area. Nothing. He had found the shelter. But he had guessed wrong on the direction the children had taken from camp. He would not find the Douglases this day.

Manfred and the children walked two miles from the camp, keeping close to the road. Sherman spotted a cove of trees surrounded by thick bush. They crawled through the bush into a small clearing underneath the trees. They gratefully ate the provisions Manfred supplied and tried to find comfortable spots to lie upon.

A little later, after they had settled down and finally began to relax, they sat somber, quiet, but happy, happy to be safe, yet still rattled by the visitor. Manfred thought about the footprints. *Was it the police, FBI or what the Bossilini called Homeland? And why only one person? Wouldn't there be several agents?* As Manfred was thinking about that and a plan for tomorrow, Carmen unexpectedly spoke.

"Manfred, ah—"

"Hmm, yeah?"

"I, ah, oh well, nothing."

"Nothing?"

"Nothing."

"Oh, come on, it was something, and something's not nothing."

"Well, okay. You know . . . today . . . when I was out there, on the raft . . . I thought I was going to drown, we all were going to drown. I mean, like, I was totally freaked out."

Manfred nodded, he knew what *that* was like.

"I knew I couldn't grab the branch. I knew I couldn't jump, my legs wouldn't move. I knew we would drown. I just knew it."

Manfred nodded. "What happened?"

An embarrassed look crossed her face. "You're not going to make fun of me?"

He shook his head no.

237

"Never mind." She looked away. But Manfred waited. She turned back.

"Okay, well, like, I saw this man. Did you see him?"

"I didn't see anybody, there was no one but us, we were alone."

Carmen looked down, shaking her head. "No, we weren't."

"What do you mean?"

"I mean there was a man behind you. I saw him. He . . . he had gray hair and a moustache. He spoke to me, didn't you hear? Oh? Well, he had a slow, kind voice, but there was something in it, I mean, I don't know who he was, but I believed him, believed what he told me." She cut a glance at Manfred. "I thought you might know him."

She continued, "I was afraid, really afraid . . . but all of the sudden I wasn't afraid anymore."

Manfred studied her. "Why would I know him?"

"He said I could trust you. I could trust myself, too. He said he had it on authority that we came from good stock, and we could be counted upon, and that we could trust ourselves. He knew your name. He said, 'When Manfred tells you to jump again, then jump, girl, jump.'"

"What did you say he looked like again?"

"He had gray hair and a moustache, maybe it was a little gray, too. He had a friendly smile . . . and I believed him. And his eyes, they twinkled when he spoke. Oh yeah, there was one other thing. He was dressed funny. He had on blue jeans, except they were green jeans."

"Green—"

"Yeah, green. Weird, huh?"

"More than you know. More than you know," he muttered absently, remembering his own encounter at the boulder. "What—what happened to him?"

"I—I—don't know. When we got off the raft and everything and were back on land, he just wasn't there anymore, he was gone."

"Did you see him, Sherman?"

"No, ah, you know I was kind of busy and everything. Did you see him, Manfred?"

"No. No, I didn't. Not there, anyway."

Manfred sat staring ahead, blankly.

Carmen awoke from a late afternoon nap. She sat up. Manfred sat a few feet away.

Carmen glanced at Manfred's profile. Something was different about him. Oh yeah, he did cut his hair, she realized. But it wasn't just his hair. He really is kind of good-looking, she thought, but quickly looked away when Manfred turned toward her.

Manfred glanced at Carmen. Something was different about her. She seemed more grown-up. He could see the woman waiting within her, but he quickly looked away when she turned back toward him.

CHAPTER 37

A SECOND PINT
October 1945
The Crooked Dart Pub
London, England

Evening GMT

Cuthbert ordered a second pint of Stout. He sat in a rosy pub with a cheery fire in the corner. Yet he did not feel cheery even amidst the crowd of boisterous Yanks—American soldiers—filling the pub. They were young lads who had won the war, pressing the Allied campaign across the Channel, through Holland, Belgium, and France, onward into the heart of Germany. They were the ones who lived, the ones going home; they were jubilate and young and irrepressible.

Cuthbert had no one to go home to. He was lonely. These days he worked alone in the lab at Cambridge. He still had the Watch. But it wasn't the same. Oh sure, he now had a circle of Officers and Agents in the League—their ranks had increased since 1929—and they did good work, just as Nigel and he had planned. But he had no *colleague*. No one to challenge him, no one who could mentally gallop with him side-by-side in an uproarious gambit to steal mother nature's secrets from her bodice.

Sir Nigel was dead.

He died in his sleep after giving a lecture at a physics convention in Chicago. Ten years had gone by, and Cuthbert alone headed the League of Privacy Sentinels. He felt alone. Cuthbert's curly blonde hair was now weeded with gray, his moustache as well. He was lithe for his age and still took long walks for his constitution, but his step had lost a little spring. He knew it would lose more.

The past was much on his mind of late, as he frequently thought of Nigel and their string of magnificent discoveries. But his mind, too, lingered on the future and what it held. With Nigel gone and himself not getting any younger he often wondered what would become of the League? He could not bear the thought of it withering away after he was gone.

And just as had the Great War, this war, too, showed the need for the League, the guardians of privacy as Nigel had seen it. The British Secret Service, the American OSS, the German Abwehr and OKW, the Russian NKVD—all had raised the ante on intelligence operations to new, unimaginable levels.

Now that Stalin was squabbling with the Allies over Berlin, it was unlikely these powers would mothball their intelligence capabilities. Orwell had already used the description "cold war" in an essay in the *Tribune*. Cuthbert predicted, as had Nigel back in 1920, that surveillance and spying would only escalate henceforth, the institutions evolving new unimagined tools of intrusion and observation, with genuine privacy becoming elusive.

That prospect nagged him like an aching joint. He had no one to really talk with as he had with Nigel, no incisive conversations to draw the ache from the joint. However, just this night an idea arose, perhaps one that could assuage his worry. He realized he had isolated himself at the top of the organization. *But what would happen to the top when he was gone?*

What he needed was an Heir. An Heir to whom to entrust the League. An Heir to whom to entrust the Watch. Nigel and he had spoken of that in the early days. But Nigel died before they made a selection, and Cuthbert had been ignoring the task. But with the passing days, he no longer had that luxury.

As he was mulling over this thought, by chance, Cuthbert struck up a conversation with an American serviceman.

Unlike the young boy soldiers, he was older, maybe around forty. Though happily smiling, he was more reserved and contemplative than his young counterparts. Nonetheless, when a pretty barmaid passed by, the man with a warm smile called out, "Bring my friend another Stout and an ale for me, please."

"Why, thank you," Cuthbert saluted.

The man nodded.

When the barmaid brought the mugs, Cuthbert again nodded to the man, tipping his head as he raised the mug to his lips. Sitting elbow-to-elbow at the next table, the man with a big smile leaned over, clinking his mug against Cuthbert's, and shouted over the din, "To Victory—ah, and to King and Queen. Is that how you do it over here?"

Cuthbert smiled. "Indeed, that is quite how we do it." The drink and budding conversation kindled Cuthbert's old gregariousness. "Next round's on me," he shouted. The man nodded in pleasure.

Cuthbert took a long draw from his mug. He hadn't felt this good in ages. After a few more swigs of Stout, he engaged the soldier in conversation.

"In what unit did you serve?"

"Armored division. Fixed tanks, at least the ones the German 88s didn't completely blow apart. The ones with direct hits were not pretty sights. Our boys had been inside." He shook his head.

Cuthbert asked, trying not to be awkward, "Surprised to find a private at your age, though no offense intended."

The soldier smiled. "None taken." Looking around, he said, "I am a little older than most of the lads . . . and I wasn't on the front line."

"No?"

"No. The most pressing danger I faced was skinning my knuckles when my wrench slipped." They shared a laugh. More seriously, he added, "Though it was nerve-wracking removing unfired rounds from the magazines of gnarled and twisted tanks."

Cuthbert raised his eyebrows. "That sounds rather harrowing."

The man smiled. "I was a mechanic. Ran a crew that patched up the American tanks and kept them running, trying to kick the Third Reich back to Germany."

Cuthbert nodded that he understood. "How did you join?"

"The service?"

Cuthbert nodded.

"When the war broke out, one of the government defense contractors came recruiting at the railroad, wanting mechanics to keep the tanks and armored trucks going. They had a program to recruit workers who would enlist, but remain employed by the company. As official army personnel, we were assigned to motorized and armor units, but also to stay in close contact with the company, usually weekly. The company had people coming over all the time."

"What on earth for? It was a war zone."

"I heard the selling point to the army was we could get battlefield performance information back to the company directly, much faster than

243

normal channels. That way the company could make production adjustments and changes to improve the fighting equipment. Or so they said."

Cuthbert stared at him, absorbing the information.

"I didn't see a lot of changes. But I did see company pitchmen hanging around the army brass buying a lot of drinks." He shrugged. "But it let us mechanics help the war effort even if we were too old to carry a rifle." He shrugged again. "So I signed up to help my country. And I did."

"And I am sure that, indeed, you did. Here's to you Yanks and your country. We'd been in a devil of a fix without you."

They both laughed and drank deeply.

"You know, I just realized I have not properly introduced myself. My name is Cuthbert Wagnon. You know I was actually born in America, but came to England as a young boy."

"Really? I was born and stayed all my life in Ohio, and I plan to get back there just as soon as I can. Got my old job at the railroad waiting on me—I've had enough of government contractors." The American took another gulp of ale. "Oh, by the way, I'm Hobart Greenjeans."

The man stuck out a big, strong hand and vigorously shook Cuthbert's. Cuthbert felt something good and strong in the man's clasp.

Their introductions were interrupted when a couple of GIs who had a bit too much engaged a table of Royal Marines. The proprietor pulled a cricket bat from underneath the bar to squelch the melee and chased out the lot.

"Well, I dare say it will be a bit easier to hear, now," Cuthbert grinned.

"Yes, seems our boys were a little over enthusiastic tonight."

"But who could blame them?"

"Certainly not me. Barmaid, over here, please, another round."

"Capital idea."

Over their mugs they talked about the war, what it had been like for each of them. What they expected for the future. After another round or two they had become friendly and comfortable with each other, discovering they had more in common than would have first appeared. Cuthbert had not had such stimulating conversation in what seemed like ages.

"Mr. Wagnon—"

"Please, call me Cuthbert."

"Cuthbert—how do you view the *new world order* rising out of the rubble of the war?" The man pulled out his pipe. "Seems we're already squabbling with our allies. I don't know about eastern Europe. It looks like the Russian Bear is on the move. Scuttlebutt says Stalin got the best of Roosevelt at Yalta." But then as if he were talking too much, he waved his hand, chasing the thoughts away. "Oh, never mind, we should be happy, after struggling for victory all those years. Things should look bright, shouldn't they? Cheerio, that's what you say."

"Hobart, you should not feel guilty. You are thinking carefully, and that's important. In the glow of victory, the people only want good news, their loved ones returned, and the end of bacon rationing." He chuckled. "But that does not mean all is well with the world. The fact there is good news does not mean there cannot be bad news."

Hobart smiled. "It's nice to talk with someone who thinks realistically." His face changed. "And I *am* optimistic about America. We came out pretty good."

They wound up talking till closing time. Cuthbert found himself drawn to this man, Hobart Greenjeans. There was something solid, strong, and endearing in this man who had left a wife and job in middle-age to serve his country, and the free world, in their time of need. Yet he was nobody's fool, either. The man had a shrewd awareness of the forces jockeying for power in the post-war world. And perhaps, he seemed to have a sharp eye for what some called an emerging union of the military and government contractors.

Cuthbert mused, *maybe this Hobart Greenjeans would be willing to serve in other capacities?*

Cuthbert had been thinking for some time of returning to his birth country, recruiting American personnel, and maybe basing the League itself there. It appeared the United States was the new world power now that Europe was devastated and the sun, it seemed, could actually set on the British Empire.

Cuthbert casually mentioned he was a member of a lodge that held these kinds of discussions, and occasionally, wrote an editorial or ran a petition when the government at home rose up too much like a bully. Cuthbert urged that, perhaps, the lodge could be useful in other countries.

Hobart listened politely, but Cuthbert sensed he was only mildly interested in his *lodge*.

"Well, in any event, Hobart, I am thinking of making several trips to the States over the next few years. May I look you up on a visit if that is agreeable?"

"Certainly," Hobart responded warmly. "If you have a card I can write my address." Cuthbert retrieved a notebook from his breast pocket, and Hobart scribbled his address and telephone number.

Finally, the pair bid each other a warm farewell at closing time. Hobart pumped Cuthbert's hand good-bye and was off.

Cuthbert stood watching till he was no longer in sight. He shook his head, for there was something about the man. *Maybe? No.* Cuthbert quickly chalked up the thought to too much Stout. Walking a little unsteadily home he reminded himself to take two aspirin before retiring.

CHAPTER 38

THE FRONT PORCH
1949
The Greenjeans Porch
Lionel, Ohio

Evening EDT

The selection of an Heir weighed heavily upon Cuthbert's mind after that night in the pub.

After some hesitancy, wondering if it is wise to ever go back, Cuthbert made the trip to the States. He pressed his face against the window of the airplane eagerly like a child searching for the Statue of Liberty and other iconic landmarks. When the green lady, then the Empire State, passed across the little window, a lump formed in his throat and, strangely, tears budded in his eyes.

He had been a ten-year-old boy in knickers when he and his mother left in 1905, sailing on the great ship, leaving behind his father's grave in a cemetery by the Hudson. His mother was marrying a man with a clipped, proper accent to live in the countryside outside London where it always seemed to rain or promised to do so.

Now he had parents buried on both sides of the Atlantic, and he himself was fifty-nine-years old, thinking of his own burial someday and that he'd better settle things securely before that inevitable rendezvous.

He did not visit Hobart Greenjeans on that first visit back, nor the second. But by the third visit he was confident the League needed substantial operations in America.

The Eagle and Bear were now more than wary allies. They had drawn a line between them that could not be crossed. It was obvious to Cuthbert this "cold war," as Orwell had so aptly named it, would produce new, modern methods of surveillance, censorship, and threat. It was equally obvious America was infected with a growing paranoia, as the Soviets detonated their own atomic bomb rumored to have been developed with secrets stolen from the very United States.

And Cuthbert could see that paranoia spawns a compulsion to unearth traitors, real or imagined, who are subverting the country. That compulsion spawns spying. And spying catches all within its viewfinder—including the innocent. And the innocent can be destroyed along with the guilty.

Yes, the United States was the battleground. And Cuthbert had an idea of just who should head operations.

So it was that he visited Hobart Greenjeans on that third trip in 1949.

He found that, indeed, Greenjeans was back working on the railroad. His daughter was visiting. She had delivered Hobart's grandson the spring before. Cuthbert sensed, but was not told, there was some tension with the father who was absent.

Cuthbert and Hobart wound up rocking on the porch after supper, Hobart contentedly smoking his pipe after a good day's work and his favorite supper.

Their friendship from the pub quickly rekindled.

After a lull in their conversation, Hobart began. "Cuthbert, I am glad you are here. I can talk to *you*." Hobart chuckled with his eyes twinkling.

This is a good man, Cuthbert thought.

Hobart looked around to make sure they were alone. "Cuthbert, everybody here is caught up in the business about the communists. Now the Russians have the bomb. Some quarters in Washington say we need an even stronger bomb, talking about a hydrogen bomb, as if we needed a weapon to kill even more humans at a time. I saw death in Europe. I thought the world was pretty good at killing back in '41 to '45."

Cuthbert noticed the lines of concern on Hobart's face. What was it? Frustration? Wariness? He sensed his friend Hobart was approaching a turning point.

Hobart fiddled with his pipe. "There's this hardness forming here. A suspiciousness. There's this Senator McCarthy who's beginning to make some noises. I don't mind telling you I don't like it. That's not the way we are. But there are people in Washington stoking it like a steam engine. And like an engine, it can blow if the pressure rises too high."

Cuthbert nodded.

"Everywhere you turn, people are beginning to talk about communists. It's like every ill in the world is communist subversion. Some of the fanatics are suggesting we watch each other—*each other*. Can you believe it?"

"It's not so bad in England, Hobart. We come at things from a different perspective." He laughed. "You Yanks always have been a touch reactionary."

"Every country has spies. But it's not the American way to poke into other people's business. Ah, Cuthbert, you came by for a friendly visit and here I am complaining."

Cuthbert smiled. He couldn't have been more pleased with the conversation.

"Not at all, Hobart. I think you are right on point. Remember my lodge that I told you about, let me tell you a little more. . . ."

The two friends talked for hours, as Cuthbert explained Nigel's concern after the Great War, their conception of a League and their work to balance government "curiosity." When Cuthbert thought Hobart had become interested enough to take it, he told him about the most amazing part—the invention of the Watch.

Hobart was astonished. His mouth fell open, and he almost fumbled his pipe. "Cuthbert, that sounds impossible." He stared at his friend, waiting for the mirth to light in Cuthbert's eyes with a slap on his thigh, exclaiming, "Got you this time." But Cuthbert only returned Hobart's stare.

"Cuthbert, you're serious?" Cuthbert just steadily held his gaze. "You do work in the lab—Cambridge—I heard it's a pretty impressive place. You're not joshing me, are you?"

Cuthbert simply turned his head from side to side.

"My god!" Was all Greenjeans could say. He sat too shocked to speak for minutes. "I can trust you about this?"

Cuthbert nodded up and down this time. "Can I trust *you*—that is the real question, Hobart?"

"What do you mean, trust me? You mean, trust me not to go blabbing about this to the paper or something?"

"No, that is not what I mean."

"Well, what?"

Cuthbert paused, feeling the tension. Everything rode on what they next said to each other.

Cuthbert began. "When I become too old, I want you to take over for me, to run the League, to keep the Watch. I have met many, many people

249

around the world since Nigel and I began our odyssey in 1920. I have become a good judge of men. You are the man. I am sure of it."

His companion looked stunned. "Would I have to quit my job?" he stammered.

Cuthbert burst out laughing. "God, no." He tried to recover himself. "You may keep your job at the railroad, actually it would be a good cover. The main responsibility is to select good people and approve strategy for operations. You could do that within the cover of your railroad job. But it takes patience. I think you have what it takes."

"I would go forward in time . . . by *myself?*"

"We will send a trusted Agent with you."

"What if I get lost, I mean, in time, if I can't find my way back . . . I have a wife, daughter, and now a grandchild?" He had become pale.

Cuthbert answered him calmly. He did not want to lose Hobart. He was convinced he was the Heir.

"You will not. If you can work a locomotive, you can work the watch. It is foolproof. I can show you. All you will have to do is use your good sense, Hobart. Your good sense is why I need you. I need somebody with sound judgment to help the League persevere, and ultimately and most importantly, choose his own successor one day. Our work is important. It must continue."

He looked steadily at Hobart.

"*The destiny of civilization has to point toward freedom and away from repression.*" Cuthbert spoke with such forcefulness it took Hobart aback. But he was impressed with Cuthbert's strength, his convictions, his will to persevere.

"Tell you what, Hobart," Cuthbert said slapping his knee, judging his friend had had enough for now, "it's getting late. Why don't you think about it overnight. I will do some checking myself. I'll come by in the morning before I leave. We'll talk then."

Hobart only nodded, his thoughts far away.

"Well, goodnight, Hobart."

"Ah, goodnight, Cuthbert."

At precisely nine the next morning Cuthbert walked to the Greenjeans' porch. His gait was unsteady and he appeared greatly shaken. His knock on the front door was heavy with reluctance.

Hobart answered the door himself. He stepped out onto the porch and softly shut the door.

"My god, Cuthbert, you look frazzled. Poor night's sleep at the hotel?"

Cuthbert returned a pale smile. He wished that was all it was.

"Come my friend, let's sit down." He took Hobart by the arm and gently guided him to one of the rocking chairs. He took the other.

"Cuthbert, what's the matter?" Hobart asked, alarmed. "I planned to tell you I thought about your proposition carefully, long into the night. I was to tell you, yes, I will accept the position. But I am now concerned for you. Tell, me?"

Cuthbert paused a time before beginning. He did not know how to begin, so he just started talking.

"Hobart, while you were thinking last night, I decided to do some checking. I was so certain you were the one, the Heir as I call him, it never occurred to me to research my conclusion, to check it out. But I realized I needed to."

Hobart looked at him, not understanding.

"Hobart, I went forward in time, to research how things would go for you, to verify I had made the right choice."

Hobart looked at him seriously. His brow furrowed. "But you saw something?"

Cuthbert nodded.

"Cuthbert, are you all right?" Hobart asked, leaning toward his friend.

"Yes, yes." He turned to look squarely at Hobart, gathering his courage to speak. "My premise in selecting you was that you were younger than me, that after me, you would have a continued service before the need to select *your* Heir. But—"

Hobart waited for Cuthbert to continue. But, with a look of realization, he finished the sentence, "I . . . I . . . didn't outlive you?"

"It was a terrible trip, unlike any of the others. Not at first, but later. My dear Hobart, I am so sorry . . . sorry to have to tell you."

"I die before you. That's it, isn't it?"

Cuthbert swallowed, nodding, yes.

251

Greenjeans tried to nod stoically. He opened his mouth as if to ask, but Cuthbert interceded.

"You want to know—but that I cannot and will not tell you."

Hobart slumped into his chair. He said, sounding numb, "It's better that way. It's not good to know . . . when your time is coming." He was utterly deflated.

"You do not travel alone in that, Hobart." Cuthbert sighed. "My trip started like usual with the beautiful colored bubble. But it began to change. After I learned about you, I . . . I went forward to conduct certain investigations of my own. As I moved forward in time, the bubble began to change. It seemed to become less flexible, as if losing its elasticity, the colors began to lose their luster and some sections became shaded in sepia. Finally, some parts of the bubble seemed to wither like a dead root altogether. I became frightened and rushed back to the present."

"What do you think it was?"

Cuthbert frowned, a brow raised. "That I traveled forward beyond the life of the League. Something happens in the future bringing about the extinction of the League. What, I do not know. I fear it is too dangerous to explore now. The bubble was withering. If it popped, the occupants could be stranded in time. Perhaps we can investigate at a time closer to the demise."

After a few minutes of mutual silence, Cuthbert continued. "But Hobart, I did go far enough forward—I think I found a future Heir— though that's when the deterioration began."

His friend sat up.

"Who?"

"I cannot tell you." He watched his friend, reeling, trying to accept that necessity. "But I will tell you one thing." Hobart looked up at him. "You will have a part to play."

In the next year, 1950, Joe McCarthy burst onto the national scene, and Hobart Greenjeans joined the League of Privacy Sentinels.

But he was not to be the Heir.

VI.

REUNION

CHAPTER 39

NO I CAN'T GET AWAY FROM YOU
April 12, 2019
A dark alley
Newark, New Jersey

2:00 a.m. EDT

Bossilini was stuck in a Cole Porter song. In his head, Sinatra sang the mutated lyrics, *No, no, I can't get away from you.* Bossilini frowned. He did not need the additional complication.

She slinked toward him, smiling, a combination of ruthless efficiency and striking sensuality. He recognized her shape in the black combat pants, outdoor shirt, and skull cap. She was ready for action. Bossilini jerkily retrieved a black cigarette and lit it, breathing deeply the smoke, measuring his response. The first one would be important.

"Hmmm," she purred, "still smoking those awful roots and hiding in alleys. I thought America was the land of opportunity?"

"Some habits are hard to break." He exhaled a stream of smoke through his nose. "Others much easier."

"I guess the trick is knowing which is which." She smiled.

Bossilini hated the combination of that smile and condescending yet seductive voice. He stubbed out the cigarette roughly on the concrete pavement. "Well?"

"Well?"

"Well, the League sent you."

"Is that a question or a statement?"

"Doesn't matter."

She sighed. "Are we really going to do that old dance."

"Is there a new dance you have in mind?"

"How about no dance?"

"Refreshing for a change. Possible?"

"Doesn't seem so. You're trying to control me with your surliness."

"Bah, you are impossible. You have always been impossible, you always will be."

"You used to find that alluring," she teased.

"*That* was a long time ago," he spat. But he noticed from her sneer that his strike had hit. They still knew how to cut each other.

She turned, speaking with her back to him, "So we have a situation."

"We always have a *situation*. It is what we do."

She let the hostility pass. "Yes. That is what we do. What do we do about this one?" she asked, turning back toward him.

He smiled in recognition. She was getting down to business. That, at least, would be easier.

"You know about the wreck."

She smiled, but more like a smirk, nodding that she did. He hated that smirk.

"Any indication I have been compromised?" he asked. "Anything on the traffic?"

"No, we think you are clear." She cocked her head.

He sighed uneasily. "I would have to go into exile if they identified me. We couldn't risk them drawing a connection with our other associates. No contact with anyone from the League." He glanced at her. "Maybe for several years."

She wasn't interested in his self-centeredness. "What's the plan?"

He took a long look at her before responding. She was beautiful. He brushed away the thought—and the memories.

"The Douglas family is separated. Need escorting, some more than others." She nodded. "I should go to New York, maybe others will arrive there soon. You, well, I think we need you elsewhere."

"What do you have in mind?"

"One was banged and a little, ah, broken. May need your special skills."

"Female, huh?" He nodded. "Wouldn't that Hungarian Bossilini charm be more effective?" she smiled, arching an eyebrow.

"Ah, not in this case."

"Where to?"

"Easton, Pennsylvania."

She waved a finger over her left palm and her device lit up. She quickly opened a small glowing map. "Not bad, not too far. Where are they going?"

Bossilini told her Middlebury in Vermont. He did not want to tell her more.

"Okay. We'll figure it out when we get there. Or you could let me know if you find out. Anything else?"

"No."

"See you soon." She smiled over her shoulder, and disappeared from the rank Newark alley.

Bossilini felt the whet of desire, and cursed himself for it. Then he cursed himself again for hiding in such a foul place.

CHAPTER 40

THE HONOR COURT
April 12, 2019
A room in DHS
Washington, D.C.

11:30 p.m. EDT

Marcie sat staring at the computer screen in the secret room Chambers had arranged. Her shoulders slumped.

Sealed on Order of the Department of Homeland Security.

The legend had popped up when she again tried to access the Douglases' financial records—their real financial records. She had wanted to see the records again, just once, just for a moment, just for a glimpse of truth.

She stared at the official seal of the department—the ubiquitous eagle framed in the blue circle with the scrolling words around the circumference. "US Department of Homeland Security." She had seen similar government seals a million times on a million pages. When she was fresh and new on the job, those seals meant something.

Now she stared numbly at the seal of her own department.

Now she was unsure what it meant.

She stared dully at the round stamp. It could be any round stamp, even a bar stamp, like the doorman had put on her wrist last weekend.

Listlessly, she read the words, "US Department of Homeland Security." She had been so proud to read the words when first issued her job identification badge.

Now she did not know what to do.

She did not know if she *should* do anything.

The screen went black. She had not logged out. She simply pushed the off button, until the machine turned off. That's what "off" buttons were for, she thought with a wry sneer. To turn off the goddamn machines when you were finished with them.

She stared at the seal on the wall. She had taken an oath to uphold the seal.

She had taken an oath another time, too.

It was her last year at MIT. She was on the Honor Court that year, the Chief Justice. She had taken an oath to uphold the Honor Code. She wished she had never served, never taken that oath.

That last spring semester, a complaint of an Honor Code violation was filed against her friend Darrin. He was caught cheating on a midterm. He needed to pull up the grade to stay in the top 10%, which was the key to the best jobs.

The problem was they had him cold.

He caught Marcie walking home from the library late the night before his Honor Court trial.

"Ah, Marcie—?"

"Darrin? What—you know I can't talk to you. Joe, your student Honor Court counsel—you hired a lawyer—Darrin, I can't—it's improper—"

"Marcie," he pleaded, "you got to help me out here. If they find a violation they'll kick me out, it will ruin me, I'll never get a decent job."

"Darrin—"

"Marcie, I've worked like hell for four years here. You know what we've gone through. It's a pressure cooker, only the best survive. Hell, a lot that started with us are gone. I *deserve* an MIT diploma. I . . . just made a bad decision, Marcie. I'm not a cheat, you know that. It was just the pressure. You've got to do something. Let me retake a new test or give me some assignment or campus community service or anything—but don't find me guilty. My parents don't even know about his. They'll flip. You can't do this to me."

The desperation in his voice was like a knife in her stomach. She knew he was right—a label of cheating would knock him out of MIT. It would destroy his carefully laid plans. *Oh, why did he do this?* They were so close to graduating, surviving.

She then became angry with him, cheating and putting her in this tough spot. And he had cheated. The evidence was incontrovertible. The professor was showing no mercy in pushing for his expulsion.

But the expression of panic and terror on his face made her want to cry.

260

"Oh, Darrin," she uttered, tenderly. Then, bracing herself. "I've got to go, Darrin."

She walked past him, backpack banging against her hips as she hurried away along the sidewalk. She knew he was still standing there watching her walk away. She could feel his pleading stare between her shoulder blades.

The day of the trial. The three Honor Court judges, including Marcie, conducted the trial then retired to review the evidence and reach their decision. They had no choice. But they looked warily at each other, grimly, trying to draw strength to do the right thing, but a thing that would crush a classmate's life. No one spoke, no one called for a vote. Each in his own way was searching for an out, a compromise, a way to pass that cup from their hands. Finally, Marcie took control.

"We need to make a decision. Does anyone have a question about the evidence, whether the charge was proved?"

The others shook their heads, not wanting to look her in the face. They were relieved she was taking charge. Marcie sat silent until the two looked up at her. She looked steadily in their eyes one at a time. Her voice was even as she spoke.

"We have no choice. We each know that. If we are to uphold our oath, uphold the Honor Code, if it is to be anything other than a piece of paper, then there's only one thing we can do."

One justice began crying.

"I'll announce the ruling. That okay with you?"

The girl softly crying nodded her head without looking up. "Yes."

The other, a boy, hoarsely whispered, "Yes, Marcie. Thank you."

They opened the door and filed out.

Afterward, as Darrin was pulled from the courtroom by his lawyer, screaming and fuming at the justices, he leveled his eyes at Marcie, and pointing at her, yelled at Marcie with the most venom that had ever been directed at her. "It's your fault, Marcie. Your fault! I hope you remember this the rest of your life, because mine's now ruined." He banged the door open with his fist and staggered from the room.

Marcie exited the courtroom with composure, then raced down the hallway to the nearest bathroom she could find. She lurched into a stall, doubled over, and retched and retched.

She never wanted to be faced with a choice that devestating again.

But now she had a different oath.

Back then her oath had been to the truth.

But what was her oath to now? The truth? The Department? The Secretary? The Assistant Secretary? The American people. Who? What?

She did not know.

Finding Darrin guilty was the truth.

The Douglas fabrication was not.

But she knew what was right.

Just as she had known back then.

She had deleted from the DHS system the evidence of the backup of the Douglas computers as Chambers had instructed. But she had made a copy on a flash drive she slipped into her pocket.

CHAPTER 41

IMHOFF AND TAPPY READ A MAP
April 14, 2019
Manhattan
New York, New York

10 a.m. EDT

Imhoff ushered Tappy into a coffee shop in midtown Manhattan.

Two days after the accident, Imhoff spent the day in Washington quizzing Tappy about every aspect of the Douglases' lives.

"Where are they likely to go?" he asked.

Tappy shrugged, "Throw at dart at a map?"

Imhoff frowned. "Let's think it through." He looked away, thinking. "Do they have any relatives in the northeast?"

She shook her head, no.

"Any contracts in the major cities? Or business dealings?"

Tappy thought hard. They had to get it right to save her friends. Bossilini had been off the grid since the accident. No one else with the League had made contact with her. That worried her. The silence was probably a security measure. But she still worried.

"Chicago? Detroit? Cleveland? Pittsburgh?" Imhoff tossed out cities.

"None of those...." After a moment, Tappy's face brightened. "They would go to New York every few years. Virginia liked the shopping and the shows; George maybe had a convention or business meeting. Virginia planned to take the kids there for Christmas sometime." She looked to Imhoff for his reaction.

"That walks. It's what my gut is telling me."

But Imhoff wanted check the data against his gut. Later, in the afternoon, he poured over the forensic reports of the Hummer. Not a lot there. Mrs. Douglas's purse, smeared fingerprints, the legible ones not on CODIS, trace fibers, but nothing revealing. He spent an uncomfortable night agitating over the fact that despite the lucky break of the wreck in Wilkes-Barre, they had nothing to show for it. And New York could be a wild-goose chase, leading him further away from the fugitives. They needed to move. In the morning, he would decide: New York.

So yesterday, Tappy and he traveled to New York, spending the day at the field office sending pictures of the fugitives to hotels and car rental companies, following up with calls. Imhoff supplied deploying agents with pictures of the Douglases to bus terminals, train terminals, the airports, and few truck stops outside town.

And after all that manpower, at the end of the day he had nothing to show for it.

They needed a different plan. The old ways were not working.

The next morning at the coffee shop, Imhoff announced, "We got to think differently about this, Tappy."

Settled at a table, Tappy watched Imhoff spread open a tourist map on the table. For her part, she held a cup of coffee in her hands. As Imhoff ran his finger along the map, she glanced around the coffee shop observing scattered millennials, middle-aged tourists, and hipsters trying to look original.

"What are you thinking, Frank?"

Imhoff looked up at her. "Wherever they were going before, the wreck changed that. They need to improvise now. They're here."

"How do you know?"

"I just know."

"Surely it's more than that?"

He stared at her.

"It's what I would do. The guy running them is good. He kept them off the radar. No mistakes. Blown by a random accident he couldn't control. He knows we're searching the area around the wreck. Now he's going to hide in plain sight. It's what I would do."

"But where?" Tappy said. "Plain sight is a big place."

"Well, let's just figure it out." He studied the map.

"How?"

"Thinking it through. We struck out with the hotels, plus there's just too many of them. They could be holed up anywhere. Maybe a street cam picks them up if they make a trip for food, but if it was me, I'd stay inside with room service. But they have to come out sometime."

She raised an eyebrow.

"Plus, there's a chance they had to split up after the wreck. They'll come out to meet up again, you can count on that."

"What do you mean?"

"Some witnesses say several people spilled out of the Hummer and went different ways. The accounts are all over the place. You know how unreliable eyewitness statements are, the numbers, ages, and sexes vary, but there was a consistency in the stories that the children were off away from the adults, and then the kids disappeared. One witness said the children were with a long-haired young man, but nobody else corroborated that."

Tappy stared evenly at him. He looked up at her and said, "Don't know what it means or why a long-haired guy would be with them, assuming there even was a long-haired guy."

Tappy looked concerned. "So you are saying Carmen and Junior were separated from Virginia and George . . . and the driver of the Hummer?"

"Yes. And there was at least one more in the Hummer, if not two, but again the witness accounts are inconsistent."

Tappy looked thoughtful. She did not show that she was worried.

"But the witnesses are consistent about the children being across the road. No one saw them regroup. Somebody would have remembered that. So my working assumption is they were separated for some reason after the wreck and they are to meet up here—maybe they have accomplices helping them." He shook his head.

After a moment, he said, "So, taking that working assumption, their meeting place has to be something recognizable and simple—where they can find each other and not be trapped." He chewed over the map.

"Empire State?" Tappy suggested.

He shook his head. "Couldn't go inside, too easy to be trapped. Standing outside? I don't know. That's a lot of people around. No way to blend in. Standing out like a sore thumb." He eliminated it.

"Statue of Liberty?" she offered.

"That would be worse. Stuck on a ferry." He shook his head again. "You know them. Museum, library?"

"Hmm, I don't think so, Frank. Museums are too easy to confuse with each other—Metropolitan Museum of Art, Museum of Modern Art, Museum of the City of New York." She shook her head. "The Douglases are not exactly art lovers—they could go to the wrong ones, and you can't just hang out in the library all day waiting for a rendezvous. That would stand out to the security guards."

"Radio City Music Hall?" he suggested. "They could sit in on a show, blend in. Meet in the lobby?"

"Maybe, maybe."

She looked worried. "But if they hit the streets, even to go somewhere inside, there are street cams to deal with—"

"And drones."

"Drones?" she asked, taken aback. "Surely not with all the buildings?"

Imhoff nodded. "They're everywhere now. Homeland's using spider drones over New York. Our New York field office spotted them. And we ourselves have a Flier—an FBI plane—flying out from around Wilkes-Barre."

Tappy stared at him.

He nodded, as if believe it or not.

They worked the map furiously for another ten minutes, batting ideas back and forth and rejecting each in turn.

Finally, Tappy announced, "They need to meet outside Manhattan, Frank. Even if they regrouped here, the crowds, the traffic snarls, too much unpredictability, transportation delays getting out of the city. We need to look in the boroughs. Less surveillance, more room to negotiate, easier to leave."

"Okay, that walks. What're you thinking?"

"I'm . . . not . . . sure."

She frowned over the map while Imhoff went for coffee refills. Tappy was frightened by the prospect the children had been separated. The long-haired person was Manfred, of course, but he hadn't been trained yet. He was flighty, and that could be fatal. She tried to conceal her anxiety when Imhoff returned.

He set her cup over by her right hand, "Thank you, Frank." Returning to the map, and without looking up, she said, "Frank. I think I've got something. Queens."

"What's in Queens besides Shea, I mean, Citi Field?"

"Actually, it's right next door. She looked him directly in the face. "The Unisphere."

"The Unisphere?"

"Yes. It's public, in a park, spacious, you can observe it from a distance, can linger for hours without standing out, places to hide, botanical gardens, a museum, open walkways and streets for escape. It would be easy to find for out-of-towners, but is not overridden with tourists. I think it is exactly what George or Virginia would pick."

She stared at him, sitting expressionless. Then his eyes met hers.

"I think it walks."

She smiled at him.

"Does your map there, Tappy, tell us what line to take?"

"Indeed, the map does."

"You lead the way."

"Frank."

"Yes?"

"Let's hurry."

CHAPTER 42

ANGIE
April 13, 2019
A motel
Easton, Pennsylvania

9:00 a.m. EDT

Her name was Angie. She was the Operation Agent in New Orleans, the striking black-haired beauty in the Ritz who had posted the video of Imhoff taking Tappy into custody.

Angie would never admit to Bossilini that she volunteered to help in Pennsylvania. She was not even sure why she did. It would have been easier to do nothing, go about her duties, relegating Bossilini to her past where he belonged. But the intense feeling . . . their failed romance . . . for reasons she didn't understand it. . . .

Angie had no plan as she sat sipping the last of her coffee at a Denny's in Easton. That always annoyed Bossilini. He liked at least the basics of a plan. She smiled. She would improvise. She would be "on" when the time came.

It always got Bossilini that she was.

Angie instantly spotted Bodhi going back into the hotel with a carton of bagels and coffee. She followed.

When he turned to look behind him, she gave a quick signal. He nodded. Bodhi continued toward the hotel; she waited outside.

From the hotel, Angie followed the pair to a retaining wall where they stopped.

"Oh, who are you?" Virginia startled when Angie suddenly appeared.

"This is my associate," Buddy said.

"You know Buddy? And Bossilini? You are here to help us?"

"Bodhi, I don't—"

"They call me Buddy."

Angie raised an eyebrow at him. "Well, okay, Buddy. Yes, I know him. I'm here to take you to Vermont where you'll be safe with Bodhi, er, Buddy. Then Nitko and I will bring the rest of your family to you."

Virginia frowned. "No. We are supposed to meet in New York."

"Virginia, plans change. You have to adapt," Buddy tried to counsel.

"*NO!*" Virginia's face went almost plum.

"Virginia—"

"No! We are supposed to go to New York. I am *not* leaving my children again." She looked at Buddy. "You promised to help me."

"I am. But—"

"We *are* going to New York to meet like we planned. I want my children back." She became teary, but she gave them a sharp look framed with defiance. "Take me to New York." Turning to Buddy, "If you don't, I'll go myself. You know I will."

Buddy gave Angie a sour glance.

"If you two don't like that, *you* can go to Vermont and I will meet you there after I collect my children and husband." She crossed her arms.

Angie looked at Buddy, who shrugged. She could tell if she pushed it Virginia would make a scene. Angie had to improvise. She was good at that.

"Okay, okay. New York, then."

She looked at Virginia and Buddy. "That good, Virginia?"

Virginia did not reply, but nodded.

"Okay, good, then let's go."

As an afterthought she added, "When we get there, Virginia, we will separate for security. You and I will stay together, Buddy will find George, then we all will get the children. That's the way it has to be."

Virginia chewed her lip, thinking a moment. "Okay," she finally agreed. "But we're not looking for George for long. I *will not* miss the children. At three o' clock tomorrow I'm at the Unisphere. Then we can find George, if he's lost."

CHAPTER 43

CAPTAIN KANGAROO & OVALTINE, TOO
April 13, 2019
Hitchhiking
I-81
Wilkes-Barre, Pennsylvania

10:00 a.m. EDT

When they awoke the next morning, Manfred announced, "Guys, we got to hitch to New York."

Sherman said, "Cool."

"Hitch?" Carmen asked, frowning. "You mean like hitchhiking, riding in some stranger's yucky car?"

"Yeah, I thought it through. It's our best chance."

"Okay," she said sullenly. "But I'm not sitting in the front seat with a stranger."

They stood for an hour at the I-81 exchange near the now-cleared accident scene as an endless stream of cars ignored them. Manfred thought about taking a break to get some coffee when a large pickup truck pulling a fifth-wheel camper turned onto the entrance ramp. The truck stolidly passed them, and a woman stared squarely at Manfred.

Whoa, Manfred thought. She looked like the women when he was a child—sprayed, bouffant hair; makeup compacts; and Lucky Strike cigarettes. He smiled, watching the truck pull away.

But out of the corner of his eye he caught the truck stopping. It paused for a moment, then carefully pulled onto the shoulder of the ramp. An arm came out of the passenger window waving for them.

Manfred leaped. "Come on, kids, this may be it. And act right, damn it."

They rushed up to the passenger window and were greeted with the friendly, smiling face of Martha Bunnion. "Howdy, need a ride?"

"Sure do."

"Hop on in the back," Martha said. It was a four-by-four; Manfred opened the back door, and they hustled in. Manfred had just slammed the door shut when the woman turned around over the seat, with a big smile. "We're the Bunnions, Martha and Horace, from McKibbon, Kansas."

Manfred quickly gave her first names only. He then pitched a lame story how he was their uncle taking them to a Junior Achievement Convention in New York when the car broke down and they had it towed to a dealership.

But Martha seemed to buy it. "That's sweet of you, taking time with your niece and nephew." She beamed at Manfred. "We need more of that in our country. Family taking care of family. It's not the government's job to take care of family, there's too much government these days anyway."

Boy, if you only knew, Manfred thought. He wanted to change the subject. "What takes you to New York?"

Martha laughed. "Honey, we're not going into New York. It's our charitable duty to help others. But we can let you off in Passaic, I bet it's a pretty close bus ride over."

Alarmed, Manfred asked, "Passaic? What's in Passaic?"

She looked at Horace, and smiling, back to them. "A big, ole time religion tent revival."

Manfred thought, *hew boy.*

"Manfred," Martha mused. "I haven't heard that name since the old Captain Kangaroo show. Remember, Horace?"

"Sure do. Watched it every day at your house while our mothers had coffee."

"Oh, there was Mr. Greenjeans, the Captain, Grandfather Clock, and Manfred the Wonder Dog—"

Carmen snickered.

"—and the show's sponsor, Ovaltine." She went on how she and Horace had a cup before bed every night. "You kids, you had Ovaltine?"

"No . . . I mean, no ma'am," Sherman answered for them.

"Oh, goodness," Martha exclaimed. "We'll just have to take care of that."

Barely taking a breath, Martha continued, "Manfred you look like you got a Beatle haircut." She looked at Horace for ratification.

"Yes, he does, Martha."

"Oh, that was back when the Beatles were fun and exciting, when the music was clean. Kids, Horace and I were in high school just when Beatlemania hit, we graduated 1965, know what Beatlemania was?"

"Sure," Sherman answered, "we've seen it on TV, it was all in black and white."

"It was living color back then, Sherman. Oh, it was so exciting. There were the Beatles, the Beach Boys, and Paul Revere and the Raiders, that cute Mark Lindsay, they did the *Where the Action Is* show in the afternoons with Dick Clark. You should've been around for that, Manfred." She laughed.

Martha, I was, Manfred thought. *I began high school the same year you did.*

"Everything was so fresh and exciting, even the black-and-white television seemed to make everything fresher somehow. You know we had the space program and were going to the moon, there was progress everywhere and polio vaccines, and the cute and funny Beatles, the dances, remember Horace, first there was the Twist, then all those others, the Swim, the Monkey, the Watusi."

Martha's reminiscing began to affect Manfred. While Martha was buoyed by her memories, Manfred sank with his.

The things Martha talked about framed how out of time and place he was. He didn't belong here. To Manfred all those things had just happened. Hell, the moon landing was a *month* ago. But for everybody else it was a half-century past.

Damn, everyone who had seen the Beatles invade and Neil Armstrong on the moon now were old or dead. But Manfred had had no adjustment period, no sense of the years rolling past in waves, no rosy glow on the past. He simply was there one moment, and the next he was not. He was on the wrong side of the memories, the wrong side of time, the wrong side of life.

Martha must have sensed Manfred's subdued mood, for she sat uncharacteristically silent for a few miles. Carmen and Sherman stared out the windows. Horace kept steady at 65 mph.

Horace reached to turn on the radio. He was usually glued to FOX talk shows, but Martha knew that soon he'd be ranting about the federal government and liberals. She was becoming tired of the anger and negativity.

"Horace, let's just ride a while." He replied with a frown but let the radio alone.

Martha turned with a smile to stare out the passenger window, her face becoming wistful. Martha preferred to remember things, to daydream about things she had not thought of in a long time. When she found a good, old memory, she was pleasantly surprised to find that it often led to other good, old memories. She could turn the pages of these memories like a scrapbook in her mind, lovingly looking at the pages for hours, remembering how fun it had all been. She enjoyed reliving how better it had all been, and how people were better back then, even when times were hard, and how better it would all be if we acted like we did back then, savoring the candy-coated feelings until it was time to close the scrapbook for the day.

The group settled down in the lull of late afternoon. They rode east as the sun set behind them, with Horace and Martha eager to meet up with the flock, where once in the fold again they could pluck the old, better memories from all their friends' minds, and create a stage upon which to play them, almost making them real again.

Manfred slumped in the seat, resigned to spending the night among the Revivalists, as Horace said they were called. Manfred hoped the Douglas clan would wait for them at the Unisphere.

At Camp, Martha had arranged for Horace and her to stay in another couples' RV that the Bunnions jokingly, or maybe not, called the Taj Mahal, so Manfred and children would sleep in the Bunnions' trailer.

Martha fed them.

"Well, it's almost time to go," Martha announced, staring at a giant tent pitched in a clearing. Manfred had heard the clanging of metal folding chairs as they were set up inside.

"Thank you, Martha," Manfred said. As an excuse for skipping the revival, he offered, in case she expected them to go. "We're tired and ought to rest. But we appreciate your hospitality."

She smiled and patted on him. "Well, if the spirit moves you, come on in."

Later, the children looked at him with wide eyes as loud voices and strange shouts escaped from the tent. "They're speaking in tongues," Manfred explained.

After the Revival, the Bunnions looked worn out from the day's travels and the night's excitement. Martha readied the trailer for bedtime, as Horace sat pensively in his lawn chair. The children began to slump in their chairs. Martha startled Manfred when she appeared at his side with three steaming mugs. "Thought you'd like to try the Ovaltine."

"Yes, yes, why thank you, Martha." Manfred reached for a steaming mug, and the children sat upright for theirs.

Soon she was back with her mug and one for Horace. She blew across the top of the mug to cool it, then took a dainty sip, careful not to burn her lips. She closed her eyes, savoring the rich chocolate taste with a hint of malt. It was her routine, her coda to the end of the day, all the days in the procession of her life.

"Martha, this is pretty good," Manfred exclaimed.

"Told you so," she said, pleased.

"Children, what do you say?" Manfred turned to them.

"Thank you, Mrs. Bunnion."

"This is one of the things I miss most about my children being far away. Of course, I make it for my grandchildren when they come. It's special with them, and the tradition goes on. Or at least I hope it does."

The warm drink soothed Manfred, and his limbs relaxed. He began to feel reflective.

"You know, the traditions are important," Martha continued, "especially as fast as the world is moving with technology and everything. That makes it especially important to keep the traditions. That's what Horace and I do with the Revivalists. You can't stop progress from going forward, and you shouldn't if you could. Surely God wants us to learn and grow as much as we can, like we want our children to grow and lead good lives. But the traditions are like a brake to keep us from growing too fast, out of control."

She took a bigger sip from her mug.

This Revivalist thing with the sawdust and tent and running around the countryside was strange, Manfred thought, but he realized he liked Martha Bunnion. He realized something else and was surprised he hadn't sooner. If life had gone normally, if there had been no time travel, he, too, would have gray hair and some wrinkles and maybe a slight stoop, for they were the same age.

"That's partly why Horace and I have gone back to some of the old things and ways," Martha continued. "We canceled our cell phones and got old, rotary dial phones. It's nice, kind of slows you down, to put your finger in the dial, turn it around to each number one by one. We got a percolator coffee pot at a yard sale, too, you know, the kind you heat on the stove and coffee perks up in the plastic bubble. When the grandchildren come, we make them put away their electronics and play board games again." She smiled and looked down at her cup. "They actually like it once they get used to it." She looked at him shyly. "Hope you don't think we're crazy."

"Not at all," he replied.

Manfred smiled with her. Martha Bunnion, Homo sapien female, living on a dirt clod spinning through space, trying to make sense of it all, trying to find Nirvana through the simple, everyday things, through Ovaltine. *Very Zen*, thought Manfred. *Very Zen.*

"It's just that yesterday's rainbows seemed prettier, the colors brighter somehow, you know? Like the old Technicolor movies," she explained.

"I know."

"Well, guess it's time for us all to turn in," Martha announced. "Need anything else?"

"Nope. You've taken good care of us. Thank you."

There was one last thing he realized he wanted to tell her. Manfred called softly, "Martha."

"Yes."

"Ah, I don't mean to seem ungrateful, but, ah, watch that religion— what I mean is, don't let it become hard or mean, you know, some folks get brittle, rigid, there's a saying that goes something like a tree that sways with the wind is stronger than one that stands rigid."

Martha, with a hint of a condescending, though kind, smile, answered, "Righteousness is bestowed upon those who remain steadfast in the way of the Lord. Good night, Manfred. Sleep tight."

Manfred watched her turn and walk away as Horace rose and followed. He noticed the day's tiredness on their faces made them look old. They were his age, they were old, but he was not.

Watching them, a question flashed in his mind. It was so simple it stunned him: Why go back?

Why go back?

Did he really want to go back now he had seen the future? Did he really want to go back to black-and-white TV's, coffee percolators with Maxwell House, the Lone Ranger and Tonto, seeing the USA in your Chevrolet, and the possible re-election of Nixon in '72, though surely *that* couldn't happen?

Watching the Bunnions head to bed, Manfred realized he had received a gift. He should look like Martha and Horace, a little gray, a little stooped, a little high blood pressure, a little pill here, a little pill there. But he didn't. He had cheated time by fifty years.

It's true he had been in suspended animation for those years, but so what—he was awake now and it all lay before him. Now they had all those Star Trek gadgets. What else would they have? Who wouldn't want to live a hundred and forty years into the future? Who wouldn't want to see what happened? Maybe Martha Bunnion would not. But then again, maybe she would if she was twenty-one. *Maybe the rainbows were just as pretty tomorrow, maybe it was young eyes that made all the difference.*

The next morning, they rode the transit bus toward Manhattan. He sat next to Sherman with Carmen seated in front of them. Carmen turned back toward him. "The Bunnions were strange."

"How so?"

"Well, they just were." She tried to figure how to put it in words. "Well, that church *thing*—in a tent, like can't they afford a building?" She thought a moment. "And Mrs. Bunnion—she was nice and everything but—well, all she talked about was old things, like she wished to go back, I mean,

277

you can't go back, but it was all she could talk about. It was, like, ancient history."

Manfred smiled.

"Why do people, I mean, why do adults do that?"

"I dunno."

Carmen wasn't satisfied. "Mrs. Bunnion was going to something she really wanted to do, the revival and hanging with her friends, I mean, they'd driven from *Kansas,* but the whole time she was talking about percolators and dial phones, whatever they were, and she was obsessed with Ovaltine, I mean, it was okay, but you don't make your life about it."

Manfred realized he would have to try for some answer. "Carmen, you'll see it better when you're grown up. For now, do you have some nice memory when you were little, that you like to think about and sort of miss and wish you could live it again?" She thought, creasing her brow.

"Ah, yeah, I guess." She chewed on her bottom lip as a tear budded from an old memory of Virginia and her in the park, just the two of them, Virginia was hers and she was all Virginia's, before Sherman was born, before she lost the specialness.

"Why—why do we do that?" she tried to control her voice.

"Don't know. But we do. Maybe it has something to do with loss. Or time. Or our misperception of both." They sat back and watched the road.

Sherman hadn't been paying any attention to them. Instead he was fixated on a thought.

I have to go to the sunflowers. I have to go to the sunflowers.

CHAPTER 44

IS THAT GEORGE?
April 13, 2019
Secret DHS Office
Manhattan

5:00 p.m. EDT

Marcie had not heard from Secretary Ogilvie in what seemed like forever. Chambers was her contact. And Chambers was now sending her to New York to man a spider drone.

Marcie was not so sure the Douglases would risk a big city. It seemed the open spaces of rural countryside would be better. She did not know that Chambers was monitoring Bart Cummings's communications and New York was the FBI's target.

There, Marcie sat in a small booth set in a row of small booths working controls guiding a drone. She was flying it around the Empire State Building. Chambers had told her there was some possibility the Douglases had been separated in the crash, and if so, they would rendezvous at a common tourist attraction that would be easy to find.

She was in her third hour at the controls.

She had lost focus. The motor part of her mind still directed the controls on auto-pilot, but her attention was blown from image after image of people swarming Manhattan sidewalks with nameless faces and faces and more faces. So it was that she missed George Douglas walking toward a McDonald's near Time Square lugging an old-fashioned suitcase by the handles.

George had found a crummy hotel the night before.

He startled awake about nine. At first, he did not remember where he was. When he did, he moaned. Wearily, he rose, stepping stiffly to the bathroom where he climbed out of the dirty, sweat-stiff clothes he'd slept in and took a long, long hot shower. He stood under the spray of needles soothing his aching muscles, warming him, restoring some measure of vitality.

He rubbed the fogged mirror with a hand towel, staring at the face flushed from the hot shower but still lined with weariness. He shaved, put on the same grimy clothes, and checked out of the hotel.

George grabbed a quick breakfast near Broadway and 45th. Carrying his suitcase by the handles, with the case banging his legs, he realized he had to ditch the suitcase. He found a cheap souvenir shop at Times Square and bought a crummy black backpack with a big red apple stitched on back. It didn't register with him that the red apple would be like a bull's eye for those who, with malice, searched for him.

George hurried out of the store to the end of the block. When he looked up at a street sign, he stared straight into the lens of a street cam with the little red light shining brightly. It was on. His face fell. A sinking feeling filled him with a stark coldness. *Caught on camera.* They had him for sure now. Sadly, he shook his head and slumped, maybe the others could carry on after his capture . . . he had so looked forward to seeing them today.

But someone rudely bumped into him, knocking him roughly aside. He felt a spike of anger, which became a gift. The anger cleared his head. George grabbed hold of himself, and with a surge of adrenaline, muttered, "No, you're not taking me—not without a fight." He burst off down the street.

The camera relayed images to monitors. They showed the harried flight of a middle-aged, fair colored man weaving in and out of pedestrians down Broadway. The camera got a clear shot of a black backpack with a big red apple on it. A few minutes later Marcie's phone rang.

"Marcie. Dick Chambers."

"Yes, sir."

Chambers liked the "sir." Maybe she could be salvaged after all, he thought.

"Marcie, a street camera located George Douglas in Manhattan near Times Square. He was last seen going south on Broadway. He has a backpack with a big red apple. Switch your drone there immediately. Stay focused working outward from Times Square."

"Any hypothesis where he is going?"

"No. But Marcie."

"Yes, sir?"

"Find him."

Hustling down the street in the stiff-legged walk of a man with tight hamstrings George desperately sought cover. With head down he frantically stole glances to the sides, and once behind, to see if anyone was coming for him.

How could he have been so stupid? He flailed himself at his stupidity. He should have known street cameras were everywhere in New York. The first thing he should have done was buy a hat, anything to block his face from those roving eyes. But he wondered, would that even have been enough. *With the new, advanced facial recognition software was it even possible to hide anymore?*

George scurried down the street looking left and right for a sanctuary, some crack, some crevice in which to hide. There! An opening! Stairs leading down, underground. A subway station. George rushed forward, then he high-stepped down the steps into the tunnels and away from the marauding street cams. He pressed flat against a tiled tunnel wall, trying to catch his breath, his heart racing.

George's breath began to even, and he could think again. With sweat running down his face, he realized he had to get out of Manhattan. And quickly. Maybe in Queens there were fewer cameras, more spaces without NSA watching his every move. The Sphere was in Queens. There he must go. He worked up his nerve, pushed off the wall away from the sanctuary, and strode awkwardly to find a subway map.

George, panting, stood on the subway platform waiting for the train. He wiped his face with a handkerchief as his chest loosened and he breathed deeper. He didn't think he had been followed. The couple times he checked he saw no one behind. Now he felt safer, relatively so, in the middle of a crowd on the platform. He swiped his face once more with the handkerchief.

The train whisked up, the doors whooshed open, and George leapt aboard. He flung himself onto a rare empty seat, staring numbly ahead. He had survived. *Survived.* At least for the length of the train ride.

George had lost track of time when the train pulled into the Flushing Meadows Corona Park station. Outside, George felt light-headed as he stumbled toward the park. In the background the Unisphere rose above the tarmac with its three rings.

George took a deep breath and heaved off for the Unisphere, striding gallantly down the walkway to turn on the tree-lined concourse a distance ahead.

George looked at his watch and frowned. *Twelve noon. Three hours to kill.* Some he killed by slowly eating a real New York Rueben sandwich at a deli. The rest he tried to pass by sitting on a bench staring at the silver Sphere off in the distance. Off to one side were the three towers—the observation decks.

The Unisphere and decks had been built before George was born. But he had learned about them in middle school. "Class," his teacher had explained, "the Unisphere was designed for the 1964 World's Fair. It symbolized the progress of civilization, mankind's promise in reaching for the stars. It was built as a shrine to the optimism of the early sixties."

But George also had learned that promise and optimism had become broken by end of the decade. As he stared at the Sphere, George thought the jury was still out on mankind.

The observations decks, however, did not look promising like the Sphere. Observation decks were for "observation." And "observation" could mean spying. The decks were run down and decayed, the perfect cover for NSA agents staring at him through high powered lenses, waiting for his family to catch them all.

George needed to move, he needed to hide from their prying lenses. He looked around, *where to go?* His head stopped. Across the way he saw the entrance to the Botanical Gardens. Foliage—he could hide there.

Deep inside the gardens, George found a secluded bench, concealed among a row of shrubs under a canopy of leaves. He sat down wearily. Resting there, hidden, surrounded by greenness, he felt safe for the first time since this ordeal began. He listened to insects buzzing a short

282

distance away and grew drowsy. His head drooped and soon he was deeply asleep.

George awoke, startled, not knowing how long he'd slept. Where . . .? He was in the gardens, he realized.

He looked at his watch.

"*My god,*" he uttered. It was ten of three.

He bolted up, took the wrong path, realized his mistake, and went rushing back toward the garden's entrance.

I'm late, I'm late, he fretted.

He burst from the Gardens, shirttail out, looking frantically around.

He raced to the Sphere where he arrived panting. He checked his watch.

3:02.

He chewed his lip. *I'm late. Have I missed them?* His heart raced as he strode around the Sphere's circumference, staring ahead expectantly for Virginia and the children.

George completed the circumference, rounding the Sphere to where he had begun.

3:08 . . . 3:09 . . . 3:10.

Where are they? he fretted.

George tried to fight off disappointment.

He made a few more revolutions around the Sphere, then sat on a bench, waiting.

Are they coming?

Finally, at 3:30, he slumped.

They were not coming.

He collapsed, head hanging, forearms resting on thighs. He sat motionless with his eyes tightly closed. *Why weren't they here? Where were they? What had happened to them?*

He rose but couldn't stand the thought of being cooped up yet in another hotel room. He had to avoid that as long as he could. He picked up a map of the park and studied it assiduously, killing fifteen slow minutes. He walked around the park, focusing on trivial features.

He stabbed a point on the map with his finger. There, he thought. He could stay in there for a couple more hours. He rose, stumbling off toward the glass building housing the Queens Museum of Art.

Inside, George found a Men's room and washed his face. He stared at a reflection in the mirror. In the mirror was a pale-faced man with deep circles under his eyes, his face made harsher by the glare of fluorescent lights. This man was at the end of his rope. He could not go on.

George stared at that man. Was it him? He hoped not. That man had given up.

George stared numbly at the face.

Was that his face? Had he, George, given up?

As he continued to stare, George wished he was not that man. George could not be that man, because it would mean he had given up on his family. But his family, even if not here today, was still out there somewhere. He must find them. No, he could not be that man.

George spoke to the man in the mirror. *"Can I trust you to find my family? Can I trust you to go the distance?"*

The face was expressionless.

George turned and left.

In the hallway George found a vending machine and chugged a Coke. He crushed the can in his hand, squeezing violently, and hurled the can in a waste receptacle. He dropped on a bench.

"Oh, god, what am I going to do," he groaned, putting his head in his hands.

After several minutes, he looked up, telling himself, "I guess whatever I have to."

CHAPTER 45

THE ENTROPY OF CYCLES
April 13, 2019
The Queens Museum of Art
Queens, New York

5:00 p.m. EDT

George drug himself upright, uttering a quiet groan, and looked around the museum. Outside it was still daylight. It was safer inside until dark. So he numbly staggered into the galleries.

George found a panoramic black-and-white aerial picture of Manhattan that he liked and studied. George moved to a section with a new exhibition on loan from a London museum. One painting immediately caught his attention.

It was a large painting of a series of circles on a washed out rose and pale yellow background. The circles overlapped at the edges, like a Venn diagram. The circles were not in a line but formed a larger, linked chain of circles.

The individual circles were filled with pleasing pallets of color. Looking closer, George saw the colors were brightest inside the circles and most intense in the center. The colors then began to fade from the center toward the overlap with the next circle. In the overlap, the colors leached to neutrals shades of tans, grays and charcoal. But in that next circle, fresh color began at the edge of the overlap, becoming brightest in the center, only to slowly fade towards the next overlap where they browned again. The pattern repeated throughout the circle of circles.

George was mesmerized by the picture. He stood fascinated by the cycles, first the neutral colors, the burst of color, then again the fading of color, as if in decline, the pattern repeating over and over without end. He looked down at the placard for the title of the work. *The Entropy of Cycles* by Cuthbert Wagnon, Cambridge, England, 1935.

He stood motionless, drawn into the painting.

He did not know for how long he had stood. But after a time a friendly voice floated from behind, breaking the spell.

"He was an English physicist. You like his work?"

George's heart raced. The voice sounded familiar. Not daring to hope, George flung himself around, staring into the mirthful eyes of Buddy. George's mouth fell open, but words wouldn't come. George clasped him as hard as he could, squeezing him. Buddy's face looked painfull from the pressure, but he made no complaint.

"It's good to see you again, my friend," Buddy said, finally released and stepping back, his eyes brightly shining at George.

"How. Where . . .?" George exclaimed, his face a mixture of astonishment and joy.

"Reinforcements," he laughed. "An ally joined to help us—"

"Virginia?"

"Yes, she is safe. We drove from Easton. There was bad wreck on I-78 . . . a truck. It took two hours to clear it."

"But Virginia . . . why isn't she here? Where is she?" George asked, becoming anxious.

"George, George, she is safe." Buddy lightly touched George's forearm, his face happy and smiling. "Rest assured she is fine. Better to take our time tonight and make sure all is safe."

George looked at him, disappointment filling his mouth. *Virginia was so close, but close wasn't enough.*

Responding to the look on George's face, Buddy added, "They are safe. They have a room in Manhattan for the night. It is a good precaution. If I were caught searching here for you, they at least would be free to carry on."

"And the children," George blurted, "they are safe with Virginia?"

Buddy saw the deep need in George's eyes. He tried to appear calm, positive, though even as he answered, he could not completely hide his concern.

"Not yet, George. Not yet." Watching George begin to collapse, he added, "Hold up, George, be strong. You will join your wife tomorrow, and your children then or certainly the next day."

"Virginia . . . tomorrow . . . the children the day after . . . what . . . why . . .?"

Buddy answered quickly to regain control. "George, it's better we try not to move this evening. There are drones flying the streets of Manhattan. They could be in the boroughs soon. Inside a hotel room

Virginia is safe, as we should be soon ourselves. Tomorrow they will be on the street only for a minimal time. Angie will get them hats. Do you have a hat, George, for street cams or drones?"

George shook his head numbly.

"Well, George, come. Let's find you a hat. And after that we can get a hotel room. I will stay with you and keep you safe through the night. But first, come with me, George, let's enjoy the exhibits while it gets a little darker outside."

Buddy hooked his arm through George's. "Let us sit a moment and admire this interesting painting." Sitting nearby on wooden blocks that served as benches, they had a good view of the painting.

George nodded, yes, that would brief, though nice, escape from his fears.

Buddy asked, "Do you understand the painting, George?"

"I like the colors, but I don't know why it's called the *Entropy of Cycles.*"

"I am sure you have heard of entropy, George, it is a principle we deal with in mathematics and physics." George nodded. "You know, then, entropy is the nature of a system to devolve into increasing states of disorder unless energy is added." That sounded right to George. "Energy has to be added to a system to counteract entropy and prevent the system's decline." George nodded again. He had heard something like that.

"The artist is suggesting to us, George, that entropy applies to civilizations, too. Do you understand his point, George? What do you think he means?"

George shrugged his shoulders, but face showed intense thought.

"Reason with me, George." Buddy wanted to draw George further away from his thoughts of disappointment and fear. "What is common about the great civilizations?"

"Well, ah, they start out strong but eventually decline. Like the title of that book says, *The Rise and Fall of the Roman Empire.*"

Buddy nodded, signaling George to go on.

George encouraged for a change, continued. He had to think for a few minutes, trying to collect some thoughts. "I . . . guess . . . the civilization starts out industrious . . . good, unselfish leaders . . . common purpose and goodwill . . . strong character among the people . . . unity?" George looked at Buddy for approval.

"But what changes, George? Once established, why don't they just go on and on, building and thriving forever?"

George thought hard about the different civilizations he knew.

"Well, with the Romans, it seems it was power and gluttony and, ah, somehow they get weak and stopped doing the right things?"

Buddy laughed. "Exactly. Industriousness, common purpose, and strong leadership produce success, stability, and economic well-being. People acquire things and improve their lives."

George nodded yes, that seemed true.

"You know, companies are like this, too," George added, eager to make a point

"Yes?"

"Yes. Often it's a business the grandfather started but by the third generation the heirs are more interested in their lifestyles and image than the business. Or the business leaders can't adapt to changing consumer desires and markets. They lag behind. I guess you could say they lose the insight to innovate or they never had it."

"Exactly, George! Companies are like civilizations in a way. At some point—the point of declination—the civilization, or company, becomes more preoccupied with the fruits of labor than the value of labor. Acting for the common good gives way to individualism, self-centeredness, and greed—cravings for wealth and power, cravings for more and more and more. Wealth disparity, erosion of character, and corruption follow. See?"

George nodded, he has seen that clearly with his accounting clients.

"See the painting? The overlap of the circles is one civilization ending while another begins to emerge. The emerging civilization breaks into its prime as shown by the increasing bright colors in its circle. But notice, George, about midway through the circle, the colors begin to fade and by the circle's edge they are washed out. This is the civilization declining through entropy, the entropy of self-centeredness flowing from the twin preoccupations of greed and power. Then, you see, it follows the path of the civilizations before it, finally becoming dark—brown and gray—the overlapping part representing its decay. Then another civilization begins to emerge. Its circle becomes bright as it matures until it, too, begins to fade and finally dim. It is entropy George, the civilization losing organization to entropy."

"America, too?"

"No one is immune."

"So, is it hopeless?" George asked, feeling again depressed.

"No, not hopeless. Just predictable, George." He paused to let George absorb the lesson. "But remember, George, energy can be added to a system, energy combats entropy. Adding energy allows the system to return to increasing states of order. It is not inevitable."

George rose staring at the painting. Finally, he asked, "But how do you add all that energy?"

Buddy smiled. "One person at a time, George. One person at a time."

George, dejected, sat back down.

"Come, George," Buddy said, the tenderness in his voice soothing George, "let me tell you another story." George nodded.

Buddy began. For another hour, they sat on a bench in the museum before the painting. Buddy told George an incredible story of those who had for generations banded together in a League of sorts. This became a League dedicated to protecting the privacy and freedom of individuals, for privacy and freedom allowed people to think and act independently, to break their cycles of consumption and cravings, to help stem the current of increasing disorder—and to add energy by their actions and examples of building good things, for it all began with one person at a time.

"Is that story true?" George asked.

Buddy laughed. "I don't know. But George . . . I know what is true."

"What?"

"All it takes is one person at a time."

VII.

INTO THE PARK

CHAPTER 46

A DAY IN THE PARK
April 14, 2019
Flushing Meadows Corona Park
Queens, New York

Daytime EDT

Imhoff called Director Cummings to report.

"I think the place is Flushing Meadows—at the Unisphere."

"Frank, are you sure?"

"Not at all."

The Director was silent.

"Frank, a street cam caught George Douglas near Times Square yesterday. Homeland did not share the information. We got it through our own sources—"

"Was he apprehended?" Imhoff interrupted, his voice tense.

"No. He disappeared." The Director paused, then added, "They apparently have not picked him back up. We don't know where he is or any of the others. But Frank, it proves you were right. It was New York. What is your plan now?"

"I'm going to Flushing Meadows to stake out the Unisphere. And wait. If they're not gone already."

"Want help?"

Imhoff looked at Tappy. He decided to omit that he was taking her. He knew the Director would never consent to introducing an untrained civilian into this situation—there was the legal liability—not to mention the publicity if she were killed.

"No help, Director. I can handle it alone."

"I don't know, Frank. This sounds like a long shot. The Unisphere is out in the open, they will be exposed. Doesn't sound like good tactics."

"They won't know any of that. They just want a landmark."

Imhoff heard the Director sigh. "All right, Frank. Give me regular reports. If something more promising breaks we'll call you. If you *do* spot them do not approach. Call for back up. And Frank. . . ."

"Yes, sir."

"Don't screw this up."

"Wouldn't think of it, Director."

Imhoff ended the call, and turning to Tappy, said, "Let's go."

A communications officer knocked on Chambers' office door.

"Come in."

The door opened and the officer rushed in. "NSA sent over a call that it picked up between Director Cummings and Special Agent Imhoff." He handed Chambers the record of the call.

"Has it been delivered to Secretary Ogilvie?"

"No, sir. Secretary Ogilvie is in a closed-door meeting, no interruptions, so I rushed it immediately to you."

"Good work. The Secretary and I are to meet in a few minutes. I'll give this to him."

"Yes, sir."

After the officer left, Chambers walked again to his wall safe. Perhaps this would be his last walk to the safe, he thought.

He pressed the numbers and brought the phone to his ear. He waited patiently for an answer, his breathing regular.

"The Unisphere," he said when the call was answered. "Yes, Flushing Meadows." He ended the call.

Chambers carefully removed the battery from the phone and faithfully counted the seconds. Ogilvie burst through the door just as he had replaced the books on the shelf in front of the safe.

"*Preston*," Chambers said, startled.

"Oh, sorry, Dick. Look, this thing may be working itself out."

"How so."

"We've been kicking it around. Suppose we catch George Douglas— that's good press—we captured a domestic terrorist, and pretty quickly too. But—here's the good part—we don't *have* to catch them."

Chambers looked at him, puzzled.

"Suppose the Douglases escape the country and disappear. There's no one to interview, no story, the media races to the next drama, and the Douglases . . . just . . . fade . . . away. The privacy hacks have nothing to write about."

Ogilvie actually smiled. "We would be sitting pretty either way. We don't have to find them. We could actually *let* them get away."

Preston beamed. He looked the most relaxed Chambers had seen him in days.

"Yes, yes, I see what you mean, Preston," Chambers replied, but without enthusiasm. He had become preoccupied.

"Preston, I hope you will excuse me, I have an important call to make. Please keep me posted." Then trying to add more brightly, "Preston, this may be just the solution we've been looking for."

Preston beamed and walked proudly out of Chambers' office.

Chambers reached for the arm of a chair to brace himself. Preston was right. *It was so simple. How had he missed it?*

They could have clandestinely aided the Douglases in leaving the country while the Douglases thought they were escaping the manhunt on their own. Soon the Douglas' and their story would be reduced to speculation, conspiracy theories, and ghosts. The Douglases would not dare risk publicity overseas for fear of extradition. They would not know DHS preferred to leave them be.

The termination order was a mistake, he now realized. A serious mistake. He had reacted too aggressively. It had seemed so simple—eliminate George Douglas, or maybe all of them. There would no longer be a problem, no embarrassment to the Department. That was the way they did it in the old days.

But it is not the old days. And that realization made him weary.

He removed his glass, rubbing the bridge of his nose trying to massage away the tiredness.

Chambers felt uncertain. Would the Douglases be content—or scared enough—to simply disappear? Or would they try to reclaim their lives and wealth once safely sequestered? They could be dealt with then, off American soil. He had ordered the terminal solution too soon. *What had he set in motion?*

It was so important to protect the Department to protect Preston, the next generation for the party. Had he lost sight of everything else? Was he getting old, too old for the game now?

With alarm, Chambers realized he needed to stop the operative. A public shooting, with cops, autopsies, and press would prolong the Douglas story not end it.

Chambers bolted to the bookshelf, racking off an armful of books. He fumbled with the combination dial, having to start over twice. He jerked open the safe door, yanked at the sealed bag, and tensely punched the digits. He pushed the phone to his ear, impatient for the answer.

"Yes," Finnegan answered.

"Ah, a change of plans," Chambers said trying to regain composure as sweat beads formed on his brow.

"What change?"

"Cancel."

There was a pause. "The order's already been sent."

"Cancel it."

"I can't, Dick. That's not my relationship with the, ah, individual. You can try directly but good luck."

Chambers paused. A direct contact was risky. It could leave trails that could be followed. But, "Okay, okay."

"I'll patch you together, his number is confidential."

"Certainly. And no recording?"

"Dick, you have to ask?"

"I do now."

"Hold on."

To Chambers, the call sounded as if he were on hold, then a single voice, said, "Talk."

"The assignment is cancelled."

Silence greeted Chambers from the other end.

Chambers fidgeted. "Did you hear me?"

"Yes. I heard you," the voice said, a new coldness in it.

"Well, good then. Assignment terminated."

The man laughed.

"What?"

"The money is en route."

Chambers heard a ding in the background.

"Well, what a coincidence. The money just arrived in the account. That was the confirmation."

"Well, consider it an advance for the next job."

"That would put me in your debt."

Chambers did not answer.

"I don't give refunds, because I don't owe people. It gives them the illusion of power over me. So my rule is that when I have been paid for a job, I finish the job," the man said, his tone light. "It would be bad for my reputation otherwise. And my reputation is my stock in trade." He resumed a more serious tone, "So watch the news. Good day."

The connection went dead.

Chambers stared at the phone as if it were a snake. He removed the battery, placing it in his coat pocket. He placed the cell phone in his brief case where it would seamlessly fit with the other business accoutrements. He would burn the phone in his fireplace when home.

Chambers walked to his desk, feeling light-headed and disoriented.

Imhoff and Tappy made an initial stroll through the park. He had bought Tappy a hat and she wore her sunglasses. Imhoff did not want Virginia, or George, recognizing her and rushing impulsively to them, attracting attention. Imhoff planned to control this scene. Tappy could help him secure the Douglases, but it had to be controlled. That's why he didn't want other agents around who could be spotted and spook them or make a public arrest rousing the press and social media.

The park was not particularly crowded, yet Imhoff and Tappy took their time walking to the Unisphere. Imhoff unobtrusively watched ahead and to the sides. Tappy picked up the rhythm from him, as she casually looked around, checking park benches, the long mall, and the approaches. She'd be a good agent, Imhoff thought.

At one o'clock they decided to eat at an outdoor café.

At two o'clock, Angie and Virginia left the hotel, both wearing big sunhats obscuring their features. Angie quickly hailed a cab and the pair jumped in. Maybe in forty-five minutes they could step out at Flushing Meadows undetected.

Last night Buddy had conferred with Angie on the encrypted phone, advising he had found George and they'd be ready tomorrow.

She asked, "Any news on the children?"

He was quiet, then replied, "No."

"Virginia, as you may expect, is highly anxious to see her children. She wants to come over with George to be there in case they arrive early. It is all I can do to keep her here. Should I knock her out?"

"No, Angie, that is not necessary. Just keep doing your good work."

For their part, Buddy and George sat together in yet another motel room, trying to pass the stubborn hours.

After hanging up with Angie, Buddy said, "Virginia, is well. She is strong, George."

George slumped with relief. "I was so worried. If that—if that were our last time together that night in Easton—our fight—I didn't want it to end that way."

"We will reunite you two tomorrow. Maybe with luck . . . the children . . . but if not tomorrow, then the next day."

"You said that once already. How can you be so sure?"

"It is my pledge to your family." He paused, staring at George. "George, your son, Sherman, he is special."

"He's a good boy." George smiled at Buddy, bashful about his pride in his son.

"Yes, that. But more. He holds promise."

"Why thank you, Buddy. Virginia can be a little hard on him. But he'll come into his own, I think."

Buddy nodded, rocking in his chair.

George exhaled a long breath. "Buddy, I feel so much better with you here. It was lonely."

Buddy thought George looked better. "Loneliness is the breeding ground of fear."

George became still.

Buddy, still in his white shirt and black pants, looked George firmly in the eye, "We are with you, George. Me, Angie, Nitko, and many others. Trust in that."

George's eyes became moist, he shook his head. "No one has ever done anything like this for me before. This whole event—it's a nightmare, just a nightmare. I—I don't know how to thank you—you and Bossilini—you both came to our aid—risking everything for strangers. It is remarkable, and I am grateful, my family is grateful however . . . however this ends."

George rose and shook Buddy's hand.

Buddy smiled up at him. "Let us hope tomorrow is a good day, George." George nodded, his head too filled with gratitude and hope to speak.

A few minutes later George began looking around. "Buddy, I can't find my backpack. I must've left in the park."

"Did it have any identification," Buddy asked, eyebrows drawn.

George shook his head, no.

Buddy sighed with relief. "Sit here. I will get you essentials from the hotel commissary. Back in ten minutes."

In fifteen minutes George heard a room card inserted into the lock. He tensed. But the door opened and Buddy's face peered around. "Everything okay, George?"

"Ah, sure, I guess."

"Well, here is something to make you feel better."

Buddy handed him a Styrofoam container. George lifted the lid and smiled, "Thanks, Buddy."

"Warm apple pie and vanilla ice cream on top. Guaranteed to make you feel better, yes?"

"Yes, indeed," George said.

"And some things for overnight in the other sack."

"Buddy, you shouldn't have. This . . . this. . . ."

"Consider it a favor from a friend."

"Well, thank you *friend*." George genuinely laughed and took a big forkful of pie.

Buddy smiled. That was the first real laugh he'd heard from George.

The next afternoon.

In the cab, Virginia tried to dampen her expectations—but she couldn't help flashing a big Alabama smile to Angie.

"Virginia, you know it could take another day. Are you ready for that if it does?"

"It will be today. I just know it."

Angie pursed her lips.

In their room, George was a mix of excitement and worry. His shoe constantly tapped the floor as he compulsively ran the channels on the TV remote.

Late morning, Buddy had gone out to the edge of the park to look around. He found nothing out of the ordinary, no signs of surveillance. When back, he said to George, "It's a go."

They left the hotel at two-thirty. As a show of confidence to George, Buddy left the room key on the hotel desk.

The man wore a black raincoat into the park. Underneath, his rifle was slung over a shoulder and resting in the crook of his arm. Nobody noticed it.

He walked calmly down the mall from the Pool of Industry toward the Unisphere. He left the path seventy-five yards away and took refuge in a copse of trees. He removed the rifle scope from an outside coat pocket, and peered through it at the Unisphere. Perfect. Good lines of sight. Little wind. Level elevation. Clear, slow moving targets. He moved out of the trees onto a bench and casually watched the pedestrian traffic.

He watched Imhoff and Tappy walk the circumference of the Unisphere. He immediately recognized Imhoff as an agent. Probably former military, too, he smiled, but not a sniper like him. *What amateurish moves.*

When Imhoff and Tappy walked to the back side of the Sphere, the man followed. The man was deciding whether to take them out first before disposing of the Douglases.

By the time the man reached the Sphere, the pair was entering the Queens Museum of Art. He took a bench to one side of the Sphere. It gave him good sight of tourists approaching from different directions, while enabling him to keep tabs on the Special Agents, mistaking Tappy for an agent.

He smiled. He had nothing but time.

He knew how to do the time. He knew time was not real. He could empty his moments, where he just sat or lay empty. It was motion and doing that gave the illusion of time. When the moment is empty and without motion, there is no time. One occasion, he had lain hidden in the mountains of Afghanistan for days waiting for his target to stick his head out like a gopher. Then the golden moment—slowing of the breath, feeling his heartbeat, and squeezing, just squeezing the trigger almost caressing it in between heartbeats, and watching the target's head explode in the crosshairs of the scope.

The man kept a relaxed focus, watching the residents and tourists flow by. He decided to try a different vantage point. He checked the museum and saw Imhoff through the glass trying to look out, unobtrusive. He smiled.

Walking along the pavement toward the National Tennis Center, the man liked this approach better. The clumps of trees were wider, providing better cover. He stepped off the pavement into the trees. Yes, he thought, this would do nicely. After the shot, he could easily exit the park along Perimeter Road going against the grain of pedestrian traffic and navigate to his car parked near Cedar Grove Cemetery, then quickly onto the Long Island Expressway . . . and disappear.

CHAPTER 47

IN THE CROSSHAIRS
April 14, 2019
Flushing Meadows Corona Park
Queens, New York

3:00 p.m. EDT

Imhoff missed it.

After several uneventful hours in the park, it was mid-afternoon, and Imhoff wasn't sure anything was going down today.

Now just ambling around the park, he stopped at a coffee vendor's stand. His back was to the Unisphere as he fumbled in his pocket for correct change. He slapped the coins on top of the counter and without turning handed Tappy her cup.

She didn't take it. Her eyes were frozen on the Unisphere.

Buddy and George had entered the park a few minutes before from the southwest side, heading on a northeast diagonal toward the Unisphere. They wore baseball hats Buddy had bought tugged low over their eyes. They walked unnoticed to the left of Tappy and Imhoff.

George and Buddy casually approached the southeast side of the Sphere when George saw a woman wearing a big hat walking along the mall toward Buddy and George about forty yards away.

George's heart leapt. Although the big, floppy Hollywood hat obscured much of the woman's face, George would recognize that walk anywhere. *Virginia*. He could not contain himself. A surge of relief and love flooded him.

"Virginia, Virginia. Over here!" George shouted, waiving his arm back and forth above his head, as he strode quickly toward her. Buddy reacted in alarm, trying to yank George's arm down. After a couple of hard tugs, George looked back at Buddy and dropped his arm.

"That was foolish, George, very foolish," Buddy chastised him, his face harsh.

George dropped his head, uttering a sheepish, "I'm sorry." But then eagerly he looked forward, "That's Virginia, I just know it is."

"Okay. If it is, let's just take it easy. Just walk toward them very easy and we will see." Then he admonished, "Do not attract attention."

George's excited waving had caught the man's eye as he stood sheltered in the trees. He peered intently through the scope. He smiled at the baseball hats.

With a practiced and expert skill, the man quickly attached the scope to his rifle, pulled back the slide, and after taking a careful look around, slowly raised the rifle to his shoulder.

Virginia, attracted to the hand waving, immediately recognized George, along with Buddy, and began running toward them with all her heart, the hat blowing off to the ground, as she shouted, tears running down her cheeks, *"George, George."*

"Virginia, No," Angie shouted. But Virginia had bolted. Angie shouted again, with a new fierceness in her voice. *"NO!"* But her warning went unheeded. *These foolish people.* Angie leapt in pursuit.

As Virginia and George ran toward each other with oblivious jubilation toward the front of the Unisphere, the man in the trees made final clicks to the adjustments on this scope. An easy kill shot. His face was expressionless in contrast to joy on the faces of George and Virginia.

Buddy and Angie tried to close on their charges.

Angie caught Virginia by the arm, but Virginia shook her arm fiercely, breaking Angie's grip and causing her to stumble.

At the Unisphere, Buddy was a step behind George.

The man slipped his finger through the trigger guard, placing only the slightest pressure on the trigger.

George felt a hard shove on his shoulder that stopped him short. A man walking the other way with his head stuck in a tourist map had bumped into him.

"Sorry," the tourist looked up, and then with his head back in the map strode off. However, he had saved George Douglas's life.

George, standing still, his head turned watching the rude man walk off, felt something whiz by eight inches in front of his chest. That must be *some* bee, a distant part of George's mind thought, as he turned to move forward.

But on the opposite side of the Sphere, pink spray burst from a woman's head. She crumpled to the ground. Another woman who had been walking with her began screaming at the blood pouring from her friend's temple.

Buddy knew something had gone wrong, deadly wrong.

He saw George, still standing in place, looked up, and saw Virginia running toward them, arms outstretched. He did not see Angie, on all fours, struggling to rise in pursuit. Buddy watched George step toward his wife.

Buddy saw a little red dot waver on George's chest, then settle right in the middle. Buddy instantly reacted, rushing forward, knocking George hard out of the way. But the little red dot now rested on Buddy's right side.

Buddy's back arched as the projectile struck him, twirling his body a half turn and knocking him to the ground on his back. A red spot began seeping on his shirt, soon spreading to the size of a softball.

"Get down, get down!" Angie, stumbling on her knees, screamed at Virginia, but the pandemonium erupting at the Sphere engulfed her voice.

Virginia stared wide-eyed at Buddy lying bleeding on the ground ahead of her. She raised her head, eyes locking on George's, the shock and terror communicating between them.

"George, Virginia, get down, you both get down! Now!" Angie frantically waved at George, who stood numbly thirty feet from his wife. "Who—?"

Angie, scrambling, had almost regained her feet when someone banged into her hard from behind, pinning her to the ground. She squirmed to break free.

Virginia staggered to George, clutching him fiercely. George, now understanding, took them both forcefully to the ground.

Kneeling, clutched in her husband's arms, head pressed against his chest, Virginia stared straight at Buddy's crumpled form on the ground a few feet away.

"BUDDY!" she screamed.

Virginia broke from her husband's clutch and crawled over to Buddy, who lay gasping. Staring at the blood seeping through his shirt, she looked down into his face.

"Buddy what . . . why?"

Buddy coughed, his spittle mixed with blood bubbles. He gave her the slight smile that was so often on his lips.

"Who would shoot you?" Virginia asked, uncomprehending, horror on her face. She turned back to George still kneeling an arm's push away from Buddy, and it hit her. She turned back to Buddy.

"Oh my god! Oh, Buddy! You saved him . . . you saved George."

Buddy smiled at her. "I promised Carmen I would take care of your family. Let her know please that I fulfilled my promise."

Virginia began crying, and through her sobs, moaned, "Oh no, oh no, oh no." Fixed on Buddy's paling face, she made herself strong. "We have to get you a doctor . . . to the hospital." She looked around frantically for assistance. "Help, help, this man's been shot!"

The scene was a mosaic of bedlam. People hugged the ground for cover, parents lay over children, others screaming hysterically, a few ran crazily out of the park, others lay still on their backs, fingers working cell phones propped on chests. But nothing yet bearing even the semblance of organization—or help.

Virginia looked back down at Buddy. "Hold on, hold on. We'll get you help. Hold on," she pleaded as her eyes darted different directions for hope of some kind of medical assistance.

"Virginia." He coughed again, the spasm racking his body. More blood trickled from the corner of his mouth. He now looked pasty. "Virginia, please look at me. It is important."

Virginia looked down. She reached for him, cradling his head in her hands, tears in her eyes.

"Virginia . . . do not worry. Life . . . existence . . . it all is impermanent . . . that is the heart of the Buddha's teaching . . . do not worry." He coughed again, his upper body rising off the payment from the force. "It is important. . . ."

"Shhh, save your breath, Buddy."

Buddy tried for two deep breaths before he could go on.

"Sherman—it is important to keep him safe." A cough racked him again. Buddy looked back up into her face. "Promise me that. He will do great things. Trust me, you must believe that. He is a remarkable young man." His eyes closed.

"Buddy," Virginia screamed in panic, certain he had died.

Buddy's eyes fluttered open.

"And . . . Virginia . . . don't be too hard on Manfred. He is important, too."

"How could you possibly—"

"Shhh." Buddy exhaled with great effort. "Just trust . . . Manfred doesn't know it . . . but he has come a long way to help. . . ." His eyes began to film over and close.

"Buddy, Buddy," Virginia shrieked, gently shaking him. If he did not close his eyes, she just felt, he would not die.

Buddy's eyes briefly opened again.

"*Om mani padme hum.*"

After chanting the phrase, a great sigh escaped his lips and his head fell limply to the side, his eyes looking out, unseeing.

His spirit was gone.

Virginia cried, "*NO,*" and clutched him fiercely to her breast.

"My god, Frank," Tappy said. "They're falling . . . what . . . is someone *shooting?*"

Imhoff whirled, dropping his coffee and reaching for his gun.

Tappy began running for the Sphere.

Imhoff chased her, and when she bucked his hand off her shoulder, he grabbed a handful of hair and twisting it quickly in his hand, yanked hard, bringing her to the ground.

"*OW!* What the hell, Frank?" She glared at him.

"It was the only way I could get you down. Now goddamnit, stay down. This isn't some damn movie."

"But they're my—"

"Stay down," he shouted.

"Okay. Just go on. Hurry." Her face was grim.

He registered she had begun to cry, but he didn't stop.

He rose to one knee, gun drawn, scanning the perimeter of the park. He was looking for the assassin, or his trail. Nothing. In a crouch, he ran toward the Sphere, with a two-handed grip on his weapon, pointing it at the ground.

He arrived at the Sphere, breathing hard, looking around in quick, sudden jerks. People were beginning to rise, to hug each other, and to try to cope with the terror. He heard sirens in the distance.

Goddamnit, why didn't he request backup? That was basic. How would he explain *this?*

He berated himself, even as his head swiveled, searching for some trace of the sniper. If he could catch him here it may play toward redemption. But he saw nothing. He was a fool.

He stared at the two dead bodies lying on the ground. They lay completely still in death.

The sniper was gone. He sensed that, too.

He shook his head.

The Director's last words had been, "Don't screw this up."

Imhoff grimaced as he holstered his weapon.

CHAPTER 48

BOSSILINI RETURNS
April 14, 2019
Flushing Meadows Corona Park
Queens, New York

3:00 p.m. EDT

On the southeastern edge of the mall at Flushing Meadows Corona Park, Bossilini sat on a small three-legged stool behind an easel on which he drew erratic lines and figures with pastel chalk. He wore a beret, capping off his disguise of a disheveled, dirty-clothed street artist. With the dark sunglasses, even his acquaintances would not have recognized him. That was good, for he did not want to be recognized.

Angie had advised over the quantum encrypted phones that, notwithstanding the wreck and the attention it drew, his identity appeared to be undetected. Now that he had broken away, he wanted to remain aloof, at a distance, watching, observing. He was more valuable as a free agent, moving through cracks and seams as needed.

Angie, in a later terse message, had alerted him the Douglases were trying to meet at Flushing Meadows this afternoon. Bossilini arrived early.

Bossilini cursed the strain and tightness in his lower back from sitting at the easel for hours. As he rubbed his back for some relief, he had no trouble spotting a man who he quickly identified as an FBI agent. He knew that because he knew the woman walking with him.

Bossilini casually watched the agent and woman move round and round the park, trying to act casual, tying to blend in. They were losing focus, he could tell. They had been there too long with nothing happening, no indication anything *would* happen. Even the best were susceptible to the undertow of monotony. It was inevitable. And most got away with succumbing to the dullness of the drifting hours.

He, however, despite his aching back, despite hating drawing the ridiculous crude shapes on the canvas, did not have the luxury of dullness. He remained vigilant, waiting for Angie escorting Virginia. He could not pinpoint their arrival, so he dared not give in to monotony.

He looked for them coming from Citi Field. Angie would be careful, he knew. She would take the longer approach from the Mets Stadium past the tennis facilities, allowing her to observe the landscape, discern any problems ahead—and avoid a trap—before it could be sprung. Yes, he knew she would do this. He had taught her. He had tried to teach her more. But that undid them.

Bossilini was less concerned with George and Buddy. Buddy had trained for this mission. It was the view of Angie, walking exposed with Virginia across the park, in the open, that worried him. Bah, he was becoming an old woman.

He bent over to release the strain in his back. With head hanging down, he watched a bead of sweat drop off his chin, falling to the pavement where it made a tiny wet circle. He watched another drop fall, joining the other. He allowed his head to hang loosely, releasing the tension in his neck, watching the drops evaporate until they were simply no longer there.

When he looked up, it had begun.

Bossilini watched with horror as a man that looked like George waved his hand crazily in the air, shouting as another man, who he instantly recognized as Buddy, tried desperately to stop him. Bossilini turned his head to the right to see the subject of George's foolish attention, but from George's exuberance, he knew it was Virginia. He couldn't believe his eyes. "Imbeciles!" he thundered, watching Virginia run to George.

A horrible foreboding seared Bossilini. He watched, as if in slow motion, Angie starting after Virginia.

Bossilini bolted up, knocking over the easel, sprinting toward the two women.

He watched Angie grab Virginia and then fall as Virginia shook her off. "Stay down," he called under his breath. "*Stay down!*"

On the left side of the Sphere a woman's head exploded. She dropped like dead weight. He saw the look of confusion and then horror on the face of the woman next to her. He pumped his legs harder, feeling them burn.

The sound roared toward him, as if launched from an explosion, the screams, shouts, yells, and wails of fear and confusion from unsuspecting, panicked people.

His only thought was Angie. To get to her as fast as could. And make her safe.

Bossilini ran, his breath coarse in his ears, legs in agony.

Angie was just standing up to try for Virginia again, when in his wildman rush he reached out, grabbing her around the waist, and flung them both to the ground. They landed with her on top, and in one quick motion, he rolled so that she was under him, his broad back protecting her.

Startled, Angie made quick, jabbing moves to escape, catching him squarely in the ribs with a sharp elbow. Bossilini grunted. "It's me, Angie, stop for god's sake before you puncture a lung. It's me, Nitko."

Wrapped in his strong arms, Angie ceased to struggle, though he could feel her coiled to strike again. Good girl, he thought. She wriggled hard, twisting her upper body until she could see the face of the man holding her.

"Nitko. Let me go. I have to get to Virginia."

"Not until I am certain there are no more shots."

Angie squirmed again with renewed vigor to escape the coil of Bossilini's arms. She spat at Bossilini through clenched teeth, "Let me up. Now. I've got to get to Virginia. They don't have a freaking clue—"

"No."

"—and I don't want to tell the children their mommy was shot at the Unisphere."

"*NO*," Bossilini thundered. "I will go. Stay here. I will bring them. Then we all will escape the park, quickly, up to Vermont. I have a car two blocks away."

Angie let go. "Okay. But Nitko, hurry, damn you." She slammed a free fist into his bicep.

Bossilini, crouching, ran around the Sphere, past the dead woman with the friend screaming at her side, past the live bodies huddled and scattered around the Sphere. As he rounded the far side, Special Agent Frank P. Imhoff, with weapon drawn, ran past him heading in the opposite direction, oblivious to the fact he had just run past the driver of the Douglases' escape vehicle.

Ten steps later Bossilini pulled up short upon seeing Virginia crouching over Buddy. Bossilini stared somberly. The racking of her

311

shoulders came from sobs. Bossilini ran his eyes around the crimson circle on the side of Buddy's shirt. And he knew.

Bossilini leaped to Virginia, clasping her by the arm.

He called gently in her ear, "Mrs. Douglas, we must go. George, too. We must leave quickly."

Virginia looked up through a tear-stained face. "You. You . . . came back? I didn't. . . ."

Bossilini looked over his shoulder, locating George. "Mr. Douglas. Come please. Hurry. Hurry. Help me with your wife."

George rose and staggered numbly to Bossilini.

"Good, Mrs. Douglas—Virginia—please stand." He gave her a gentle tug up.

"But—" she said turning back, looking at Buddy's lifeless body. "We have to do something for him. We can't just leave him out here. Who will take care of his body? Who will make the proper arrangements?"

"Come—" Bossilini said, turning back to Virginia.

"No," she said, her jaw set firmly. "We must see that he is properly taken care of. It wouldn't be right."

Bossilini answered her, the evenness of his voice, a lack of emotion for his colleague. "He chose this life. He understood the dangers—and the consequences. He is—was—a professional, Mrs. Douglas."

"But leave him just lying here?" She looked at him uncomprehending.

"Yes, leave him lying there."

Bossilini stared her in the eyes, uncompromisingly.

"He would not want you hurt by lingering, worrying over him, Virginia. If you care to honor him at all, then you will leave with me now. You will only dishonor him if you remain and are caught. Now come."

Bossilini reached his hand out for her.

Virginia Douglas stared at his big hand tentatively. She did not move. She could not move. Vaguely she heard George's voice, but could not tell what he was saying. How can you leave a dead friend—no, not a friend, but someone special, she realized—just lying in the park? How will they know his name, she wondered? How will they know who to contact?

"I killed him. I killed him," George repeated numbly, horribly recalling his waving hand.

Virginia looked at him, puzzled.

312

Suddenly, a caring hand touched her shoulder, followed with a gentle whispering in her ear.

Tappy.

Virginia turned to find Tappy looking at her with deep concern. Tappy nodded at Bossilini. Turning back to Virginia, she said, "Go with Nitko and Angie. They will take good care of you."

"Tappy—what are you—"

"Shhh," Tappy said gently, as if comforting a child. "Go now, Virginia."

"How do you know them?" Virginia cut her eyes toward Bossilini.

"Later. Now go. I will join you soon." Looking up, she asked, "Nitko, where to?"

"Vermont."

"Middlebury?"

Bossilini nodded."

"Virginia, sweetie, let's go now."

Virginia at first seemed not to hear, but she slowly turned and whispered in Tappy's ear. Tappy looked up at Bossilini and nodded.

They rose, Tappy holding Virginia's hands in hers and speaking in a comforting voice to both Virginia and George standing behind her. "Go with Nitko and Angie, I'll join you soon."

"But, but—" George and Virginia uttered in unison.

"We will find them and bring them to you," Tappy answered. "Now go."

Bossilini quickly ushered the couple away from the Sphere to where Angie was waiting. Angie put her arm around Virginia's shoulder. Bossilini linked his arm through George's, and the Operation Agents whisked the couple away.

CHAPTER 49

CHAMBERS
April 14, 2019
Georgetown
Washington, D.C.

Imhoff searched the park for Tappy, his eyes slits, breaths short and shallow.

He needed to secure her safety. *Jesus, the Director.* He'd have to call. But first he had to see that Tappy was safe.

The Douglases had to have been in the park. Nothing else walked. The op had turned black. He had sensed that. Why hadn't he taken precautions, arranged backup? Now two civilian casualties on him. Where was she?

"Frank. Oh, Frank." He heard his name called, feeling a mixture of relief and exasperation. Turning, he exhaled as Tappy Montgomery walked slowly toward him with the Sphere offset in the background.

"You okay?" he asked, studying her, his chest loosening.

She nodded that she was, but he wasn't convinced.

"You look a little shaken."

"Honestly, Frank, who wouldn't be?" She stared at him, her face hard.

"Yeah, I guess so. Now I know you're safe I gotta call in."

"Wait a minute, Frank. There's something you should know first."

He looked at her, impatient. "Okay, what?"

"I know where the Douglases are going."

Imhoff startled. "Why haven't you said something before now, before two are dead on the ground?" His face flushed.

"Because I didn't know this would happen," she snapped, looking hurt by his accusation. "Did you? *You* knew it was an open park."

Pain crossed his face.

"I'm sorry, Frank, you didn't deserve that."

Imhoff blew out his breath. He looked down at the ground, then back squarely in her face.

"Okay, okay. Let's just start over," he offered. "I'm glad you're safe. I was worried about you."

Imhoff waited for her reaction.

Finally, she answered, "Okay."

Tappy seemed to slump, and a tear rolled down one cheek.

Imhoff handed her his handkerchief.

"How old-fashioned," she tried to keep her voice light through the tears. "A gentlemen providing his handkerchief to a crying woman. Who are you, Frank? Robert Taylor? Dick Powell?"

Tappy dabbed her face. She returned the handkerchief, and raising her shoulders, took a deep, composing breath.

"I found them. Virginia told me the address where they are going. I promised I'd bring the children to her—"

"We don't have time," Imhoff interrupted, a plan forming in his mind.

"No, Frank."

"Tappy—we have to beat him there. The man who did this won't stop. He's trained to never stop."

Tappy's face whitened.

"Give me the address. We'll head straight there. But first I need to pick up something from the FO."

"FO?"

"Field office."

Secretary Preston Ogilvie sat at the head of the table in the private conference room adjoining his office. Assistant Secretary Richard Chambers sat at his right, and the Department heads filled the remaining seats.

Ogilvie looked shaken, though stern. "Two dead at Flushing Meadows? One a real estate agent from Queens. But the other? Unidentified, no records, no trace. But of Indian ancestry. The phenomena at the Douglas house . . . two dead at Flushing Meadow . . . only days apart . . . and no group claiming credit . . . were they related?"

"I don't know, Preston, what's the connection, how do we put these two events together?" Bob Harley asked.

"Richard, we pick up any video from the park?"

316

Whitmire shrugged. "Not much to go on. That lawsuit by the privacy fanatics a couple of years ago made NSA take out the cameras from the park. The judge said lack of compelling interest, but he did leave cameras over by the National Tennis Center and Citi Field as a compromise. Tough break they filed the suit in that district."

"How do they expect us to keep Americans safe if they won't allow us the tools to do the job?"

"This judge was a baby-boomer. He remembered Watergate. But, we got something, I don't know if it's anything, but. . . ."

"Well, what," Ogilvie pressed, annoyed.

"We got a shot from the Billie Jean Center camera. It's grainy, but it shows four people leaving the park. It's unusual, that's what got our attention, because otherwise the people were running around like ants out of an anthill."

Ogilvie looked over at Chambers, who he thought looked a little pasty.

"What was unusual?" Ogilvie asked.

"They moved out, calm, professional. Two of the party seemed to be helping the other two out of the park. The calm ones were on the outside, holding onto the middle two. When one of the middle ones looked up, the outside guy pushed his head down, like he knew there were cameras around."

"Hmmm."

"Oh yeah, and the middle two, they were a man and a woman."

"A man and a woman."

"Yes."

"Children with them—ahead or behind?"

"Nope. Just four adults. But the middle two fit the sizes and ages of Mr. and Mrs. Douglas, as far as we can tell."

"What happened to them. Where did they go?"

"Unknown, Preston, they moved off camera and that was it."

"Dick, what do you think?" Ogilvie asked, turning to Chambers.

Chambers had not been paying attention. He was distracted by the horror of two innocent bystander deaths. He had let loose a monster and now had innocent blood on his hands. George Douglas was one thing; that was necessary to protect the administration, to protect its power— or at least he thought it had been— but the others. He had tried to call it

317

off. But this man . . . his type . . . he had made a deal with the devil, and as always, the devil took his due.

"Dick, are you all right? You look a little pale?"

"Preston, I am not feeling well. I think I need to go home. A little rest is all. Be fit and ready to go in the morning."

"Sure, Dick. Sure. We have been under a strain since this whole business began. Let me know later if you need anything."

"Thank you, Preston."

Chambers summoned his driver and was soon pressing the key into the lock of his Georgetown home. He opened the door and the silence surrounded him even before he was inside.

Chambers stepped past the doorstep and paused. He did not want to shut the door behind him and be alone, cut off in the silence. He stared at the grandfather clock that stood still, mute, its hands fixed at some random time, marking the moment it finally wound down, forever.

He thought of Martha.

Chambers shook his head. He walked unsteadily to his library and turned on the gas starter jet for a fire. He had placed fresh logs on the grate the night before. Chambers went to the kitchen while the logs caught. He returned with the bottle of scotch. He poured his regular measure.

After a steadying sip, he reached in his coat pocket, removing the battery and retrieving the cell phone from his briefcase, Chambers put the plastic phone on the logs. He deposited the battery in the kitchen trash.

He watched the flickering fire for a long time. A faint smell of burnt plastic lingered.

He looked up. He smiled fondly at a picture on his desk. It was one of Martha and him taken at a party on their last wedding anniversary together.

"Ah, my dear Martha," he uttered, "I miss you so."

They were his last words.

The assassin stood silently in the doorway to Chambers' study. He raised a black Steyr 9mm pistol with a silencer.

The explosion blew Chambers' head to the side, turning and slamming his body into the back of the chair, with the recoil knocking him forward, his forehead banging the desk hard where his head came to rest, blood pooling on the desktop.

CHAPTER 50

REQUIEM
April 15, 2019
Department of Homeland Security
Washington, D.C.

1:45 p.m. EDT

"We don't know," Ogilvie answered.

His department heads sat stone-faced around the conference room, the seat to Ogilvie's right empty. That was Chambers' seat.

"All we know is his housekeeper found him late this morning when she arrived. She called 911. The DC police called us."

"Do we have any people on the scene?" Bob Harley asked.

"Yes. I—we—are waiting to hear."

"What does it mean that he was shot?" the general counsel asked. "I mean, was it a burglary or a murder . . . or some type foreign retaliation? Do we need to be concerned?"

"Of course, we need to be concerned," Ogilvie snapped, not trying to hide his irritation. "The Assistant Secretary of the United States Department of Homeland Security has been shot to death. I would say that is definitely something with which merits concern, wouldn't you?"

"Sure, Preston, sure," the counsel said, sitting back in his chair, looking sheepish.

"We need—"

The conference room phone rang, interrupting Ogilvie. He quickly answered.

"Yes . . . I see . . . are . . . are they sure? I want you to check behind them, make this a joint investigation, review everything with a fine-tooth comb . . . no, do *not* involve the FBI . . . keep it out. I don't care how you do it." Ogilvie hung up. He sat motionless, staring grimly at the telephone.

"Preston . . . Preston?" Harley gently prodded.

Ogilvie looked up. He went around the table, looking each in the eye in turn, trying to steady them . . . or perhaps himself.

"That was McElroy. He says the DC detectives say it was murder. No stippling. No weapon found. No shell casings, so either the killer used a revolver or he policed his brass."

"Any idea who? Leads?"

"No."

"Related to the Douglases?"

"How could it not be?" He thought, ruefully, *no Plan B for them to leave the country now.*

They sat silently around the table with their own thoughts for several minutes. Then Preston began.

"We can mourn, and we should mourn, but we also have business to attend to." His voice was heavy, hoarse. Looking over at the press secretary, he sighed, "We need a press release. Something good, that does Dick proud, and no mention of . . . well, just say he died unexpectedly." The press secretary nodded. "Get me a draft in an hour."

"Yes, sir."

Ogilvie looked around the room.

He dismissed them.

Preston remained, sitting alone in the conference room. He stared at Chambers' empty chair. He felt empty like the chair. It hit him how much he had relied on Chambers—and how much he would miss him.

Preston felt a stab of uncertainty. Preston had been a rising star, with Dick always just off the stage, always pulling the right strings, giving him the right lines, never seeking personal attention, just serving his party and his country. That had a quiet nobility, Preston thought. Now when he would look offstage, the wings would be dark, empty.

A deep regret filled Preston, tightening his chest and throat. He realized he had never thanked Dick. He had never even acknowledged the man's contribution to his career. He always thought it had been his own ability. Now, alone, head of the one of the most important departments in the world, he did not feel so able. And now it was too late to properly thank the man who had guided him without his even knowing it.

Ogilvie could not take his eyes off the empty chair, even when regret slid into sharp concern. He was now alone at the apex of this mammoth organization headquartered in a city of Byzantine ambitions. Harley was a good man and seemed the right choice to replace Chambers, but he hadn't yet been put under fire—and he had yet to be tempted.

"Oh, Dick, I am going to miss you," Preston called to the chair as his eyes became moist.

Preston thought about the future, his career. There were still rungs ahead on the ladder he wanted to climb. He did not want to remain in place, or worse, start the climb back down.

He wished the Douglas business had been finished. Soon, perhaps it will, but not yet. And he did not want the origins explored too closely, the launching of the *Wildroot* alert that began everything. Space tunnels? It sounded ridiculous now. But on the bright side, it smoked out a domestic terrorist. They had found solid connections with the Middle East, the basis for Chambers' press release. Preston felt much better with that chit in his pocket.

Yet good press—or at least sustained good press—was a rare thing in this town.

He sat still a long time staring at the empty chair as the sun crossed toward the west, with shadows from the east following closely behind.

The ringing of the phone jolted Preston from his thoughts. More bad news? He tensed. He glanced at his watch. The press release was past due. He answered the phone.

It was his secretary. "I am sorry to bother you, but one of our techs has been calling every fifteen minutes since the email to employees advising of Mr. Chambers, ah—"

"Yes, I understand. Who is this person and what is so blasted important?"

"She said she had to speak with you about Mr. Chambers and she could only talk to you and no one else. She said it was urgent and concerned a secret project Mr. Chambers gave her about the Douglases and since Mr. Chambers' demise, she thought she should inform you directly . . . and no one else."

"Who is this person?"

"Ah, Marcie Beethoven, an Intelligence and Analysis supervisor."

What would she be calling about? What was so urgent to warrant an interruption outside the normal channels at such a time? Maybe she had found new connections?

"Give me her number," he said quickly.

"Yes, sir. It's her cell. Mr. Chambers sent her to New York on the drone team."

Thirty seconds later Marcie answered.

"This is Secretary Ogilvie. I understand you have been trying to reach me. This is a difficult day, so it better be important." There was silence at first. Then she began with a slight quiver in her voice.

"You know that project on the Douglases?"

"Of course."

"Sir, I haven't known what I should do since I got the news about Assistant Secretary Chambers."

Ogilvie remained silent.

"After we searched all the Douglases' computers and electronic connections—well, there's a problem."

"So that was when you found George Douglas' terrorist connections, that's why Dick—Assistant Secretary Chambers—issued the press release. So how is that a problem?"

"Well. We didn't. And that's the problem."

"You didn't what?"

"We didn't find anything like that. They were a normal family. There was no terrorist or Middle East connection. No money transfers. No affair. I told Assistant Secretary Chambers that."

Ogilvie was stunned. It took him several moments to recover.

"They had connections," Ogilvie struggled, as if Marcie's information could not be true. "Chambers' press release said we had tracked the money to the Middle East."

"Assistant Secretary Chambers did that on his own . . . I think. He was sure there was a connection, but we had not yet found it. I told him they were clean, there was nothing there, but he said you and he knew things that were above my security clearance. Now he's dead. I don't know what it means."

"You mean—"

She shuddered when it hit her.

She spoke. "Ah, sir, are you saying there was no evidence above my security clearance?"

Preston felt a pounding in his temples.

"Secretary Ogilvie?"

"No, no, I'm not saying that at all. I was just thinking. Who knows about this?"

"Just my team. And, of course, Mr. Chambers. But, er, you didn't?"

Ogilvie did not answer.

"Who is on your team?"

"Jenkins and Hattaway."

"Have you told anyone else?"

"No. Chambers told me to keep our findings to our team. And I did. I was afraid Chambers would put us all in Gitmo if anybody said *anything*. Sorry, sir, I mean Assistant Secretary Chambers. Anyway. I'm scared."

"That's okay, Ms. Beethoven."

"Sir, what do I do now?"

"Nothing."

"Nothing?"

"Nothing, Ms. Beethoven."

She hesitated. "There's one other thing."

Ogilvie cringed.

"The Department has the Douglases' computer and data records before Wildroot. You know, we started searching them right after this happened. But sir, we have a new finding."

"Huh?"

"There is a record showing that someone outside the Douglas house backed up all their devices before the *Wildroot* alert."

"Before—?"

"Yes."

"So what?"

"Ah, well, the Douglas records are now sealed. I cannot see them. No one can. But, ah, sir, if the Douglas records are now dirty when they were clean before, then the backup would expose that somebody altered the records."

"How could someone do the backup. Why?"

Marcie paused, deciding whether to answer. She proceeded cautiously. "Well, one possible reason is someone knew this was going to happen, I mean, the Wildroot alert."

"This was before the particle detection?"

"Yes, sir."

"How could someone possibly know? That's incredulous."

"Yes, sir. Unknown, sir."

Silence.

"What should I do, sir?"

"That entry or code or whatever it is, isolate it and find out who did it."

"Sir—" she began to say that was impossible, but instead, she replied— "Yes, sir, will get right on it."

"I want this sealed up tight like it never existed. No one knows. This will be discussed at the highest levels of authority. Ms. Beethoven, you do not want to screw this up. Do you understand?"

"Yes, sir, absolutely."

"Does your team know this last piece, about the hack?"

"No, sir."

"Are you certain Ms. Beethoven?"

"Yes, sir. Just me." Her hand started shaking. Suddenly she felt very alone—and exposed.

"Okay, then. No else is to know. Do you understand your freedom is at stake?"

"Yes sir."

He was pleased with the sound of fear in her voice.

"Good, then, I will be back in touch."

Ogilvie hung up the phone. He felt anger rising like a fever.

"What in the hell were you up to, Dick?" he asked the empty chair. He kicked the chair away from the table. It rolled on its casters to the window.

This was a disaster. A bogus *Wildroot* alert, now followed by a fake terrorist profile on an innocent *American* family. A press release full of lies that will be exposed? Someone had the Douglases records *before Wildroot?* What in the hell had Dick been doing? It had to be some breakdown, some stroke, he reasoned, maybe a tumor, otherwise it was too inexplicable.

"Damn, Dick, you've put me in a fine position," he said angrily across the space to the chair. But the words faded into silence.

He fumed, running his hands through his hair, mussing the neat grooming. But in a moment he raised his head, smiling. He realized Dick could do one final thing for him.

On the phone, he had almost told Marcie to destroy the record of the data backup, that had been his first reaction. But that could trap him. If he destroyed the evidence, it could be turned on him, he could be charged with obstruction of justice, they would argue it showed he was complicit with Chambers, the destruction a cover-up, a guilty act.

But Dick's death had now become a hook upon which Ogilvie could hang the whole Douglas affair. The story would play that Chambers was behind the *Wildroot* alert. Chambers was adamant the *Wildroot* alert was absolutely necessary to protect the country. The scientists said this was real. Chambers persuaded them that urgency prohibited consultation with coordinating agencies and the White House. So they went along. He had the experience, after all.

Now they know something had been wrong with Chambers. He had been into something that got him murdered. The rush to Alabama and the terrorist fabrications were the actions of a man with dark secrets. Or maybe better yet, an ill man. Yet Preston and the others knew none of that in the exigencies of the moment. If the Douglases surfaced, the government could only too willingly make satisfactory reparations.

Ogilvie cast a last look at the empty chair. The dead cannot defend themselves. With that thought, he rose and left the room.

CHAPTER 51

SHERMAN SPLITS
April 14, 2019
Manhattan
New York

11:00 a.m. EDT

Sherman stared straight ahead while Manfred bounced in the next seat as the New York skyline appeared in the bus window.

"This is going to be cool, guys," Manfred said, smiling. "First time I came here was the '64 World's Fair—guess it didn't turn out like all those futuristic exhibits predicted, but the Fair was still far out—missed the Beatles at Shea in '65—really wish you hadn't told me they broke up."

"Ancient history, Manfred," Carmen said lightly. He flashed her a big smile. She didn't respond, but she did like his smile. She smiled back, thinking her mother couldn't stand him and enjoying the thought.

Their banter annoyed Sherman. He was absorbed in thought. He did not want distractions.

Manfred, noticing the boy's mood, said, "Hey, dude, like, this is the day." Manfred put his arm around the boy. "It's gonna be a *good* day, I can tell."

Sherman looked in his face without expression. "It's not time for good days yet."

"Whoa," Manfred protested.

Sherman pulled Manfred's arm off his shoulder. The boy turned forward, returning to his petulant stare. Manfred looked at Carmen who shrugged.

"Sherman, you're not getting sick, are you?" Carmen asked.

The boy sat as if of stone, refusing to answer.

The bus bounced across the George Washington Bridge. Carmen, wide-eyed and up on knees, looked out the window. *New York.* She turned back to Manfred and giggled.

Sherman ignored them, as if in a trance.

The bus pulled into the terminal. Sherman was oblivious to the passengers collecting their things and marching off the bus. He did not react when Manfred, said, "Okay. Let's go." He paid no attention to Manfred and Carmen skipping down the aisle and bustling off the bus.

Sherman sat alone amidst dust mites floating in the stale air. It was quiet inside the bus, with the outside noises muted, though he didn't notice. He was absorbed by the images in his head. He watched them, the bright, happy colors, as if projected on a screen. Sherman had a problem to solve, and he would focus on nothing else until he did.

"Sherman. *Sherman*!" he barely heard his named called. He broke awake from his reverie. It was Carmen's voice. He looked up. Carmen stood at the front of the bus with a frightened look. Manfred stood tall behind her.

The boy shook his head. Sights and sounds flocked into his consciousness. He stammered, "Ah. . . ."

"Sherman?" Manfred called, puzzled. "Come on," Manfred waved him forward.

Sherman looked around, as if noticing for the first time the bus was empty. He slowly walked to Manfred.

"Let's go," Manfred said. He ushered Sherman ahead of him. "What happened?"

"Ah, I was thinking about something. I had to think it through . . . and I kind of lost touch."

"Well, it's time to get back in touch. We gotta stay together."

Sherman was annoyed at Manfred bossing him.

Outside the bus, Manfred bounced along the street, talking in a barrage. "Hey, let's hit Times Square and read the ticker-tape news screen, see what's happening. Maybe pick up a paper and see if the enemy is up to anything."

"Sounds cool." Carmen smiled at him. "Who's the enemy?"

"The government, man. The government." He smiled at her.

"Manfred, I don't know if you're serious, or you just say those things to get a reaction."

Their banter bothered Sherman. He needed to finish thinking. He flinched when Manfred leapt forward, pointing toward a pretzel cart. "Hey, let's get one of these. You guys want mustard or cheese?"

"I want sugar and cinnamon," Carmen called, gaily skipping to the cart.

Sherman, hanging back, answered, "I'm not hungry."

"Come on, man," Manfred cajoled. "You got to have one." He and Carmen rushed to the cart, eagerly bending over the glass case.

Sherman realized this was his chance.

He had already made up his mind to leave. Manfred and Carmen— their excitement distracted him. He did not want to be cross with them. Plus, he knew they would be caught if they remained together. Three of them would never make it to Vermont. So he was going alone. He had to get to the sunflowers. Manfred and Carmen would be okay, they could meet up with Mom and Dad. He saw how they now made eyes at each other.

Vermont. That was what he had been thinking of so hard on the bus ride. How to get there on his own, which was a big problem he had not yet solved. And what to do when he got there. He hadn't solved that, either. But he needed to split while their backs were turned, and he could get a good head start. He felt badly about leaving them, especially without saying good-bye or explaining why.

Sherman took two quiet steps backwards while Manfred and Carmen leaned over the pretzel cart, then he pivoted and began sprinting down the sidewalk. He was half a block away when Manfred turned to where he had been standing, calling, "Sherman, sure you don't want—"

"*Sherman,*" Manfred bellowed, as he watched Sherman sprint away. After a split second, Manfred tore off after him, startling Carmen, who turned, wide-mouthed, watching her brother run away.

"What's he doing?" Manfred shouted back at Carmen.

She shook her head. "I don't know," she shouted, watching her brother pull away from Manfred.

Manfred tried to catch up, but he was out of shape, and Sherman, a block ahead, suddenly disappeared in a crowd of pedestrians at a street crossing. After few steps Manfred slowed, then stopped. Carmen caught up.

"He's gone," Manfred said, turning to her.

"Oh my god."

Stunned, Manfred and Carmen found their way to a bench and sat, not knowing what else to do. Things had gone so well, Manfred thought, we were almost there.

"Manfred?" Carmen asked in a small voice, incomprehension changing to fear. She looked into Manfred's face for an answer.

He saw her fear but shook his head. "Carmen, I don't know . . . he acted strange on the bus, but I had no idea."

"What are we going to tell Mom and Dad?" She sounded as if she would cry.

"Jesus, I don't know."

In a sinking mood, they sat lost, in a stupor.

Carmen worried that Manfred would now leave, too. He was closer to Sherman. She would be alone on the streets of New York. But she took a deep breath and reached over, patting Manfred's shoulder. He smiled, briefly touching her hand. He shook his head, "I'm not going anywhere." She nodded, then gave him a quick, thankful smile.

They sat dejectedly, but at least together, as the sun beat down upon them and the exhaust from an island full of cars enveloped them in a pale brown cloud.

Many blocks away, Sherman panted to catch his breath and, hopefully, to cool off as he was drenched in sweat. He knew he had lost them. So he had time to try to figure out where he was.

He shuddered, realizing how alone he was, standing by himself on an unknown street in New York City thousands of miles from home, not to mention the whole United States government searching for him. He felt dizzy and his legs wanted to bolt and run again. But though his heart raced, and he could barely hold his legs still, he forced himself to stay in place. He had to figure out where he was. That was the first step.

A part of his mind, fancifully, wished he could find Bossilini. Hope rose that maybe Bossilini had come to New York to see if the coast was clear. Bossilini would know what to do and would help him. He stood hopeful. But only a moment.

"That's bullcrap," Sherman told himself, his expression stern. He must figure out on his own where he was and how to get to Vermont. He remembered his dad had once told him the city was a great grid of avenues and streets, like graph paper. The thought of his father made him teary. But he shoved the tears away.

Sherman stared up at a street sign a short distance away at the corner. Fortunately, it did not have a street cam. If he could find a map, he would pretty much know where he was.

He walked unsteadily toward the corner, as guys from electronic stores called out for him to buy something. A few steps later a street person in a doorway asked him for change. The man had parchment skin, yellowed scummy teeth, a decrepit frame, and gray, dirty clothes. When Sherman, feeling politeness required him to respond, quietly said, "no," the man gestured toward him as if flinging some medieval curse, mouthing syllables Sherman could not understand. Sherman, filled with terror, began running again. Running, running, was all he knew. Running away, away, away. He ran full out for two long city blocks.

Finally, worn out, he realized he had to stop, he was going crazy. The boy spotted a deli across the street and headed to it. Inside, he ordered a Coke and sat at the counter by himself sipping it slowly. His breathing began to steady. The fatigue from running calmed him. He soon began to think again.

Thinking is what he had done on the bus.

He had thought hard about the sunflowers. He didn't have to try to think about them, for images of the sunflowers kept popping into his mind at regular intervals. Sherman knew he needed to understand them, for he thought they were a signal.

But he hadn't gotten much farther than that. He didn't understand what he was supposed to do with the sunflowers. Or what was supposed to happen at the sunflowers.

Sherman picked at a scab on his wrist. He didn't know how he'd got it.

On the bus, Sherman had thought as hard as he could, that's why he was so preoccupied he did not notice the bus had arrived and the passengers had filed out. He was simply sitting, with thoughts flowing around in his head as if he were on a merry-go-round, round and round, each revolution passing a field of sunflowers.

333

Bossilini had told him at the electronics store shortly before all this began that should Sherman have a special feeling or intuition or vision, he should pay careful attention. *Special attention.* Bossilini kneeled down on Sherman's level and looked at him sternly.

"It is imperative that you follow the feeling or image. You cannot dismiss it or say it's no big deal. It *is* a big deal. If it happens, you will come to see that."

"What am I supposed to see?" Sherman asked, slightly alarmed. But then he smiled casually back. "Is it some vision quest, like in my PS 6 game, *Return of the Magus?*"

Bossilini, staring sternly at the boy, reached out and gripped firmly Sherman's shoulders. "This is nothing to take lightly, boy. This is serious as life or death." His tone startled Sherman. "You must promise you will do as I say, that you will obey me." The man's eyes bored into Sherman till he thought he would fall backward.

"Do you promise?"

Sherman blinked.

"Tell me, do you *promise!*"

"Ah, okay, okay. I promise."

Bossilini stared intently at Sherman. That was not good enough.

"Do you promise?"

"I guess I promise."

"No. Do you promise?"

Sherman took a moment, a new firmness arising in his voice. "Yes. I promise. I promise."

Apparently satisfied, he released his grip on the boy.

The encounter had made quite an impression on Sherman. When the sunflowers arose in his mind, he knew to follow them.

But what did they mean? What was he to do? What was to happen?

CHAPTER 52

MARCIE BEETHOVEN WATCHES THE NEWS
April 14, 2019
DHS Control Center
New York

1:00 p.m. EDT

Marcie watched the Special News Alert on CNN on her smartphone. Her coworker Paul had texted her to check it out.

"Oh, my god!"

The broadcaster was a blonde thirty-something who, after informing the hungry public in dramatic tones of Breaking News, broke the news that the Assistant Secretary of the Department of Homeland Security, Richard X. Chambers, had been shot to death in his home."

Marcie furiously texted Paul back at DHS. "Shot?!"

Her phone beeped a second later.

"Marcie, can you believe it?" Paul asked, sounding incredulous. "He was shot. Not a heart attack or a stroke, but shot. Like, who did it? Is somebody taking out the top leaders? ISIS? Al-Qaeda? Russia?"

"I dunno. It could be something simple like a burglary."

"Naw. This is something big. People are going crazy over here. When are you coming back?"

"I don't know. Chambers sent me over here. I guess I'm here until we catch the Douglases or somebody tells me to come back."

"You got a big fat expense account," he said slyly, changing subjects. "Staying somewhere ritzy? Need some company to spend the Department's money?" She could sense his leering through the phone.

"Not really. It's not a lot of fun over here. Listen, I got to get back to the drones. But if you hear something, let me know."

Marcie placed her phone on the desk. She had been flying the drone absently while talking to Paul and watching the newscasts. She briefly focused on the images from the drone, but they were not what interested her. What interested her was a change of plans.

She thought, a frown marking her face. One finger tapped the table in a staccato rhythm as she pumped a foot in matching time. Something was wrong, she knew. Really wrong. She could feel it.

What had Chambers been doing? Why did he lie to the Secretary? Ogilvie did not know what was going on. Why did someone shoot Chambers? Did this project get him killed—was that it? Why? Her foot pumped faster.

She knew about the Douglas download. She told Chambers. Then he was shot. She told Ogilvie. They both had asked if she told anyone else. *She answered no.* She had a creeping feeling that answer was a mistake. With Chambers dead, if she were eliminated, no one would ever know, any loose end would be sealed off. Ogilvie? Could she trust him? She had thought she could. But if this special project got Chambers killed, was she next? Was she in danger? How could she find out? She did not know. She did not know who to trust. But she knew what to do. She had to get out.

The feeling to flee, and flee quickly, gripped her. It was not safe to remain in the office. She turned anxiously, checking the cubicles around her and then the hallway. Empty. But that didn't mean danger was absent.

She rose, reaching for her purse . . . then sat back down. She had something to do first. Someone else was in danger.

Hurriedly, Marcie checked the battery level on the drone. It would need a recharge soon. That gave her just enough time. Marcie leaned over the console and rapidly worked the drone controls, systematically searching the streets out from where George Douglas had been identified on the street cam.

"Where are you . . . where are you?" she softly uttered. She chewed her lip in concentration. Leaning forward, she furiously examined the screen, searching block to block. Without looking, she reached over, clicked a switch, and activated the facial recognition software. She rapidly scrolled and selected a file picture for comparison, then her eyes re-fixed on the screen.

Her foot tapped as she searched while every few seconds checking her watch.

"Too long, it's taking too long," she fretted.

When ten minutes later the drone battery was down to 3%, she sat upright.

"My god!"

She glanced at the facial recognition screen. The screen was split. On one side was a school picture of George Douglas, Jr. On other side was a boy standing outside a deli. The border of the deli screen flashed an emerald green color—a positive match.

Marcie quickly canvassed the block with the drone, but there were no other Douglases that she could see. Is he alone? she wondered, as her foot tapped faster. Marcie almost drew blood from chewing her lip. She needed to contact the boy, but how?

"There!" she exclaimed, sitting upright and touching an image on the screen. The image was a payphone, a remnant, ten steps from the deli. In a flash, Marcie turned to her laptop, fingers flying over the keyboard as she rapidly scanned the databases for the number of the phone.

"Found it," she announced with determination. She dialed the line from her computer.

It rang. And rang. And rang.

"Come on, buddy, come on, put it together, put it together," she called softly, willing the boy to the phone. A quick glance at the battery level— 2%. "Come on, come on now, before I lose you."

She could hear the phone ringing and ringing from the laptop's little speaker. She leaned forward, elbows on the table, staring at the boy. She did not realize she was holding her breath.

Ten steps from the phone, Sherman stood under the shadows from the canopy of the deli, puzzling what to do next.

Gradually, a noise intruded on his thoughts. He didn't pay attention to it at first, but after a few moments he registered it was a ringing sound. It sounded like a phone ringing. Cocking his head, he triangulated the sound and spotted the payphone a few feet away.

Blast, it kept ringing and ringing, the ringing becoming jarring, and no one stopped to answer. He should walk off, he knew. People hung up after a few rings when no one answered. Yet this caller, apparently, was not hanging up. He stared at the phone.

"That's not random," he said to himself.

He tried to reason it through. If it's not random, then it's purposeful. If it is purposeful, maybe it's about us—or me? Maybe it's Bossilini, and he's trying to contact me. Sherman's face brightened. Almost involuntarily he began walking toward the phone. A few steps later he stopped. *What if it's a trap?* He felt caution. But in two more big steps he was there.

He stood before the phone staring at it as it continued to ring. After two more rings, he carefully lifted the receiver. He tried to dampen his expectations—what were the odds Bossilini would find him, and then call him on a payphone?

He had to find out.

Sherman stopped breathing as he nestled the receiver to his ear. He tensed, and said, "Hello."

"George Douglas, Jr. you don't know me but my name is Marcie and I'm here to help you. Don't hang up. Please."

His heart sank. It was not Bossilini.

And it was a girl, he could tell that much—and likely her job was to trap him. He slumped, still holding the phone to his ear. He furiously racked his brain for spy shows he had seen to figure out what to do, how to avoid a trap, or turn it on the other person, but he came up with zip. He was about to hang up. But he decided to test her.

So he asked directly, "How do I know this isn't a trap?"

"Because if it were, I would have already sprung it, and you'd be in custody. Think about it."

He did. He realized she was right.

"You're a girl. Why are you calling?"

Marcie actually laughed in the receiver.

"What's so funny?"

"Well, for starters, I am a little older than a girl. I'm twenty-six."

"I . . . I never talked with anyone that old before."

"Really? You've never talked with your mother or teachers at school?"

The boy blushed. "Yeah . . . ah . . . course I talked with *them*. I mean, I never talked just by myself with a girl . . . or woman, I guess, or whatever you are." His voice trailed off; he blushed at how stupid he sounded.

"Don't worry. I know what you mean. I won't tease you."

338

She sounded warm. And friendly. He opened his mouth to reply, but froze. His mind wouldn't work. He couldn't think of what to say. Anything he said would be stupid, he knew.

"You are George Jr.," she said, filling the silence.

She sounded nice. He wanted to trust her. And she was right—he would already be arrested if she was out to get him. He decided to try again.

"I . . . I don't go by George, Jr. anymore."

"Well, then, what do you go by?"

He blushed. "You promise not to laugh?"

"Promise and cross my heart."

"Uh, Sherman." He added quickly, "It's a nickname a friend gave me."

"Okay, then . . . Sherman," Marcie said evenly, smiling at his shyness.

But with a new seriousness in her voice, she went to the point. "Sherman, you're not safe."

"No joke."

"Seriously, you are not safe. I need to come get you. Just me. I can take you to someplace safe. You can trust me. Where is the rest of your family, do you know?"

Suspicion shot through the boy. *Was she trying to dupe him into giving up his family?*

"Sherman, I'm not trying to trick you. I am not playing you to catch your family. I assume you are separated from them, and that is why I think you are in danger. Is that right?"

He didn't know what to do. She sounded straight. But agents could be tricky—they were trained in how to do that. He squeezed the receiver to his head.

If she was telling the truth, she could make him safe. But if she was tricking him—and he fell for it—they could torture him to tell where his family was, and when they figured out he didn't know, they could use him for bait to capture them. He rocked from one foot to the other, frantic, trying to figure it out, trying to decide the right thing. Oh, he wished Bossilini was there.

A recorded voice interrupted. "Place three quarters in the slot to continue the call for another three minutes." He stared at the phone, and was about to say to Marcie, "I don't have three quarters," when a buzzing tone filled his ear. He knew that was a dial tone. The call was over.

Anger rose from his toes to his head as he slammed the receiver into the cradle where it bounced off, jumping and dancing on its cord. He roughly replaced the receiver in the cradle, staring at the phone and numbered buttons, his face red. He was just about to get somewhere, damn it—and if it worked out, get a ride to the flowers that would have solved a lot of problems.

But now nothing . . . because he didn't have any quarters. He dug in his pockets just in case, but nothing but a ball of lint. He didn't know the freakin' number to call the girl anyway.

He banged his hand on the booth, and shuffled away, shoulders slumping. But three steps later the ringing started again. He whirled, diving towards the phone to make sure nobody else got it.

"Is that you?" he asked, almost out of breath.

"Yes, it is, Sherman. It's Marcie."

"Whew, I thought I lost you. That's good. That's good."

"Why is that good, Sherman?"

"It just is, just because it is."

They were silent on the phone. He wondered if she were leaving it for him to begin.

After he settled down, he asked, tentativeness filling his voice, "Why? Why are you helping . . . me? What . . . what is your job?" The boy tensed.

Another pause. "I work for the Department of Homeland Security."

The boy's whole body twitched. "Oh my god. Are y'all about to nab me?" He almost let go off the phone and started sprinting.

"No, no," Marcie almost shouted through the phone, "nothing like that. Don't hang up, please. Don't hang up."

Sherman realized he was being stupid. She knew *exactly* where he was. He sighed, "I guess there's no point. You can probably see where the phone booth is on your screen. So, if they're coming, then they're coming."

"They're not coming. Sherman, can I tell you something?"

He didn't answer.

"Listen, I think something is very wrong here. Somebody has made a big mistake about your house and family and they're trying to cover it up.

340

I don't know everything, but that's the only explanation that makes sense." She paused for him to respond. He didn't. "Sherman? Sherman, are you still there?"

"Yeah."

He heard her exhale.

"Anyway, I think you and your family are in danger. I've decided to go underground. Like I said, there's something really wrong, I think, and I'm leaving New York. I want you to come with me. I want you safe."

The boy tried to analyze what she said, his brow deeply furrowed. This was too weird, he thought. A DHS worker going underground and trying to help him? That had to be the biggest trap in the world, and he had to be the biggest idiot in the world if he fell for it. But, he *had* seen enough spy shows to know that sometimes the good guys had to hide out because some bad guy in the agency was trying to take them out. He had watched that old Robert Redford movie on Netflix, *Three Days of the Condor*. And then there was the whole Jason Bourne thing. But what was she—good guy or bad guy? He decided to test her.

"Explain something. Why me? Why risk your job and getting into trouble for me? If they catch us you're toast. Why?" He pressed the received as tightly to his ear as he could; he wanted to hear every nuance in her voice when she answered. Then he would know.

"Well," she paused. "I read you essay."

"What essay. What are you talking about?"

"The essay, you know, that one for English. You titled it, *The Grandfather I Never Knew*."

The boy recoiled from the phone, his face blushing. "No, no. You didn't read *that*. How did you get it? Nobody could get that."

"I have access to a lot of data in my job."

"Yeah, but. . . ."

"Sherman, you really can't fathom the breath of our information on *every* American?"

"I dunno. But, nobody was supposed to read that but my teacher." He hated the whiny sound of his voice. "I made Mrs. Andrews promise she wouldn't read it in class. I let her keep it so even my mom wouldn't find it rummaging through my backpack. She said she'd keep it safe. How'd you—?"

"Sherman, relax. It was the sweetest piece I ever read. So tender . . . I cried at the end."

He was now really embarrassed.

"I can't believe you read it, I can't believe it," he blushed.

"You should be proud, Sherman. It was written by a sensitive, thoughtful boy—it's one of the most poignant pieces I have ever read. The depth of your feeling. I knew then that any boy who wrote that could not be mixed up in anything bad and the family that nurtured such a boy could not be bad, either. I cannot let that boy fall into the wrong hands. I *won't* let him fall into the wrong hands. Not now." He heard the determination in her voice.

And he was beginning to believe it, as his embarrassment faded. Finally, he stuttered, "O-okay."

That was all he said for a moment. Then he added, his ever practical self, "Where do you want to pick me up?"

Marcie saw the battery level on the drone had fallen to zero. The drone began falling sixty feet above the payment. She fully intended to let it fall, the impact breaking the camera lens. She watched with pleasure the last few seconds as the pavement rushed up to the meet the drone, then a burst of static followed by darkness. *Good,* she thought, *one less pair of eyes.*

With a wry smile, she placed a flash drive with the record of the pre-Wildroot Douglas download into her purse. She *was* going underground. She could emerge once this was figured out. But she wasn't taking the chance that she was next. She had seen all the movies, too.

She pulled out of the parking garage in her car. Using her car was a chance, she knew, but she reasoned it was too soon for anyone to discover she was AWOL. Plus, everyone was still reeling over Chambers.

Several blocks later she pulled up, double-parking by a deli. She reached over, pushing open the passenger door slightly. She motioned to hurry to a boy with a backpack standing under the awning of the deli. He spotted her and ran to the car, jumping in, slamming the door shut. He stared at her.

"Hi, I'm Marcie."

"Hi, I'm Sherman Douglas."

"I know." She smiled and quickly accelerated away.

CHAPTER 53

AN AFTERNOON IN THE PARK
April 14, 2019
Flushing Meadows Corona Park
Queens, New York

5:00 p.m. EDT

Manfred and Carmen were hot, tired, and forlorn. They had waited together on the bench as long as either could take it, hoping against hope that Sherman would walk back, saying, "Sorry guys. I freaked out."

But no Sherman.

Manfred looked at Carmen. "It's after two. What do you want to do?"

She chewed her knuckle, looking away.

"Carmen, what do you want to do?"

She turned toward him, and he saw the fear in her eyes.

He offered meekly, "I'm sorry. It's hard, I know."

She nodded.

"Manfred." She looked up, slowly taking his hand. "We have to look for him, one last time. I can't face Mom and Dad if we don't."

Manfred nodded. "But Carmen, there's not much time."

"I know. But we have to."

"Okay, then." He rose. "Which way?"

Carmen looked both directions and shrugged. "I guess the way he went."

And they took off together in search of the boy.

They searched blocks and blocks, at right angles, at diagonals, tracking parallel streets. But no Sherman. No towheaded boy. Finally, Manfred stopped in the middle of a sidewalk, where they were jostled and nudged.

"Carmen, we'll never find him," he said, exasperation in his voice.

She said, taking him aback with her firmness, "We have to keep trying."

"But the time—"

"We have to try, just a little longer." She choked on the last words, imagining the reality that Sherman really was gone. And there was no explanation.

He shook his head, sighing.

"Don't act like that with me. He's not your brother."

"Sorry." They moved on.

Finally, they ran out of time.

"Carmen."

"Okay." She glanced at her watch. "Oh, god, Manfred, we're really late." Carmen looked as if she would cry. "Have we missed them? Do you think they'll wait for us?"

"If they can. We did the best we could for Sherman."

"Did we?"

He nodded.

"It's doesn't feel that way."

"Come on, this way." He led her down the street to the subway.

As they walked up the subway steps into the slanting late afternoon sunlight, they stopped, turning hesitantly to each other. Locking eyes, Carmen gently reached out her hand and Manfred took it. Taking a deep breath, together, they turned into Corona Flushing Meadows Park to face what awaited, and hoping . . . hoping.

Finally, over two hours late, they stood on the mall, with the Sphere in the distance as if in a haze. They suddenly stopped still, as if frozen, mouths and eyes wide open.

They stared at a sea of blue—blue police uniforms, blue crime scene technician jackets, and others in blue armored vests. And yellow—reams of yellow crime scene tape marking a perimeter sixty yards around the Unisphere.

"What . . . what?" Carmen uttered, shocked. She had worried about missing her parents. But this?

"I got no idea," Manfred answered numbly staring ahead.

Manfred grabbed the arm of a passerby.

"What happened?"

"Shooting. Two people got shot today. Dead. Where you been? Under a rock?" The guy brusquely strode off.

"Oh, Manfred. Do you think. . .?"

"Naw, it couldn't be them."

346

"How do you know? Who else could it be?"

"It could be anybody, anything." He looked around, irritated by his own fear. "Come on. Let's find a newspaper. There's got to be a stand somewhere around here. This way."

Late edition newspapers were extinct, but they found a barrage of TV trucks, masts high in the sky, flinging up-to-the-minute broadcasts to the hungry public. Tables with mass of cables and equipment sat outside the trucks.

There, a television monitor sitting on a nearby table tuned to a news broadcast. Manfred and Carmen moved to it. On the screen, a reporter with a microphone stood next to a lady who looked in shock. The reporter identified her as Dolores Humbolt, friend of the deceased woman Jessica Bons. The reporter advised the dead man apparently was an unidentified man of Indian ancestry and no more was known of him at that time. Carmen squeezed Manfred's hand so hard he thought she crushed the bones.

Delores Humbolt stood earnestly looking straight into the camera, dressed in tan pedal pushers, a sleeveless madras blouse, and white tennis shoes. She wore wire-rimmed glasses, and her hair was light brown, parted on the side, hanging straight to about chin level. Her blue eyes looked oversized through her thick glasses.

"Dolores, can you lead us through the events of this shocking afternoon."

"Yes. I certainly can. Jessica and I walk every day in the park. It was our New Year's resolution, and we walk every day but Wednesdays, so today was a walk day."

"Okay, Dolores, you were walking, then what happened?"

Dolores frowned, looking at the reporter. "Oh, it was just awful. One minute we were walking and talking—she was talking about her grandchildren, they were coming to visit this summer, she was so excited—then the next moment, she just fell over, just like that." She snapped her finger. "I wasn't looking right at her when she was hit, thankfully, but there was all that blood everywhere. She . . . she must've been dead before she hit the ground. My god, it could have been me." Delores shook, pressing a hand to her forehead, pausing to compose herself.

Turning to the reporter, "I know you want to know if I saw the shooter, but I didn't." She added, shaking her head, "I don't know where the shot came from, either."

"Did you know the man who was shot? Had you seen him around the park before? The authorities say he appears to be from India."

"No, I don't."

"Do you have any information who may be responsible for the shooting? No group has yet claimed responsibility."

"No, I don't." Looking straight into the camera, she announced firmly, "But I feel it was one of those domestic terrorists, you know, the kind that are now acting alone or in those cells."

"Do you have any evidence of that?"

"No, no evidence, but you know, they recently found out about that horrible man from Alabama, pretending to be a normal American family, fooling everybody, when all the time he was sending American money over to radical Islamists."

The reporter tried to interject a new question, but Dolores was on a roll.

"And I'd like to say this to our government, that shows we need *more* surveillance not less, we need to ferret out traitors like that Alabama man . . . and the man that murdered Jessica, my friend." She pointed into the camera as she spoke.

"This shows how wrong those liberal privacy extremists are, and that Mister Snowden and his crowd. I want my country to be safe. I'm tired of taking my shoes off at the airport. The government can know anything it wants about me. I'll tell you that. It can search my cell phone and computer, look in my closets, look in my drawers, anytime it wants. If you're a loyal American, you got nothing to hide, the ways I look at it. And maybe they can prevent something like . . . like this." She turned toward the Unisphere, and clasped a tissue to her eyes.

"Thank you," the reporter said, pulling the microphone back, quickly ending the interview. "This is Roger Ford interviewing shooting survivor Delores Humbolt at Flushing Meadows Corona Park, site of the shooting earlier today. Now back to you, Selena."

"Thank you, Roger. To recap . . ."

"Manfred," Carmen whispered urgently. "A man with no identification from *India*. Do you think—?"

"What would Buddy be doing out here by himself? He was with your mom and dad and Bossilini. They all would have been here. If it was him, they wouldn't have left."

"But what if they *all* were here. And somebody shot at them and Buddy was the one hit. Oh, I hope it's not him. He was really nice to me. He helped me see something about myself . . . and about Mom."

Manfred put his arm around her shoulder, surprised at her fondness for Buddy. "Naw. Don't worry. The odds of that are infinitesimal. Besides, they shot a lady that has nothing to do with your family. For Buddy to get shot they'd all have to get separated, which wasn't going to happen with Bossilini there. Then, somehow he'd have to come to the park all by himself." Manfred shrugged like, why would he do that?

Carmen thought for a moment, then looked up at Manfred. "He would come here if they *were* separated. This is the *meeting* place."

Manfred frowned, but quickly waved his hand dismissively. "That's just being paranoid. *Whoa—what's that?*" Manfred leapt, pointing over nearby rooftops where a swarm of drones hovered and darted singly and in pairs. "It's *War of the Worlds.*"

Carmen couldn't help a brief, small smile. "They're drones. They're everywhere now."

"Drones?"

"Yeah, flown remotely. There's big ones that launch bombs."

"What do these little guys do?"

"The fly around, a lot have cameras."

"Cameras?"

"For public safety, the police and military can monitor them."

"*Police?*"

"Yeah."

"*Carmen, we got to get outta here.*"

Carmen's face froze at the realization of the danger.

Manfred grabbed her arm and they beat it out of the park.

A few blocks later, Manfred spotted a Dunkin' Donuts. "There," he pointed.

Soon they were seated at a table with two chocolate-covered doughnuts each, a coffee for Manfred, and a large bottled water for Carmen. Manfred hadn't gotten into bottled water yet. He didn't see the point.

Carmen sat still, breathing rapidly, staring down at her untouched doughnuts. Manfred had already crammed down one. As he swallowed, he looked over at her. "Hey, you okay?"

The old Carmen answered, "How could I be okay after *that*?"

He nodded. He looked outside. "We gotta make a plan."

She nodded. "We need to get to Vermont."

"How? I don't think we can hitch out of here, especially after the thing at the park."

"It wasn't a *thing*, Manfred, two people were shot to death."

"Ah, sorry. Maybe we can take a bus again. Yeah, that's the ticket. But we need to go back to Manhattan to catch it. I bet they're shutting down everything here."

They had tickets for the 8:30 p.m. bus to Hartford. It was the best they could do for the night—and they *had* to leave that night. From Hartford they'd figure how to get to Middlebury. Carmen figured that's where they needed to go.

They sat together in the very back of the bus staring straight ahead, expressionless, as the bus rolled along the highway. Manfred turned to Carmen.

"This is like the last scene in *The Graduate*—you know, when Benjamin and Elaine rode off in the bus."

"Who are they?"

He looked at her.

"Hooboy." He shook his head.

350

VIII.

MIDDLEBURY

CHAPTER 54

YOU SHOULDN'T HAVE COME HERE
April 15, 2019
Rose Street
Middlebury, Vermont

12:15 a.m. EDT

"I'm sick and tired of riding in cars," Virginia said. Scowling, she rubbed her temple.

"Indeed. About as sick as I am of driving you," Bossilini retorted.

"Maybe we *all* should be thankful we're not back at the park in handcuffs—or shot dead," Angie interrupted them. She wasn't in the mood for these two bitching.

"Yes, yes, you're right," Virginia quickly agreed, shaking her head. "We don't want to be disrespectful to Buddy."

"What do you think will happen to him?" George asked.

"Well, he's dead, George, so obviously not much else," Bossilini replied, sharpness in his voice.

George blanched. "I'm sorry—I didn't mean—what I meant—do you think they will investigate him, trace his background?"

"That will be a little hard to do," Bossilini said.

Angie shot Bossilini an angry look.

Virginia broke the tense silence. "I am so grateful for him—he helped us—and it took his life. I—can't make sense of this." Virginia, shook her head, eyes leaking tears.

Bossilini sighed.

Angie sighed. "Nitko, we can work the mission and still mourn for our comrade. You are in charge now."

"Yes, yes, you are in right. I am sorry if I sounded callous. This . . . was quite a shock to me. And I am supposed to be used to shocks. He was a fine man."

Virginia looked to the seat next to her. It was empty, though it shouldn't be. She saw only the vinyl seat and unlatched seat belt hanging listlessly. No person, no spirit, no presence filled the seat. She turned away with eyes wet and shiny.

Finally, in the dark of night, after all the miles and the turmoil, the death of a comrade and the lost children, the sign read, "Middlebury City Limits." Bossilini sat straighter, clenching his jaw. It ends here one way or the other.

Not too long after midnight, they pulled onto a quiet, dark street. The house was quaint, wood painted yellow with white trim, pots with ferns hung from the arch over the front porch where two white wicker rocking chairs sat invitingly.

George and Virginia looked at each other, but neither moved.

"So are we sitting in the car all night?" Angie asked. When no one moved, she said, "Well let's just go knock on the door and see what happens." She shoved open the car door. Bossilini frowned at her.

At the doorstep, George and Virginia pressed Angie aside and looked at each other, something unspoken passing between them. George nodded. He raised a hand, and fully extending his index finger, pressed the doorbell.

George tried to carefully listen for sounds inside, and after what he thought was a polite interval, if ringing a doorbell at midnight could be considered polite, pressed the button again. This time a light somewhere in the house came on. He heard footsteps, coming closer, then a voice, "Hold on, I'm coming, I'm coming."

The porch light suddenly bathed them in yellow light. The door chain slid, scraping, then the deadbolt clanged back into its housing. The door creaked open and an older woman with graying hair in a granny nightgown cocked her head, blinking, and asked, "Who's there?"

George answered for them. "It's me . . . us . . . George and Virginia. And, er, some friends."

The woman paused a moment, peering out at the persons standing in her doorway. She tilted her head back for a better look through her bifocals and recognized her son and daughter-in-law.

"I can't believe you decided to show up here."

George looked sheepish. "Well, er, we really didn't have anywhere else to go, really."

"I can believe that."

"Is there any chance Sherman and Carmen are here?"

"Who's Sherman?"

"Ah, George, Jr. It's a new nickname . . . it's a long story . . . I can explain later."

The woman stared at him.

"No, your children are not here." Then, peering at them, "Why would you ask that?"

"Well, er, we don't exactly know where they are."

"You've *lost* your children?"

"We did not *lose* them," Virginia answered sharply, stepping up next to George.

"Did they run away?"

"No."

"Well, you lost them, then."

"Ooo, George, coming here was a mistake. I knew it."

"I was so sure they would be here," George said numbly.

"You going to stay on the porch all night?" the woman said grumpily, holding open the door. "They got the house under surveillance. Government car's been down there on the next block since the news broke about you. But from what I can tell, the pair they sent aren't too sharp. They're asleep now. Obviously, government didn't think you'd be stupid enough to come here, or they would've sent the A-team."

"It's not true," George protested. "None of what they said about me is true."

"None of its true," Virginia corroborated.

"I know *that*, George," the woman said with irritation. "You're not crafty enough to be a spy."

Virginia's eyes narrowed.

"And besides, you would never have done those things. You're a conformist."

"What's wrong with conforming?" Virginia demanded.

"Nothing, unless—"

"Hold on, hold on. We forgot introductions," George said, trying to diffuse the brewing argument. "Bossilini, Angie, this is my mother, Star Douglas. Mother, this is Mr. Bossilini and Ms., ah, Angie. They helped us. Actually, saved us is a better way to say it."

"Saved you from the government?"

George nodded.

"Well, then, very glad to meet you indeed and thanks for taking care of my family. Now, where are the children?"

George and Virginia paled, and answered in unison, "We don't know."

"Lord."

Later, after Star was in the kitchen brewing hot herbal tea, Bossilini sat filled with pessimism along with Angie and George in the living room.

"Where's your father?" Angie asked George, knowing the answer, but wanting to change the subject before Bossilini fell completely into the pit of his dark Hungarian mood.

"Don't know," George answered, looking embarrassed. "I never knew him. Star—"

"You call your mother Star?" She knew that he did.

"Yes. She was a hippie, Woodstock and all that. She always insisted I call her Star. She wouldn't answer to Mom. Anyway, she hinted he may have been killed in the Vietnam War. I saw my birth certificate once when she had to turn in a copy for Little League. In the box for father it just said, 'The unknown soldier.'"

Bossilini could only shake his head.

George answered, "Sherman said we had to go to the sunflowers. Star has a huge garden of them in her backyard. But he's not here. Do we stay?"

"We must give the children more time, but, really, our time has run out," Bossilini said flatly.

"What does that mean?" George asked. "The children will show up here, surely?" hopefulness lighting his face.

Bossilini shook his head, shrugging. "I want to have a look at the sunflowers," he said.

"You can go out the back door in the kitchen." Angie nodded her head toward the back of the house.

In the kitchen, Star didn't think much of his poking around in the dark. "There's nothing out there but flowers and you can't very well see them at night. But suit yourself . . . and here's a flashlight."

"I'll come with you, Nitko," Angie said, walking toward him.

"No, I want you in here with them . . . in case. Thank you," he said, turning to Star. "But I will not need the flashlight. It would only signal my location."

"The boys down the street?"

"Maybe."

He stepped outside.

Virginia took her herbal tea and sipped it alone in a living room chair while the others remained in the kitchen. She did not like herbal tea but didn't want to begin a new argument with her mother-in-law. In fact, Virginia did not like much of anything about her mother-in-law, beginning with her name. Virginia found the name Star distasteful and everything about the sixties it signified. *What a ridiculous name for a woman her age*, she thought. It wasn't even her real name. George said her given name was Cheryl Laura Douglas. *Star, really?*

The truth, which Virginia did not know, was that during the sixties—specifically the last night at Woodstock—Cheryl Laura Douglas had taken the name Star when, lying on a blanket looking up into the black inky sky, she saw a star that looked like a shimmering diamond bubble. Gazing at it, and thoroughly stoned, she thought the star was cosmic. When the sixties ended, she kept the name. She thought it helped keep alive the spirit of the sixties even if only in a little, personal way. Besides, she liked it a lot better than Cheryl, though as the years passed it became incongruous with her aging face.

Bossilini probed in the dark around the rows of giant flower stalks, pushing a few aside, peering inside, stepping in a short distance, then walking around their perimeter, finally standing still and listening carefully, staring at the big flower heads. There was only silence. Minutes later he returned inside.

357

Angie looked expectantly at him, but he shook his head. Nothing.

She frowned. She was angry at Bossilini. She felt trapped, with a government car down the block. They couldn't hide from prying eyes forever; it was just a matter of time. Her anger at Bossilini was irrational, she knew. But he was a familiar focal point. After the sweetness between them died some time back, they simply argued like angry pit bulls. She gave him a hateful glance now.

Bossilini gave no reaction. He was used to it, though he never liked it. It was their dance. It always ended this way.

"We need to get some sleep," he barked. "Tomorrow will be a challenge and we need all our wits about us. I would expect a raid at dawn."

"I'll take the first watch," Angie, said, ice in her voice.

Bossilini nodded. "We need a contingency plan for the middle of the night. Our code word is *Birmingham*. If something happens, the person on watch yells *Birmingham*. Everyone runs to the bedroom away from the woods—I think George and Virginia's room—and go out the window. I checked. It will open and has no screen. It's only a short jump to the ground."

Angie rolled her eyes at his need to always have a plan.

"Okay, then. The rest of you get some sleep—while you can."

"Come on everybody. I'll get you situated," Star said.

Later, in the guest bedroom with the lights out, Virginia turned to George. "Why did Sherman tell us to come here. It feels like a trap."

"He didn't actually tell us to come *here*. He said we needed to go to the sunflowers. I just assumed—" George began to feel sick. Had he misunderstood the boy? Had he led them into a box canyon?

"Come on, George, this is where he meant. He's never seen sunflowers anywhere else."

"Anywhere else we know of."

"George, you're being ridiculous. Sherman meant here, but why? George, do you think there is something wrong with Sherman? What if he has a brain tumor or something? Would—"

"He doesn't have a brain tumor, Virginia."

"Don't be cross with me. It could explain—"

"There're no symptoms. There would be symptoms. He's fine. The sunflowers are the only thing. We just don't understand. Yet. Maybe we will. Don't worry yourself anymore. We've got to get some sleep like Bossilini said."

"Bossilini was agitated."

"What do you mean?"

"Did you see the way Angie looked at him."

"I—"

"She looked like she wanted to kill him."

"I didn't—"

"You never do, George. You're not good at reading women. Go to sleep."

"How do I go to sleep with *that?*"

"You just do, George. You certainly don't have a problem falling asleep at home." With that, she turned over, pulled the covers to her chin.

"Don't hog all the covers," George mumbled, then he was out.

Sitting on the living room couch next to Angie, who had moved a chair by the window, Star stirred her coffee to dissolve a clump of brown sugar. Under the circumstances, she had switched from herbal tea to coffee.

Star had changed into blue jeans and a Middlebury College sweatshirt. Angie noted she was trim, with angular lines, pale gray eyes, and gray hair with a nice wave to her shoulders. She looked young for her age, with soft, fair skin. She was attractive, but not pretty.

The two women were silent for a few minutes, Angie barely nudging the curtains to look out.

"Are we in Dutch?" Star asked.

"Seems like it."

"Oh, well." Star sighed, resignation clear in her voice. She looked at Angie, "Who are you and why are you helping my family?"

Angie took her measure. They were in a fix, there was no need for reticence. They'd all be incarcerated or dead in a few hours.

"We are a group that watches out for unnecessary or excessive government intrusion into personal lives and privacy. We believe in a

359

strong nation, but we believe in individual freedom. Spying on the enemy is one thing, but we don't believe in government spying to gain power over its people. Your family got caught in a government cover-up to avoid embarrassment. Some high-up officials made a bad decision that has now spun out of control with a life of its own."

"Thank god someone still understands and carries on the fight."

"We do not fight, unless for self-defense. We work behind the scenes to try to rebalance situations, to restore equilibrium."

"At least you're doing something. Everyone else has been asleep since 1980. That decade killed America."

After a few more moments, feeling she could trust Angie, Star began talking. Angie didn't mind listening. It would help keep her alert.

"I guess you can see Virginia and I have a little tension."

Angie turned, looking at her evenly.

"I didn't want George to marry her. She's not a bad girl, but god is she self-centered—and conservative as hell. She's obsessed with her children climbing the ladder of success. As you can see, that's the opposite of me. The alphabet generations laugh at us now, but we really believed we could change the world back then, that we could live in peace, and be real. But you know how that turned out."

Angie thought she looked deflated. She asked, "So what happened?"

Star studied her.

"I knew whoever George married wouldn't be like us, you know, us sixties folks. The times had changed. Carter was a President before his time, then Reagan swept in, and people wanted to forget the sixties and the despair from Vietnam, Chicago, riots, and the Iran hostages—it was Yuppies spending and Wall Street on steroids—Madonna and *Miami Vice*, with Ferraris and white jackets over pastel shirts. No more paisley. Little did they know. The young women George's age never heard of Betty Friedan. I thought Michael J. Fox on that show *Family Ties* was supposed to be a comedy, but it turned out to be a true prediction." She shook her head. A strand of gray hair fell across her face.'

"I always hoped I'd have a daughter-in-law that was thoughtful and sensitive. Virginia was sensitive all right," she said with a rueful edge. "It built up, you could see it coming, then the big blowout five years ago. I don't even remember how it started. I'm sure it was over Carmen. I probably said something I shouldn't, like Virginia was raising Carmen to be a neurotic social-climbing perfectionist—the implication was she'd grow up like her mother. I didn't say the last part, but Virginia understood my condemnation of her. I can be pretty awful, don't you think?"

"Not if it was true," Angie said neutrally.

"I was scared," she said, placing the cup firmly on the coffee table, as if for some justification. "I was scared for Carmen. And I was scared about everything I cared about. It seemed that everything important, everything we'd worked for, that some people had died for, was just washing away, washing away with the conservative, materialistic tide without a trace. Carmen, I thought, had real potential to do something. But I worried it would be wasted with Virginia turning her to into a little material bitch."

"Anyway, I just lost it. I packed my bags, visit over. At the door when the taxi pulled up, I said, 'I'm never coming back *here*. If you want to see me, you can come to Vermont where it's real.' Virginia said in the most hateful voice I'd ever heard, 'Don't hold your breath.'"

That was five years ago. Haven't seen or talked with them since. I tried to call for the children and George, but I think Virginia screened the calls on the answering machine. Then they got smartphones with new numbers, kids too, didn't bother to give them to me, well, George did his for emergencies, but Virginia didn't know."

She took a deep breath. "Anyway, I sent presents to the kids on Christmas and birthdays. They'd send little thank-you notes in child scrawl. But nothing else. George probably couldn't help it. Sometimes a man's got to choose between his wife and his mother. I guess I know how that came out."

Star shrugged, folding her arms across her chest. "It still hurts, deep in my soul, though. With all I stand for, with all the spiritual work I'd done, in the end I was just as nasty as the most unenlightened, ah, whatever. I nuked her and I shouldn't have, and I'm paying for it. Some karma." She tried to make a wry smile, but the sadness and tears would not let her.

"Sorry," Angie said. There was some sincerity in her voice, but she was focused on the business at hand. "You need some sleep."

Star nodded. "Too many unhappy memories for sleep now."

Angie saw that Star now looked embarrassed. Angie looked to the window, but turned back to Star.

"You know you two are alike?"

Star looked puzzled.

"You and Virginia. You are just alike."

"Virginia and I are *nothing* alike," Star crossed her arms in definance.

"Not on the surface. But you are both strong-willed, opinionated, and just plain stubborn at times. You are just opposite sides the coin. One heads, one tails. One on the left, one on the right. That's what makes you think you are different. But you're cast out of the same metal."

"Hmph." Star turned her head to the side.

"You really see, don't you? You know what they say. Boys pick a girl just like dear ole mom." Angie laughed.

"That's the first time you've laughed. Or smiled. You have a pretty smile."

"Don't change the subject."

Star frowned but Angie gave her forearm a little squeeze.

"Now," Star took over, "let me give you some advice. I don't know what this is all about, and I don't completely understand why they are chasing my family, but I feel they are in good hands with you and Mr. Bossilini. Don't be too hard on him. All time together is precious. *I know.* You were together once." It was a statement, not a question.

"Once."

Star watched her.

"Yes, we were together once. It was intense, we were intense. But we worked together. He my superior. Our intensity on the job—and off—destroyed us."

Star nodded, thinking of Virginia. I know how that goes, she thought.

CHAPTER 55

THE NAMELESS ASSASSIN
April 15, 2019
Rose Street
Middlebury, Vermont

2:00 a.m. EDT

"Let's go over it again," Imhoff said, his voice all business.

"I got it, Frank."

After picking up the gear at the FO, he drove fast as he could to Middlebury, only stopping at a convenience store to buy a thermos in which he poured a whole fresh pot of black coffee.

"Better watch out, Frank," Tappy commented. "You'll be stopping every twenty miles to pee."

He gave her a sneer. He could hold his coffee with the best of them. *How'd she think he made it through all the stakeouts?*

In Middlebury he flashed his credentials and "commandeered" a yellow taxi. He had Tappy sit in the backseat like a fare passenger as he drove, using his phone to navigate to Star's house. Now four blocks away, he pulled to the side.

Turing back to Tappy, he said, "Let's go over it once again. I will pull up to the house, stopping at the curb on my side. You exit on the driver side. I will lower my window and you approach. Pull your wallet out of your purse, act like you're giving me money for the fare, snap your purse shut, don't look back, and walk as fast as you can to the front door. Go in quickly when it's opened."

"Frank, really. This man—he may not even be here. He could—"

"He's here."

"How do you know?"

He stared at her evenly before replying. When he did, his voice had a ruthlessness that took her aback. "Because I would be here."

Tappy blinked at Imhoff.

"Okay, Frank. I understand. I'll play it by the book."

"And remember. You have to convince them to stay inside, that it is dangerous outside, that a sniper is waiting for them, particularly George.

Tell George and Virginia, and the people with them, it is the man in the park. That ought to scare them enough."

She stared at him.

"It's on you, Tappy. No one goes out. Not to check the weather, not to get the newspaper, not to the corner store for milk. Nothing. And they stay away from the windows. Pull all the curtains. Got it?"

"Got it. When *do* we come out?"

"When I tell you it's clear."

"What if we don't hear from you?"

"Then you really better not come out."

They locked gazes, then he started the engine and pulled away.

Five minutes later, the front door of Star's house opened, and Tappy stepped inside, quickly shutting and locking the door behind her.

The man watched impassively through the night-vision scope. The headlights from the taxicab erupted in a flare of light, momentarily searing his eyes, but the pain quickly passed. His eyes adjusted and he watched a woman pay the cab and enter the house. She carried no luggage. He noted that detail.

He lay in a stretch of woods on the edge of a field at the end of Star Douglas's street. The woods grew perpendicularly from her street for two blocks in each direction and two blocks deep. The trees gave him cover for his shot and for his escape to his vehicle parked at the opposite edge of the woods. He had positioned himself at an angle from which he could see the front and side of Star's house. He could see enough of the backyard to reposition for a quick shot there if the target presented.

He had watched the Douglas entourage arrive, but as they walked to the door in a clump, he could not get a clear shot at his target. When he took the shot, he intended for it to count. He was patient. Patience is everything.

He had repositioned once already when alerted by a wash of light as the backdoor opened. The man in the backyard must have thought he was crafty moving in the dark among tall growing plants that at first appeared to be corn stalks, but he realized were sunflowers. He couldn't tell if the man in the backyard was armed, but he seemed to be examining

364

the flowers. The man returned empty-handed to the house. He smiled. *They would never know when it was coming.*

Wearing dark clothing, he blended perfectly into the foliage. He would wait patiently until his primary target—George Douglas—appeared, either at a window or in the backyard, where an amateur like him would think he was safe. The man felt derision for his target. That was against his training. He was supposed to invent stories about the target. That enabled him to remain alert and focused for days. He didn't care. He was doing things his way now. And he found derision was just as effective for alertness and focus.

The woman from the taxi was a puzzle, however. He had to assume she was a conspirator with the fugitives. The only weapon could be a handgun or H&K MP5K in her purse. That would be no match for his Vanquish Nemesis Mini rifle. He decided he would take her out, too.

At three-fifteen, when the house was finally dark, he saw movement at the edge of the flower patch. Two shapes moved forward into the stalks. They were small. Then he realized one was a child, the other maybe a woman.

He watched intently for five minutes, but there was absolutely no movement, no rustling of the stalks, no sound, nothing. That was strange. He decided he needed to position himself closer to the backyard.

He set up fifty yards from the flowers, rifle pressed to cheek, barrel resting on its bipod, peering through the scope. And he waited.

CHAPTER 56

THE SUNFLOWERS
April 15, 2019
The Woods at Rose Street
Middlebury, Vermont

3:00 a.m. EDT

"Park here," Sherman told Marcie. "We'll walk through the woods."

"What?"

"We don't want to drive up. Someone may be watching."

"True," she acknowledged, though the prospect was chilling.

"Besides, we're going to the backyard."

"Lead the way. Hey, how are we going to make it in the dark."

"No problem. I explored all over these woods last time I was here. There's an old deer trail that runs to the house. I blazed a tree over here to find it."

"Well, okay." She shrugged, took a deep breath, and started forward.

Marcie had successfully driven them out of Manhattan. Speed was essential. She had to get them away from peeking street cams and curious drones. Then maybe they would make it. Maybe. Marcie drove fast and efficiently. She intended to race ahead of the discovery of her "departure," ahead of the storm. It would help that Vermont was an unlikely destination.

When the concrete city was behind them, Marcie stopped and poured a bottle of water on dirt by the shoulder of the road. She quickly made a mixture of mud, took a clump in both hands, and smeared it over half the numbers on her license plate. She washed the mud off her hands with a second bottle of water.

"That was really rad," Sherman said, admiration in his voice, when Marcie returned to the car.

She simply smiled and gunned the car back on the interstate. Speed was their savior.

They talked along the way, though Sherman had moments of embarrassment that were simply awful. He had never spent a lot of time with pretty girls, not to mention being cooped up with one in a car for hours.

Marcie sensed his awkwardness and smiled as she pressed on.

The miles relaxed Sherman making him more comfortable with her.

"Uh, you mind if I ask you something?"

She turned to him smiling. "No."

"Well, like, what was your job at Homeland?"

She turned with a tense smile. "I was in Intelligence and Analysis."

"What does that mean?"

"It means I used information technology to analyze data trails—cell phones, texts, emails, video, whatever—looking for patterns and chains. When I found one, I tried to find a link with a bad guy, and follow the link back to the bad guy's leader."

Sherman's eyes grew wide. "Would you then go blow him up with a drone?"

Marcie did not smile this time. "No, not me."

Marcie stared back at the highway.

Sensing her discomfort, Sherman asked, "You don't like your job anymore?" He added, "You don't have to say if it's uncomfortable or something."

Marcie shook her head. "No, it's not that. I'm just trying to find the words."

She turned toward him with a grave look. "It used to be simple. We all were on the same team, we had the same mission, we worked together."

"What happened?"

"Something changed."

"What?"

"I don't know."

"When?"

"I don't know that, either."

"Why?"

"Their power was not enough, I suppose."

"Whaddya mean?"

"They wanted control."

"Control of what?"

"Everything."

"Everything?"

She nodded.

"Oh."

"My turn now." She changed the subject. "Why the sunflowers?"

He swallowed. "I don't know," he lied. It was not completely a lie. He knew where to look, but not what he was looking for.

"You don't know?"

He shook his head that he did not, then stared at the road ahead.

As they drove along the miles toward Middlebury, they settled into an easy, quiet companionship. They could not anticipate what was waiting for them.

A deer trail is not very wide, especially when abandoned for years. Marcie, and to a lesser degree, Sherman, stumbled along the trail, with roots grabbing at their feet and low branches pulling at their arms and faces.

"Ouch," Marcie complained, as a branch scratched her cheek, leaving a mark.

"Shhh," Sherman whispered. "We've got to be quiet."

"It hurt."

"It will just have to hurt quietly," he shot back, which he normally would never do to an adult.

Ten minutes later Sherman whispered, "Stop here."

He crouched, obscured in the woods at the edge of a backyard.

"They're real," Marcie whispered, amazed, as she gazed upon the sunflower patch, rustling in the breeze only feet away.

"Told you," Sherman answered.

"What do we do?"

"Let's wait a second to make sure the coast is clear, then we'll go in."

When the night remained still and empty, or so he thought, Sherman said, "Let's go." He rose, stepping around a shrub, parting the branches

369

of a sapling and stepping into the backyard. He turned. Marcie was right behind him. He nodded at her—*Okay, come on.*

He moved quickly to the sunflower patch but stopped short. The plants stood before him, tall, like guardians, the night painting them black and gray. The silhouetted stalks, as if standing in formation, were intimidating, taller than either he or Marcie, and bunched closely together like a dense, forbidden forest.

For a fleeting moment he wondered, once inside, if he could find their way out again. But that was silly, he thought. Yet as his eyes looked up, the giant flower heads looked like big, dark faces staring down upon them in stern disapproval. He shuddered and thought maybe they should leave. Yes, they could turn around and simply go back to Marcie's car.

Whoa, get a grip, he told himself.

"This way," he called over his shoulder.

He crouched, took two steps forward, pushed open a pathway between the outer stalks, and stepped inside.

Marcie shuddered as she stepped into the thicket of the alien-sized plants.

Sherman made their way in, pushing stalks aside with his shoulders, arms, and hips when necessary.

"Sherman, what are you looking for? It's creepy in here. Ooo, what's that? Sherman! Something just ran across my foot. This—"

"It was probably just a lizard—"

"A lizard?"

"Yeah. It won't hurt you."

Marcie didn't answer, but she stepped carefully, looking around for creatures that could run through her legs—or drop down upon her.

A third of the way in, Marcie gasped when Sherman fell to his hands and knees.

"Shhh! I told you, you can't make noise."

Sherman crawled along the floor of the flower bed, his hands extended, digging his fingers in the soil as he carefully inched forward, working the soil.

"What are you doing?" Marcie asked, fear seeping into her voice.

"I'm trying to find it."

"Find *what?*"

The boy reached out, groping the area in front of him. He stretched his arms forward as far as he could reach, feeling for the ground ahead.

"Sherman, find what?" she whispered. "I don't like it in here. The flower tops look like they're staring down on us, like they're mean. Oh my god, I'm losing my mind. Flowers are not nice or mean—"

"Don't look up, then."

"Sherman, that's not help—"

"Found it," he exclaimed.

"What?"

"Crawl up beside me. You can help."

Marcie braced herself and moved beside him. He scraped a pile of dirt and seemed to be clearing a perimeter. She positioned herself beside him and began helping.

"Sherman—"

"Shhh."

"But there's big white worm."

Exasperated, Sherman brushed it aside. "It's not a worm, it's a centipede."

"Thank you for the distinction."

Marcie returned to work. Two inches deep she felt her hand scrape across something cool and smooth, as she raked a handful of dirt away.

Sherman frantically slapped dirt off the remainder of the surface.

"Move back," he ordered.

Marcie scooted back, forgetting her fear.

Sherman seemed to be searching for something with his fingers. Suddenly he dug his fingers down and began raising a square metal sheet about two-and-a-half feet square. It screeched on rusty hinges. He threw it forward revealing an open, dark square.

"Sherman—"

"Hold on."

He leaned forward into the square, then miraculously it flooded with light.

"Come on," Sherman said, "feet first." He slid into the lighted square and disappeared.

Marcie tottered at the top, eyes big. She was not going down there, not down there where there could be lizards and centipedes—or worse.

"Come on," Sherman hissed, motioning for her. He appeared to look around wherever he was, then back at Marcie. "You can't stay up there. Somebody might see the light. Come down now."

"Okay, okay."

Holding her breath, she crept to the edge of the hole and looked down. Metal rungs ran down one side into a room of sorts. She exhaled, closed her eyes, and turned to back down the steps.

Sherman watched her. "Come on. There's nothing to it. Hurry."

"Okay." She breathed out, worrying herself down, then planting one foot followed by the other firmly on a concrete floor. Her nose twitched from a pungent earthen, musty odor. The room had concrete walls with moist spots from water in the soil. But when she turned, Sherman's face was jubilant.

Sherman climbed up a several rungs, reaching up far, and pulled the lid shut. He slid a bolt locking it.

Sherman looked around the room. It was just as he remembered.

"Sherman, what is this room?" Marcie asked, eyes wide, turning around, staring at the shelves lining it.

"I didn't know at first. But then I saw on old magazine article. I figure it's a bomb shelter from the sixties. You know, those movies we saw in school about how people thought there would be a nuclear war with Russia and built these shelters."

"Yeah, we saw the old film reels and laughed at them. Like hiding under your school desk would save you from an atomic bomb." She paused. "It's not so funny anymore with North Korea."

Looking around, they saw rows of shelves. Shelves filled with stacks and stacks of canned goods—Spam, soups, vegetables, fruits, a grocery store of cans, with rust forming round the rims. Next was an industrial-sized bin full of size C and D batteries, green corrosion on their tips and brown acid oozing out their seams. Then more shelves, one with an old battery radio with a three-foot antenna with a pretty spider-web bridge to the wall. Further down, rows and rows of plastic Clorox bottles that Sherman assumed were filled with now putrid water. Nearby sat two dust-coated gas masks with the rubber cracked and brittle.

Other shelves held knives and saws with a patina of corrosion, and a wooden tool box looking flimsy with nails partially worked out. On the floor rested two cots with dingy gray pillows and moth-eaten Army Surplus blankets. A hunting rifle with a shiny, rust-free barrel from the ample coating of oil stood propped in a corner by the edge of a shelf where a Colt .45 lay next to stacks and stacks of cartridge boxes now damp and shapeless from humidity. The rest of the room had various items with which to try to survive the aftermath of a nuclear attack.

"Did your grandmother show you this place?" Marcie asked, eyes fixated on the relics.

"Naw. I found it exploring the sunflowers. The flower patch was here when she got the house. She bought the house from an estate sale, I think, when some old geezer died. She had gone to Middlebury College and wanted to move back when my dad went off to college."

"How did you find this?"

"I was playing in the sunflowers. They were really giant like Jack and the Beanstalk except they weren't strong enough to climb. Anyway, I found this square patch and raked the dirt off and found the lid. An old padlock had rusted off, so I raised the lid."

"I looked inside, saw the room, found the light switch, and went down. That's it."

"What did your grandmother say about it?"

"I never told her. I never told anybody. It's my secret place." He added shyly, "You're the only one who knows."

"Well, I feel very honored then."

He looked up, giving her a brief smile.

"How did you know to come here?"

He paused, looking down, like he really didn't want to answer. But she stared at him, insisting. "Sherman, I think you and I are past the point of keeping secrets, don't you?"

"Well, okay, then. But you got to promise not to think I'm weird."

"Promise."

"It's like I kept seeing images of the sunflower patch. Bossilini had told me if I had images of something, or how did he say it, an intuition about something, then I should pay attention and follow it. I said, 'sure,' but he didn't like the way I said it, so he got real serious with me and everything. It was a little freaky because I didn't know what he was talking about."

"Bossilini?"

Sherman squinted at her. "Just a guy."

"Anyway, I didn't pay any attention to the sunflowers when they first popped in my mind, but the third time I wondered if this was what Bossilini was talking about. So when they kept coming, suddenly I knew it *was* what he was talking about and I needed to come here. That's why I ran away from my sister and Manfred—"

"Your sister and who?" Marcie, obviously, knew about the sister, but Manfred?

"My sister's Carmen, you probably know about her. Manfred is a guy who was helping us."

Marcie instantly stiffened. Helping? "Were two people helping your family?"

"Three actually."

Sherman saw her face draw tight. He suddenly felt the need to be very careful.

"I . . . don't know who he was. He came to help." Sherman avoided the piece about Manfred time-traveling from 1969.

"Oh," Marcie uttered absently, staring off to the side.

This is not going well, Sherman thought. He had too much explaining to do on something he couldn't explain.

Marcie's senses were on high alert. She was trapped alone in a locked underground bunker with this kid whose family home had strange happenings before the government invaded. Now there were people *helping* them. Helping with what? Was DHS right after all? Suddenly, she felt claustrophobic and her skin clammy.

Sherman sensed her withdrawing from him.

"Look, I know all this sounds crazy, and, believe me, it is. We don't know what happened. Really, you got to believe me."

He gulped. He couldn't read her. "Why don't we look around, find why I was supposed to come here. Okay?" he offered. "I'll even let you look with me. I won't hide anything, okay? You get to see it when I find it, if there's anything to find."

This could be valuable, Marcie thought. Discovery of some valuable intel could help her bargain her way back into the Department. Otherwise, she was screwed.

"Sure, Sherman," she said soothingly, smiling, watching him carefully. "What do you think it is?"

"No idea. We have to look around and see if we can find anything."

"You take that side, and I'll take this side, and maybe we can find it," Sherman said, eager to please her.

She nodded.

"I just bet there's something here for me to find."

"What could it be, Sherman?"

"No clue."

She eyed him carefully to make sure he was away from the guns. They turned their backs to each other and began searching the shelves, prodding, sliding things aside to look behind, with Marcie often turning to check on Sherman, who was painstakingly searching the detritus from the Cold War. His earnestness added to her confusion. Was she just being paranoid?

Watching him, she reached her hand to the back of a shelf, and found it. Her hand touched something metal and cool. Behind a row of woolen hiking socks was a metal box about the size of a large sheet cake. The box was new with only a thin sheen of dust, not dirty and rusty like the other museum pieces. As she reached for the box, a spider ran out across her hand. She gasped and dropped the box which clanged.

"What? What?" Sherman wheeled around.

"Sherman! Here, I found something," Marcie answered, recovering.

He was by her side in an instant. "What? What?"

She carefully slid the box off the shelf, knocking off a row of socks, and carried it to one of the cots. They kneeled down before it, looking at each other.

"It's got a combination lock," Sherman said.

Marcie stared at it.

"Let me try it," Sherman blurted, seizing the box in his lap.

His fingers flew, working different combinations of numbers, but the lock held fast.

He looked up at Marcie, but she only shrugged. She was really confused now, about the box, about the boy, about what they were doing here. But that box could hold the answer.

375

"What's an important date, Sherman? If you're supposed to find it, then shouldn't you know the number?"

He frowned a moment, then lit up like a LED bulb. "That's it," he shouted.

He quickly spun four numbers on the lock, and the latch opened.

"Sherman," she said amazed. "What was the number?"

"The first four digits of my birthday," he said brightly. "That's weird, isn't it? It couldn't be a coincidence, I mean, the odds are astronomical. But how would whoever put this here know my birthday?" He shrugged, "Let's see what's inside."

Sherman flung off the lock and opened the lid expectantly as Marcie looked on, as anxious as he was to see inside.

CHAPTER 57

THE LAPTOP
April 15, 2019
The Sunflower Patch
Middlebury, Vermont

3:30 a.m. EDT

A black laptop was inside. A thumb drive lay on top. Next sat a powerful portable battery with a connecting cord for the laptop.

They looked at each other.

Sherman carefully lifted the laptop from the box.

Marcie relaxed. Maybe she had not been played after all. She hoped not. She liked the kid.

"Power it up, big guy, and plug in the flash drive. Maybe we can figure out what is going on." She smiled expectantly at the computer.

Sherman became pensive, studying her. He looked at the laptop, back to Marcie, then back to the laptop. He frowned. He looked at her. "I'm supposed to be the only one to see this."

Marcie's mouth flew open. "*What*? How do you know?"

"I just know. I want you to go up top now," he said without looking at her.

She stared at him, speechless.

"Now."

"Sherman . . . I came all this way . . . I helped you . . . you don't trust me, you want me to leave just as you're about to discover what this is about, why things went so crazy?"

The boy looked at her without flinching.

"It's not personal, Marcie. And I really appreciate everything you did for me. We can talk later." He turned, looking at the computer, then back to her." But this is something I have to do alone—that I should do alone. So, will you please just leave. I'll catch you up top." It was not a request.

Marcie sighed, casting a him a thin, hurt look, and climbed the steps. She was able to slide open the bolt on the door after a couple of tries and climbed outside into the dark.

"Close the lid, can you," Sherman ordered.

The clanging lid was her answer. He leapt up, latching the door.

The boy could now turn his complete attention to the device. In his zeal, he did not think it could be useful for Marcie to come back if there was trouble.

"I hope this thing works." He plugged the battery connection into the laptop and set the laptop on the cot. He lowered himself to the floor and sat cross-legged before the computer. Filled with anticipation, he pressed the power button.

Nothing happened.

The screen remained black. "Oh, no," he uttered with a sinking feeling. He thought, all the effort to get here, all the running, all the time scared, now just when he made it, the hard drive had crashed. He hung his head, too dejected to cry.

But a moment later he looked back at the machine. Suddenly, the power button began blinking green, then turned solid green. He heard a soft whirl as operating system powered up. The Windows logo filled the screen. The machine was ready for business. Sherman carefully slid the flash drive into its port. When the menu appeared, he clicked "Play."

For a moment the screen turned black again, worrying Sherman the flash drive was corrupted, but quickly an image of a man in old-fashioned clothes appeared on the screen. He had wavy golden hair with streaks of gray and flashed a friendly smile. He spoke with an English accent.

"George Douglas, Jr., congratulations. May I call you George? Good. If you are watching this, it means you are a very tenacious young man and likely have overcome many difficulties to arrive here. Let me first say it is critical that you watch the entire film, or rather, I think you say, video. The, ah, flash drive, as I understand you call them, will erase if the film, that is, video, stops before the end. Likewise, it will erase at the end of its play. Thus, you cannot watch part and resume later. And no record of this conversation will survive. Understood? Good. You have demonstrated you are adept at following instructions."

Sherman thought that sounded like something out of those Mission Impossible movies. Both cool, and in real life, weird.

"Allow me to introduce myself. I am Cuthbert Wagnon. I am—I was—a physicist at Cambridge in England after World War I when I, along with my colleague and dear friend Sir Nigel Clements, made a most amazing discovery. That I will tell in time, but first let me share a story—the story of the League of Privacy Sentinels."

Sherman was glued to the video.

"You know two of our present-day Agents—Mr. Bossilini, who has been instrumental in your arriving here, and your neighbor, Tappy Montgomery—"

"Mrs. Montgomery—" Sherman blurted, astonished.

"And we brought forward an Officer Agent from my days. You know him as Bodhi Jha. I trust he and Mr. Bossilini and Mrs. Montgomery are all quite well themselves after facilitating your transportation here. Now, young man, down to business. About the League."

Cuthbert told an engrossing story beginning with the aftermath of the Great War, the rise of totalitarian regimes, the Second World War, technological revolutions, microdots, recorders, bugs, secret cameras, miniaturization, drones, IT devices, hacking, computer cloning, data theft —all the modern, fearsome tools that enable governments to peek into the nooks and crannies of its peoples' lives under the guises of preserving their safety and security.

"I assume you may have studied the McCarthy years here in the States." The man paused. "I dare say, George, intrusion into peoples' homes, where their most personal thoughts and feelings reside, does not foster liberty or happiness or safety. There is a saying, something like, 'Be careful how you fight your enemy lest in your zeal to defeat him you become him.'"

The man looked down, clasping his hands behind his back. He looked back into the screen. "Nigel saw it all coming, he saw it all—he was always brilliant, George, really brilliant. So we formed the League of Privacy Sentinels. We work in anonymity to restore balance between government's legitimate intelligence activities and unwarranted invasions of personal privacy. You can learn more about our methods later, but I assure you they are consistent with proper principles. I must stop here and make a point perfectly clear."

He stood perfectly still, then going up on his toes to his full height, his voice rising with his body. "*Balance.* Balance is the key. Balance is essential."

The boy's eyes grew wide.

"George," Cuthbert continued, his voice stressing the importance, "you must never forget this understanding. You of all people must remain balanced. The democracies need robust intelligence systems. Just as our bodies have immune systems to rid them of pathogens, our countries need intelligence systems to rid them of human pathogens. But just as our human immune system can turn upon itself causing harm, like inflammation, arthritis, or cancer, so can an intelligence system turn on its citizens with like harm. Balance, then, is essential to keep these priorities in order."

Cuthbert paused, staring firmly into the screen.

"One last point to remember, George. Paradoxically, it seems, the time to be most vigilant is when the nation is threated, and the people are only too willing to relinquish personal rights for security. But know this, governments do not willingly give up power. So our job is to nudge them, persuade them to step back. We do this by shining a flashlight, as it were, on the wrongful conduct and exposing it—the flashlight is our symbol."

Cuthbert became quiet and appeared thoughtful.

"Let us see if I can wrap this up." He clasped his hands in front of his chest.

"So, George, the League adds new personnel every ten years to continue the work. I have personally participated in selecting the constables, or agents, every ten years from 1929 through 2009. You may ask how could we possibly do that? Let me tell you a wonderful and most improbable story."

Cuthbert, his voice animated and his face excited, told the story of the amazing invention of the Watch, discovery of the Wall, and time travel. The boy's jaw dropped.

"So what we discovered, George, is that the universe is not smooth, but comes in clumps. Planck would say space is full of quanta, but now you would say space is digital, really space is bits of information. It is as if there is a big digital Wall containing all the information that is, and the Wall can be triggered to flash information—reality—outward as if it were a movie projector."

"I read about that, I read about that," the boy leaped up, excited. "I read a *Scientific American* article in the school library." He then sat, feeling foolish.

"Nigel and I accidentally learned to trigger the Wall, and for security, we house the apparatus in a big gold watch." Cuthbert held it up to the screen.

A new look crossed his face. The boy thought it looked somber.

"But . . . we have reached, er, limits for the moment." Cuthbert smiled ruefully. "Events have rendered it impossible for me to go forward to select the new constables."

Sherman sensed the man was leading to something.

"So we need someone to replace me. Nigel is gone. I will be long gone when you watch this video. Yes, I traveled forward to record it."

He clasped his hands behind his back.

"What we need is the one person, the right person, the person with just the precise combination of qualities to possess the Watch and to save the League—yes, it is in danger of perishing. In short, what Nigel and I need is an Heir, an Heir to take custody of the Watch and superintendence of the League."

Sherman wondered who it would be. Bossilini seemed a good choice to him. Maybe Buddy?

"You may be wondering who I have chosen as the Heir."

Sherman nodded. He leaned forward expectantly.

"George . . . it is you. You are our Heir. Of all the candidates, you are the one. I have selected you."

The boy almost fainted. His head swam. Stunned, he blinked, sitting mute before the screen. He blinked again. He said aloud, though Cuthbert could not answer, "You're kidding. I'm not a grown up. I'm not even in high school yet." He leaned back in shock. "No," the boy shouted as the realization grew. "I can't do that. I don't know how. *No.*"

Cuthbert stared at the screen a long while before continuing, as if he knew the boy would have to process the shock.

"Fear not, George, you will have Bossilini and Bodhi and the other Agents and Operatives and personnel to guide and teach you. Have great confidence in yourself, George. We do. You are related to a very dear friend of mine, so I have it on sound authority you come from good stock. Now, our visit must come to an end. You must acquire the Watch. That is your first official duty and the most important one you will ever perform. You cannot—must not—ever let it fall into other hands. That could be calamitous beyond imagination."

"Now, underneath the cot, there is an old electrical plug. Don't worry. It does not work anymore. Count up three cement blocks from the plug. Press the block until you hear a click. The block will release. You may slide it out—replace it when you're done, that is important—and inside you will find it."

"Goodbye, George, and may privacy's flashlight always shine brightly for you."

The screen went black. He heard a soft whirring in the flash drive then it went silent and dark.

Sherman sat staring at the black screen, sitting motionless, silent. Finally, after what seemed a long time, he stood, placing the laptop back in the box and spun the combination to lock it. But first he tried the flash drive again. Nothing. It was blank. He left it the box with the laptop.

He roughly shoved the cot from the wall and bent down, counting the blocks from the outlet. Indeed, the third block clicked when he pressed it. He slowly slid it from the recess and set it on the cot. His hands began to tremble. He carefully reached in the hole, when the thought flashed through his mind—it could be a trap with a blade that slashed his fingers off.

He shook his head, and moved his hand farther into the hole.

His fingers felt something rectangular, like a box. Gritting his teeth, his fingers lightly moved over the box, past its length, to the back end where he could get purchase and pull it out.

Carefully, very carefully, he slid the box out of the hole.

He stared down at the box nestled in his hands. It was a stout metallic gray box with a tin Victorian flashlight set in the top. Sherman did not know what to make of it.

He carefully opened the box, noting its sturdy construction and rubber gaskets sealing out moisture. Inside, lying on plush, red velvet lining, was the biggest pocket watch he'd ever seen. It was made of gold, real gold, he thought. Sherman marveled at the fine watch hands, the grooved winding knob, and the filigreed inlays. Tenderly he removed the Watch. It had heft.

He was about to replace the Watch in the box, when he noticed a small note. It read, "Dearest George, this is a fine English time-piece. Please take careful, very careful, care of it. At a later time, you will be given instructions on its many features, but you will not be allowed to use it until you are age twenty-five. Your humble servant." It bore the signature in blue fountain pen ink of Cuthbert Wagnon. Sherman whistled. He was relieved he did not have to figure out the Watch himself—the wrong twist or move and he could be sailing back to the dinosaurs. But he did feel a bit peeved he had to wait eleven years before taking his first time trip.

In awe, he gently placed the Watch back in the box and securely shut the lid. He tested the lid and found it snug. He carefully slipped the box in a compartment in his backpack.

He tried to rise, but quickly sat back down on the cot. He stared blankly, through unfocused eyes. He was numb, and in shock, as if a sheet woven from his overwhelming feelings had drifted down covering him, binding him in its fabric. He could not think, he could not feel. It was too much—the League, the Watch, the Heir. He only wanted to lie back and sleep, to curl up and sleep and forget.

But, no. Slowly, he felt two buds of feelings pressing through the numbness, feelings that reached upward toward consciousness, as tender shoots in the spring reach up through the loamy earth toward the light.

He shook his head. It was not time to sulk. Whatever this League business was it was huge. But he would have to figure all that out later. For now, his family was in danger.

The boy looked around one last time. He felt glad the old man never had to use the room for the purpose for which he built it. He scampered up the ladder, flicked out the light, and opened the lid, feeling the cool night air trying to press in.

He hopped out of the hole in one leap and turned to find Marcie.

He jumped and stood staring, confused at first, then in fright. Marcie suddenly appeared between two flower stalks, her eyes, wide and terrified, her mouth taped with a mean rectangle of gray duct tape.

"Marcie . . . *what*?!" His own terror grew as he looked down to see her hands apparently bound behind her back.

Then he felt it. A cool, metal point sticking ever so slightly in the side of his neck.

383

"Now, lad, be perfectly still. Not a sound. You understand? Don't talk, just nod your head."

Sherman did.

"Good. It's best if you close your mouth."

Sherman complied and immediately felt a sticky mess plastered over his mouth and the tearing of a tape strip from the roll. His hands were bound with tape in quick succession.

"Come along now."

Sherman stiffened. No, he shook his head. It is in there, he thought. My backpack. The Watch. I can't go with him. He could find it.

His back arched as a calculated blow to his right kidney rocked him followed by a penetrating pain in his back.

"I've not the intent to harm you. It will be better for you if you do as I say."

Sherman became still, standing tall and unmoving, like an oak.

"That's better."

The man quickly patted Sherman down. "This way, quickly. No noise. No tricks. You first," he called to Marcie, pushing her roughly out the back side of the stalks.

A moment or two later they were stumbling into the woods as the man pushed them roughly from behind.

Soon they were in a lair of sorts, up on a hill, nestled in a natural pit with a clear view of the yellow house. They could see only the back of the sunflowers in the rear.

But the sunflowers were no longer the focus of their attention.

Instead, their eyes were riveted on a rifle with scope. The rifle was nestled on the ground with the barrel raised on bipod feet. The barrel pointed down toward Star's house.

As their gaze shifted from the rifle to the man, he looked deeply in their eyes, and laughed.

CHAPTER 58

THE HILLS OF AFGHANISTAN
April 15, 2019
The woods at Rose Street
Middlebury, Vermont

3:40 a.m. EDT

Kill or be killed.

Imhoff was back there—short shallow breaths, beads of sweat trickling down his ribs, heart beating fast, the sour taste of danger. Afghanistan. Instead of New England trees along sloping hills, he faced small rocks and hills rising a hundred yards away. He hated hills. He could never see what lay over the crest, insurgents with weapons or only the blowing wind. But there was only one way to find out. *Take the hill.* Moving forward, he felt like his chest was painted with a bull's-eye.

He blinked.

He felt the same fear, now, in Vermont. But he had to step forward here, too. He had to clear the woods, find the assassin, and kill him. There was only one way to find him.

As he stepped forward, one careful foot at a time, looking around, listening for the slightest sound, then placing the next foot forward, looking around, listening for the slightest sound, he was there again.

It was later in the post-9/11 campaigns, when mistakes piled up, mistakes that had killed innocent Afghanis and Iraqis along with the combatants. The politicians thousands of miles away decided to assert control, for America had allies after all and world opinion was important. So the politicians and their bureaucrat delegates wrote protocols on killing, when it was permissible and when it was not. The insurgents had no protocols. They simply killed Americans anytime and anyplace they could. When briefed on the protocols, Imhoff had shaken his head, frustration pounding in his chest.

He was on a hill late one night along with Corporal Johnson. This time he was looking down his rifle sights not at leagues and leagues of rocks, as before, but at a clear target.

Their squad was assigned to find and kill a particular insurgent who was placing deadly IEDs along a key roadway, disrupting military traffic and killing and maiming Americans. Imhoff, with Johnson, had spent a lot of nights on the cold mountain turf watching the empty desert night while trying to stay warm.

But that night, out of the gloom, into the surrealistic green wash of the night-vision goggles, appeared two men with turbans and the long sleeveless coats over linen shirts. They looked carefully around for minutes, standing casually as if they were simply talking and smoking. Imhoff carefully positioned his M40 rifle, adjusting the sights for the conditions as he peered through the scope. He put the crosshairs on one man, then the other. He had two clear shots.

Imhoff noticed one man stood awkwardly, with one arm pressed down against his left side clamped to his body with the other arm.

"He's carrying," Imhoff whispered to Johnson. "Call it in, live target, get clearance."

Johnson spoke softly into the microphone, barely above a whisper.

"Not clear, Frank. They want identification of the men."

"Get close-ups of them and send it in. They won't be here all night. Tell the desk jockeys we got live targets and get the goddamn permission for the shot."

Johnson quickly punched a few clicks with the camera shutter. "There, Frank, images sent." Then Imhoff heard him talking furiously with someone who would relay the request to a politico for clearance.

Anxious, Imhoff watched the men move to the side of the road, look around casually, and kneel to the ground. They began scraping away dirt and sand, making a hole a few feet off the roadway. Imhoff flinched as they placed something the size of an artillery shell beside the hole.

"They're planting a goddamn IED."

He heard Johnson relaying the info, his voice strident, as his frustration grew. "They're planting a bomb by the roadside. How much more fucking identification do you need? Frank's got him in his sights and can send the guy to Allah and the virgins."

Imhoff tried to slow his breathing. Johnson's tirade was getting to him. He tried to relax as his finger rested on the trigger guard. He imposed control, regulating his breath, slowing his breathing, allowing his heart rate to drop, so he could fire in between beats.

He focused on his breathing as the men in turbans placed the shell in the hole and began covering up it up. "Johnson, is it clear? These guys will be in the wind in two minutes. Am I clear?"

"Not yet. Not clear, Frank."

Imhoff heard Johnson spit words into the mic. But he focused on the men. He had the one on the right dead in his sights, the crosshairs on the man's torso. The only word he listened for in Johnson's exasperated voice was "clear."

"Johnson, am I clear? I got the shot. I am clear?"

He heard Johnson rant something into the mic.

"No, Frank. You're are not clear. Repeat. Not clear. Hold on. Keep the target. I'm trying."

Imhoff felt the heat of rage rising through him, as the men patted the cover over the hole hiding the explosive, roughing the dirt and stray grass to erase any signs of their work. They stood, standing still for just that moment.

"Johnson, they're gonna disappear, they're disappearing. Am I clear?"

"No, Frank. Not clear. Repeat not clear."

Imhoff ground his teeth as he watched the men walk away, becoming dimmer and dimmer, finally melting into the darkness.

He stared disbelieving. He tried to swallow his rage. He thought bitterly, *how do you win when you can't kill the enemy?*

"Frank, they reviewed the images. You're clear, repeat, you're clear . . . for what it's fucking worth. I tell you, Frank, I've had it. I've fucking had it."

"Give me your headset."

"What—"

"I said, give me your goddamn headset."

He snatched it out of Johnson's hand. He didn't bother putting them on, but jammed one receiver against his ear. "Patch me into your contact."

"Frank, that's not—" the voice answered through the headphones.

"Patch me in or when I get back I'm kicking your ass across the desert."

"Okay, Frank, okay."

Someone up the line answered.

"Yes?"

"You just let two turban heads plant an artillery shell by the roadside. I had them in my sights and could have taken both out. That's the mission. To find and kill the guys planting the bombs and blowing apart our guys. I could have killed them, goddamn it. I'm not some unmanned drone dropping a bomb. I am a Marine, and I had real eyes on real targets."

"A team will remove the device at daylight, nobody will be killed."

"You don't understand. They will be back. They will plant devices when we don't have eyes on them. More people will be killed."

"I understand your concern, but we have protocols. There are political complications. The administration—"

"Fuck the administration, you bureaucratic asshole. Have you thought of the political complications if we don't win?"

"Soldier—"

"*MARINE!*" Imhoff thundered.

"Yes, Marine, I understand your frustration but there is a bigger picture here. You need to calm down and work the system. It is a good system."

"Kiss my ass," Imhoff shouted, breaking the connection.

Johnson looked at him, shaking his head.

"Frank, I don't think that was a good idea. You don't need to trash these guys. Even though they don't know shit, they're connected, got clout."

Imhoff looked at Johnson, suddenly deathly tired and black inside. He'd had enough, enough of death, the metallic taste of fear, the strain of trying to survive another day, the sand in his mouth, socks, waistband, and clothes all the goddam time, the baking and freezing temperatures, the thinning ranks of his company.

He shook his head and said, the tiredness heavy in his voice. "Let's get back in and warm up, Johnson. Nobody else is coming tonight."

The men rose and trudged back to base.

The next morning Imhoff's CO chewed his ass up one side of an Afghan hill and down the other. Johnson had a new partner, and Imhoff spent the rest of his tour riding in a Humvee and kicking in doors. He saw more Marines killed and blown apart.

Imhoff stepped on a branch that cracked. He startled, senses on high alert. He frowned. The snap of a branch could carry in the clear night. And whoever heard it now had the advantage.

The assassin looked up. *A sound?* He became still, cocking his head, listening intently. He stood motionless for two minutes, scanning with his night-vision goggles, turning his head to triangulate for sound. He had to be careful, especially with the DHS car down the block.

But nothing.

He shrugged and turned. His two captives were still bound, sitting against tree trunks.

He saw the young woman, wild-eyed, looking around like a trapped animal.

The boy was trying hard, but the man saw tears running down his checks with mucous dripping from his nose over the duct tape sealing his mouth. He knows his father's inside, the man thought. It wasn't hard to realize the rifle was for his family. The man didn't care. He was mostly empty inside, feeling only a cold, ruthless intention to complete his missions.

"Where'd you get the dog-eyes, boy?"

The boy looked puzzled.

"I shot a dog with a blue and a brown eye once."

The man sneered, turning back to his rifle. Only a couple of hours to sunrise. They would come out of the house sooner or later, he knew. With the sound suppressor on his rifle and subsonic bullet, he would be gone before the agents in the car woke up.

Earlier, upon entering the woods, Imhoff had sat on the ground in the dark, perfectly still, waiting for his pupils to dilate, the SPR A36 sniper rifle from the FO lying across his lap. He knew it would take about twenty minutes sitting there to get his night eyes. The goggles were great for close-up work but they were like looking through tubes. He had the whole woods to search for his enemy, and he wanted every last degree of vision.

He was supposed to be in Washington trying to explain to the Director how in the hell things had gone so sideways at the Unisphere. But that conversation could wait. After supplying himself at the FO, Imhoff with Tappy blasted out of New York. *If his career was over, he might as well bag this guy on the way out.*

Imhoff felt the old anxiousness to get moving, to get on with it. This was the best chance to end the sniper and the threat to the Douglases. Something had gone black inside DHS. He couldn't fathom why. But if merely flushed away, the assassin would kill the Douglases at another place another day. That much Imhoff knew for sure. The Douglases didn't deserve that. He was now certain.

The seconds dragged by as Imhoff tried to breathe deeply and release the coil of muscles squeezing his chest. Finally, time to move out. Imhoff stood with the rifle in his hand, turning to the wind, and sniffed. Nothing. He didn't expect there to be.

The woods felt dark and ominous. As he moved through the terrain tree limbs and branches seemed twisted in deformed, menacing shapes. The ground was rough, uneven, and seemed to rise and fall step by step. He stumbled several times, once almost dropping his rifle. But he didn't. A Marine never dropped his weapon. Vines and stickers, meanly clutched and tore at him. He shivered in the deathly silence.

Imhoff felt a grating fear that any moment a bullet would tear into him, and it would be over, he would have failed. With each step, he almost felt surprise he was still standing.

Imhoff kneeled, staring down at the dirt for tracks. Nothing. He breathed hard and fast trying to pump himself up, pump up his adrenaline, pump up his resolve to voluntary rise and run into harm's way, as in Afghanistan when he'd crossed an alleyway or a street or a doorway, wondering if they held a bullet for him.

In the end, the knowledge that this man would continue until he killed the Douglases—and others—forced Imhoff to move out. The memory of how he had misread the threat at the Unisphere steeled him. He could make amends.

Imhoff took one deep breath and flung himself forward. He didn't need clearance tonight. "Not Clear" was not an option. If he got the shot, he was taking it.

Imhoff turned and moved out, his jaw was set. He stepped as carefully upon the dirt and pine needles as he had quietly stepped before upon the scruff and rocks thousands of miles away.

The assassin figured nothing would happen before daylight. He was ahead of the curve on DHS and the FBI, they wouldn't put it together to search the house for a day or two. *Bureaucrats,* he smiled with derision. That's why he moved alone. That's what he liked in Iraq—a permanent green light, free to choose his targets where opportunity presented. But back stateside his freedom was stripped, taken away by the civilians deep in the recesses of the CIA who chose his targets for him, telling *him* when and where and who. So he quietly resigned, left no forwarding address, and became a free agent. Then Security Data Systems began looking for overseas security contractors.

To pass the time, the man decided to search Sherman's backpack. He quickly snatched the pack in one leap and was back at his rifle in an instant. Sherman sat up. The boy became extremely agitated, the man realized. Maybe there was something worthwhile inside.

He unzipped the top and dumped out the contents. He picked around them with his foot, spreading the items out on the ground, nudging some over with his toe of his boot, holding the pack loosely in one hand.

He found nothing of interest, but decided to search the pockets before tossing the pack back at the boy. He patted the outside pockets. Empty. He ran his hands along the front and back of the backpack.

His hands stopped, and a knowing look crossed his face.

The boy wiggled, straining against the duct tape binding his hands behind him. The man smiled.

He turned toward the boy. The man was trim but muscular. His hair was dark, and his face hard, as if chiseled from a cold stone. His lips where thin and cruel, and upturned at the ends as if in a permanent sneer.

The man reached inside the pack to a zippered compartment. He unzipped the compartment, and reaching in, touched something metallic, a small box. He grasped it, pulling it out into the green haze of his goggles. He studied the box, and then flipped it open. He smiled. The goggles made the gold appear chartreuse, but the object was unmistakable.

"What have we here?" He looked toward Sherman with mock surprise. "My, my, where did a boy get such an impressive timepiece?"

"Hmmrjgh," Sherman tried to shout through the duct tape.

The boy's struggling look told him all he needed to know. The watch *was* valuable. Maybe a family heirloom. He grinned. This bounty would add handsomely to his profits for the job. He was even more enthusiastic to complete it. "Thank, you, Richard," he said to the sky. "What an expected bonus for my services."

The man saw the boy settle down and cease struggling. Good. Resignation made the close-up work easier. He would take them with the knife. He disliked it when they struggled and cried and pleaded and made such a fuss. The end was always the same, inevitable, so why not just accept it, and pass effortlessly into oblivion.

The man could not see that Sherman was spitting saliva into the duct tape binding his mouth. Nor could the man see that Sherman's hands had found a sharp rock at the base of the tree behind his back, and that Sherman in short strokes was rubbing the duct tape against the rock. From the tape around his wrists, he had little freedom of movement and his efforts to saw through the tape were clumsy, scraping off skin along with fibers of duct tape. Sherman knew he had to ignore the pain—no matter how sharp, his hands would heal. But the world, as they knew it, could not heal if the man discovered how to work the watch and altered history and ruined the future.

Sherman felt sick. It would have been better, he thought, to have never found the Watch. Now he had led a psychopath to it. The man placed the watch to his ear. "Still ticking," he announced, with that sneer. He placed the watch in a compartment of his black SWAT pants and turned back to the house.

Sherman worked furiously on the tape binding his hands. Sherman had to get the Watch back but, as the pain made him grimace, he knew the odds were not very good. Marcie could tell Sherman was planning something. The snarled determination on his face strengthened her. She would be ready if the chance came.

Imhoff studied the terrain. To find the killer, he tried to figure where he would set up. Imhoff had stopped moving and kneeled in shrubs at a point between Star's backyard and a hill he had seen earlier. He realized it overlooked Star's house.

He studied the hill with renewed interest. *Was the killer there?* Maybe. He stared intently at the hill for five minutes, even slipping on his night goggles, but nothing. Imhoff decided to try to work his way closer to the hill to get a better look, working off to the side, carefully remaining out of sight—he hoped. The darkness helped. But it would be light soon.

Fifty yards farther, Imhoff instinctively knew the hill was the spot. It overlooked Star's front yard and enough of the backyard to provide shooting lanes at someone trying to escape. A saddle led from the hill to a small plateau a few yards away on the right that would allow quick redeployment and a fuller view of the backyard if necessary.

But Imhoff began second-guessing himself. It *was* a good spot, but how did he know it was *the* spot? Surely there were other good places. The man could be in a ghillie suit or under a camouflaged tarp anywhere. Imhoff crouched nervously, trying to conceal himself behind a shrub. He squinted his eyes shut and shook his head. *Think, think*, he told himself. He had to play the odds. If he lost, he lost. But the odds said the killer was on the hill, and the odds were all he had.

He began carefully. He planned to traverse the woods behind the hill over to its far side, and from there, he would attack from the assassin's rear as he looked down on Star's house for a kill shot.

But it would be light soon. He would be visible. Then it would boil down to who saw the other first.

The assassin surveyed the terrain through binoculars. Nothing moving at the house. Nothing moving in the woods. Good. He noticed, fleetingly, the woods were unusually quiet, no bird tweets or insect chirps, but he gave it no further thought. It was early. It did not occur to him the woods were silent because someone was moving through, stilling its inhabitants.

The man pulled a wicked knife from a scabbard strapped to his calf. As he stuck it into a fallen log next to him, he gave a look back at his two captives.

Neither missed the clear import. Marcie began weeping softly.

Sherman shot a look of pure hate at the man's back.

It was not easy going. Imhoff, pausing on all fours and breathing hard, was finally at the back of the hill a short distance from where he would climb, rising directly behind the man in his blind spot. At least, Imhoff if he had figured it right. If not, he would appear to the man's side and then. . . . Imhoff moved out, not daring to stand or even crouch, but crawling on his belly with rifle cradled forward in his arms as in basic training.

Imhoff was filthy. The knees of his suit pants were muddy and wet. One sleeve of his coat was torn and a button ripped off. Leaves stuck down in his belt at all angles from crawling. The front of his shirt was now a permanent a gray color. Briars clung stubbornly to his pants leg. Sweat made drip lines in the grime on his face and stung in the thistle cuts. He looked down at himself and cursed that he'd only had the suit three months.

Imhoff crawled another thirty feet and stopped.

This is it, he thought. Time to move up the hill to greet what was waiting on the other side—an armed killer, or only blowing wind? Imhoff inhaled and exhaled. Then there was nothing left but to do it.

He brought the rifle stock to his shoulder, peering down the sight, and in a crouch, doggedly moved forward, with his finger on the trigger.

Sherman could feel blood dripping from his hands. The pain was searing from scraping and scraping raw flesh, but he sawed back and forth, back and forth. He turned to Marcie as he worked. She tried a smile of encouragement, but he was too intent on working through the pain to free his hands to acknowledge it.

There, it loosened. His hand moved freer, still bound by tape, but now with a couple inches of range. Sherman checked the man who was still looking down on the house. Sherman gently tried to pull his hands apart to tear the last of the tape. It ripped some but still held fast enough to bind him. He couldn't use all his strength to rip the tape, because if his hands shot out when it finally tore, the motion could attract the man. So he returned to sawing on the rock. At least one hand had a reprieve from pain.

Imhoff panted heavily, sucking air through his nose and blowing it out his mouth, as still crouched, he raced as rapidly as he could up the hill. His breath became ragged and sweat poured down his forehead into his eyes. The time for stealth was past. *Now was the time for speed. Fire and maneuver. Fire and maneuver. Fast, fast.*

The man eagerly eyed the rifle scope. The gray light now completely revealed the house, and soon fresh, pink sunlight would rim the trees. "Come on, come on," he whispered toward the house. "Time to get the morning paper."

Sherman felt the tape give. Locking his shoulders, he pulled hard with his forearms and the tape broke, causing his upper body to sway only slightly. He smiled at Marcie and nodded.

He reached up carefully and pulled at a corner of tape sealing his mouth. Wet from his saliva, it easily peeled off and he cast it aside.

Sherman stared forward, at the man's back, his eyes wide. He gave Marcie a barely perceptible nod. He placed his hands on the ground and prepared to push up with his legs and arms. Sitting cross-legged, he felt the resistance from the solid earth underneath his palms as he pressed down. He began to rise and his legs uncrossed. A second later he was up in a crouch with one hand pressed on the soil for balance. His next move was to leap and sprint forward.

Imhoff couldn't get enough oxygen and felt lightheaded as he neared the top. The rifle sagged in arms heavy with fatigue. He could see the crest ahead, but not what was just beyond it. He dropped his head and redoubled his effort. Everything depended upon crossing the next few yards.

Sherman raced toward the man, the determination on his face frightful. He leaped the last few feet landing to the man's right. The assassin sensed the attack, but instinctively yanked left, leading with the rifle barrel to aim and shoot. But he turned the wrong way.

Sherman grasped the knife by its handle and yanked it out of the log, raising it high above his head. He swiftly plunged the knife down into the man's back below his right shoulder.

The man arched his back in pain, but neither screamed nor dropped the rifle. He instantly pivoted hard, striking Sherman in the temple with rifle barrel. Sherman crumpled.

Marcie, hands taped tightly behind her, crashed into the man's ribs. He staggered and expelled a sharp breath of pain. As Marcie tried to regain balance from the collision, the man backhanded her fiercely, knocking her five feet where she landed, hitting her head hard without free hands to break her fall. Stunned, her feet writhed on the ground.

The man reached back over his shoulder with his left hand and pulled out the knife. Though the pain showed on his face, he uttered no sound. He tucked the knife in his belt and turned back to Sherman's crumpled body. With a vicious look of hate, he raised his rifle stock to pummel the boy's face. He stared at Sherman with a white fury. He would disfigure the boy's face as he killed him. No open coffin funeral.

Imhoff, scrambling up like a crab, was now high enough to see the man with his rifle poised to strike down hard upon a crumpled figure. It surprised him someone else was there. Marcie lying a few feet off did not register. Imhoff reacted instinctively, fiercely swinging his rifle to his cheek, taking a quick, ragged aim.

He fired, the explosion ringing in his ears.

CHAPTER 59

GUNFIRE
April 15, 2019
The woods at Rose Street
Middlebury, Vermont

4:25 a.m. EDT

George awoke when a car backfired. He closed his eyes for more sleep.

But when he heard several more bangs, he knew they were not backfires. His eyes flew open and he leapt out of bed.

In the living room, Angie and Star watched the DHS agents running up the street toward the woods, guns drawn. Angie threw Star to the floor. "Crawl into the hallway and stay there."

"But—"

"*MOVE!*"

"O-okay."

Angie flattened herself on the floor behind the wall near the window. From there she had access to the window, the front door, and back to the hallway and kitchen.

In the bedroom, Virginia groggily called after George, "Honey, whereyougoinginsuchahurry? It's still early."

"Virginia, those were gunshots," George called back to her as he ran from the room. "I've got to check the backyard. Sherman could be out there in the sunflowers."

She called, "George?" She tried to rise, but had difficulty untangling herself from the bed covers.

George rounded the hallway door into the kitchen at something that could not quite be called a gallop before pulling up short at the scene before him.

Tappy was on the floor, sheltered by the sink counter. Bossilini was on his knees, carefully peeking out of the lower corner of a window. Bossilini turned to find a completely disheveled George in his wrinkled clothes, hair a mess, and eyes squinting from having forgotten his glasses in his haste.

"George, get down. Those were gunshots," Bossilini ordered.

"Sherman. Have you seen Sherman? The children could be out there. In the sunflowers."

"No . . . I haven't seen them out there," Bossilini answered.

But to George, Bossilini sounded noncommittal. Noncommittal wasn't good enough for George Douglas. George burst forward, unlocking the door and racing outside before Bossilini could rise to restrain him.

"George! No. George—"

Bossilini, crouching, ran to the door, stopping behind the wall, peeking out to look, and then ducking back out of the doorway.

George stopped, standing still ten feet from the sunflowers, turning his head frantically, "Kids. Sherman. Carmen. Are you there?" Silence. "Kids, if you're here, stay in the sunflowers till it's safe. Stay put. There's a gunman out here."

Bossilini took another quick look, and flinched as he saw the ground kick up two feet from George followed by the retort of a rifle.

"George, back here! Run, man, run!"

George froze.

Bossilini had a flashback of the Unisphere, a women's head exploded and she fell, the scene now superimposed with an image of George falling, falling into the sunflowers.

Cursing, Bossilini leapt out the kitchen door and sprinted to George, flinging him toward the house. Bossilini pushed him from behind like a lineman pushing a football sled, finally muscling them both inside the kitchen. He kicked the door closed behind them. Bossilini stood panting in the doorway.

Angie stood still in the dining room doorframe; Bossilini watched the fear in her eyes give way to relief.

Imhoff cursed. He had yanked the trigger and the bullet went four inches wide of the man's head.

The assassin, standing over Sherman, looked at Imhoff, startled, but recovering, flipped the rifle in his hands with the barrel forward and the stock resting in his right hand. Imhoff jerked the bolt action of his rifle, chambering the next round. But he had to dive to his left as the man fired from his waist, the bullet tearing through the flap of Imhoff's coat.

Imhoff rolled hard to his left and fired lying prone. He missed wide. He rolled two more times hard left, hugging the rifle to his chest as he feverishly worked the bolt. A bullet kicked up dirt a foot away.

At the end of the second roll Imhoff fired, the recoil kicking hard into his chest. He cursed; missed again. The man leapt over a two-foot-high berm on the downslope of the hill toward Star's house. The berm was like a small Civil War earthwork, separating the two men intent on killing each other.

Imhoff rose and darted back right, hoping to make the trees for a better angle. But the man's barrel peeked over the berm. Imhoff hit the ground, firing on his side, his right arm pinned by his body, furiously tried to slide the bolt and ready another round.

Imhoff quickly came up into a kneeling position and fired two more covering rounds. He realized a bolt-action rifle was not useful at thirty feet. He threw down the rifle and sprinted for the trees. He heard a round of fire from the assassin's gun on the other side of the berm. From the retort, it sounded like the shot was toward Star's house. He briefly heard muffled voices carrying up from Star's backyard.

Breathing hard, back resting on a tree shielding himself from the sniper, Imhoff reached to his waist holster and drew his Glock 22. He held the weapon in a two-handed grip, thankful he had two extra clips.

Imhoff peeked from behind the tree. Sherman and Marcie had come alert and were hugging the earth, terrified by the gunshots firing over their heads. Imhoff grimaced at the thought of a gun battle with innocents pinned down in between. He had to clear them first.

He called to the boy. "Hey, *hey!*"

Sherman turned only his head, pressing his cheek firmly into the ground. Imhoff pointed toward the nearby trees. Sherman nodded he understood.

Imhoff saw Sherman get Marcie's attention, then crawling to her, he wrapped his arm around her waist and drug them both to safety.

The kids are safe. Now it's time to win, Imhoff thought. *But where is he?*

Imhoff took another quick look from behind the tree. Nothing. In the distance, he saw two DHS agents running, entering the woods below. "Where are you?" Imhoff muttered under his breath.

Standing still was a bad option. He needed to move.

As Imhoff prepared to run to trees a few yards away, he saw a flash— the reflection of rising sunlight off a rifle scope. It came opposite from him down the other side of the hill. Using the berm as cover, the man had moved somewhere down on the side towards the back of the hill. Imhoff ducked back behind the tree, waiting for the shot. But it did not come. He's playing it smart now, Imhoff thought. Not giving away his position unless he has a kill shot.

As sweat ran in his eyes, Imhoff thought furiously. *Maybe?* he thought, as a plan formed.

"Hey, George, Jr.," he called, loudly enough for the assassin to hear, but not so loud as to be obvious. "Don't answer. Just listen. There are federal agents running into the woods below from the street. When they get near, hold your hands up—but keep covered by the trees—and tell them an FBI agent is up here. He said to go to the left side of the hill to towards the back and then work toward the right. The FBI agent will be waiting on the right to take the man when they flush him."

Imhoff hoped they got it right.

But Imhoff had no intention of being down on the right of a pincer trap. He knew the man would come for him, traversing the back of the hill to ambush Imhoff from behind. The man would not flee the woods, not yet. His arrogance would not allow him to play to a draw. He had to win.

Imhoff, crawling, maneuvered back to the top center of the hill. He would take out the assassin at the mid-point on his traverse on the hill's back-side.

Imhoff had retrieved his rifle, setting up on the back edge of the hill where a tree provide cover. He had a good view of the draw behind the hill. Imhoff lay, patiently looking through the scope, finger caressing the trigger.

He heard muffled voices behind him toward the street. That must be George, Jr. talking to the agents. A few moments later he heard the agents trudging around to his left. *They'd never catch the man on their own with that much noise,* he thought.

Imhoff scanned the terrain below. The assassin should appear any second, moving mid-way across the draw.

But nothing, no movement, no sound other than the DHS agents.

Imhoff became tense, sweating as the seconds flicked by. The man should be moving below by now. *But nothing.* The woods now stood deathly silent.

It was the silence that caused Imhoff to break into a cold sweat. *Silence in the woods brought death.* Too late, Imhoff realized the man was close. He was circling back from the left side for Imhoff.

Imhoff reached for his service pistol. He had the grip firmly in his right hand, pressed tightly to his stomach underneath his body when the man spoke.

"Did you really believe I would fall for that amateur trap?" The haughtiness in his voice made Imhoff feel sick and foolish.

Imhoff's body went slack, dark resignation flooding him. With a piercing sadness, he saw in his mind his wife and children, he thought of the family photograph hanging over the living room couch, then most poignant, a framed picture of his son in his baseball uniform on his office desk. The image of his son, smiling proudly in his uniform, racked Imhoff with a hopeless sob. *Why hadn't I played this smarter.* Imhoff was choking on his grief. He would never see his son grow up. There was so much he wanted to teach the boy. He would never walk his daughter down the aisle at her marriage. His eyes burned.

Imhoff turned his head to the left. The man was standing on the edge of the clearing in front of the berm with his rifle pointed at Imhoff. Imhoff heard the agents down below the hill on the backside. They had already passed.

"Yes. I will kill them, too." He laughed at Imhoff. "Thank you for setting them up so nicely for me." He let the words sink in, enjoying the despair on Imhoff's face. "And I will get the family, make no mistake about that. I will walk down to the house. And I have decided for the trouble you have given me I will kill them all—not just the father—but all of them. You will have them on your conscience. But, oh yes," he softly laughed, "you won't be alive for your conscience to be troubled."

Anger flooded Imhoff. He reacted instinctively, pushing aside the despair, the hopelessness, the sadness. Only action could save him. The Marines and Afghanistan had instilled that.

As the man taunted him, Imhoff had been sliding the Glock under his body. The barrel was now even with his left side, the side facing the assassin.

"Goodbye, Special Agent Imhoff. Yes, I know your name. You're not as clever as you think. I was in the park yesterday watching you walk around and sip coffee." He laughed.

"You're not that good a shot. You missed your target," Imhoff snapped to distract him. The man blinked. It bought just enough time.

The man snarled, jerking the rifle to his shoulder. But pain from Sherman's stab wound caused the slightest flinch slowing his motion.

Imhoff flexed his wrist, angling his gun from underneath him. Imhoff fired three rounds, the recoil fracturing two ribs and bruising his spleen.

The first two rounds hit the assassin's chest with the last going high over the man's right shoulder. The man staggered a step back, then another, the rifle slowly dropping. Mouth gaping open, his face bore the look of complete astonishment. He staggered another step back, staring into Imhoff's face, his eyes uncomprehending, his mouth twitching, as if how could this rank-and-file government gumshoe take *me*?

He then fell over, landing spread-eagle, dead, the rifle clattering away.

With the little strength he had left, Imhoff fished out his credentials in two fingers, and rolling on his back, held them as high as he could, yelling in a rasping voice, "FBI. FBI. Special Agent Frank P. Imhoff," as the DHS agents, guns drawn, finally scrambled up and crashed into the clearing on top of the hill.

CHAPTER 60

ON THE FRONT PORCH
April 15, 2019
Rose Street
Middlebury, Vermont

4:50 a.m. EDT

"Mister, mister. Are you okay?" Sherman softly called.

Imhoff looked over at the trees to his left. Peeking out from behind was the head of the boy. Imhoff sat against a log, coatless, with tie loosened half-way down his chest and his left arm clamped to his side.

"I told you to get out of here," Imhoff said.

"Are you really FBI?"

"Yes," Imhoff panted.

The boy walked into the clearing.

"That was real sick, the way you took that guy out."

"You saw?"

Sherman nodded.

Imhoff opened his mouth to bark at the boy for not running away to safety. But he thought of his own boy and was enveloped in gratitude. *He would see his son again! He would go back to his family!* Softening, Imhoff asked, "Tell me, son, do you play baseball?"

"Er, no, ah, not any—no."

"Well, that's okay." Imhoff studied the boy. He struggled with his breath. "You're George Douglas, Jr." It was a statement, not a question.

"Yes, sir. Except my friends call me Sherman."

"Sherman?" Imhoff puzzled. He nodded. "Okay, then. Sherman."

Imhoff winced from pain in his side.

"I'm a Boy Scout, I can give you first aid," Sherman offered.

Imhoff smiled. "I'm okay, son. Had worse than this."

The boy shifted around as if he had something to say. Finally, he stammered out, "Ah, is my family going to be arrested? Are we going to some secret government prison?"

The boy's expression was so earnest Imhoff had to chuckle. But he paid for it and grimaced from pain. Sherman took an automatic step toward him, but Imhoff held up his hand. "No. I'm okay, really. As they say, it just hurts when I laugh."

He said to the boy with a benign smile, "No. Your family will not be arrested. No secret prison. I know you are innocent."

It took a moment to sink in, then Sherman took a deep breath and bent over bursting into tears. Brief as a quiet summer rain, they were done, and he stood up wiping his eyes.

"Sorry."

"No need to apologize. I'm assuming your family has been through a lot."

The boy nodded.

"Where is the young lady?"

"You mean, Marcie?"

"I don't know her name."

"Yeah, her name is Marcie. She helped me." Then alarmed, "She's not going to prison, is she?"

"Nobody's going to prison. But you and I have to get something straight. Why didn't you go to the house like I said? You could've been killed coming back."

"Well, ah, I came back for something." With eyes staring at his shoes, he said, "It's sort of personal, something important."

"Okay," Imhoff nodded. "Go ahead. Where is it?"

"Well, that's the problem."

"What problem?"

"It's in his, er, pocket." The boy stuck out his arm, pointing at the dead assassin.

Imhoff frowned. "What could he have of yours?"

"He searched my backpack. He showed us his knife and was going to kill us. I guess stealing our stuff was rubbing it in."

"Where is it?"

"His pants pocket. I want to get it before those other agents get back." The DHS agents had secured the weapons from the scene and had walked down to meet the investigative teams arriving on Star's street and help cordon off the area.

Sherman tried to make himself blush as he lied, "Like I said, it's something personal, you know, my girlfriend gave it to me. I don't want anybody knowing and making a big deal out of it."

Imhoff remembered when he was the boy's age trying to figure out girls and his first crush. He nodded. "Okay. Okay." He gestured toward the body, as if help yourself. He was interested to see if the boy really would retrieve whatever it was from a dead body.

To Imhoff's surprise, the boy walked straight to the body, reached in the right-side cargo pocket, and turning his back as a shield, removed something, slipping it into his own pocket. Imhoff shrugged. Probably a charm from a girl or maybe a memento from the skating rink. *Anything from a girl at that age would be embarrassing.* Imhoff knew.

"You should go to your family now. Some of them are in the house. Also, someone else you know from home. Tappy."

"Mrs. Montgomery!" the boy whooped. "She's one of my mom's best friends. Is my mom down there?"

"Why don't you go see for yourself," Imhoff half-smiled, then grimaced.

Sherman turned to tear off down the hill, but he turned a last time. "Thanks, agent, you saved our lives. That guy really was going to kill Marcie and me."

Imhoff watched the boy race down the hill, delight on his face.

He thought, this really is a good job some days. Some days it all goes right.

Sherman burst down the hill, raced across the front lawn, took the porch steps two at a time, and burst into his mother's arms. She hugged him, crying over him, as if he were the most precious thing in the world. And, of course, he was.

His father rushed over, hugging them both, and Sherman felt like the luckiest and happiest boy in the world.

When released from the joyful embrace, Sherman happily crowed, "They're not going to arrest us. We're free, we're free." Sherman beamed, looking around the porch.

Bossilini and Angie sat in the porch swing, gently swaying, but a quick look passed between them, while Tappy sat on the porch rail with her back to the front yard.

"Hello, Mrs. Montgomery. What are you doing here? The FBI agent said you were here."

But before any explanation could come forth, he noticed someone moving off to the side. The boy burst across the porch, shouting, "Grandma, Grandma." He ran straight into Star's arms.

Virginia watched the boy squeeze his grandmother as hard as he could, the side of his face pressed against her, his expression angelic. He clutched her as if he would never let her go again. Virginia stood, silent, as a realization hit, and her face softened. She swallowed, and walked slowly to them. She reached up hesitantly, then placed her hand softly on Star's shoulder. "He's missed his grandmother." Followed by the arrival of a fresh thought, Virginia's face relaxed. *If we work hard enough, maybe we can be a family again. That may be nice.*

Star turned with the most grateful look Virginia had ever seen. "And his grandmother has missed him." Over the boy's head, she looked at Virginia with tears and mouthed, "Thank you."

When Sherman pulled free from the embrace, he looked around, "Where's Carmen? And Manfred and Buddy?"

The porch became silent. Sherman caught the adults looking to each other. Tears budded in Virginia's eyes, and she blinked quickly to dry them. Sherman, looking from face to face, knew instantly something was wrong, and his face turned grave.

Virginia nodded at George and took the lead.

"Come to me, Sherman."

She reached out with both hands placing them on the boy's shoulders, but she did not kneel down to him as she used to. She saw he was different now.

"Sherman, we do not know where Carmen—and Manfred—are. They haven't arrived yet." Her face began to crumple. She turned to the other adults for strength.

Sherman followed her gaze and realized all the adults were looking really serious. Something bad had happened. He became scared and felt like he would cry.

"Sherman," his mother called his name tenderly. "Buddy is dead."

The boy recoiled as if from an electric shock. "Dead? *No!* He can't be. How?" As the news sank in, he felt unsure, hollow, he didn't know if he wanted his mother to hold him or to stay back. He hoped he wouldn't cry. He stammered again, "How . . .?"

Virginia nodded at George who moved to the boy. "It was at the Unisphere. We were meeting there as planned. But a man shot Buddy . . . and an innocent woman."

"Why did he shoot them?"

George swallowed. "Well, son, we think he was trying to shoot at us— at me. Buddy pushed me out of the way and saved my life. But he was hit."

They closely watched the boy, concerned.

Suddenly, he erupted, pointing to the hill, lips pressed thin in anger. "I'm glad that man up there's dead. It was him, wasn't it? I wish I could have shot him, too, after I stabbed him."

"Stabbed him," Virginia uttered in horror. "After he was *dead?*"

"No," Marcie answered. She had come from inside with a glass of water and had heard the last part of the conversation.

Virginia and George turned to her, stunned. Their boy, Virginia's sweet boy, had stabbed someone? "You mean with a knife?" she asked, her voice tremulous.

"The man was going to kill us with his knife," Marcie said, emphatically, with a hint of impatience. "He tied us up and gagged us with duct tape. He was waiting to shoot someone down here at the house, then he was going to kill us with the knife." She paused momentarily. "But Sherman worked his hands free, and while the man was looking down his scope or whatever, Sherman snuck up on him and got the knife from the log where the man had stuck it, and stabbed him. I would have done it, too, if I could," she said with a sudden fierceness.

Bossilini looked at her, approving. *Yes*, he thought.

Continuing, softer now, Marcie told them, "But it didn't kill him."

Marcie added, "And, like, the man got really mad and hit Sherman with the rifle barrel and slammed me onto the ground. He was about to hit Sherman in the face with the rifle—what do you call—that back wooden part—"

"The stock," Bossilini supplied.

"Yes, that. And he was going to beat Sherman to death, I just knew it, but that's when the FBI agent came up and shot at the man. He missed. But that's when they got in the gun battle."

"*Gun battle!*"

"Yes, Virginia, that's all the shots we heard," George interrupted, impatient to hear what happened—with a growing pride in his son.

"The agent told us to run down here. So we came down."

"Let me get this straight," Virginia interrupted, speaking to Marcie. "You got here first. We didn't know who you were. You were out of breath and simply said, 'We escaped.' But when you turned around, Sherman wasn't there and it surprised you?"

Turning to her son, Virginia demanded, "Sherman, where were you?"

"Ah, I had to get something." He looked over at Bossilini, who nodded ever so slightly, as if to say, *go on, but make it good.* "Not get something, I mean, I wanted to make sure the agent was okay. He seemed hurt after he shot the man—"

"You saw him *shoot* the man?" Virginia shrieked.

"No, the man was already dead. I went back to see if the agent needed help. He had saved us, and I didn't want him to be alone, like, if he was bleeding to death or something."

Out of the corner of his eye, Sherman saw Bossilini nod again, indicating, good job.

"Oh, they're taking him now," Tappy called, interrupting.

They turned to see Imhoff loaded on a stretcher into the ambulance. He gave them a thumbs-up before disappearing inside.

"Will he be okay?" Sherman asked.

"I expect we will shall see Special Agent Imhoff again," Bossilini answered, giving Tappy a knowing look.

"His choice made all the difference," Tappy said to him.

Virginia called to one of the DHS agents, "Have you seen my daughter?"

The agent walked over. "We've cordoned off this area for several square blocks, but if your daughter's caught at a checkpoint we'll pass her through."

Before Virginia could thank him, a yellow taxi cab screeched to the curb and the back door flew open. Carmen and Manfred, hand-in-hand, popped out, looking around at the departing ambulance and the commotion of techs and agents moving along the block.

"Did we miss something?" Manfred asked.

Then, led by Carmen, they raced excitedly up the steps to the porch.

"Mom, Dad," Carmen, burst out, breathless, "Manfred and I, we . . . we're engaged. We're getting married."

Virginia looked at the two of them, a look of horror hijacking her face. Then her eyes rolled in her head, and she fainted, sprawling out cold on the gray boards of Star's porch.

"Oh, lord," George exclaimed.

CHAPTER 61

TIME MACHINES AND AMARETTO
April 15, 2019
Rose Street
Middlebury, Vermont

5:30 a.m. EDT

While George tended to Virginia on the porch floor, Bossilini stepped forward.

"Manfred, there's actually quite a lot you missed, but it worked out fine, except for one thing I will explain later." He decided to defer informing Manfred about Buddy. "We'll tell you the whole story in a little while. In the meantime, there are some people you should meet." He turned to Angie at his side. "Manfred, this is my associate, Angie. She helped Virginia get here."

Manfred nodded, but turned, excited, to Sherman. "Dude, you freaked us out in New York. Man, it's good to see you." He gave the beaming Sherman a peace handshake.

"Sorry, dude," Sherman said. "I had to split. I just had to come here."

"No sweat. But what's the big deal here?"

Bossilini interrupted, reaching out his arm for Star to join them. "And this is Star Douglas, George's mother."

An attractive woman with shoulder-length gray hair stepped forward. He saw she wore blue jeans and a college sweatshirt. She was lithe and had a sparkling smile. But it was not her smile that grabbed Manfred. As she extended her hand, Manfred leaned forward, staring intently into her face. He blinked, then stared again.

She had one blue eye. And one brown eye. Just like Sherman. He looked down to Sherman at his mismatched eyes, then back to Star with her mismatched eyes. He looked back and forth twice.

Suddenly, dizzy, he felt as if his head were shooting up off his body as flashing lights and sounds from that last night at Woodstock psychedelically cascaded through his mind. He felt weirdly split, as if half of him was here on the porch but the other half was stretched back fifty years, then suddenly he snapped all the way back.

413

Next to him on a blanket, gazing at him sweetly, was a pretty girl about two years younger with long brown hair parted down the middle. She wore a rainbow-colored headband. The girl reached tenderly for Manfred's hand. Taking his hand, she moved close and kissed him sweetly. Pulling back, she smiled at him with her eyes, one blue and one brown. She started to speak.

But Manfred snapped forward.

Quivering, he stared at the women on the porch as her image slowly superimposed over the girl's face. Manfred gulped, and with eyes wild, shrieked, pointing at Star, "*It's you!*"

Star's eyes startled wide open and she protectively leaned back.

Manfred shuddered from head to toe, then his eyes rolled in his head and he fainted, sprawling out cold on the floor boards next to Virginia.

George stared down at the pair.

"This is getting to be contagious."

"Manfred."

Manfred heard his name dimly as he began to rouse. He seemed to be lying on a couch in a living room. Maybe there was a cool compress on his forehead. He could see candles burning softly on the mantle. They were scented and smelled like jasmine.

A woman sat in a chair next to him. She was the one who had spoken. She spoke again, "Do you know where you are?"

It took a few moments for Manfred to get his mouth working, "I, ah, in New, no, Vermont. I'm in Vermont. We had to get to Vermont."

"Good. And your name is Manfred Redford?"

"How, how did you know that? Have we met before?" He was confused.

"Yes, we have, Manfred. It was a long time ago." She leaned down, looking in his face. He could see she was the one with the eyes, a blue one and a brown one. "Do you remember me?" she asked.

"Yes . . . but no, I'm not sure," he said, looking vague. But certain images were surfacing in his mind. "You have eyes like Sherman."

She smiled. Manfred was becoming more alert.

"What happened to me?"

414

"You had a shock, Manfred. A psychic shock. Probably like no human has ever had before. But you will be fine, do you know that?"

He nodded.

He couldn't take his eyes off her eyes. Intrigued, he stared at them. His mind was squirming to reason things out. "Your eyes are like Sherman's eyes. That's rare. Does that mean Sherman and you are related?" Manfred sat up as he asked.

He was coming out of it quickly now. Star wanted to proceed slowly, though, and let him process a step at a time.

"Yes, Sherman and I are related." She paused to let Manfred absorb the information. "That's lavender by the end table. It's an essential oil, good for balancing the Doshas. Do you like it. Does it make you feel better?"

"Actually, it does."

"Good. Manfred, Sherman is my grandson." She looked at him, smiling.

Much more alert now, Manfred said, "George is your son, then?"

She nodded.

"Is your husband still alive?"

She smiled at him. "Well, I don't technically have a husband. And I didn't know until today that George's father, and Sherman's grandfather, was still alive." She watched him carefully. He was doing nicely, but had had a terrible shock, and she did not want him tripping out again.

"Manfred, how are you feeling?"

"Pretty good, actually." She noticed his color had returned, and his eyes were clear.

"Where's Carmen? You know, we're going to get married when she's a few years older."

Here it comes, Star thought. "Well that's what I wanted to talk to you about, Manfred."

"You mean Virginia won't allow it?"

"It's a little more complicated than that."

"Huh."

Star looked down at her hands, then back into Manfred's face. "Manfred, where we met before, it was at Woodstock. Can you remember?"

He nodded, but his eyes were vague again.

"We found each other that afternoon. You were excited to see Hendrix and were grooving over that, but do you remember the woods before?"

He thought hard. At first there was only fog. It took hard remembering, through fifty years, back through the streaking lights, amplified music, the chaos of that last day and night. But he looked deeply into her eyes, the pretty two-toned eyes, and was jolted by the memory of looking, falling depthless into those eyes as he made love to her in the woods.

"*You.*" He stared at her wide-eyed. "How—but her—your—name's not Star. Star's not right."

"No. That came later. After the woods, we went back to the blanket to wait for Hendrix, I turned to get something out of my backpack and fumbled around with it, and when I turned back, you were just gone."

Manfred was touched by the tears in her eyes. He reached out for her hand, squeezing gently.

"I looked all over for you," she continued, "but I couldn't find you, and nobody had seen you. I thought you just got tired of me and split." She paused. "Now I know what happened. But for fifty years I have thought you just left me, you didn't like me." Her voice wavered, "That was hard. I thought we really had something or I never would have made love with you. All this time I thought—" She looked away, looking for composure. "Then when I missed my period the next month, and the month after that, I thought, what a fine fix you'd left me in. I forgave you in time. Now I am glad I did because it was never your fault."

"I remember, I really dug you, I would've stayed around."

"Maybe," she said. "But Manfred, you *know* what that means."

Manfred reasoned slowly, "I got you pregnant. I am the father of your child. I—holy shit—I'm George's father! I—oh no," he shrieked, leaping halfway off the couch. "I'm Carmen's *grandfather!*"

His face was stricken. Star thought he was really stroking out this time. His eyes were wild with panic, spittle flew from his mouth. She could see a thought cross his mind, then he blurted, "Carmen and me, like no, we didn't do anything, no fooling around, we didn't even kiss. Hell, there wasn't even time to fool around."

"I know. I pulled her aside and we talked alone outside. I swore her to secrecy until we all could talk together. I didn't want Virginia to have a stroke before Carmen got the story out. Yes, she told me nothing happened—same story as yours. She was quite stunned, but then smiled. She said, 'Well, I guess I lost a fiancé, but I got a pretty cool grandfather.'"

He was a bit relieved but frantic to be acquitted of any impropriety with Carmen. "We felt this, like, cosmic thing, we were supposed to meet—"

"Well, maybe you were. To meet that is. Not get married."

"Huh?"

Star pursed her lips. "Carmen told me something else. She insisted I tell no one else but you knew."

"What did she say?"

"She told me about the man at the creek who told her to jump to you, that she could trust you. She thinks the man saved her life. Do you know who she is talking about?"

Manfred thought about Carmen's conviction she'd seen the man. He rolled her description around in his mind. *How could he explain it?* He couldn't.

"Star," he reached out clutching her arm, "she described my grandfather, Hobart Greenjeans. But he died before I left, back in the sixties. But I saw him, too, kind of. He looked, like, translucent or something."

"Manfred, you didn't bring anything from the sixties, did you? Like, you guys turned on or were tripping?"

"No, of course not, although I wouldn't mind having a little something—but that wasn't it."

"I don't know, Manfred. It's another strange thing in all this strangeness you have brought with you." She thought a moment. "But it looks like her grandfather—and her great-great-grandfather—saved her life."

"I'm too young to be a grandfather," Manfred weakly protested.

"They all say that Manfred. They all say that."

Star and Manfred sweetly held hands as he lay on the couch a while longer. They didn't need to talk.

Finally, Manfred broke the silence, asking, "Did Carmen tell you how we got here?"

"Sure did," Star laughed. "Might've been something I would've done. You know she's *my* grandchild, too. She told us you took the bus out of New York, sleeping a few hours in a park, then hitching up to Vermont in a semi, and finally copping the ride to Middlebury from a couple of guys on Harleys. Her mother was horrified, especially that you didn't wear helmets, but Carmen did confirm that without them you really do get bugs on your teeth when you smile."

They laughed together.

"We need to get you some food, if there's any left," Star said.

"How long have I been out?"

"Twelve hours."

"Damn."

"Have you told the others, ah, about the family connection," he asked.

She shook her head and smiled. "I thought mom and dad should tell the children together."

"Oh, boy. Maybe you can do the talking."

She leaned down and kissed his forehead. He squeezed her hand.

Manfred had missed dinner, but he slid into a chair next to Sherman at the dining room table where Star handed him a glass of Amaretto. Manfred was introduced again to Angie and Tappy, then to a black-haired girl a few years older than him who looked really glum and kept to herself.

"Carmen and Sherman were just filling us in on what happened after we were separated," George said to Manfred. "They had gotten to spending the night in the woods, you going for a haircut—which looks much better I should say—and they left to look for you."

Manfred turned to Sherman, who slunk in his seat with a sheepish look.

Carmen jumped in, "Manfred saved us."

"*Manfred!*" Virginia huffed.

"Yes, *mother*, Manfred." Turning to the group, she continued, "Manfred was late in coming back, so Sherman and I went to look for him. Something didn't feel right, the woods felt spooky, so at a creek we got on a raft and pushed out into the water."

"It was real crummy and we started sinking!" Sherman burst in.

"What!?"

"But Manfred saved us from drowning," Carmen resumed. "He had tracked us somehow and bent a tree over to us and we crawled along it to the shore."

Virginia stared amazed at Manfred.

"He actually saved us a second time," Sherman said. "When we got back to camp, someone had been there and kicked in the shelter I built. Now we think it was the man looking for us."

In response to Virginia's open mouth, Carmen said, "So Manfred led us away to place hidden by shrubs and we got out of there."

"So you children *were* safe with another adult," Bossilini could not resist adding.

"So how did you get to New York," George asked, fascinated.

Manfred and the kids took turns regaling amidst laughter around the table about the Bunions and Ovaltine, the bus to New York, and Sherman running away.

Virginia turned to Marcie, her eyes moist, "Thank you for saving my son."

"I think that saved all of you," Bossilini added.

The table became quiet for a moment, as the group sat relaxed and safe.

Bossilini broke the silence, resignation in his voice. "I am sorry to spoil the mood, but there is something else. Manfred, I have some bad news." Manfred cocked his head. "Buddy's dead. Shot." Manfred flinched, then slumped as Bossilini explained the details.

"Man, I wish you hadn't told me that. That's a real bummer." He shook his head sadly. "That cat was cool, and man, we went through a lot together." Manfred looked around the table, noting the sadness in their faces. Carmen quietly cried.

"Did they get the guy who shot him?" Manfred wanted to know.

Bossilini nodded.

Manfred looked away for a few moments, composing his emotions.

Bossilini leaned forward, addressing the group, forearms on the table. "We need to talk. You deserve an explanation of all that has happened."

"You can say that again," Star carped.

Bossilini had thought about how to start—about everything. He chose to go slowly, from the beginning. "It began in 1919 in England when two physicists formed an organization—a League—that continues even today." But he omitted the Watch.

Ten minutes later when Bossilini had finished explaining the League, George asked, "So, Angie, you—and Tappy—work for this League?"

Bossilini nodded.

George asked, "What does the League do?"

Bossilini cocked his head, thinking.

"One of the first successes was here in your country. 'The Black Chamber.'"

"Sounds like a Dashiell Hammett novel."

"Perhaps. In the 1920's after World War I—as a predecessor to the NSA—a unit of Army codebreakers formed a clandestine group named the 'Black Chamber.' It spied on other nations' communications, principally through telegraphs. The Chamber pitched flag and patriotism to the telegraph companies. The pitch was to discover foreign interests posing a risk to national security.

But the companies did not limit access to only foreigner's cables, the government asked for *all* international cables—excesses attributable from the trauma of a whole world at war and the unimaginable battlefield casualties. Western Union and other companies were only too happy to comply. It was the maybe the first partnership between the government and private enterprise that—under the guise of national security—was simply an information dump on private citizens.

If American citizen Gustav in Minneapolis sent a cable to his brother Hans in Frankfurt about a birthday present for their aunt Gertrude, the government got it. Or if a French student studying in America sent a love letter to his betrothed in France, the government got it. And none were the wiser."

"How did you find that out?" Sherman perked up.

Bossilini smiled. "The League acquired knowledge of the unit's operations. There was a boy, a delivery boy, not much older than you, who for the price of a motorcycle brought us satchels filled with copies of dispatches. Our agent in New York had befriended the boy. We discovered many simple private telegrams were stamped "Classified" to prevent their release. The discovery led to a tête-à-tête between the League's Secretary General Counsel Henry P. Witherspoon and the former head of the Black Chamber, Herbert O. Yardley. Yardley had become disillusioned, and Witherspoon persuaded him to write a book exposing the unit's activities to the embarrassment of the government and Western Union. Although exposed, it was not the last of government-private enterprise spying ventures. Look at Security Data Systems today."

The group sat silently, pondering the information.

"What else?" Sherman piped up.

"World Wars seem to spawn governmental over-intrusions. 'Operation Shamrock' began in 1945. The government during the war had been granted *legal* access to the international cables of RCA Global, ITT, and our old friend, Western Union.

Of course, the program was entirely necessary during the war. But it continued it—covertly—for another thirty years. As you may expect by now, in obtaining the cable companies' consent to continuation of the program, the government omitted the small, yet important, detail that it was analyzing telegrams of Americans sent between themselves in this country.

In 1959, Congress officially closed the window, so to speak, on the then adolescent NSA's voyeurism. Yet the agency was not deterred, and it opened secret spying centers in several cities. The operation became comical at times. Once, as if from a bad 1960's spy movie, it sent operatives disguised as a television processing company who removed the computer tapes containing the telegrams, copied the tapes, and returned the originals to the telegram companies. The telegraph companies hadn't a clue and were duped. Of course, the whole slapstick scheme was illegal."

Bossilini surveyed their faces for any hostility or disapproval before continuing. "The League had agents as staff members to the Senate Church Committee that conducted hearings in 1975 exposing the breadth of the spying. Despite those successes, our greatest failure was the inability to put someone in place in during the McCarthy business in the fifties. We almost got someone in as an assistant to Roy Cohn but missed the chance. Cuthbert never got over that."

"Back in England, a League agent, working as independent journalist similar to Mrs. Montgomery today, helped break the story on the Christine Keeler scandal, or the "Profumo Affair," as it's known, that preempted possible compromise of British Officials by Russian agents. In that instance, we worked hand-in-hand with the British government, though it knew nothing of our identity. We have done similar things in different countries, and by my accent you may surmise I spent many years in eastern Europe."

"Of course, elements of the FBI have been full of mischief through the years, no disrespect intended for our new friend, Special Agent Imhoff. But the government's demand for spying, data, and power seems infinite and continues in full force today with the NSA's project 'Echelon.' The government will not acknowledge the program, but we know some about it. What we do know is frightful, as technology penetrates deeper and deeper into our daily lives, even our very thoughts, with the AI algorithms selecting what we see and what we don't see, financing it with personal data sales. And it is much more dangerous."

"What we do know is that the NSA through intercept stations is sucking data off fiber-optic splitters to be copied and stored in immense NSA databanks. We have learned of an important DHS facility in Cape Canaveral that is working on increasing the volume and clarity of the massive intercepted data. Though we know the location, its inter-workings are a mystery. More public is knowledge that the NSA and FBI have direct access to the servers of numerous tech industry giants including Google, Facebook, and Apple through the use of PRISM. We recently learned that call records of millions of Verizon customers are being harvested, sometimes through 'back doors' of which the companies themselves are unaware. And we all know of the debacle with Facebook and the fool Zuckerberg."

Bossilini looked tired, and his face sagged. "Mrs. Montgomery works tirelessly on her blog to keep these issues in front of Americans. But. . . ."

"But what?" George asked.

"I fear. . . ."

Around the table, they leaned forward, faces lined with concern.

"I fear it all will become too much."

"To much what?" Sherman asked.

"Too much *distraction*—too much artificial consciousness. Too much technology; too much usage; too many phones; too much data; too many tweets, chats, emails, searches, sites, data, AI, and devices; too much people not talking *with* each other, too much obsession with it all, just all too much, *too much*, till no one cares, no one can see it the problems, no one wants anything to change, they just want more and more and more technology to feed their obsessions and avoidance of real life. Bah."

As Bossilini looked grave, Manfred finished the thought. "Then Big Brother will really be here. But not on a screen hanging from a wall, but on Captain Kirk things in our own hands."

Bossilini nodded without looking up. Tappy sat silent, simply staring at him.

But a moment later, Bossilini looked in their eyes, with some energy returning. "But for now, we still work, we still strive, we still think freely."

"Here, here! George shouted, unable to contain himself.

"But what's that got to do with the government chasing my family?" Virginia demanded. "We don't have any secrets."

He looked straight at Manfred. Everyone turned to stare at Manfred.

"What?" Manfred asked, protesting any guilt.

"There was a cosmological event that we were powerless to prevent or alter," Bossilini began to explain. "It is called a disaccordian resonance bubble. Manfred became trapped inside one. It is what set all this in motion." He gave a short-hand explanation of the quantum bubble.

"So that's what happened to Manfred," Sherman asked. Marcie looked at the boy, then to Manfred.

"That is exactly what happened. At first we thought Manfred was lost . . . gone . . . but later we learned he would reappear in 2019 and the government would misinterpret the event as a threat against the United States . . . and things would rapidly spin out of control."

"They sure did," Virginia confirmed.

Bossilini continued. "You see, Manfred was to be an Agent in the League—in 1969. His grandfather, Hobart Greenjeans, was selected in 1949 and could have succeeded to head of the League following Cuthbert, but—"

"He died out on that train track," Manfred interrupted, but proud his grandfather was an agent and he was to follow in Hobart's footsteps.

"Yes. We knew Manfred had many of Hobart's qualities—but in our effort to find Manfred after he disappeared we disc—"

Virginia interrupted, "So you and Tappy are agents? Ya'll were selected in these decennial, ah, whatevers?"

Bossilini smiled and nodded. "I was selected in 1989. Tappy in 1999—and Angie in 2009."

"Let's get back to Manfred," Star said, elbows leaning onto the table. She gave a raised an eyebrow to Bossilini.

"As I was saying," Bossilini resumed, "in searching for Manfred we discovered by chance that Manfred's grandson would be superior. The boy's potential was off the charts. He is the one we had to protect at all costs."

"I still don't get it," Star said. "Who's it going to be this year, 2019?"

"Sherman."

They could have fainted. Marcie raised an eyebrow.

"But, but . . . ," Virginia sputtered.

"I know, he's only a boy," Bossilini finished her sentence. "He was slated for 2029. But events have interceded."

"Manfred was the triggering event. His catapulting forward in time set off the events. If Sherman had been captured, he could never have become a member of the League, the timeline of his life would have been inextricably altered. We believed the League was tied to the boy somehow, and it would have withered and died without him. We could not allow that. So we mobilized Angie, Tappy, Buddy, and myself to come to your aid."

"But how did you know all this was going to happen?" Virginia asked. "I get how you could find out Manfred had disappeared in 1969. That was that bubble thingy. But how did you know in advance this was going to happen—or even that Sherman will be important in the future? You pulled into our alley in the Hummer like it had been planned out."

"It was," Sherman announced.

"It was what?" his mother turned to him.

"Planned out."

"Not completely, Sherman," Bossilini gave him a warning look.

"But how in the world?—I mean, you could only do that with a time machine." Virginia quipped, as if that were the most outlandish possibility. When Bossilini remained silent a look of incredulity crossed her face. "OMG, you didn't invent a time machine—you couldn't."

"Not me," Bossilini said.

"Not a machine, Mom. A time Watch." Sherman flashed a mischievous look, pulling the gold Watch from his pocket and holding it up for all to see.

"SHERMAN!" Bossilini thundered. Sherman's flamboyance was unacceptable. He did not intend for the family to know of the Watch at this time. The Watch was perilous, as proved mere hours ago by the assassin. Bossilini had wanted to introduce the notion of the Watch more slowly, over time. But the cat was now out of the bag. Bossilini exhaled in frustration, waving his hand. "Bah. You may be safer knowing than not." He looked sternly at Sherman a last time, then turned to the others. "Again, we go back to Sir Nigel and Cuthbert. . . ."

George and Virginia shook their heads in shock. "This is true?" Virginia asked.

"Every word of it." Bossilini stared evenly at her.

"Time travel?" George muttered, incredulous.

"If you knew this was going to happen, why didn't you fix it," Virginia asked. "I mean, we could have been out of town on a college visit for Carmen, or done some house remodeling, or explained it to the government in advance—no, I guess not that," she quickly added, noticing Bossilini's look. "You could have warned us or something."

Bossilini shook his head. "No, we couldn't."

"But—"

"We didn't know, Virginia. Remember, a disaccordian resonance bubble is subject to the laws of quantum mechanics. The uncertainty principle was in play. We thought the same thing, but as we went back and forth in time with the Watch over the six months from January to June the bubble popped spilling Manfred out at different times and

425

different places. Once in January, twice in March, three times in June. And different times of night and day and different locations, but all within five miles of your house. If we calculated a high probability *when* it would pop, we had no idea *where* it would pop. If we calculated a high probability of *where* we had no idea *when*. That is the quantum conundrum. All we could do was be vigilant and wait. And hope Sherman took seriously enough my admonition to call me if something strange happened. We could not watch over you all the time at all places. So we watched and planted a message for Sherman."

"That's sneaky. What was the message? Oh," he realized, "is that how come I kept having the thoughts to come to the sunflowers?"

Bossilini smiled. "Subliminal messaging."

"Huh? You mean like some movies theaters got in trouble for subliminally advertising their Cokes and popcorn back in the fifties or sixties?"

Bossilini smiled at him. "We intercepted your *Deadly Combat XXXIII* game and inserted pictures of Star's sunflower patch. The images were too quick for your conscious mind to notice, but your subconscious did. Each time you played the game, the subliminal message was reinforced."

"That was sneaky."

"We have to be resourceful."

Marcie interrupted, "How did the gunshots in the wall happen? The perplexed us."

"I can answer that," George said. "It was random. The neighbor called my cell phone, the shock caused Manfred to scream, and his scream startled me causing me to clinch the trigger. Totally random. It didn't have to happen at all."

"Wow. The investigators were sure it had significance. That really threw them for a loop."

Sherman had a final question. "Who put the CD and Watch in the shelter under the sunflowers?"

"Cuthbert and I. Again, we did not know when you would need it. I used the Watch to first go back for Cuthbert. It was his last trip forward." Sherman thought Bossilini's face changed with the memory. He looked sad.

"Why didn't you just keep the Watch and give it to me in person? It would've been a lot easier."

"Too risky. If I were caught with you, which was likely—all of you don't know how lucky you are—the Watch would be lost to the League forever, owned by the type men who are chasing you. Buried in the sunflowers, the Watch was safe."

The table was silent when Marcie, shoulders slumping, asked, "What's going to happen to me?" She looked around the table. "Best I can figure is I committed treason against the United State of America."

"No way," Sherman said, emphatic.

"Marcie, we are indebted to you. Through Ted Montgomery's firm—Tappy's husband—we are working on something for you. We would not have had this conversation in your presence otherwise."

Angie spoke, "We have 'Subcontractors,' as we call them, who work in business and government and help us but they don't know about the League or its, ah, capabilities with time. But we could create a brand-new position for you. You have unique qualities and have proven yourself quite capable with good judgment. The position would be called Supernumerary Agent—a person who is not a member of the League but who knows about the League and actively helps us. No one has ever done that before."

"You gotta be a Supernumerary Agent, Marcie. It's written all over you," Sherman almost leaped from his chair with enthusiasm.

She gave a shy smile for the first time.

Bossilini took command. "In fact, you all are now tapped into the League of Privacy Sentinels—you, too, Marcie, as Supernumerary Agent. You must—you will on your sacred honor—maintain utter secrecy of everything that has been revealed to you tonight." His fierce stare around the table bore into each of them. They did not dare withhold their solemn assent. They did not want to guess what Bossilini would do to them if they did not.

"Changing the subject, Star has something she'd like to share with you." She shot him a thanks-a-lot grimace.

"Star, I need another shot of Amaretto," George started to reach across the table for the bottle.

"You're gonna need a shot of something stronger than that," she challenged.

The table became quiet and they all turned towards her.

She took a deep breath, looked at each of them around the table, and said, "Well, there's no point beating around the bush. George, meet your father."

"Where?" George blinked, utterly astounded. There was no man present old enough to be his father.

"Over there, sitting next to Sherman." George, astonished, turned to Manfred, his face draining.

"H-him? How? *What?*"

"We met at Woodstock, fell in love, made love, and he disappeared in that goddamn bubble. Nine months later you were born."

George blanched, his voice weak, "You mean my father was not an unknown soldier in the Vietnam War?"

"Oh, George, please." Star shook her head.

"Jesus Christ," Virginia blurted, a stricken look of horror on her face. "Manfred is my children's *grandfather?* They have his … his *genes? Carmen was to marry him!* She looked as if she'd just smelled the most ghastly, putrid, horrid smell straight from hell. Her eyes rolled and she fainted dead away, falling from the chair and striking the floor hard.

Star looked down, then back over the table. "She did it again. She's out."

"Just leave her there this time," George said, face in his hands.

Later, the Douglas family and guests numbly stumbled to bed with, as Star said, "their minds blown." But there was not room for everyone, so Bossilini and Angie took their leave for a local hotel. Star raised an eyebrow as they slipped quietly out the front door.

Under a waxing Vermont moon, they walked slowly across the yard toward the street to await the taxi. Angie reached for Bossilini's hand, and upon finding it, stopped, turning him toward her. "You were strong tonight, Nitko."

She looked up into his eyes, and he smiled at her.

"And you came for me—in the park," she said.

"Yes."

"Despite our bickering these past years, when the bullets flew, you came to save me, you pushed me down and went after Virginia yourself even though you could die. You have been dismissive of me on this mission, but that it is not how you feel."

He held her eyes evenly.

"You have been so strong to save the League, so strong. Cuthbert and Nigel would be proud of you, Nitko."

"And you came to help the Douglases—and me—despite my, ah, surliness."

"Yes."

She reached her arms around Bossilini's neck pulling him gently to her and gave him a sweet kiss. As she separated, he felt the warmth of her breath.

"I am older now," she said to him. "I always loved you, Nitko. That is why I have been so irritable with you. I just had . . . things to prove. It took time." He smiled. "I think it's different now, do you? Do you feel it?"

He answered by gently encircling her in his arms and giving her a long overdue kiss, one he'd saved just for her.

CHAPTER 62

NOW AND THEN
The next day
Rose Street
Middlebury, Vermont

Daytime EDT

The lawyers swung into action. The head of Ted Montgomery's firm, Henry P. Witherspoon, VII, arrived from England to personally oversee the acquittal of the Douglases from any charges. He then planned the campaign to fully press the Douglases' claim against the government for its many wrongs against them. He expected that within a fortnight the government would pay damages, which he described in English understatement, as "a rather substantial sum indeed." Of course, the payment would be under a non-disclosure agreement.

Ted, along with Witherspoon, had talked with government officials most of the day. Around suppertime Ted arrived at Star's house.

"You're in the clear," he informed George and Virginia as they sat around the table. "It's over."

"It's over?" Virginia uttered in disbelief. "You mean it's *really* over—once and for all?"

"Really. Once and for all," he laughed.

"Oh, Ted, you're the best." Virginia flung herself at Ted, hugging his neck.

George beamed. "I can't believe it."

"Believe it, George."

"Well, I'm going to the Kroger for champagne," Star laughed.

Marcie, sitting alone at one end of the table, looked forlorn.

Ted, noticing, turned to her. "I have taken care of you, Ms. Beethoven. No adverse action, Secretary Ogilvie promised. He sees that in a way you helped apprehend the rogue assassin. They think he may have killed Chambers. They figure Chambers must have known something and they sealed a potential leak, but there aren't any leads. You understand there's no going back to DHS for you. Preston has to clean up the Chambers mess—and they don't trust you over there, and they never will again. Nor will the other agencies. You're done in D.C."

She hung her head.

"Get your head up, girl. You're moving," he said brightly. "To the land of free enterprise and the big bucks. New York. I've got you in the IT branch of XRT Technologies. They are licking their chops to get someone with your level of high security government work."

"No more chasing turbans," she said, unsure.

"Turbans?" he asked, puzzled.

Marcie looked up, her face a conflict of emotions. "Thank you, Mr. Montgomery. It's a shock, that's all."

Sherman, however, gave her a thumbs up and big smile.

Turning to the table, Ted announced, "Oh, yes. I'm pleased to report your friend Imhoff will make a full recovery. I actually spoke with Director Cummings. That was quite a conversation. He said, 'That godamned Imhoff screwed the pooch after I told him not to. But then he stuck in his thumb and pulled out a plum. Hey, hey,' he chuckled, 'NSA and Homeland have black eyes, while the Bureau's sitting pretty. I'm suspending him six months without pay to teach him a godamn lesson. But he's good—I'm moving him to FBI headquarters after that. Special position under me.'"

Sherman whispered in Marcie's ear, "Don't sweat it. If you don't like the corporation gig, I got an Operation Agent job waiting for you. Bossilini and Angie are a lot sicker than corporate suits."

She turned, smiling at him in spite of herself. She realized she had been right. There was something special about this boy.

Marcie turned back to Ted. "One more thing."

"Sure."

"What's going to happen about Secretary Ogilvie?"

Ted looked at her thoughtfully. "Ogilvie is working the PR machine. A story will come out that Chambers was under psychological distress—maybe from his declining health and his wife's death—that affected his rationality. His murder will simply remain a mystery for the conspiracy theory camp."

"So, he's the scapegoat."

Ted smiled, admiring her sharpness. "Yes, the powerful always have a scapegoat, Marcie. Truth does not sustain wealth and power."

"Does Ogilvie just get off," Star demanded, scowling.

"This is a tough bunch," Ted answered lightly. "No. He may think that. But no. I have sources that give him six months, then there will be a surprise announcement that he is resigning to pursue other opportunities. He will give a smarmy speech about the privilege of government service, proud that the country remained safe on his watch, and he'll wrap it all up in the American flag. But, politically, he's dead."

The next day George walked into the kitchen. "Where are the children?"

"Out back," Star answered. "*Granddad* is teaching the kids how to throw a Frisbee. We may have a sixties renaissance on our hands," she chuckled.

Bossilini had a more serious conversation with them that night.

"There is one more thing we need to discuss." He looked at them around the table. "It has been decided." His face became somber. "We must go underground."

"Underground?" someone asked.

"Yes. We are on a leave of absence from the League. We are prohibited from any contact or activity for five years during which time we will have no contact with each other. We are to separate when we leave here, and we will neither see nor hear from each other for five years—no contact."

Star watched Angie dab her eyes with a handkerchief. She could understand Angie's anguish.

"You mean—" Sherman blurted.

Bossilini held up his hands. "Through some miracle—especially for Angie and me—we managed to preserve our true identities and the League's secrecy through this wild chase and escape." They nodded, pleased, as incredulous as it was.

"But now is different. The events we have been through will attract a firestorm of media intrusion. Also," he smiled, "we tweaked the noses of

433

some at highest reaches of government. They will not easily let the slight pass. So the level of scrutiny and investigation for the next six months will be unimaginable. We cannot permit a connection to be made—discovery of the League. Our work is too important. Were the League to be destroyed there is no other organization to take its place. And there is only one Watch. So we—Angie, Tappy, myself—must have no association with each other. Angie and I must scatter on the wind."

Angie uttered a muted groan. Bossilini's jaw clenched and unclenched as he stared down at the table.

"Of course, this does not apply for obvious reasons to the Douglases and Montgomery families who must obviously have contact in Birmingham—and with Star."

"But five years—" Sherman whined.

"Yes. Five years."

"I can't see you for five years?" Sherman blurted, his face turning red as if he were about to cry. "When does it start?" he asked with trepidation.

"Tomorrow."

Sherman looked around the room at Angie and Bossilini. Marcie had left yesterday. He suddenly bolted up, running from the room, covering his face with his arm.

"Well, what do we do?" George asked.

"There is nothing you can do but take care of the boy."

Bossilini continued matter-of-factly. "In five years you will be contacted. Manfred will then begin his training. Sherman will also begin training."

Bossilini looked around the room, staring each person in the eye. He turned to Manfred. Manfred felt something bad coming.

"Manfred, you must leave, too."

"Dude, I just got here. No way."

Bossilini stared him down.

"Manfred, your arrival started all this. You are an anomaly—you have a fifty-year gap in your background. That's too enticing for an ambitious reporter. In five years we can build you a sufficient identity. And you can return then."

Manfred turned in a panic to Sherman, forgetting the boy was gone. He turned to George, Virginia, Star, with a plea in his eyes that prayed, "Help me."

"No way," he argued. "They need me. I just found them. I'm not going anywhere."

He turned to Star again for support, but she looked white-knuckled, shocked beyond speech.

"We will force you if necessary." Bossilini looked at him sternly.

Carmen stood in the doorway perfectly still, having heard the conversation.

She walked to Manfred and patted him on the hand.

"We will wait for you," she said tenderly. "We will not forget you."

Manfred looked up at her face, his was flushed with a tender anguish. "You won't?"

"No, we won't. All of us." She smiled at him. "I have it on authority we come from good stock. You can trust us to be here for you."

He hung his head and his shoulders racked with a sob or two.

All he had wanted was to go back.

Now all he wanted was to stay.

435

CHAPTER 63

RAINBOWS FROM THE PAST
Rose Street
Middlebury, Vermont

Afternoon EDT

Late in the afternoon, Manfred sat in the porch swing while Star faced him in one of the rockers. She held a cup of tea. She had given Manfred a cup of tea, too, with honey. She told him George's family would be staying in Vermont for a while at least. It would be too hard to go home now with all the questions, all the suspicions. She looked at the travel bag sitting on the swing next to him.

"I'm catching a bus tonight. Too hard trying to delay leaving. Better to get on with it." He looked at the porch floor as he rocked slightly. "I wish I had the Watch all to myself. I could go back in time. I could help you raise George. We could be together."

"But you don't and you can't." She looked at him a moment, letting the silence lay between them.

"You haven't aged a day, Manfred. You look just like you did that day, that last time I saw you." But she pulled her graying hair. "Don't try some smarmy compliment how young I look for my age. You're still twenty-one, I am sixty-nine, and those numbers don't equal."

She felt sad when she said it. And he did, too. But she had needed to say it. She gave him a straightforward look. "You had a fleeting thought about us, now, whether we could pick it up, and I did too." But she shook her head, no. That said it all.

They were quiet, a fifty-year silence between them, when a song came on the radio, the music carrying through the open window from the living room. The DJ said the song was titled *Savior* by Rise Against. They were drawn into the song. It was about lovers who were separated over time, trying to figure it out. The woman said she did not hate him, she just wanted to save him while there was still somebody left to save. The man said that he loved her, but he was not the answer for the questions she had.

As the chords from the song faded, Star smiled at Manfred, saying, "We're kind of like that couple in the song. I could see you had a dark place. I'd have wanted to save you, boy."

Manfred looked sad. She thought that was sweet.

He said, looking not fully at her, "And I wasn't the answer to the questions you still had. I was really kind of messed up back then."

"There was more to you than that, you just didn't know yet. I could tell. And you *were* good-looking, with all that beautiful hair. Still are," she said, joining him in the sadness, their shared knowledge they had been cheated. "Didn't you feel the spark, the last time we kissed, before. . .?"

He smiled. He did remember. He thought a moment. "You know, if I hadn't sat in that particular place . . . if I'd stood up or walked three steps forward or talked to the people on the next blanket or taken a leak behind a tree, I mean, who knows what would have happ—"

"Oh, the sixties," she sighed. He heard the wistfulness in her voice.

There was nothing for him to say.

With a look tinged with melancholy, she said to him, "We have a wonderful child and wonderful grandchildren . . . but we never had ourselves. I wondered about you all through those years."

Manfred looked down, considering the hurt that had sawed on her through the decades, and tried to blink away a tear. Turning back to her, with one lone streaming tear, a tear full of the most affection he'd ever summoned for a woman before, he said, "Someone told me rainbows looked prettier in the past. Maybe looking back makes me look better now than I was."

"Yes," she smiled, "maybe so." But she shook her head, no, as if she knew. God, how he loved her smile. Then a little forlornly, she tilted her head, "Manfred, we can't go back. It's gone, not meant to be. But it can still be good between us—different, but good. You know? Like I told George and Virginia, you got to ride easy where you are."

He took a sip of the warm tea. The tea was sweet, like her, and he felt such a fondness for this woman. "Yes, I do. Different but good." Then he added, "And maybe there are no questions you still have."

She laughed deeply and returned his look with equal affection. "And maybe you have saved yourself while there is still plenty left to save."

She looked at the father of her child and lamented life's strange timings.

EPILOGUE

The Drake Hotel
Chicago, Illinois
1935

6:15 p.m. CST

The man in the fedora walked into the hotel bar.

He stood in the entranceway for a moment, surveying the tables and chairs before him. Off to the side stood the empty bandstand with a single microphone pole in front of a few rows of padded chairs with music stands. A saxophone lay across one of the front chairs. The band would play later.

A cigarette girl in a red saloon-style skirt came by with her tray, stopping before the man. "Cigars? Cigarettes? Tiparillos?" No thanks. The man shook his head, he knew what those things did to you. She flitted to a different table. "Cigars? Cigarettes? Tiparillos?"

The man in the hat walked to the bar. He was of medium height, a little dumpy, not athletic. He looked about twenty-five. He wore round glasses. He took the last open seat at the bar and ordered an Early Times on the rocks. While he waited on his drink, he pulled a chain with a heavy gold watch from his vest pocket and checked the time. *Six-fifteen.* He absently wound the watch then placed it back in his vest pocket. The backside of the watch had a small glass-covered hole, as if it were some sort of lens.

"Would you get a load of this?" The man next to him swatted a page of the *Chicago Tribune.* "They got a new G-Man."

"Who?" the man in the hat asked, but with no real curiosity.

"This guy Hoover. He's head of the new Federal Bureau of Investigation."

"Hmmm."

"You'd think the Bureau of Prohibition—those *prohis* would be enough. Eliot Ness and the Untouchables helped take down some bad guys like Capone and Nitti, but they caused a mess doing it."

"How so, do you think?"

441

"Well, for starters, they didn't care a bit about getting innocent bystanders caught in the crossfire with gangsters. I remember, buddy, I was *here*." He tapped the bar three times with his index finger for emphasis.

The man in the hat did not doubt he had been here.

Sitting back, the other continued, "I guess you could call that being in the wrong place at the wrong time. It did clean up the town. But, you know, what I didn't like was what do they call it—yeah—wiretapping, you know, listening in on people's private telephone calls. I mean, that don't seem right, the government listening in on your private business and stuff. I know I don't want them listening in on me and Cutesy on the phone— that's my girlfriend," he beamed. "You know."

"Yes. Indeed, I know quite well."

"You know, I also heard they weren't beyond steaming open an envelope and reading people's private mail."

"You don't say?"

"I sure do say."

Staring at the picture in the article, the other said, "This guy Hoover looks like a bulldog. No, more like a Pekinese. You know he started that scientific crime lab in '32."

He folded the paper and tossed it onto the bar.

"We don't need a new—what do they call it—" He reached for the paper. "—yeah, *Federal* Bureau of Investigation. You know," he continued, "first they passed the income tax laws to get their slush funds for the elections, then FDR got to regulate commerce, and now they're starting this federal police force, maybe even with branches all over—and to top it, Hoover's had this 'scientific crime fighting lab' for three years now. I'm not sure I trust that lab. I bet they're working on things way beyond steaming open mail. All in the hands of the federal government." He took another long draught of his drink. "Yeah, I heard this Hoover's like Ness and them, he likes—what are they again, oh yeah—wiretaps. What they gonna listen to now that Prohibition's over and Capone's up the river?"

"Maybe they'll listen to us," the man in the hat offered softly.

"Huh? You mean sit in those offices listening to me make a date with Cutesy?"

442

The man in the hat sipped his Early Times with a smile and answered quietly, "Who says they will stop at listening?"

"Whaddya mean?" the other looked sharply. "You saying spying on us—on American citizens? You're beginning to give me the creeps. America's a free country, Bub. The government can't snoop in our lives. We're not Germany."

"Hmmm, maybe." The man in the hat thought about saying the next part, and decided to say it. "Watch out for a new book in a few years. I think you may be interested in it. Its title will be a simple date."

"Yeah. What date?"

"1984."

"That's a helluva long time from now."

"The book will come out sooner than that. But it doesn't really take long for the government leaders to change. They are like that now, even, it's their nature, it's their ambition, really. The technology enables their ambitions. It's when the technology comes—"

"Technology?" he said, as if the word was sour.

"Technology plus ageless human nature. You need to pay attention."

"You mean like peep out my curtains, see if anyone's watching?"

The man in the hat smiled. "You'll have to figure it out. But I can suggest it's a little more complicated than that."

The man in the hat politely smiled, and took another polite sip of his drink. He looked from his drink, and said, "Just keep paying attention."

"To what?"

"You'll see."

"Aw, you're putting me on," the man said. A moment later, he changed the subject, "What you in town for, Buddy?"

The man in the hat paused, different feelings washing over him. Finally, he answered, "I was here for a lecture given by a dear friend. Perhaps you've heard of him, Sir Nigel Clements, a renowned physicist?"

"Naw. Sorry. I don't go to no physics lectures." His face wore a grimace as if the subject were distasteful.

The man in the hat nodded, fingering his pocket watch. If he pressed the filigrees on the watch in a certain order, a beam would shine out of the tiny lens on the back of the watch activating a two-dimensional sheet of digital information, which he could run forward or backward. If he then pressed the winding knob, he could enter into the stream of time.

To change the subject, and fill the silence, the fellow asked the man in the hat, "What business you in?"

The man in the hat paused. "The privacy business."

"*The Privacy Business?* What the hell does that mean?"

"What do you think it means?"

"Well . . . ah . . . I don't know."

"Try harder."

"Gee . . . I . . . I guess it's like taking care of people, like people's private business, like keeping us a free country?"

"Yes. You could say it that way."

"Well . . . I suppose that is a good business."

"Yes. I find it so."

The man gulped. He stuck out his hand as if he didn't know what else to do. "Frank Dominick."

The man in the hat shook Frank's hand while smiling warmly into his eyes. Frank instantly felt better, his eyes cleared, and a feeling of *purpose* momentarily floated through his mind. He had the sudden feeling that if things were important, one should stand up for them, and that maybe, he, Frank Dominick, could stand up for something important one day. He would find courage and would stand up.

The man in the hat rose, leaving a five-dollar bill on the bar.

"Hey, you never told me your name," Frank said.

"Oh, I didn't, did I? It's Douglas. Sherman Douglas."

Frank asked, as if not wanting the man to quite yet leave, not ready to break contact with this unusual man, "Do you have a business card or something?"

The man in the hat smiled, reached in the breast pocket of his suit coat, and gave Frank a card.

It read, "Privacy Consultant."

Frank blinked. He stared at a little drawing of a flashlight on the bottom of the card. When he looked up the man in the hat was gone.

Outside the hotel, Sherman walked a few blocks toward the lake. After gazing at the pretty colors of the evening sky filtering off the water, he pressed the filigrees on the watch in a certain order. Rows of digital data reflected on the lens of his glasses. He pressed the watch knob, holding it for a few moments then quickly releasing it on coordinates for January 1, 2039.

In the next step he was gone.

THE END

ACKNOWLEDGEMENTS

Thanks to all who lent a helping hand with this book. First, to Bobby Frese, a true Renaissance Man, whose talks with me in his wingback chairs gave life to Manfred and Sherman and their adventure. Gwendolyn Hart helped create the Watch for the book's cover. Anna Owen provided assistance and cheerleading to keep me going. Mark Terry taught me helpful lessons about writing. Tom Ward, Alabama author and impresario, took the book from my closet shelf into print and beyond. And to my love Cynthia who allows me to be the absent-minded writer I am at heart.

The idea of the Watch arose from a Scientific American article authored by Michael Moyer in the February 2012 issue titled "Is Space Digital?" The article presents the exciting work of Craig Hogan of the University of Chicago and Director of the Fermi Lab Particle Astrophysics Center on ideas about the interrelation of information, space, and gravity.

ABOUT THE AUTHOR

J. Mark Hart has been an Alabama lawyer for 42 years practicing in the field of insurance coverage litigation. Growing up, he witnessed the struggle for civil rights in the South, which experiences led to his first novel, *Fielder's Choice*. That story follows a white teenager in Birmingham, Alabama in the late 1960's who befriends a new black teammate on the high school baseball team only to face a raw backlash from his steel worker community. *Fielder's Choice* is available in book or kindle at www.amazon.com/Fielders-Choice-J-Mark-Hart/dp/1975751760.

Made in the USA
Columbia, SC
19 December 2020